A KILL
IN THE SUN

ROBERT F BARKER

By Robert F Barker

The DCI JAMIE CARVER SERIES

LAST GASP (The Worshipper Trilogy Book #1)

The last time Jamie Carver let a would-be victim as bait for a serial killer, it ended badly. Now they want him to do it again, only this time the 'victim' is a dominatrix.

FINAL BREATH (The Worshipper Trilogy Book #2)

A monstrous killer, safe behind bars, but just how safe is 'safe'? An archive of debauchery and murder, poised to ruin reputations, carers, lives. A detective, running out of time to find what he seeks

OUT OF AIR (The Worshipper Trilogy Book #3)

One City; Paris. Two killers, one in hiding, the other stalking the streets. An innocent young couple, bewitched into the deadliest danger. The detective who must find them before the worst happens.

FAMILY REUNION

How do you save a family from slaughter when you don't know who they are, and you're not allowed to find out?
A killer is coming, and Jamie Carver has to to stop him. But how?

DEATH IN MIND

"Five minutes before she killed herself, Sarah Brooke had never had a suicidal thought in her life."
A mind-bending psychological thriller with a terrific twist. 'A treat for all Derren Brown fans.'

FREE DOWNLOAD

Get the inside
story on what
started it all...

For those friends and family who share my love of Cyprus, and who through their knowledge of the island, its customs and traditions, have helped in the development of this story.

This Englishman's 'Place In The Sun' is his

castle.

And he wants it back.

Part One

OFFER/COUNTER OFFER

CHAPTER 1

The gleaming, black Mitsubishi pick-up rocked and thrummed on its chassis, like a wounded bull in the ring, pawing the ground before one final, fatal charge. And with each renewed vibration, Nik Klerides's anxiety crept up a notch. He shot another nervous glance to his right.

'I think, perhaps we should go now Mr Murray?'

The man in the driver's seat didn't move, but remained draped over the steering wheel, his right foot riding the accelerator. His gaze was still locked on the house at the end of the kilometre long track, as it had been since he'd swung the pick up left off the main road ten minutes before, jerking to a stop in a cloud of dust that drifted away on the light breeze.

In that ten minutes, the man called Murray hadn't uttered a word. His attention was focused on the white-walled property that, perched above the locally-famous Sea Caves, looked out over the sparkling Mediterranean. Two storeys high, but with Roman-style turrets that gave an impression of more, its terracotta tiles contrasted sharply with the sky's clear blue.

The fact that, though the truck was Nik's he wasn't driving, was just one source of Nik's anxiety. Caught out by his former client's sudden lunge for his keys and surprise suggestion that it was, 'Time to see how this new truck of yours goes,' Nik had found himself

3

relegated to the passenger seat. There, he was uncomfortably aware he was no longer able to follow the dictum property developers along Cyprus's southern fringe live by; *Whatever the client does, stay in control.*

The other source of Nik's angst was the knowledge that whilst he could imagine what Murray might be *thinking*, he had no idea what he was *planning*. It meant Nik had no choice but to watch and wait while Murray decided his next move. But unsettling though the continuing silence was, Nik didn't feel like breaking it to ask, 'What are we doing here?' To do so risked prompting another outburst of the sort Nik witnessed when he first described the 'rather unfortunate problem,' that had developed around the project. Given a choice, it was something he would rather avoid.

Chancing another glance, Nik noted that despite the heat, Murray was barely sweating. Even with the air-con turned right up, stuck out in the glare of the baking sun as they were, the temperature was well above the '24' showing on the control setting. Nik's shirt was already sticking to his back and chest, rivulets running down his face into his collar, a glistening veneer over his hairy, builder's arms.

But as he waited and fumed, Nik knew he had only himself to blame and cursed his own stupidity. He should have seen it coming the moment his former client asked to take, 'One last look at the place.' He had seen enough of Murray the past couple of years to know that the quiet reserve that seemed so typically English was, in fact, a front. Even during the early days, when they'd haggled over the likes of the purchase price, contracts, delivery dates, and the all-important, profit-enhancing extras, Nik had seen signs of the steely resolve that by all accounts came to the fore in the days and weeks following the tragedy involving his family.

Even back then it made Nik wonder what, exactly, Murray was leaving out when he spoke of the, 'bit of military work,' that preceded their decision to settle on what Nick always referred to as, 'Our Beautiful Island Of Cyprus,' - force of salesman's habit. He should have realised that any man who could come through what Murray had suffered without crumbling, wouldn't be the sort to just chuck things in with a, 'Ah well, never mind,' and walk away. Christos had warned as much.

Christos was Nik's brother. Between them they owned and ran Klerides Development and Construction, Nik building, Christos designing and planning. Over the past ten years, they had seen the small building company they'd set up following their National Service grow into the burgeoning property development business it was today. And while it was still far from being a threat to the 'Big Three', it was, nonetheless, attracting an increasingly large slice of the market in overseas property investment centred around, Pafos, the popular resort on the island's south-west corner.

As he glanced at his watch, Nik wished that right now, Christos was here. Three years older than Nik, and the lead decision maker when it came to the Big Issues, Nik was sure Christos would know what to do, especially given the way time was ticking. But the Englishman seemed in no rush to be going anywhere. Rather, he was just sitting there, immobile.

Apart from his right foot.

Nik was just thankful that, so far at least, there was no sign of movement up ahead, either around the wrought-iron gates that had caused his blacksmith cousins, George and Evsan, so much trouble, or behind the two-metre wall surrounding the property. But despite the apparent lack of activity, there was no question that whoever was at home was aware of their presence. Nik had seen the camera atop the nearest telegraph-pole swivel in their direction seconds after they pulled off the main road. Even if whoever was on watch hadn't actually seen them swing in, they couldn't have failed to see the dust cloud that spilled down the track after they stopped. Nik knew the Englishman had spotted the cameras as well, though Nik hadn't mentioned the security measures he saw going in the week before the new occupant arrived. The knowledge they were being watched only added to Nik's discomfort. With the temperature rising, and not just due to the heat, he knew there was nothing else for it. He cleared his throat.

'Have you seen enough now Mr Murray?' He turned in his seat, as if it might add weight to his suggestion. 'I think perhaps we should not stay here much longer?'

But if Nik's words registered, Murray showed no sign. His gaze didn't shift from the property Nik and Christos had once hoped to use, with permission of course, in their next marketing campaign. *So much for that idea.*

He tried again.

'Mr Murray?' Murray half-turned towards him, but it was obvious his thoughts still dwelt elsewhere. *A dream turned nightmare perhaps?*

As Nik took in the stony features, he thought he caught a fleeting glimpse of something he hadn't seen before. Something other than just the cold stare. The idea came there was something dark in it, but he dismissed it. Apart from the connection with the British Sovereign Base Garrison at Episkopi and the sad fate of his wife and son, Nik didn't know much about Murray. Nonetheless, he was pretty certain that despite all Murray had gone through - crowned as it was with the house problem - the man wasn't suicidal. Not yet at any rate.

6

But even as the thought settled, reassuringly, in Nik's brain, Murray did something that sent the builder's stomach sliding towards the hand-stitched Gucci shoes he'd picked up in Nicosia the week before. Murray straightened in his seat and, quite casually, slipped the shift into 'drive.' The truck gave a slight lurch as the transmission engaged.

'Wh- what are you doing?'

At first Murray said nothing. Then, to Nik's growing horror, he turned to him, smiled, winked, and floored the accelerator.

The truck's back-end slewed side-to-side as the engine roared and the Pirellis with the legend 'Rough Terrain' gouged into the walls fought for purchase in the loose gravel. Stones, dust and burning rubber spewed behind. Then the tyres bit and, before Nik could voice any protest, they took off.

CHAPTER 2

Nik hung onto the grab-handle as the pick-up hurtled down the track. Missing a brake pedal, he pressed his feet against the bulkhead, forcing himself even further back. He tried to shout, 'STOP', but his parched voice was drowned out by the engine roar and the clatter of stones, hitting the undercarriage.

The track was pocked with potholes. Some were deep and more than capable of bouncing them into the ditches lining the fields either side. But as Nik glanced right, he was horrified to see that Murray barely had a grip of the steering wheel, which was sliding easily between hands that seemed far too low for Nik's reckoning. It made him think of the complimentary Off-Road Course that had come with the Mitsubishi but which he'd never taken up. Had he done, he might at least have some idea whether the technique signalled someone adept at off-roading - or a man made reckless by anger and despair. Either way, Nik doubted it mattered. The track was raised several feet above the fields. Images of what would happen if they left it at this speed – they were already nudging sixty - flooded Nik's brain. But as they bore down on the villa – they must have already covered a hundred metres - other images swept aside those of them leaving the track and somersaulting through the fields. And these were worse.

When they'd set off, Nik had no clue as to Murray's intention, his face showing only grim determination. But as Nik took in the set features, the thoughts of suicide he had dismissed so casually came flooding back. His natural instincts for survival fought against the reflex to panic, and his mind raced as he calculated consequences, possibilities.

Though the heavy iron gates wouldn't stop the Mitsubishi outright if they hit at this speed, there was no way it, or its inhabitants, would be good for anything afterwards. And though the truck was equipped with the latest life-saving technology – safety cage, all-round air bags, collapsing steering column – he seriously doubted they would survive such an impact. For an instant he thought about leaning across and wresting control of the wheel from the madman next to him. Murray was tall and had a good physique, but Nik was bulkier. And though he had given up hod-carrying long ago, he was, probably, the Englishman's match if it came to a tussle of strength. But even as the thought settled, he realised that the consequences of such an act would be no better than the alternative.

We're still going to die, he thought.

But then, shocked that he could accept his impending fate so clinically, Nik gave it one last try.

'YOU'RE GOING TO KILL US,' he yelled.

The Englishman kept the pick-up pointed straight, accelerator hard down. The engine rose, then fell in pitch as the auto-change shifted up. Their speed increased.

Whatever else he might be, Nik was a pragmatist, and no coward. He knew that whatever course the Englishman was set on, there was nothing he could do to stop him. He turned to face the inevitable. As he did so, he saw movement within the villa's compound as those within finally responded to what would, to them,

9

look like a direct attack. From his raised position, Nik could just see the tops of figures behind the wall, rushing to and fro. Men appeared at the gates, pointing, spinning, yelling to each other. They were still a good two hundred metres away. Even so, Nik read panic in faces and bodies as the truck bore down.

Transfixed as Nik was by the sight of the gates rushing closer, he was dimly aware of figures emerging round both corners of the perimeter wall, running forward as if bent on intercepting their charge. And he sensed rather than saw that the implements some carried, and which another time he may have taken as gardening tools, had a more serious purpose. As if to confirm it, a figure off to the left hefted something long and heavy to his shoulder, bringing it up to bear on them. Nik screamed. 'LOOK OUT.'

Even as the words leapt from Nik's throat, Murray stood on the brakes. Still wearing his seat belt – some instinct had made him keep it fastened - Nik was thrown forward. He grunted in pain as the webbing dug deep into his shoulder and chest. But he knew it was too late. Though he could feel the vehicle's ABS working at maximum as it responded to the maniac's belated change of heart, they were still bearing down on the villa at breakneck speed. Clouds of dust and gravel flew everywhere as their charge slowed, rapidly.

Not enough…

Now Nik could see fear as well as panic on the faces of those manning the gates. He glimpsed weapons. *We're still going to die*, he thought.

As the gates loomed, filling Nik's vision, the Englishman pressed down even harder. At the same time he spun the wheel anti-clockwise then, as the truck began to slew broadside, quickly back in the opposite direction.

Nik's first thought was he was trying to roll it, so it would career, tumbling over and over into the gates, the guards and the pink-painted walls - the last act of a demented soul. But to his astonishment, the truck didn't roll. Instead it began to slide over the loose surface at the same time dipping, sickeningly, to its offside but remaining upright until with a final rock it came to a bone-jarring halt, less than three metres from the gates.

Choking dust-clouds enveloped everything and everyone. And as Nik waited for it to clear, too shocked to be grateful he was still alive, he looked to his right at the man in the driver's seat.

Murray's hands were now resting at six-thirty, like some commuter stuck in slow-moving traffic. His expression, which before had been set like concrete, was relaxed, his head angled towards the villa as if waiting for it to emerge from the dust so he could gaze on it, admiringly. He wasn't even breathing heavily.

Nik knew that his response right then should be to vent his fury for having put him through such a terrifying ordeal. For coming so close to killing them both. For whatever damage he would later discover had been caused to his mechanical pride and joy. But he didn't. Right now, Nik was just grateful to be alive, and still too shaken to do little more than wonder over the man's cool demeanour. It was then Nik realised.

Whoever Murray was, whatever his background, suicide had never been in his mind. And as far as losing control was concerned, Nik now suspected that given the way he had brought the pick-up to such a precisely-gauged stop, there had never been the slightest danger of such a thing happening.

But even as comprehension dawned and the dust began to clear, other matters grabbed Nik's attention, making him realise that while he might still be breathing, his ordeal was far from over. A face appeared at his window.

Shaven headed, with high cheek-bones and a livid scar running vertically from his left eye to his jaw, Nik recognised the giant Siberian he had met twice before. On each occasion his looming presence had made Nik feel uneasy. Now Nik saw he was brandishing some sort of automatic rifle.

Before Nik could move, the man – Lantzeff, Nik suddenly remembered his name - yanked the door open so it swung back on its hinges in a way that made Nik want to shout, 'HEY. Be careful.' But he said nothing and simply stared, for the first time since his National Service, down the barrel of a gun.

'OUT,' Lantzeff barked.

CHAPTER 3

Still shaking, Nik half-stepped, half-fell out of the truck.
As his jelly-legs began to give under him, the giant
Siberian's paw dug into his shoulder and lifted, forcing
him to stay on his feet. The sight of angry men
brandishing guns made Nik's head spin more, and as he
struggled to orient himself, he glanced back at Murray.

The Englishman was still just sitting there, watching
as the men outside banged on the window, pulled at the
handle, demanded he open the door Nik hadn't seen him
lock. But then the fingers gripping him spun him round
and he found himself staring into Lantzeff's angry face.

'KLERIDES?'

Nik sighed in relief. At least the man remembered
him. But it did nothing to quell the Siberian's fierce
anger.

'WHAT MADNESS IS THIS?' Lantzeff yelled.
'What brings you here?'

Before Nik could answer, his interrogator glanced
over his shoulder into the pick-up. Nik saw the gun
come up, pointing at Murray. And there was no doubting
the threat in Lantzeff's voice as he addressed the
Englishman.

'Out,' he said. 'Now.'

Still in the Siberian's fierce grip, Nik managed to twist
enough to see Murray give the Siberian a long stare, the

half-smile now gone. But though Nik was as scared as he could ever remember, Murray didn't seem the least bit intimidated. Eventually, he pulled the lever and stepped down from the cab.

Immediately he was surrounded by clamouring, gesticulating figures demanding to know who he was, what he thought he was doing. Like a doll in the hands of a child, Nik felt himself being half-dragged, half-carried round to the other side of the truck to join the man who had brought them to such a plight. The others stood aside as the Siberian jammed Nik up against the Englishman.

'Tell me,' the Siberian growled. 'Why are you here? And why did you come at us like that? You are lucky we didn't blow you and your truck up before you got to the gates.'

Nick saw Murray turn his gaze on the men surrounding them. He seemed to be weighing them, their weapons, their capabilities. Nik wasn't interested. And when Murray didn't rush to provide the Siberian with the information he had demanded, Nik decided he ought to offer some sort of explanation.

'You know me,' Nik gushed, just in case the Siberian might have forgotten in the half-minute since he'd said his name. 'I'm Nik Klerides. The builder.'

'I know who you are,' Lantzeff barked, 'But who is this?' He jerked the gun at Murray, who turned a stony face to him. Nik knew enough to recognise a potential stand off when he saw one and wondered again if the Englishman had taken leave of his senses. Surely Nik had told him enough to know these were not the sort of people you mess with.

'This is Mr Murray,' Nik said, keen to pacify his inquisitor, calm things down and just get the hell out. The Siberian looked blank. 'You know, Mr *Murray*. The man I spoke to your employer about?'

The Siberian's eyes narrowed and his head lifted as he subjected the Englishman to a scrutinising stare. Nik held his breath, hoping things were starting to register in the ape whose fingers were still digging into his shoulder. In their limited dealings, Nik had gained the impression that whatever position Lantzeff held within his employer's organisation, it was not one that required a great deal of reasoning ability. Slowly, the big man nodded, realisation seeming to dawn, at last.

'Ach. HIM' He said it almost dismissively. He turned to Nik. 'So why have you brought him? What does he want?'

About to protest his innocence – the idiot could see who was driving – Nik opened his mouth, only for Murray to cut across.

'He didn't bring me. I brought him. And I'm here to see your boss.'

Inside, Nik groaned.

Lantzeff looked at the Englishman as if he was mad. 'You are not expected. It is not possible.'

'That's alright,' Nik said. 'We understand.' He turned to Murray as if to say, *That's it then.* But Murray was returning Lantzeff's stare with interest.

'Tell him I'm here. He'll see me.'

The Siberian stood over the Englishman by a good six inches, but the way Murray was looking at him it didn't seem to mean a thing. It prompted Nik to wonder again about him.

Eventually Lantzeff turned, and barked something at one of the men at the gate, clicking fingers and holding out a spade-like hand. The man reached behind the gatepost then jogged over with a mobile which he placed in it.

Lantzeff walked away a few paces, making the call. As

he waited with the phone to his ear, he turned to stare at the two visitors. Someone answered. There was a jumble of conversation which consisted on Lantzeff's part of little more than a series of guttural grunts and growls, none of which Nik could translate into anything meaningful. It ended with the Siberian barking a sharp, 'Da!' into the phone before he tossed it back to the gateman. He sauntered back over, eyeing them both as if they were bugs he would take great pleasure in squishing, before nodding back over his shoulder towards the house.

'He says he will see you.'

As the Siberian led them through the gates and up the block-paved driveway towards the villa's front door, Nik saw Murray's gaze roaming everywhere. The now landscaped garden. The child's bat and ball awaiting its owner's return. The custom-built Monaco-Blue BMW X7 xDrive that Nik so admired. Parked outside the double garage where it looked like someone might have been polishing it, it was now covered in a film of dust. As Nik watched, Murray transferred his attention to the front of the house, his gaze lingering somewhere high. Looking up, Nik just caught a glimpse of the blond woman before she slipped out of sight behind the master bedroom's curtain. Nik bit his lip. Truth be told, she was probably to blame for everything.

As they passed the circular pond and fountain in the turning circle at the bottom of the steps that led up to the wide porch, Murray stopped so suddenly the man behind bumped into him. For a moment his features seemed to soften as he gazed into the gently splashing water and the careful arrangement of plants and grasses. As he saw the almost imperceptible nod, Nik thought that for once he could imagine what might be going on inside Murray's head. An imagined conversation with someone who would, Nik was sure, have appreciated the care that had gone into achieving just the right balance between water and greenery. To his regret, Nik had met her only twice, yet it somehow felt as if he knew her well. Then they were up the steps and through the darkened doorway.

But inside, the hallway was light and airy in the way that most traditional Cypriot houses are not. After the baking heat of outside it was wonderfully cool. As he looked around, and despite his anxiety over what the next few minutes might bring, Nik indulged his craftsman's feelings of self-satisfaction. Unable to resist, he turned to check out Murray's reaction.

The Englishman was standing in the middle of the entrance hall, at the bottom of the wide staircase. As Nik watched, he made a slow, full turn then tipped his head back to stare up at the coloured-glass dome in the middle of the high ceiling. An extravagant touch that was Nik's own idea - he had stood to recover less than half its cost in the final settlement - Nik remembered how pleased he had been the day when, having overseen its fitting, he stood halfway up the stairs, admiring the way it diffused the light just the way he had envisaged..

'This way.'

Lantzeff's gruff command snapped Nik out his reverie. He followed as the Siberian led them to the carved wooden doors to the main lounge. He knocked once then, in response to the muffled hail from within, threw them open. They trooped through.

The Russian was over to their right, in front of the long sweep of curved windows that gave the room its panoramic sea-view. As they entered, he snapped his mobile shut and turned to them.

Valerik Podruznig was tall, slim and sharp featured,

with high cheekbones and a hawk nose. His light brown hair, greying around the edges, was cut short in what was almost a schoolboy-style, making him appear younger than his actual age. But it was the eyes - strangely lifeless, like a dead man's - that drew people's attention the most. Dressed in grey linen slacks and a long-sleeved white shirt, open several buttons to reveal a thick, gold chain, his relaxed, hand-in-pocket stance made him look every inch the wheeler-dealer businessman he nowadays professed to be.

Despite it being Murray's first glimpse of Podruznig, Nik was surprised to see that at least part of his attention seemed focused on something beyond the windows. Laid mainly to lawn – the swimming pool was further round to the right – but dotted here and there with angular flower beds, the garden shelved gently to where it met the cliff-top. There, an old carob tree stood guard over the small cove that Nik had always felt was an excellent selling point. For a fleeting second, an expression Nik couldn't quite place flitted across the Englishman's face, then he was turning to give the Russian his full attention.

'Mr Murray,' Podruznig said as he crossed the hardwood floor, hand outstretched. 'We meet at last.' His mouth was set in a smile that wasn't reflected in the eyes, and he withdrew the hand as soon as it became clear Murray intended to ignore it. Nor did Murray return his greeting. Podruznig turned to Nik.

'You should have told me you were coming, Klerides. We could have been expecting you.' Though the words were those of a gracious host, disappointed at not being given enough notice to lay on lunch, Nik had little difficulty reading the message they contained. The Russian was not pleased to be interrupted this way.

Like at the gate, Murray wasn't going to let blame fall

anywhere other than where it was due.

'He couldn't tell you because he didn't know.'

Murray tossed the words out, casually, as he gazed about the room, taking in the elaborate décor and furnishings that were in a different league to those on the original plan.

But at least it had the effect of drawing Podruznig's scrutiny away from Nik. For long seconds Podruznig watched as the Englishman completed his appraisal. Eventually, his reconnoitring finished, and presumably aware of the silence that was now hanging, Murray turned to face the man he had come to see.

Less than thirty seconds had passed since they had first laid eyes on each other, but it was already clear to Nik there was to be no pretence at amiable politeness on either part. Nik knew it would not trouble the Russian - Podruznig hadn't made his fortune by prevaricating – and he was beginning to think the same about Murray.

The Russian's smile disappeared, replaced by a cold stare and an icy manner. 'Why have you come, Mr Murray?'

When Murray replied his words were clear and calm. And as far as Nik could tell he seemed entirely serious when he said, 'I want my house back. And I would like you, your family and your associates to leave. Now.'

CHAPTER 4

Efrosine Philippou's eyes widened as she leaned over her desk.

'And how did he react?'

Despite her client going completely against all her advice, 'Fofo', as she was more commonly known was, nevertheless, engrossed. And though she was doing her best to maintain the professionalism for which she was known, she also knew that her taste for the dramatic - and which she shared with many of her fellow country women - was in danger of showing.

'He laughed in my face,' Murray said. 'I guess he thought I was joking. When I told him I wasn't, he got pissy and started ranting.'

'About?'

'Oh, solicitors, contracts, not-so-veiled threats. That sort of thing.'

At the whiff of an opening, Fofo sat up, pen poised again. 'He threatened you?'

But Murray shook his head. 'Nothing you could make anything out of in court. But they were there. It's the way he operates.'

Fofo frowned, annoyed by his casual dismissal, and not for the first time since he'd begun his narrative. For some reason, her client seemed intent on playing down anything that could hint at a bargaining point. It was as if he had already decided that court action was not the way forward, though she couldn't imagine why. It made her wonder again whether he was simply cynical of Cyprus's legal process - given his army/police background he would know it well enough - or if what he'd been doing these past few years had turned him into one of those 'actions speak louder than words' ex-service types she met occasionally. The sort who think that because of their background and contacts, no one would be stupid enough to mess with them. They all rejoin the real world eventually, of course. Though by then it is usually too late. Certainly in Murray's case, whilst his anger at the wrong done to him seemed as strong as ever, there were times when he seemed, just a little too understanding of the grab-it-while-you-can mentality that seemed to underpin the Russian's actions.

Masking her disappointment, Fofo checked her notes again, hoping to spot something she might convince him to let her use, but there was nothing.

Eventually she said, 'So how did it end?'

'I guess you'd have to say he threw us out.'

'Physically?' One last try.

He gave it some thought. 'It depends on your definition of physical.'

Glaring at him, she chose not to press it.

She sighed and leaned back in her chair. 'What did Klerides say?'

Murray thought a moment. 'I don't think he'll let me drive his truck again.'

For the first time since he'd arrived to tell her about what she wasted no time in labelling, 'An entirely ill-judged intervention,' Fofo failed to stop the smile that was never far away from breaking through. Having been told many times how it changed her - radically most said - she didn't let it linger. Then it was back to business. She shook her head.

'You are sure there was no violence of any sort?'

'None at all. I couldn't even say if the guns were loaded.'

She froze. 'They had guns?'

He half-smiled, like it had been a joke. 'I'm kidding. There were no guns.'

For a long time she let her gaze linger on him, trying to decide whether the innocent look was genuine. She had learned long ago how he seemed to enjoy winding her up - the way some men do. But given how she had committed herself to his cause, if she thought for one moment he was keeping stuff like that back from her, she would not be pleased. She liked to think that after all this time he trusted her, and that the same went for Penny, her ex-pat English secretary, though she was aware he was less sure of some of her colleagues. He made no secret of his reluctance to share information with those who don't need to know. To some extent she understood. Pafos was a place where many of the locals either know each other, or are related. Secrets tend not to stay that way. And whilst she knew he'd also taken the matter to the police, he had, it seemed, even been reluctant to say too much to them. Why, she still wasn't sure. She eyed him, coolly, before putting down her pen.

'Peter.' She paused while he gave her his full attention. 'Why is it I have the distinct impression you are not telling me everything?'

He didn't avoid her gaze. 'I am telling you everything you need to know as my solicitor.'

'But shouldn't it be me who decides what I need to know?'

In truth, Fofo was beginning to feel more than a little patronised. With an LLB from Oxford, she was rightly proud of her hard-earned reputation as one of the island's best litigators outside Nicosia. But there had been occasions when he had said things that left her wondering if he was trying to protect her from something. Yes, the information she had garnered on Podruznig so far was alarming, particularly the bits about his penchant for violence and - assuming it was true - young girls. But whatever the fate of those who had previously tried to get Podruznig into court - she hadn't mentioned that side of things to her Italian boyfriend, Franco, yet – it would not stop her from following her principles, or doing the job she had trained so long and hard for.

Murray leaned forward. His face said, *'Time for some straight talking'*.

'I'll tell you what,' he said. She arched a wary eyebrow. 'You tell me what you were going to tell me before I mentioned going to see Podruznig. Then, if there is anything I know that might change things, I promise I'll tell you.'

She gave him the sort of look she usually kept for opposing counsel. But eventually, she caved, and shook her head, exasperated. As she did a spray of her thick, dark hair fell across her face. She swept it back with the practised gesture she was aware many of her clients seemed to like. Murray didn't move.

'The next time I see Nik, I am going to tell him he must never again send me clients like you.' Ignoring the wan smile of apology, she commenced to give him the opinion he'd come for. It was in two parts.

First off, she told him how she thought he had a strong case. True, they would have to concede that, technically, he *was* in breach of contract for failing to make the last two stage-payments within the periods stipulated. However, assuming he could prove the, 'extraordinary and extenuating circumstances beyond his control,' he claimed had prevented him from making the necessary arrangements, *and* that his claim to have contacted Klerides' office by telephone to inform them the payments would be late held up, then there was a fair chance a court would find in their favour. Klerides' sudden voiding of the contract – particularly his failure to give reasonable notice - would, in all the circumstances, be adjudged a disproportionate response to something that developers operating within Cyprus's dynamic property market were well-used to.

At this point Fofo emphasised that she was putting her trust in his claim to have good reason why he could only reveal the nature of the 'extenuating circumstances' to a Judge in his or her private chambers. She had tried pressing him on the matter of course, but he had been insistent. And it was only his reference to 'sensitive military matters' that finally persuaded her to drop it. It is widely accepted within Cyprus legal circles that the island's strategically-significant location, as well as its historic links with the British Armed Forces, generate any number of legal anomalies. European Union and UN-sponsored negotiations over the island's partitioned status are always on-going, and given the country's interest in maintaining its strong links with Britain, the courts tend to be sympathetic towards those who find themselves disadvantaged as a result of performing some duty that is, in some way, conducive to Cyprus's longer term interests. It certainly wasn't beyond the bounds of possibility that whatever work Murray had been involved in, a judge may well be persuaded to rule him a 'Special Case.' And if that happened, there was an excellent chance the court would find in their favour. The contract between Klerides and Pudruznig would be voided and the property would revert to Murray's ownership. She paused to sip from her water bottle.

'I sense a 'but'.' Murray said.

'I have researched Podruznig. And this so-called Security Chief of his-.' She searched through her papers.

'Lantzeff,' Murray reminded her.

'That's him. First of all, you were right. Podruznig does have connections with several of those people nowadays refer to as, "The Oligarchs".' Murray nodded, clearly not surprised. It was he who had first suggested she may want to check it out. 'In particular he worked for someone called-' She searched through her papers again, found it. 'Anatoly Kaskiv?' If Murray had heard the name, he didn't show it. 'He is in shipping, as well as other things. Anyway, it seems that Podruznig started off acting as a... I think you would call it, a *fixer*, to some of these characters?' She looked up, caught his affirming nod. 'I haven't been able to get hold of a police record yet but there seems little doubt he was involved in some very dubious activities. He has a reputation for extreme violence.' She looked up again, saw his face. 'Am I boring you or do you already know all this?'

'Carry on.'

She took a deep breath not at all sure she wasn't wasting her time. 'A few years ago, it seems Podruznig decided to go 'respectable.' I am not sure why. He invested in some companies Kaskiv and a couple of others had inherited during the soviet upheavals, motor manufacture, gas production, that sort of thing. He also, somehow, ended up with a stake in the privatisation of Aeroflot. I won't bore you with the details.'

As Murray nodded again, Fofo wondered once more how much of what she was telling him he'd already gleaned from his own sources. Most of what she'd discovered was even in the public domain. Thanks to the dedicated efforts of a handful of stalwartly-patriotic Soviet exiles around the world - some of whom were now dead – much of it was now on-line, especially Wikipedia. Over recent years such people had made it their mission in life to expose the stinking corruption that had allowed the former wealth of the Soviet Union to fall into the hands of the relatively small number of entrepreneurs who just happened to be in the right place at the right time. Still more could be gleaned reading between the lines of what they had written. People like Kaskiv - and those feeding off him, like Podruznig - weren't subject to assassination attempts because of the equitable way they ran their business affairs. But Fofo wasn't stupid. If this was just what she had been able to find out, there had to be more, lots more. She wondered what Murray had been doing since she saw him last, apart from acting like an idiot. She got to the nub of it.

'The main point is, over the years several people have tried to sue Podruznig through the courts.' She gave Murray a loaded look. 'He seems to have a knack of making enemies.'

'Is that right?'

'But as far as I've been able to find out, no one has ever got their case before a judge. Sooner or later, people always drop their cases, quite suddenly in some instances, and before any bargaining has even taken place. Either that or they, or their witnesses, *or* their legal representatives, disappear.' She looked for a reaction. When there wasn't any, she carried on. 'It doesn't take a genius to work out that Podruznig, or more likely this....'

They said his name together. 'Lantzeff.'

'...this Lantzeff, employ some rather questionable methods to dissuade litigants from pursuing actions.'

'So what are you telling me?'

Fofo took a deep breath. It was what she had been leading up to. In fact, she had been thinking of little else for days, mulling over her decision, what it may mean. 'As your solicitor, I have to advise you that you should consider pursuing your claim against Klerides. There is every chance a court will find in your favour. And if that is what you want to do then you can rest assured I will do everything in my power to get the case into court.'

This time she didn't wait to be invited to give him the, 'but.' 'I must also tell you, quite frankly, that things are likely to get rough. You must be, we both must be, sure we understand what we could be getting into if we take Klerides, which means Podruznig, on. You could end up paying a higher price than you bargained for over what some might see as simply a point of principle.

'Is that how you see it? A point of principle?'

Seeing the look in his face she softened, searching for the right balance between professional advice and compassion.

'I know what the house means to you, Peter. And what it meant to Katherine. But you have to remember that Klerides did offer you another property. Okay, it's not the one you originally signed up for, but it's comparable in many ways. And he's probably right when he says it is worth more. Some legal advisers would see it as a fair offer, and would advise you to take it.'

'I asked if you think this is about a point of principle.'

She took a deep breath. 'No. I believe this is more than a point of principle.' For once he gave her something back, not much, but enough.

'Thank you.' She nodded her acknowledgment. He continued. 'So, seeing as we both agree this isn't just about principles, what are you advising me to do?'

Fofo Philippou sat back in her chair. For several

seconds she tapped the rubber end of her pencil on the yellow legal pad in front of her, at the same time subjecting him to a long look. *Would he be up for it? More to the point, was she?*

Eventually, her attractive face broke into the sly smile some people said hinted at something dark within her. She sat forward again, and as she did so she thought she saw something in his face that told her he knew exactly what she was going to say.

'I hate these *Pontians* who come to my country and think that just because they have money they are above the law. If you are up for it, I think we should sue.'

CHAPTER 5

Murray waited for the clattering noise to stop. The dive shed was made of breeze-block topped with fibre-glass sheeting and had a corrugated iron roof. The generator powering the Max-air Scuba Compressor was running full-on. There was no chance he would be heard over the din bouncing off and around the walls.

Across the other side, by the workbenches, a man was filling air-tanks. Back to Murray, his attention was on the row of pressure gauges on the wall above. Tall and gangly, his still-damp, ginger hair hung in rats' tails. The top half of his wet-suit dangled behind, like a withered, con-joined twin. As he monitored the dials he seemed as oblivious of Murray's presence as Murray appeared to be of the small Nepalese in bright blue Bermuda-shorts and carrying a spear-gun who crept up behind and prodded the point squarely into his belt. At the same time the man working the compressor released the trigger so that the noise suddenly cut off.

'That belt cost me twenty euro on Pafos market,' Murray said without looking round. 'If you mark it Kish, I'm going to stick that spike so far up your arse the only job you'll be good for will be as a spit.'

Chuckling, the ginger-haired man didn't turn as he hung up the hose. 'Jesus, Kishore, you make more noise than a crate of roller-skating monkeys.'

Behind Murray, the former Ghurkha corporal with the spear gun shrugged, and put up his weapon. As Murray turned, he ran a finger over the smooth leather, checking. The man called Kishore smiled, displaying prominent white teeth.

'You fucking fairy,' Kishore mocked. His voice was a mix of native Nepal and East-end cockney. 'Since when did you worry about poncy belts?'

Murray looked threatening. 'Since a little buck-toothed bastard thought he could creep up on someone without being heard.' He made a grab at the spear-gun but the smaller man was ready, and jerked it out of his reach.

The toothy grin showed again. 'You've slowed up, Plod. You've lost it.'

Murray turned to the other man, now sauntering over, wiping his hands on a rag.

'It's time you drowned this runt and got yourself a proper pet,' Murray said.

The man nodded, accepting the truth of it. 'Aye, but he does a good job keeping the rats down.'

Murray shook his head, not convinced. For several seconds the two men faced each other, noting the changes.

Red's hair was longer, if thinner, but his face was as tanned and weathered as it had always been. Several days' grey stubble lightened his chin and jowls. Murray had put back on some of the weight he'd lost. He still had a way to go yet, but he knew he looked better for it.

After a few seconds' inspection, both men caved, stepping in to embrace each other. The man in the wet suit was taller and older and before they broke he clapped Murray's back in a way Murray read as, *I miss her too*. He cocked his head to one side. 'How are you, Pete?'

Murray shrugged, took a long, deep breath. 'Getting

there, I guess.'

Former SAS-Sergeant Mike 'Red' McGeary nodded, letting his silence substitute for words their reunion would otherwise have merited. Then he turned to the still-grinning Nepalese.

'Kish. Go tell that lot out front the dive is cancelled. Tell 'em there's a storm brewing. Then break out some Keo.'

Some minutes later, the three popped Keo cans as they sat at the plastic table in the small courtyard out back. It was private and, under the vine-laden trellis, welcomingly cool.

'Yamas,' Red said, raising his beer.

'Yamas,' the other two answered. As cans clinked, condensation dripped onto the table. They all supped, long and slow.

'So,' Red said eventually, pulling another chair round and putting his feet up. 'Tell us.'

Over the next few minutes Murray gave his ex-colleagues further details of the problem he'd first sent word of in an email, weeks before. In particular, he described what he'd discovered about how the Russian had accomplished it, the veiled threats he now knew Podruznig had made towards the Klerides brothers and their families - not that they had reported anything to the police. He told how, finally convinced they had no choice, Nik and Christos had voided the contract with Murray in favour of the Russian. Murray spoke of the anger he'd first felt at being cheated, and how he'd been on the point of setting out to convince the builders of the error of their ways when he caught wind of what had actually happened.

Red snorted. 'No excuse as far as I'm concerned. If it had been me, I'd still have buried the bastards.'

But Murray shook his head. After listening to Nik's story and checking a couple of details, he was satisfied the pair's actions were nothing to do with greed, rather simply making sure their families stayed safe and the business viable. It wasn't their fault. He said so.

Red interrupted again. 'But why your house? Why didn't the Russian just get Klerides to build him a new one? There's plenty of land out there.'

'His wife, Klerides reckons. Apparently she took one look at it, or rather the location, it wasn't finished then, and decided it was just the place she was looking for. It's the most prominent point along that stretch of coast.'

Red nodded. 'The view's spectacular, that's for sure.'

Murray stopped his can an inch from his lips. 'You've been out there?'

Red swigged some beer before answering. 'Not to the house, but we dive along that stretch all the time.'

Murray nodded. The calm, crystal waters north of Pafos are well used by the resort's several dive schools. He continued. 'Podruznig's wife is a former beauty queen, or model, or something. But from what I've heard, the marriage is a sham. He treats her like shit, but still likes to show there isn't anything he can't get if he puts his mind to it.'

Red spat in the dust. 'Women. They cause more fucking trouble....'

'I doubt she even knows what he did,' Murray said. 'Apparently Podruznig went looking for her when he decided to become respectable, and didn't hang about trying to romance her. The word is he just uses her to show people that the rumours about his other interests are bullshit.'

'And are they?'

Can to his lips, Murray shrugged. 'I'm still working on that one, but I wouldn't mind betting they're true. From what I know, he's not exactly what you'd call well-balanced.'

'Like us you mean?' Kishore said, grinning. Murray ignored it.

'Anyway, it appears his wife isn't the sharpest tool in the box. She wouldn't have given a thought that the house might already be spoken for. My fight's not with her.'

'Guess not,' Red said.

After popping more cans, Murray brought them up to date, describing his abortive visit to the house the previous morning. Red and Kishore sat up, more alarmed, it seemed, than Murray thought it merited. After all, he was still here wasn't he? He moved on to recount his morning meeting with Fofo. On hearing of her enthusiasm for doing battle in court, Red looked sceptical.

'That could take a long time.'

Murray wafted his concern away. 'I can't let her take it on. It's too dangerous and I'm not going to let her expose herself that way.'

'Have you told her?'

'Not in so many words. I said I'd think about it and get back to her.'

Kishore chipped in. 'So you've come to us instead.'

Murray turned to the diminutive Nepalese. Excitement already showed in the beady eyes. He was probably already imagining them teaming up again, what it might mean, what it might bring.

'Don't get ahead of yourself Kish. I'm still weighing options. And I'm not ready yet to start something that could well turn nasty. Kathy wouldn't want that.'

At mention of her, the atmosphere around the table changed. Red and Kishore had known Kathy. Kishore adored her.

'You're right,' Red said. 'She wouldn't.'

They finished the rest of their beers in silence. Eventually, Red broke it.

'As a matter of interest, what was the set up at the house?'

'He's well dug-in,' Murray said. He described his welcome committee. 'Since leaving Ukraine, Podruznig keeps a small army of ex-military around him. For personal-protection supposedly, but they come in handy for other things, too, I imagine.'

'Like putting the squeeze on people.'

Murray twitched an eyebrow. 'Podruznig got Klerides to extend the basement as well as the house. It's a lot bigger now than we originally planned. According to Klerides there's accommodation down there for twenty or more, as well as a state-of-the-art security system. He likes his privacy. It's why he's come here. Things were getting a bit too hot back home it seems, but he's close enough here to keep in touch if and when he needs to. He's still got fingers in plenty of pies around the Russias.'

'So what's your plan?' Red said.

Murray stood up. 'There's someone else I've got to see. Then I'll decide.' Crushing his can, he tossed it to Kishore. 'Don't fall asleep, Goofy. I still owe you for ruining my belt.' Then he marched out, ducking under the vines as he headed towards the Dive Shop's front,

'Prissy wanker,' Kishore called to his back. Murray didn't turn.

From under the shade of the front awning, the pair watched as Murray threaded his way through the tourists milling around the bric-a-brac and souvenir shops lining the arcade down to the sea-front. As he disappeared, Kishore turned to his partner, all trace of humour now

34

gone.

'What do you think?'

Red took his time. 'Not sure yet. Let's wait and see. It might all just sort itself out.'

'And if it doesn't?'

A broad grin split Red's weather-beaten features. 'In that case me old cocker, you, me and our mate Plod may have to resume where we left off.'

Kishore's eyes widened and his brows jerked up and down, several times. 'Can't wait.'

CHAPTER 6

If the Pafos Divisional Police Headquarters were situated in some sandy desert, rather than the centre of the Old Town, looking down on Kato Pafos - the tourist area around the harbour - it could pass as some Foreign Legion outpost. Square, and plainly built around an inner compound that is used for everything from mustering-parades, to car parking, to volley-ball, the station's wide, outer, stone wall is broken, here and there, by green-shuttered windows. Around the inner square, wooden steps lead up to the walkway that gives access to the second storey offices. Almost completely enclosed, the square is a natural sun trap. Not yet ten o'clock, the temperature outside was already into the high twenties.

The Divisional Commander's office is situated on the North East corner where it catches the least direct sunlight. As Murray waited in the small ante-office, he was grateful for the barest breeze coming off the ceiling fan. He was trying to remember if the Police Chief's office had air-con, but he'd last visited in April, long before a local would have felt the need to use it.

Murray checked the clock on the wall behind the desk where Woman-Sergeant Andri Pahiti sat at her keyboard. He had been waiting nearly a quarter of an hour now. It made him wonder what was happening behind the door Andri guarded.

Andri's initial pleasantries - 'Nice to see you again Mr Murray. How do you like our Cyprus sun?' - had finally dried up as she got back to typing up the summaries for the stack of Court Files on the table beside her. A middle-aged career officer and, as she had disclosed during Murray's last visit, married to a Limassol-based Inspector, Andri had the air of someone who had been around long enough to have seen it all. Attractive, in a motherly sort of way, her quiet efficiency reminded Murray of some of the spinsterly types he had come across during his own police service back in the UK. It prompted thoughts in Murray's mind about how, though the island's system of policing was based on the British model, the local force seemed to operate in a time warp that mirrored UK Policing thirty or more years earlier. He wondered if the cult TV drama from years back, 'Life on Mars', had ever been popular here. Even if it had, most Cypriots would probably never get the jokes.

And though the Island-state was gradually catching up with all the so-called 'modernising' EU legislation – Health and Safety, Human Rights, Diversity training, et al - for the time being things remained much as they had always been. Which included Divisional Commanders having no compunction about keeping visitors waiting. Murray was about to ask Andri how much longer, when a shadow fell across her desk, announcing the arrival of another visitor. He looked to his right.

Framed in the doorway, with the sun behind so he couldn't make her out properly, Murray nevertheless knew at once she was a looker. Dark hair fell in waves onto tanned shoulders that were bare but for the thin straps of her bright summer dress. Cut low enough to tantalise, but not so much as to draw disapproving comments from those of a more conservative nature, it showed off a figure whose curves, his instincts told him, owed nothing to motherhood. The way Andri's face lit up when she looked up and saw the newcomer, Murray could tell she was, Somebody.

For nearly a minute, a staccato of indecipherable Greek rattled between the two women. And though Murray understood barely a word, he sussed enough from the way Andri kept shaking her head and gesturing at first him, then the door to the office behind her, to know that whoever the visitor was, she also wanted access to the Commander. He could also tell that unlike him, she was not inclined to wait.

Even as his suspicions formed, she confirmed them. Waving away Andri's protestations, she crossed the room and headed straight for the door. Andri looked horrified.

'*Gina*,' she hissed. 'NO.'

As 'Gina' turned, finger to her lips to give Andri a conspiratorial, 'Ssshhh,' she seemed to notice Murray for the first time. She threw him the sort of smile he couldn't remember being on the receiving end of in a long time.

'You do not mind do you? I will be only a moment.'

He opened his mouth to say something, but wasn't quick enough. Spinning on her heels, she knocked once on the door, loudly, and walked straight in. She closed it, firmly, behind her. At once, echoes of voices sounded through the door - Gina's and a man's. Both were loud. Andri covered her face with her hands in horror at the crime that had just been committed. But between the covering fingers, Murray spotted traces of wry amusement.

'She is *so* BAD,' Andri said, turning to him and shaking her head. 'He will be furious.'

For several moments the voice Murray assumed was the commander's lent truth to Andri's assertion. When it suddenly quieted, Andri span round to face the door, as if expecting to see it spring open and the invader be ejected by the man who was apparently still too busy to see Murray. But it stayed closed. Eventually, she turned back to Murray, biting her lower lip to stifle a smile. 'I think she wins. As always.'

As much amused by the young woman's bravado as interested in who she might be, Murray was getting around to asking when the door flew open. As explosively as she had entered, Gina came out.

'Thank you Papa. See you later,' she said, before closing it behind her as firmly as when she entered.

Andri attempted a scolding look and launched into what Murray assumed was supposed to be a severe ticking off. When she lapsed into English, Murray wondered if it was for his benefit or just that the language suited better.

'You must not do this, Gina. Every time, it is me he shouts at. Now I will be in trouble again.'

But if Gina was concerned at all that her actions may bring problems for the sergeant, she didn't show it, waving away Andri's protests with a carefree flick of the hand that sent sunlight dancing across her several rings.

'Don't worry Andri. I told him you did your best. If he says anything, you let me know and I will speak with him. Besides, it is his own fault. How am I supposed to know what he wants for dinner when he does not answer his telephone?'

Andri looked aghast. 'THAT was what you needed to see him about?'

'Of course. What else?' Gina's face made clear that nothing was more important than dinner.

'*Gina.* You are *terrible*.'

Gina shrugged, and surprised Murray by rounding on him. 'You would not mind being interrupted at work to be asked what you want to eat, yes?'

Caught off-guard he just managed, 'I, er... suppose not.'

'There. You see Andri? It is not a problem.'

Andri shook her head, and groaned.

'And now I must go.'

But at the door she stopped. 'By the way, Andri.' She flicked her head in Murray's direction causing her dark tresses to bounce and swing. 'He said to send him in.'

'GINA.'

Turning, she flashed Murray a smile that hit him between the eyes. 'Nice to have met you.' Then, like a whirlwind, she was gone, leaving everything in her wake upside down, the people she had touched gasping.

But before Murray could ask what was uppermost in his mind, Andri was on her feet.

'This way Mr Murray.'

CHAPTER 7

The office was longer than it was wide. At the far end, the large desk stood under the only window, which was open. The man sitting at it rose as Murray came in. As Murray strode down to take the hand the man held out, he noted that the air-con unit above and behind the desk wasn't operating. Nevertheless, it was a couple of degrees cooler than the ante-office.

'Welcome again Mr Murray,' the man said as they shook hands. 'Please, sit.' He gestured to the chair already pulled up in front of the desk.

Murray sensed the difference in him at once.

Superintendent Pippis Iridotu, Divisional Commander for the Pafos Police Division, was an imposing figure. Inches over six feet and broad shouldered, his thick, black hair was flecked with grey, matching the moustache that entirely hid his top lip. At their last meeting, Murray had gleaned he was around fifty, though the rugged features gave an impression of someone older. Nevertheless, Iridotu lacked the self-important air some senior police officers carry. His face was the sort that, in repose, fell naturally into an easy smile. But Murray could already see that, unlike last time, he seemed to be doing his best to not let it show. He wondered what lay behind the change.

'Would you like coffee?' Iridotu said.

'No, thanks,' Murray said. Given the length of time he'd had to wait and the policeman's changed manner, he was interested to hear what he had to say without further delay.

Reaching down, Iridotu opened a drawer and took out a plain buff folder which he placed on the desk in front of him. About to open it, he paused to give Murray a look that suggested he was thinking, carefully, about how to proceed. As Murray waited for him to decide, he noticed the empty coffee cup that was closer to his chair than that of the Divisional Commander's.

'I have made many enquiries since we last met, Mr Murray.'

Murray didn't respond. Iridotu had indicated his intention the last time they met. He continued.

'And I have learned much.' He tapped the folder with a fingernail, as if to warn its contents before he opened it. Lifting the topmost sheet, he perused it for several seconds.

'As you suggested, this Podruznig is an interesting character.' He stopped to look up. 'You are aware that he spent time in a Russian prison?'

Murray nodded. Most of his sort had done so, one time or another. It was how they forged their connections.

Iridotu hesitated again, which was when Murray realised. This wasn't just going to be about Podruznig. The policeman shuffled the papers before him. 'There is much information here, Mr Murray. About Podruznig's background, and how he came to be what he is today.' He glanced up again. 'But there is nothing, I fear, that can help you.' Murray said nothing, still waiting. 'Like you, I am not happy about the way this man does business. But as far as the Cyprus authorities are concerned, he is legally entitled to be here. And he has been granted the necessary approvals to purchase property.'

Still Murray didn't react. So far, it was all pretty much as he had expected.

'As far as his dealings with the builders are concerned, my Chief of Detectives has spoken with both of the Klerides brothers. They deny that Podruznig subjected them to threats of any sort. They say you were in breach, and therefore they acted within their rights.'

Iridotu waited, as if expecting a response. When none came he continued. 'I do not want you to misunderstand me, Mr Murray. I do not take kindly to foreigners coming to my country and acting as if they think they can tread all over our laws just because they have money and power.' He paused again. It made Murray wonder. *Was that a message?* 'But like any policeman, I can only act on what I can prove. I have no evidence that this Podruznig has committed a crime in my country, therefore I cannot intervene in your dispute.'

Dropping the paper he was holding, he spread his hands to show open palms. *And there you have it.*

Murray nodded. 'Did your Chief of Detectives say if he believed the Klerides brothers?'

The way Iridotu took his time, Murray guessed the answer.

'Like me, he can only go on what he can prove, not what he believes.'

'I understand.'

The policeman shuffled through more papers, as if thinking about sharing some of their contents. But then, with a finality that caught Murray off guard, he closed the folder.

'I do not think there is anything here that can help you, Mr Murray.'

Murray stared at him. For all that much of what

Iridotu had said came as no surprise, he had, nevertheless expected at least a little more. Clearly, Iridotu was closing him out. He wondered why. When he'd first approached the commander with his story, he'd come away with the impression that the Cypriot was keen to do whatever he could to deal with one of those he referred to then as, 'The land-grabbing *Pontians* who think they can run our country.'

Murray was familiar with the term, 'Pontian'. Originally ethnic Greeks from Pontius, on the shores of the Black Sea, nowadays Cypriots use it, disparagingly, to refer to those from the former Soviet regions around Georgia and Ukraine. Having ancient Cyprus blood in their veins and therefore the right to a Greek passport, they see themselves as having an even greater claim on the Island of Aphrodite than its present incumbents - Greek *and* Turkish. Despite its holiday-resort credentials, Pafos is home to a sizable Pontian Community. They complain, frequently, about police harassment.

Murray waited, still saying nothing.

Eventually Iridotu said, 'There is another matter I must discuss with you, Mr Murray.'

Here it comes.

'Podruznig is not the only person about whom I have made enquiries since our last meeting. I also took the trouble to enquire into your own background.'

As would any policeman with any sense.

'It seems that our Mr Podruznig is not the only one with, how shall I put this? An interesting history?'

Murray nodded slowly. It was the policeman's play. He would let him run with it.

'I understand you did some work with the military.'

Murray nodded again. 'I left the army several months ago.'

'I know. You were a policeman as well, of some sort?'

Murray hesitated, careful as always about discussing his past. For all he knew, Iridotu might now know of it, though he doubted it.

'I was a policeman back in the UK for a while.'

'But not now.'

'No.'

'So what sort of work were you involved in with the army?'

'I'm sorry, I can't say.'

'Undercover work, I believe?'

Murray came on alert. Now where had he got that?

Iridotu seemed to sense his reaction. 'You were in Iraq and Syria. During the Isil wars I understand? Some sort of… secret operation?'

Murray's mind began to work. It wouldn't have been recorded on any personnel file.

'Like I said. I can't talk about it.'

'I also believe… you fell out with your employers.'

Murray tensed.

'Something to do with some property that went missing?'

By now Murray's brain was racing. There had to be a leak somewhere. Senior though Iridotu was, Murray was pretty sure a Cyprus Police Commander wouldn't be vetted for that sort of information. A thought sparked.

'I believe it involved a consignment of gold?'

The spark fanned into a flame. Murray crossed his arms.

'Who told you this?'

But it was Iridotu's turn to say nothing. And the voice, when it came, sounded from behind him.

'I did.'

Murray glanced at the empty coffee cup.

The flame turned into a conflagration.

CHAPTER 8

As Murray met Iridotu's gaze – he was checking his reaction - he felt no antipathy towards the man who had set him up. Had the roles been reversed, he may well have done the same. Behind him, the sound of the voice's owner rising, coming forward. He must have been tucked away in the corner when Murray entered, shielded by the bookcase to the right of the door.

He understood now why Iridotu had kept him waiting. They would have been talking about how to play things. And though Murray's instincts still told him that Iridotu was a man he might trust, he was glad now that he had chosen not to say too much. If the time came for the two to talk about these things further – though after this meeting it was probably unlikely - he would rather do so knowing that only the two of them were present.

The man who had spoken came level with Murray's field of vision.

'Hello, Peter.'

Murray didn't reply, nor did he turn to look at him. It was a complication he should have anticipated, been prepared for. But he wasn't going to grant the sneak the pleasure of seeing him acknowledge his mistake.

The man came around to stand next to the Police Commander, where Murray could not avoid looking at him. Before switching his gaze, Murray noted the policeman still weighing him, and was glad. It meant he was still interested in gauging things for himself.

'Hello Glyn,' Murray said at last.

'Surprised to see me?'

'Not really. It's hot and humid. Worms surface.'

The man smiled.

As they regarded each other – how long had it been? Two years? – Murray wondered if the Special Investigations Branch man was still part of the Cyprus Joint Police Unit, or if he had returned because he'd heard of Iridotu's enquires. In the intervening period, Major Glyn Westgate hadn't changed much. Tall, athletically built, and with a receding hair line, he still had the superior, self-assured look that comes with a commission in the Royal Military Police. And as they checked each other, Murray realised that his attitude towards the man who, had he had his way, would have seen Murray put away long ago, had changed not one bit. Murray still felt he could cheerfully plant a fist into the smug face.

Not yet ready to acknowledge his tormentor, Murray spoke to Iridotu. 'There is another side to it.'

Iridotu gave a knowing smile, 'Of course. It is always so.'

'Oh, I was quite fair Peter,' Westgate chipped in. 'I did tell the Superintendent that nothing was ever proved that would have stood up in court.'

Murray eyes stayed on the policeman. 'Nothing was ever proved, period.'

Westgate continued.

'But I was interested to hear about this house of yours. The Superintendent tells me you put your deposit down about two years ago? Now there's a coincidence. Come into some money did you? And you seem very determined to get your property back. Makes me wonder what's so important about it, especially seeing as how I understand you've been offered fair compensation.' Westgate placed his hands flat on the Commander's desk and leaned forward. 'So what's it all about Peter?'

Murray's hands balled into fists, but he stayed put, keeping them down at his side. *When the time comes…*

'Not that it's any business of yours, but yes, as a matter of fact *we* did come into money. An aunt of Kathy's who died. As for my interest in getting the house back, well you always were an insensitive prick.'

Westgate put on a hurt look. 'Oh I'm sorry, Peter. Of course I remember now. It's got no connection with anything that happened back then. It's just about keeping promises to your dead wife.'

Before Murray could move from the chair, the policeman leaned forward in his, putting out a staying hand. 'Please,' was all he said.

Wound like a watch-spring – *the bastard always did know which buttons to press* - Murray practised what he had forced himself to learn long ago. After a few seconds, the urge passed and he settled back. The policeman turned to Westgate.

'The loss of a man's wife is not a thing to speak lightly of Major. Not under such circumstances. I think perhaps that if you wish to discuss such matters with Mr Murray, you should do so outside this office?'

Westgate responded like the officer he was. 'Of course Superintendent. I'm sorry Peter, my remark was uncalled for. Please accept my apologies.'

Iridotu turned to Murray. 'The Major contacted me after I enquired about you with the military authorities.' *I'll bet he did.* 'Pafos is my town. I am interested in anyone and everyone who comes here, particularly people who may cause trouble.'

'You don't have to justify anything Superintendent,'

Murray said. 'And I am not looking for trouble.'

'Perhaps not. But from what I hear, trouble seems to have a habit of finding you.'

'If it comes, I deal with it.'

'Then please Mr Murray, do not deal with it here. After my enquiries I know some of your background. But what happened when you worked for the Army is between you, them and the Major here. Pafos is a nice town. That is why the tourists come. Please do not do anything that would spoil it. I would not like that.'

For several seconds, Murray let his silence serve as acknowledgement of the policeman's warning. Eventually he said, 'I'll do my best.'

Iridotu fixed Murray with a stare that left him in no doubt about the message he wished to convey.

'Do not do your best Mr Murray. Do as I say.'

Ten minutes later, as Murray stepped out into Ypolohagou Avenue where his jeep was parked, he stopped, closed his eyes, and turned his face up to the sun, letting its fierce heat burn away the memories his encounter with the Special Investigations Branch man had resurrected.

Westgate.

If there was one person he had neither expected, nor hoped to see, it was him. Sorting out things with Podruznig and the house was going to be difficult enough. To have the Special Investigations Branch man dogging his footsteps, waiting to see if Murray would lead him to what he had failed to find years earlier, would only make it more so. Murray was in no doubt that Westgate's carefully choreographed reappearance was meant to send a signal. He was back, and wasn't going away until he found what he was looking for. He was probably hoping that his return might fluster

Murray enough for him to slip up, perhaps even reveal what he was after.

He thought about whether, had he been more upfront with Iridotu to begin with, Westgate's return might have been avoided. But from what he'd gleaned, the policeman was the sort who played things straight. Whatever Murray had told him, he would still have made enquiries. The outcome would have been the same. As he crossed to where he'd parked under the shade of the jacaranda trees lining the pavement, he thought on what it meant. One thing was for sure. If the time came that he had to do what he still hoped to avoid, he would need to be on his toes. Which would mean keeping track of where Westgate was, and what he was up to. He was still musing on it as he climbed into his jeep and started the engine.

Unfortunately, Murray's commitment to stay alert related to the future. Had he applied it at once, he may have spotted the two men in the silver Toyota Rav 4 parked further along the avenue and who watched him get in, start his jeep, then followed as he headed back down to the harbour area.

CHAPTER 9

Murray parked in the small car park at the back of the Dive Centre. The middle of the day, its aluminium shutters were down, everyone out on a dive. It was Thursday, which probably meant the Zenobia, the favoured spot for wreck-diving along that stretch of coast. He wrote a quick note, jammed it between the shutter's slats, then headed down to the municipal lido on the front.

There, he changed in one of the wooden cubicles before diving off the stone platform into the sea's crystal waters. After the early afternoon's heat, the water was wonderfully cool. He swam three, fast sprints out to the safe-swimming marker buoy, before emerging, comfortable and refreshed - apart from Westgate's smirking face popping into his head every few minutes. After showering and changing, he strolled up Poseidon Avenue to Dorinda's Place, the deli-restaurant opposite the Aphrodite Hotel.

In the full heat of the afternoon sun, the blue-gingham-clothed outside tables were unoccupied. But inside, the air-conditioning and ceiling fans were helping ensure good business. Dorinda's greeting when he walked in was over-the-top, as usual.

'PEEEter,' she gushed, deftly manoeuvring her considerable frame between the tables to plant wet kisses on both his cheeks. She turned scolding. 'You are too long not here. Now I must make you a special lunch. And you did not tell me you were coming.'

'Sorry, Dorinda. If it's too much trouble….' He made to turn towards the door.

'PHWA,' she snorted. 'Stupid. You know it is not. Look.' Turning, she pointed to a corner table by the window. He had checked it was free before coming in. 'See? I keep your table, just for you. As always.'

After sitting him down, she tried to be discreet, turning away so he would not notice. Nevertheless, he saw her right arm lift and her hand dart across her chest in a hasty Sign Of The Cross. A lifelong agnostic, Murray nevertheless appreciated it, conscious of the sad-but-warm feeling the prayer triggered. After the tensions of the morning it felt good to be in a place where, for a little while at least, his biggest problem would be choosing between the seafood, or cooked-meat platters. And deciding which of Dorinda's delicious cheeses would best accompany his choice.

For the next hour, Peter Murray, ex-soldier, policeman, father and husband, took simple pleasure in working his way through the ridiculously-large helpings of mussels, prawns, crab and oysters Dorinda kept replenishing whenever it appeared he may be in danger of catching up with Pedro, her Mexican-Cypriot chef. When they were gone, she brought out the meats. Not in the mood for big decisions, he had opted for surf and turf. As the feast wore on, and washed down with glasses of Vasilikon – Murray's preferred white - it had a surprising effect. Bit by bit, he relaxed.

Two things helped. The first was Dorinda's carefully-judged nurturing. Mother to four girls, she knew, instinctively, when her cajoling banter was welcome, and when he needed space. The second was re-living, in a way he had not allowed himself for some time, the sort of experience he and Kathy had used to savour. A warm welcome, with good food and wine in a convivial atmosphere. At that moment, a burst of laughter from a group of women, sitting at a table across the other side of the restaurant and enjoying a leisurely lunch – mainly liquid it seemed - served as example.

By the time Dorinda brought out the baklava she was known for, followed by coffee along with a brandy bottle - seven-star Greek Metaxa, rather than the local Keo - Murray was feeling mellower than he had in a long time. Now mid-afternoon, the restaurant had quieted, the only customers remaining being a couple of older British tourists, and the group of women - who seemed set in for a long session. When Dorinda appeared in the chair next to his and covered his hand with her own, he surprised himself by not moving it.

'It is good to see you again, Peter.'

'And you Dorinda.'

'How are things?' Suddenly, the showy, front-of-house-manner used to draw in the tourists and locals alike was gone, replaced by an earnestness few beyond Dorinda's family ever got to see.

He swirled his brandy, checking out its honeyed depths.

'I'm doing okay. Thanks for asking.'

'And the house?'

'Still working on it.'

'I hope you can sort it out. You deserve it.'

'Thanks,' he said, glad she hadn't added, *After what you've been through*. 'I appreciate it.'

They were still reminiscing when Red and Kishore showed up. They must have found his note. For once, Red had showered the salt off. He'd even run a comb through his hair. Dorinda was in-role as soon as they came through the door.

'If you think I am going to open my kitchen again just for the likes of you, you can think again.'

Red growled at her. 'Just bring whatever you've got woman. We've no time for your nonsense.'

A couple of the women in the group turned to see what was going on, alerted by Red's menacing tone. But seeing Kishore's grin and Dorinda's mock defiance, they returned, smiling, to their gossip. Making one last show of high dudgeon, Dorinda brought them over ice-cold beers, banging the bottles down along with chunky glass tumblers, which would not be needed. Pausing only to throw Red the challenging look he was due, she retreated into the back to see what she could find. Red turned to Murray.

'Any luck?'

Murray shook his head. 'As I expected. The police won't move unless Klerides complains.'

'Which isn't going to happen,' Kishore said. For once, he wasn't grinning.

Murray let them swig their beers before saying, 'Westgate was there.'

Both men froze, bottles to lips.

'Was he now?' Red turned a thoughtful look on him. 'How did he get involved?'

'It seems our friendly neighbourhood Superintendent made enquiries about me. Westgate must have heard. Wants to know what's going on.'

'Shit,' Kishore said. Red threw him a look.

'Doesn't matter,' Murray said. 'He had his chance. If he wants to waste his time hanging around, it's no skin off my nose. At least not until I decide what to do about the Russian.'

Red looked less certain. 'I'd rather not have him mooching around thank you very much. It was bad enough last time. I take it he hasn't changed?'

Murray nodded. 'I'd guess so. The superintendent was a lot cagier than last time, which probably means Westgate must have blown us out.' Then he added, 'Or just me, maybe.'

Kishore glanced at Red before asking. 'Did he mention us?'

Murray shook his head. 'And neither did I. But I'll be surprised if he doesn't know you're here.'

'Shit,' Kishore repeated.

'Don't let it bother you, Kish,' Murray said. 'It's me he's after.'

'But if he knows we're here, he'll assume we're back together. He's bound to start poking his nose around.'

'So what's there for him to find? Let him waste his time. He'll give it up eventually, like last time.'

'Last time, the operations had ended and he didn't have much choice. Things are different now.'

Murray shrugged, surprised to see Kishore so unnerved. *Too long missing the sort of action he likes*, he thought.

As Red and Kish supped their beers, Murray helped himself to more brandy. Dorinda arrived with a huge platter of meats, cheeses, breads and salads. She plopped them down between Red and Kishore - 'THERE. Enjoy,' - before moving over to join the group of still-chattering women whom she obviously knew.

'So what's your next move?' Red said between mouthfuls.

Murray breathed deep. 'I'm thinking I'll give the Russian one more try. If that doesn't work... We'll see.'

Red didn't glance up from his eating, and tried to make it sound casual as he said, 'Want us to come with you?'

Murray shook his head. 'I'd rather keep things low-

55

key. For the time being.'

Red feigned indifference. ''Kay.'

Half-an-hour later, plates cleared, drinks drunk and with work to do, they rose to leave. Murray left money on the table to cover the bill, then wandered over to where Dorinda and her companions were discussing in more subdued tones than before. As he neared, conversation seemed to falter and the sudden outbreak of fidgeting made him think about what - who - they'd been talking about.

'Thanks, Dorinda,' he said, resting a hand on her shoulder.

She rose, reaching up to drape her arms around him.

'Take care, Peter.'

'I will.'

As they hugged, Murray saw sympathy reflected in some of the women's faces and realised. She *had* been doing a number on him. Slightly irritated and a touch embarrassed, he struggled to free himself from the clinging embrace. It was then his eyes lit on the woman at the far end of the table and whose back had been to him the whole afternoon. It was all he could do not to react.

Gina Iridotu - if she wasn't married - was looking at him in a way that reflected as much interest, as sympathy. Her sparkling blue eyes were narrowed, as if appraising. And the way she wasn't rushing to acknowledge their earlier meeting made him think she hadn't yet mentioned it to her friends. He was thinking on whether to let on to her when Dorinda released him. Turning, she presented him to the group.

'This is Peter. He is nice.'

The warm smiles and chorus of 'Hello Peter,' confirmed Murray's suspicions. Dorinda had told them enough to appeal to their motherly instincts - for the time being at least. But as he nodded and returned the friendly smiles, Gina continued to say nothing, regarding him with the sort of look that suggested she at least needed to know more before taking Dorinda's commendations for granted. He wondered what, if anything, she may have picked up when she walked in on her father's meeting with Westgate that morning.

'And I'm nice too.' Appearing from behind Dorinda, Red's wide smile evidenced he was looking for similar treatment.

'PHWA,' Dorinda chided. 'This man is a pig. Do not have anything to do with him.' But the laughter round the table showed they weren't fooled. As Red registered his protests and the banter between him and the women threatened to delay their leaving, Murray looked up to find Gina's gaze still on him. He flashed her a neutral smile, but didn't wait for a response. Grabbing Red's elbow, he steered him towards the door, conscious of a sudden desire to be gone.

'See you soon, Dorinda.'

They were thirty yards down the road, Red still berating Murray for spoiling his chances, when a call - 'Mr Murray?' - made them turn.

It was her.

Murray retraced his steps to meet her halfway. The suspicious look he had seen was gone, her face now more inviting, but not that way.

'I am sorry,' she said. 'I thought it best to not mention having met. It may have raised questions about matters private to you.'

He tipped his head in thanks. 'That's fine, it doesn't-.'

'I know a little about the trouble you are having.' He started. 'And I can imagine what my father has told you.'

He shook his head, not looking to discuss it with her. It wasn't like he blamed her father for anything.

'It's not a-.'

He stopped as she held something out to him. It was a business card. He took it. *Gina's Taverna.* An address up in the Old Town. A simple map on the back.

'This is none of my business of course, so please, if you do not like, I understand.' He looked at her, puzzled. 'But if you wish to talk. I am there most evenings. Perhaps I can help?'

'That is good of you, er… Gina. But I don't think-' Again she didn't let him finish.

'I know my father. Like you, he is not happy with this thing. But he has to show he is doing things the police way. Perhaps there is another?'

Not at all sure what she was hinting at - if anything - he tried again to speak. As now seemed her habit, she wasn't interested.

'I also do a very good Meze. You should try it.'

And with that she turned on her heels and headed back to her friends. As he watched her go, he thought her catwalk sashay oozed confidence, along with other things.

As Murray re-joined his companions, Red's lingering gaze past his shoulder, registered suspicion. 'Who's she and what did she want?'

Murray turned to look back, but she was gone. 'Just someone I met.'

Red sent him a long, hard look. There were few secrets between them. Murray sensed what he was thinking.

'You don't think I'm going to give you an in with a woman like that, do you?'

Red and Kishore looked at him uncertainly, before turning to each other, shrugging.

'Well it's nice to see you may be thinking of rejoining the land of the living,' Red said.

Murray said nothing.

CHAPTER 10

Not yet eight, the temperature outside was already nudging thirty. In the sleek, black-and-white-and-steel kitchen however, the atmosphere was chill. As Podruznig paced, back and forth, surveying the scene, the other three present waited, not moving. Two of the three were petrified. They had witnessed their employer's displeasure too many times not to be. The third, Lantzeff, simply waited. He hadn't been on watch, and although security was his responsibility, he knew he was safe as long as there were others on whom blame could fall.

Still pacing, Podruznig's gaze remained fixed on the abomination that, when Lantzeff had seen it last - on his final rounds the night before - had been a pristine, white wall. The Russian either wasn't aware, or couldn't give a rat's shit that with every step, he was walking more of the blood-red paint into the grouting between the Italian floor-tiles that, when Lantzeff first heard their unit-cost, he thought was a joke.

Suddenly Podruznig stopped. He stared up at the wall one last time before turning to Lantzeff, face contorted, lips trembling and twisted. Lantzeff readied himself, grateful there were no baseball bats to hand. But all that escaped the audibly gnashing teeth was a single, half-strangled word.

'How?'

Lantzeff made sure not to be seen to wilt in the face of the anger he knew the man was holding in check until certain who to turn it on. Now was not the time to show weakness. And Lantzeff had his answers lined up. As soon as he'd arrived and seen what had happened - rocketed from his bed by the whore's wailings - he had wasted no time conducting an investigation. Of necessity it had been quick, but thorough. He knew he only had the time it would take his incandescent boss to calm his hysterical slut-wife. As it happened, ten minutes was enough.

As soon as he reached the CCTV room in the basement and saw the blank middle screen, Lantzeff knew exactly where to look. He didn't stay to listen to the pair of bleary-eyed night-duty guards' almost blubbering attempts to explain themselves.

'It went last night,' one of them tried. 'We checked but couldn't see anything.'

'We assumed it was the monitor again,' whined the other as Lantzeff headed straight back up the stairs. 'We said the stuff you get here is crap.' Lantzeff wasn't interested. The two would soon be history.

In daylight of course, the shattered lens on the camera fixed high up on the South-East corner was clearly visible. The fact that it was so high up and inaccessible, even he probably wouldn't have seen it at night, was neither here nor there. It wasn't Lantzeff's job to defend others' cock-ups. They were all well paid, housed, and fed for their services. They also knew that mistakes were costly.

But as Lantzeff turned, searching for the vantage point that would have given the shooter the right angle – the nearest was way up on the hillside, well over a kilometre away, he realised how badly he had underestimated. There and then, Lantzeff resolved not to make such a mistake again. As he skirted the house, checking for signs, he was met by Ivan.

For once the dark-skinned Mongolian had been quick-witted enough to spot an opportunity to gain some credit with the Big Man – even if it was at the expense of his soon-to-be-ex-colleagues. As Lantzeff had been checking the CCTV, Ivan had double-checked the Alarm station and found the Bypass Switcher-Relay attached to the window of the small utility room next to the kitchen. It was a sophisticated piece of kit, and Lantzeff would not imagine his number one suspect having easy access to it, never mind being familiar with its use - another underestimation.

By the time he returned to the kitchen, dragging the now wide-awake night men in to confront them with the result of their failure, he had a pretty good idea of how it had gone down - with the exception of the paint. No one was certain yet whether it was from the store under the swimming pool, or if the vandal had brought it with him. It was a detail he didn't worry about. If necessary he would wing it.

Now, as he started to give his glowering boss the information he had requested - starting with the neglectful response of the night duty team - he tried to stop his eyes drifting to the message clearly visible over his boss's right shoulder. Painted in metre-high red letters, it read;

'LAST CHANCE. LEAVE NOW.'

The hapless guards - both Siberians, to Lantzeff's shame - tried to defend themselves. But when Lantzeff pointed out to their still-livid employer that even the most cursory check of the house's security systems should have uncovered the discrepancy in the Alarm Feedback Readings, they lapsed into silence. Lantzeff wondered if they'd suddenly woken up to the fact that rather than trying to defend the indefensible, their time would be better spent working out how they might escape what would - on past experience - most likely follow. Though on the evidence of last night, he thought, they were probably incapable of managing even that.

As he waited for Podruznig to announce his decision - he was ranting now about how was it, given the fortune he had spent on security, one man could bypass the sophisticated systems that were in place, to threaten him and his family, to say nothing of how much it would cost to re-furbish the kitchen. Lantzeff made a mental note to speak to the ex-KGB 'Security Consultant' through whom he recruited. Another failure such as this and he may wake up one day to find himself in the hot seat, and that would never do. If there was one thing he had learned over the past five years, it was that, in the Russian's view of the world, only one thing mattered. Getting the right result - every time, and with maximum efficiency. He wasn't aware that words such as 'loyalty' and 'sentiment' were even part of the man's vocabulary. He sometimes wondered if, and when, the slut would realise.

Finished interrogating the by now, all-but quivering Siberians, Podruznig turned to Lantzeff. Flecks of foam showed at the corners of his mouth.

'Get them out of my sight. I will decide what to do with them later.'

'Sir.' Lantzeff snapped to attention, and nodded the men towards the stairs leading to their basement quarters. They didn't need to be told a second time. As they scampered down the steps and Lantzeff made to follow, he stopped to raise a quizzical eyebrow to his boss.

Podruznig nodded. 'But quietly,' he said.

At the bottom of the steps, Lantzeff was about to disappear when he heard Podruznig call, 'And Uri.' He looked up, saw his employer looking down. 'Afterwards, I would like to speak with the Englishman, again.'

Lantzeff gave a sharp nod. But before taking his final leave, he let his boss see his leering smile, so he would know how much pleasure he would take in arranging such a meeting.

CHAPTER 11

Murray left Fofo's office, pleased not to have fallen out with her. He'd expected she might rail against his decision, try to talk him into letting her pursue the case. But his mind was clear - on this at least. He gave no hint that concern for her safety had influenced his decision. That would really have upset her.

And while he told her he simply needed more time to, 'think things through,' he knew she saw through his words. Fofo knew him well enough to know that indecision wasn't part of his make-up. If he didn't intend court action, he had to have an alternative in mind. But professional discretion - or the survival instinct - prevented her delving too deep. He imagined her at home later that evening, glass of Agios Fotios in hand, confiding to her Italian lover her relief at having been spared what could have turned into the most troublesome - and dangerous – piece of representation she may ever have taken on.

For his part, Murray was grateful for the way she played it. After presenting all the arguments she could muster, only to hear him dismiss them one by one, she eventually let it go. Reluctantly it seemed, she agreed to accept his 'instructions' in the matter. He'd hated lying to her.

Now, out in the fresh-but-hot air again, he felt freer

than he had in a long time. Having made his decisions, the way was clear to let instinct dictate how best to achieve the result he was after. And while it wasn't wholly without danger, he felt better knowing Fofo would play no part in it.

About to cross the street to where his jeep was parked, he remembered that Patrick's Bar was only a short walk away. It could be a while before he had time to sample one of the Irish-Cypriot's coffee and whiskey-chasers again, while being lectured to about the state of local politics, global warming, or some new concern. Turning left, he headed for Kennedy Square. But, intent on making the most of the rest of his morning, he failed to spot the bulky figure that stepped out several doorways to his right, and followed behind.

He had covered less than thirty yards when a black four-by-four coming from behind pulled into the kerb beside him, the nearside doors already opening. Recognising the tactic, he started to divert away. Too late, he sensed someone behind and to his right just as the blow came up and under his ribs, knocking the wind from him. Even as he doubled-up, two burly figures in jeans and tee-shirts were out of the car and, in a well-practised sequence, took him, one under each arm, and bundled him into the back. Face down and hanging half-on, half-off the seat, Murray made to pull himself up. But as he lifted his head he saw only the rapidly-closing fist which exploded into his face with the force of a jack-hammer and turned everything black.

Head still spinning, Murray reached out to the kitchen work-top for support. His vision was yet to fully clear, but he had no trouble making out the blood-red letters daubed on the wall before him.

'So?' he managed.

A blow to his head, from his left this time, sent him reeling again. When he recovered enough to turn, Lantzeff was standing there.

Podruznig's face, red with anger, appeared in front of his.

'How did you do this?'

Murray took his time, breathing deep, forcing back the doughnut and coffee breakfast that was threatening to reappear. He met the wild gaze.

'Much as I'd like to take the plaudits, I'm sorry to say, it wasn't me.'

This time, Lantzeff's fist buried into his stomach. He doubled-up, but hung onto the counter so he wouldn't fall.

'Do you expect me to believe that?' Podruznig all but spat the words into his face as he came upright again.

'Believe – *gasp* - what you like.'

One of the pair he remembered from the pavement stepped forward and threw something onto the floor in front of them. It took Murray a moment to work out what the expanse of grey was. Eventually he recognised the felt-mat lining from the boot of his jeep.

'And this?'

The tip of Podruznig's shoe waved over one corner of the mat. Murray shook his head, trying to focus. Eventually he saw what everyone else could see quite clearly. Two overlapping half-circles of red, smudged with drips.

Murray smiled, tasted salty blood in his mouth. 'Clever.'

Podruznig misunderstood. 'We are not idiots Mr Murray. What did you think? I would just pack up and leave?'

'That would save us all a lot of trouble.'

As Lantzeff made to move Murray steeled himself,

but Podruznig held up a hand. Looking up, he saw the Russian eyeing him with a puzzled expression.

'I am confused Mr Murray. When we last spoke I had the impression you were a man of intelligence. Yet you seem to think something as crass as this is the way to get what you want?'

'Well, like I said-'

This time it was the back of Podruznig's hand that came up and lashed across Murray's face. Something stung even worse than the blow itself and Murray remembered the heavy gold ring he'd noticed during his previous visit. He felt blood run down his cheek.

Podruznig's yelled reply bordered on the hysterical. 'DO NOT INSULT ME BY LYING TO ME.'

Murray remembered the accounts he'd read of Podruznig flying into uncontrolled rages at the slightest provocation. And this definitely didn't come under the heading, 'slight'. Sense told him not to push too far.

'Who else is going to break into my house and threaten me like this? Klerides?'

Murray made sure he met the man's stare. He'd seen eyes like his before. 'We both know it wasn't Klerides.'

'Yes,' Podruznig said, beginning to pace again, as he had been doing when Murray was first dragged in and dropped onto the floor at his feet. 'That is right.' He was nodding, over and over. Coming to a decision. 'It was not Klerides. As you say, we both know that.' Without warning he rounded on Murray. But Murray was waiting for it and didn't flinch. 'I had thought we could solve this amicably Mr Murray. That between you, me and Klerides we might work something out.'

'Somehow, I doubt that.'

Podruznig ignored it. 'But I cannot let something like this go. This is not just an attack on me. It is an attack on my family. My reputation.' Murray waited. The

Russian was raving now. Beyond talking. 'I have already dealt with those who let this happen. I can do no less with the man responsible.'

Murray awaited the verdict, knowing he would need to be ready.

When it came, it was quick, professional and without any of the dramatic accompaniments that feature in the movies. Turning to Lantzeff, Podruznig said simply, 'Deal with it.' Then, without a backward glance, he turned and walked away, business done.

As before, Murray's captors weren't going to give him any opportunity to work out a plan. Before he could even look round to see what was coming, something hit the sweet spot at the base of his skull and the blackness took him once more.

CHAPTER 12

Murray fought his way back to the land of the conscious. The spasmodic jolting and side-to-side lurches, together with the bitter taste of small-arms cordite in the back of his throat, made him wonder what he was doing back in the Al Laiyah hills above the Bay of Kuwait. But as his senses returned, he knew something wasn't right. The spec of Military snatch-Land Rovers doesn't include the sort of soft-feel upholstery he could feel on his cheek. Another thing. Back then he always did the driving. Then there was the fact that his hands were somehow locked behind him.

Suddenly his transport dropped, violently, and his head jerked up off the seat. Coming down, his right temple banged against the hip of the man next to him. The contact marked something harder than bone and he realised the cordite smell was coming from the recently-fired side-arm tucked in the man's waistband.

Murray squeezed his eyes shut while he worked it out. It took only seconds. Suddenly, everything that had happened since he'd left Fofo's came rushing back. And he knew he was in trouble.

The last few years he'd learned enough about how men like Podruznig deal with 'business problems' to know he couldn't afford to wait to find out where he was being taken, or what awaited him when he arrived. The way the truck kept lurching, it was obvious they were off-road somewhere. Probably the wilds of the Akamas, the area of unspoilt wilderness along Cyprus's west coast. Its furthest reaches are only accessible by more sturdy four-wheelers – most often the ubiquitous 'Jeep Safaris' that do good business in the resort areas. Inhabited only by wild sheep and goats, the rugged terrain is ideal territory for a 'disposal' op.

In the way he'd been taught, Murray swallowed his tongue.

The choke-reflex made him spasm, gag, then retch, which brought up the remnants of his breakfast.

'ACCHH,' the man next to him cried. 'You fucking English BASTARD. He's spewed all over my pants.'

He gave Murray a violent shove which sent him sliding down onto the floor. Laughter came from the front of the truck. Two more there. Three altogether.

As he fell, Murray made sure he managed the half-turn he needed so that he landed almost on his back, hands hidden beneath. He lay there, to all intents semi-conscious but seeing enough through half-closed eyes to recognise the face above him as one from the bunch at the gate a few days before. It had been angry then. Now, it was twisted into an expression of distaste as he wiped at the vomit clinging to his trousers, sending bits of half-digested bread roll into Murray's face, flicking the foul-smelling goo out the window.

'Bastard,' he said again, then jerked a boot into Murray's side, before leaving his comatose captive to stew in his own sick. He turned to look out the window, still muttering oaths.

Murray waited until he was certain his guard's interest was elsewhere, then began fishing. He knew the bill-fold was still there, could feel its reassuring presence through the thin material of his baggies. And by good fortune, his hands were tied in such a way he barely had to move to slide the folded-leather out of his back-pocket. He checked again, but the man was still looking away, his rancid hand stretched out, away from his nose.

Murray rummaged inside, pulling out the batch of notes he'd stuffed in there that morning. As he poked around the pockets he gave thanks that Podruznig ruled by fear. His captors wouldn't risk incurring their employer's wrath by robbing their victim - not without express permission.

But his twisted position meant that whatever was round his wrists – it felt like hemp – was now biting deeper. He could feel the needling pain that presages numbness creeping into his fingers. He needed to work fast before he lost all feeling.

Running a finger around one of the linings, he felt the cold metal. He slid it out, gripping it between his fingers. As he did so, he made a mental note to thank Stu Whiteside if they ever met again. The lanky SAS trainer had drummed into them the value of always keeping a craft blade about your person when engaged on an op. And though Murray wasn't planning to ever be involved in those sorts of operations again, he was glad he'd stuck by the principle, even if it did mean having to regularly replace the billfold whenever the razor-sharp edge sawed through the silk linings.

Keeping a half-closed eye on the figure looming over him, Murray worked at the rope. It wasn't easy. In the months it had languished, unused, the blade had dulled, which he noted for future reference. And in order to not draw attention, he could only work across the strands in short bursts. He also had to take care not to let the blade slip from his fingers. If he dropped it now, he would struggle to find it again. Even as the thought came, he felt the thin metal becoming slippery in his grasp. Blood.

Rope wasn't the only thing he was slicing through, though the numbness prevented him identifying the source. He just hoped it wasn't an artery. But suddenly, the pressure on his wrists eased. He was free.

He waited another minute, letting the feeling come back into his hands, so they would do what he wanted when they had to. As the numbness ebbed away, he could tell the cuts were to the fleshy parts of his palms, a couple of fingers, nothing serious. When he was ready, he groaned and, as if finally waking, rolled onto his side so that his weight fell against the legs of the guard above him, at the same time making sure his hands remained out of the man's sight.

'I think he's coming round,' the man said. Murray felt him take his upper arms, making ready to pull the weight off his legs and bring him to a sitting position. It meant he would be leaning forward and down. Suddenly Murray felt the man freeze, and knew he'd spotted the severed ropes.

'FUCK, HE'S-.'

Murray exploded upwards. He caught a brief glimpse of a shocked face before he rammed his forearm up and under the man's chin so that the man's jaws snapped together with a painful-sounding, *CLACK*. The man's head whipped back against the head rest before bouncing forward again, when Murray thrust the point of his elbow straight into his throat. There was a dull, splintering sound as cartilage shattered.

Sounds of movement up front and more 'FUCK's, signalled the other two reacting. He had only seconds. Even as his victim's eyes rolled upwards and he began to slide down the seat, Murray was groping at his waistband. Feeling for the weapon's butt, he whipped it out, at the same time spinning round and pulling the automatic's slide back so that when he jammed it into the cheekbone of the still-turning front-seat passenger, it was ready and cocked. The man froze. The driver - another face Murray recognised - glanced round.

'SHIZER,' he yelled.

As the truck lurched to the right to bounce off a rut and the driver fought to keep control, Murray weighed his options. Outside, bleached rock, dramatic gullies and low scrub rushed past the window. He'd been right. It *was* the Akamas. The bare coastline away to his left told Murray they were driving through the area's most isolated parts to the far north. The old British Army firing range. No witnesses.

'STOP THE CAR,' Murray yelled.

As he gave the order Murray saw the driver's eyes swivel front, searching, gauging. A quarter mile ahead, on a rise, the dark shape of another four-by-four waited. Murray remembered the BMW X7 he'd seen parked outside the garage. Maybe Podruznig had decided to take a personal interest in seeing to the man he held responsible for re-decorating his kitchen. Either that or it would be Lantzeff.

Sensing the driver weighing options, Murray moved the barrel away from the passenger's cheek long enough to squeeze off a single round that shattered the driver's door-window. In the confined space the explosion made his ears ring. Both men yelped in shock and the way the man in the passenger seat clamped a hand against his ear, groaning in pain, Murray guessed a ruptured eardrum. He didn't dwell on it.

Having got the message, the driver stamped on the brakes. The truck slid to a halt amidst a cloud of dust.

Keeping the gun on the pair, Murray stepped out. The sun blazed down and the sudden heat made him catch his breath. Pulling the passenger door open, he motioned the man out. He didn't argue. As soon as his feet touched ground, Murray span him round, spread his legs and frisked him. The gun was in the small of the man's back, under his shirt. Murray tossed it high and far into the bushes. Keeping his eye and gun on the driver, he marched the first man round to the other side then went through the same procedure with him. Up ahead, Murray saw the dust cloud that indicated whoever was in the BMW had seen what was happening and was on their way.

Murray made them lie face down in the gravel road, hands on heads before jumping back in the truck and turning it round. Giving the BMW one last check – given the state of the track this far out it would still be minutes away, which should be enough - he jammed his foot to the floor. As he sped away, he checked his mirror and saw both men racing off into the bushes in search of their weapons. Further back the fast approaching dust cloud told of the X7's approach. Someone wasn't going to be pleased, which probably meant there would soon be more vacancies on Podruznig's team.

As he pushed the truck along as fast as was safe, letting the training he now rarely got a chance to practice take over for the second time in a few days, he forgot about the danger behind and turned his mind to what his next move was going to be. Whatever had gone before, his judgement that morning while talking to Fofo had been right. Though it had happened sooner than even he had expected, there was no doubting. The gloves were now, well and truly, off.

As he rounded a sharp left hander, Murray just had time to swerve out of the path of the jeep racing in the opposite direction. There was a sharp 'CRACK' as the wing mirrors clipped and shattered. He jerked to a stop, waited as the other driver made a fast three-pointer, then pulled up alongside.

'You okay?' Red said from behind the wheel of Murray's jeep. Kishore peered round beside him, grinning.

'No thanks to you two,' Murray called. He jerked a thumb behind him. 'They're right behind.' He looked ahead of him. The road narrowed round another left hander, a steep rise on the left, an even steeper fall-away to the right. Murray nodded at it. 'Pull up around that bend.'

Looking ahead, Red twigged his intention. Wheels spinning, he shot forward. Murray followed but as he reached the turn he spun the wheel and pulled on the hand brake. The back of the truck slewed round, stopping across the road at its narrowest point where there was no room for a vehicle to pass. Only a half-track would manage the steep slopes either side. Screwing the front wheels round so they jammed against rock, Murray locked the steering, remote-locked the doors and lobbed the keys high up into the scrub.

As he jumped into the back of the jeep he heard the roar of the X7 coming up behind, fast.

'GO,' he yelled.

As Red took off, Murray had to hang onto the roll bar to keep from being thrown out.

CHAPTER 13

Whatever Red and Kishore were talking about under the shade of the awning at the side of the house, conversation died as Murray returned from Red's bathroom. The cut to his cheek still seeped through Kishore's field-training stitches, but it would do. The pains in the rest of his body would take care of themselves.

'Better?'

Red held out a bottle. Murray took it. The Keo's refreshing coldness was reviving.

'Next time, let me do the planning. You were too far behind.'

'Just be grateful I twigged the bloke driving your jeep wasn't you,' KIshore said. 'Otherwise we wouldn't even have known there was a problem.'

For once, Murray found Kishore's toothy smile strangely reassuring, confirmation of his narrow escape.

Earlier, the Gurkha had told how his chance observation while out picking up air cylinders, had alerted him that something was wrong. When he followed and saw the Mongolian dump Murray's jeep behind the Pafos Aquarium before getting into the black 4x4, he put things together. After calling Red and collecting the jeep, they'd headed out to the house just in time to see the four-by leaving towards the peninsula.

Guessing right, they'd followed.

'And we had to hold back, or they'd have seen us,' Kishore defended his tactics.

Murray didn't complain further. He *liked* to think that if he hadn't managed to free himself, the pair would have come up with something before Podruznig, or Lantzeff, or whoever, put a bullet through his head.

'So where does this leave us?'

Red's serious expression reminded Murray of Iraq. They all knew that events had moved onto a different level.

'Keeping our heads down for starters,' Murray said. 'We have to assume they've made our connection, so that puts you in the frame as well.'

On the way back to Red's house in the hills above the village of Timi, over-looking Pafos International Airport, Murray had ruminated only as long as necessary over his failure to spot he was being followed. And after everything they'd been through, he was annoyed it was a Russian goon, of all people, who got the better of him. Neither Red nor Kishore made too much of it. After this long, they were all out of practice. Nevertheless they didn't have to discuss things to know they had been careless. They had underestimated Podruznig, and got lucky. If it had been Syria, or Iraq, one, or all of them would be dead.

'Guess that means the dive business is fucked for a while,' Red said.

Murray looked rueful. 'Sorry.'

Red waved it away. 'Not your fault. Speaking of which, where will we find the bastard?'

Murray shook his head. 'If he's got any sense, he'll be staying on the base. But we've no proof the kitchen paint job was anything to do with Westgate, remember. It's just a theory.'

Kishore's face twisted into an angry sneer. 'Sounds good enough for me. It's the sort of thing he'd pull. Kick the can, and see what jumps out.'

'Maybe,' Murray said. 'But let's not go planning any rendition ops until I've had a chance to run things down. Like I said, while I don't see anyone else in the frame, I'm not convinced Westgate is up to something like that. Getting into Podruznig's and out again without being spotted smacks of Special Forces. Westgate may be a cunning bastard, but he's only SIB.'

'Yeah-but,' Red came in. 'There're plenty up at Dhekelia or Episkopi who'd be up to it. Even if it wasn't Westgate, he could have sent someone in. Officially or otherwise.'

For several minutes they discussed possibilities and theories. Afterwards they were none the wiser. Red mused on whether it was time to call for back-up.

'Like you said Peter, the gloves are off. And right now there are a few more of them than there are us. The last I heard, Billy and Wazzer are still working out of Limassol. And I can always look to see who's around the bases. You know what those guys are like. Anything for a few extra bob.

Murray looked across at the man who'd twice saved his life, before shaking his head. 'I know what you're thinking, but I'm not ready to go to war just yet.'

With studied deliberation, Red put his bottle down. 'I probably don't need to mention this, but weren't those Russkis about to see you out?'

Murray looked thoughtful. 'That was for the kitchen paint job. I'd rather be sure there's no other way of sorting the house out before starting something that'll only end one way. Besides, I'd like to know who did it before making a move. And there are a couple of other things I need to run down first.'

But Kishore was also clear on the matter. 'If you ask me, we already know all we need to know. There's a bent Russian living in yours and Kathy's house, and the only way we'll get him out is to carry him out. Seems simple enough.'

Murray fell silent, as he still tended to when her name was mentioned.

Red gave his partner a look that said, *'Stupid twat.'* Kishore shrugged, feigning innocence.

Eventually Murray said. 'When I'm ready guys, okay?'

In the silence that followed, Red and Kishore communicated through looks and nods.

Eventually Red said: 'You mentioned running some things down?'

Murray nodded.

'Need our help?'

Murray knew he was probably being more po-faced than necessary when he said, 'Thanks, but after today's performance I'm quite happy to manage this one on my own.'

He saw the suspicious look that passed between the pair, but gave nothing away. They would work it out when they saw him showering and shaving.

CHAPTER 14

Murray found the taverna tucked away up a side street in Chlorakas, a 'traditional' village adjoining Pafos' old town. Shortly after seven-thirty, it was already busy, the tables out front packed-out with a mix of local families and ex-pat residents, which is always a good sign. Wandering through, he found a table inside at the back, ordered a Keo off the pretty, young East European waitress who brought him the menu, and settled back to study it. The girl must have reported his presence straight to her boss - despite Kishore's ministrations he still looked like he'd gone ten rounds - as she appeared, hovering over his table in less than a minute. When he looked up from the menu and she saw his face, her look of amused curiosity vanished, replaced by one of concern.

'OH MY GOD,' Gina Iridotu said. 'What has happened? Are you alright?'

'I will be,' Murray said. 'Nothing a good meze won't cure.'

Ignoring his flippancy, she turned to bark something at the white-shirted waiter about to enter the kitchen. When he made a quick reverse to head over to the bar and she pulled out a chair, Murray guessed she'd just put herself off-duty. Sure enough, the waiter returned with a bottle of Metaxa Seven-Star and two glasses.

Pouring them both a generous measure, she leant forward, eyes roaming his face, assessing the damage. As he drank his brandy and waited for her to complete her appraisal, he was surprised to realise that the feeling triggered by her interest in his welfare, reminded him of how he sometimes felt in Dironda's company, only he'd known Dironda years.

'Tell me what happened,' she said. 'And don't try to tell me you were in an accident. I've spent enough time around policemen to know the difference.'

Murry knew it was pointless him lying. 'I guess you could say my problem took a turn for the worse.'

Her eyes narrowed. 'The Russian, or the Army Policeman?'

Surprised by what she seemed to know - he wondered what else - he reminded himself he still needed to be careful. He had no idea yet how much she may report back to her father.

'Maybe a bit of both,' he answered. It prompted a sideways look that said she didn't like to be patronised. About to give him another chance, she was interrupted by the waitress arriving with Murry's Keo, who spoke to her in Greek.

Irritated, Gina rose. 'I am sorry. There is a problem in the kitchen. We will speak later.' She turned back to the waitress. 'Irena. Look after Mr Murray. Give him whatever he wants. His money is no good here.'

As Gina disappeared through the door to the kitchen, Irena turned her gaze on him. Her face said she was impressed. In accented but good English, she said, 'She does not do that often. You must be important.'

Murray smiled at her. 'I'll have the meze,' he said.

It was a good decision. Over the next hour, Irena - who he learned was Polish - kept him well supplied with the full range of dips, salads, vegetable and meat dishes that mark a chef who knows how to put on a good meze. Gina floated in and out now and then to check on him, but spent much of the time in the kitchen where, Irena confided, they were having to cope with, 'a bit of crisis'. It seemed the Head Chef's wife had gone into labour, causing him to rush off to be at her side.

But despite the disruption and the place being all-but full, Gina was showing she knew how to run things. Her ready smile and soothing attentions easily charmed those customers who were having to wait a while longer than usual. It helped that on a warm summer's evening, no one seemed bothered. Like many Mediterraneans, Cypriots regard eating as a leisure activity, and not one to be rushed. Besides, from what Murray could tell most appeared to be regulars. He doubted they would complain if they had to wait until midnight.

Eventually, the busiest part of the evening over, Gina managed to free herself. After checking with Irena that everything front-of-house was under control, she returned to Murray's table with glasses and a bottle of red to wash down the carafe of village wine he'd ordered after his beer. She poured two glasses and they chinked each other. By now he was onto the 'mains' - a succulent selection of roasted and grilled meats and wonderfully-flavoured vegetables. Already feeling like he'd eaten a normal meal's worth – there was still more to come - he didn't object when she picked up a fork and proceeded to help him out.

'You should do that more often,' she said between mouthfuls.

'What?'

'Smile. It is good for you.'

It brought him up short. A reminder of how he'd changed. Smiles and laughter were once the default. At that moment the face of a young boy swam before him.

He had to take a quick breath to stifle the melancholy that usually only came when he was alone. And he was shocked to realise that on this occasion, it could easily have turned into something else.

Gina sensed it. 'It is normal to grieve, Mr Murray. But it does not mean you cannot enjoy yourself, every now and then.'

He gathered himself. 'I'll try.' Then, eager to divert conversation somewhere safer, he waved his fork over the lamb dish he'd been enjoying when she arrived. 'What's the marinade?'

The look she gave him said she wasn't fooled, but she played along. 'Commanderia. You like it?'

He nodded, enthusiastic. 'This is the best meze I've had in a long while. Maybe ever. Compliments to the chef.'

She inclined her head in graceful acknowledgement. 'I will pass that on to Pepe when he returns. He will appreciate it.'

For several minutes they talked food, eating and the Taverna's history. She told how it still belonged to her grandfather. Now in his eighties, he'd given the running over to her the last couple of years.

'He still cooks?'

'Only when family come. He likes to show he still can.'

Murray nodded. He'd attended many Cypriot family gatherings in his time. Her father being Chief of Police, he suspected hers would probably fill the place, and imagined Pippis Iridotu, lording it at head of table. It triggered a flush of guilt. He'd been on the verge of thinking he was there to enjoy a hearty meal in the company of a woman who, the more he saw and heard, the more he imagined liking. Time for business.

'Last time we spoke, you seemed to think you may be

able to help with my problem in some way?'

The sudden switch brought a look that made him wonder if it was disappointment. She put down her fork and sipped at her wine. Her eyes bore into his. 'First, you must tell me honestly. What happened?'

To his surprise, he didn't think long on how much to say, but let his instincts dictate. In the end he didn't hold much back. Her eyes grew wide as he recounted the tale. When he got to the part about them taking him out to the Akamas, he had to, 'Shush' her, sharply, when she gasped out loud, 'THEY WERE GOING TO KILL YOU?'

After she calmed down and the faces at the tables had turned away, he said, 'I don't think they were taking me to see the Lara Turtles.' Lara Bay is a renowned Loggerhead nesting ground. 'On the other hand,' he mused. 'Maybe they were.'

'But that is awful. Surely you must tell my father?' She looked horrified.

For a moment, Murray feared he was being too open. Her father's work would have given her many insights as she grew up. But this was still Cyprus, and while it had changed much over recent years, it was still a long way from being some drug-dealing gangster hot spot, like Miami. Nor did he want her to think he had no faith in her father. During their limited dealings, Murray had formed the impression he was the sort of policeman who could be depended upon. He could even be one of the honest ones. But neither did he want to get into a debate about legalities, and the realities of dealing with people like Podruznig.

He shook his head. 'It would come down to my word against the Russian's. And you can bet he'll have witnesses prepared to swear I'd started any trouble. The message on his kitchen wall points to me. Involving the police wouldn't achieve anything, even with your father pushing it.'

'But your face. Your injuries-.'

'Inflicted when I tried to force myself into the house, or some such excuse. I'm sure others have bruises they could show.' He thought of the man whose throat he'd shattered - a detail he'd glossed over - though he suspected he was probably no longer around to lay any claim of assault.

She still wasn't convinced. 'You don't know my father. He is a good man. He wouldn't let them-.' She stopped, staring at the hand he'd placed, lightly, on hers.

'I'm not saying your father isn't a good man, Gina. And I'm sure he would want to do something if he could. But men like Podruznig don't worry about the law. And this isn't the sort of situation that gets resolved by the police knocking on the door and advising people against taking things into their own hands.'

As she sat back, thinking on it, Murray took his hand away. It had been a reflex contact, but one that, for as long as it lasted, felt good. She drank her wine.

'Tell me about this money, or whatever it is.'

For a split second he almost froze. When he spoke he did his best to sound casual. 'What money?"

'The money you are supposed to have stolen and which this Army policeman is looking for.'

He sighed. It was the subject he'd hoped he could avoid. But she'd either dug more out of her father, or overheard, than he'd realised. More than ever, he could see she was not the sort he could easily keep secrets from. And she clearly wanted answers before agreeing to help.

'What do you know about me?'

'What makes you think I know anything about you?'

He gave a rueful look. 'You obviously know

something. Besides, your father will have told you.'

'Why would he tell me anything?'

'Because you asked.'

She camouflaged her smile behind her glass before setting it down and looking directly at him.

'You were in the Army, but left to become a policeman, back in England. Then you came back here to do some special work of some sort. I don't know the details but my father said you were involved in something during the war in Afghanistan and the fighting in Syria? Something happened. Some money, or something, went missing?' She paused to see if he wanted to correct her on anything. He didn't, so she continued. 'I believe this Army Major, Westgate? believes you were involved.' At this point she hesitated, uncertain whether to mention it. Murray guessed what it might be. 'When you came back here you started to have this house built. Your wife and son were living here then. There was an accident. They....' She stopped unsure about going on.

'A road accident. They died.'

Her hand found his. He didn't return the squeeze but appreciated the gesture.

'Afterwards, you finished whatever work you were doing then came back to settle here. But by then this Russian had arrived and moved into your house. You asked my father for help but he says it is not a criminal matter and he cannot do anything.' She took up her glass again. 'That is as much as I know.'

He nodded. About what he'd expected.

'Now, it is your turn.'

He remembered their bargain, yet still he hesitated. There were still things he had never told anyone, not even Kathy.

'Before I tell you what you want to know, may I ask a

question?'

'Go on.'

'I'm sure your father warned you against having anything to do with me.' The slight lift of her eyebrows confirmed his suspicion. 'So what is the Chief of Police's daughter doing, meeting with someone her father thinks is a criminal?'

She put on a determined look. 'My father is a policeman. He thinks like a policeman. I however am a woman. I think like a woman.'

He frowned. 'What does that mean?'

'Dironda has known you a long time, yes?'

'My father was in the army. We were stationed here when I was young. I have been coming here for many years.'

She gave an affirming nod. 'Dironda says she knows about you.'

'About me?'

'Dironda has a way of *knowing* about people. You understand what I mean when I say, 'know'?'

His eyes narrowed. 'I think so.'

'And she is always right. She knew about my sister-in-law before she married my brother. The rest of us only realised later.'

Murray thought it best not to ask.

'And she knows about you. She said you would not do anything….' She hesitated, searching for the right expression.

'Against the law?'

'Ummm… not quite. She said you would not do anything… *bad*.'

'Er, wouldn't stealing be bad?'

'If you stole something and were caught, that would have harmed your family. Dironda says you would not do such a thing.'

He nodded. He'd never realised Dironda gave him so much thought.

'Now, you tell.'

He thought about where to start. Eventually he said, 'Alright, but on two conditions.'

'Yes?'

'First, you must not repeat what I say to anyone. And that includes your father.'

'Of course. And?'

'When I've finished, I will ask you if you feel you can trust me and you must answer honestly.'

She gave him a quizzical look. 'Agreed.'

He told her.

CHAPTER 15

He didn't tell her everything, they'd have been there all night and into the morning. He told her what she needed to know. He started with Rowan Grantham.

Grantham was a low-level drug dealer around London's Streatham district when Murray was attached to the Metropolitan Police Plain Clothes Branch. Murray busted him for possession and some minor supplying. It turned out Grantham was an ex-squaddie who had served in Cyprus. He also had links into the London drugs scene that Murray thought he could use. Though a junkie, Grantham was still managing to hold down a job with a national transport company which he stood to lose if he was convicted. Unusually for someone with a habit, he was surprisingly desperate to hang onto his position. On realising Murray was also ex-service, he offered to become a street informant if Murray could cut him a deal. Murray agreed. In return for regular cash payments, Grantham began putting Murray onto other, higher level dealers, as well as some of the *Capos* running street-gangs in the areas south of the Thames who had long been a cause of so much trouble.

For nearly a year it remained a mutually-beneficial arrangement, one of several Murray and his team were managing. Then, one evening, Grantham turned up at Murray's station fearing for his life and begging protection. He told Murray he had, 'A story to tell. Something *big*.' Murray took him to an anonymous Travelodge beyond the M25. There he began to coax the terrified dealer to spill.

The transport company Grantham joined on coming out of the army specialised in placing ex-servicemen. The reason soon became clear. It turned out it was the London end of a smuggling operation between Europe and the Middle East. Lured by the promise of big rewards and a never-ending supply of opium - Grantham became addicted to heroin soon after his discharge - he allowed himself to be sucked in. For two years everything ran smoothly. But two weeks before, a big deal had gone south when the product was intercepted, en route, by a rival gang. Word went round that Grantham was responsible, having taken a bung to set up the intercept. The night before, Grantham had learned there was a contract out on him – something Murray was able to confirm was true. Such was Grantham's paranoia about not trusting anyone, not even other policemen, it took Murray three days to get all the details out of him. When he eventually did, he understood a little better Grantham's assertions that the smuggling operation was too big for even the police to tackle. For the gang behind it was, the British Army.

In telling Gina the tale, Murray glossed over most of the secretive enquiries he later carried out with a select group of police and army investigators - Murray was himself, ex-SIB - he knew he could trust. Grantham's contention that the operation involved people in senior positions – perhaps even within Special Investigations Branch itself - meant that everything had to be kept especially tight. But eventually Murray uncovered enough to show that Grantham's story was substantially true.

Grantham's company had contracts with NAAFI, the

official trading organisation for all UK Armed Forces. A consortium of British and mainly Saudi gangsters, working with a network of corrupt servicemen, were using army supply routes between the Middle East and the UK as cover to smuggle in everything from drugs, to stolen art-works, to counterfeit retail goods. Officials and clerks on army payroll in bases around the Med had been bribed or threatened into supporting the operation, which had been going on for years using Grantham's company's drivers, especially planted for the purpose.

It was immediately clear to Murray that uncovering the full extent of the operation and bringing those involved to justice would require a great deal more than the sort of routine anti-smuggling operation usually carried out under the joint auspices of the Police, National Crime Agency and HM Customs. It was decided, at the highest Police, Home Office and Whitehall levels, that a joint operation was needed in which a police investigation could be supported by the Army know-how necessary to identify those involved.

A special unit comprising Police and Army investigators, as well as carefully-chosen, for the most part ex-Special Forces, was formed to work out of Cyprus to investigate the gang's activities and bring them to justice. From the beginning, it was recognised that given where they would be operating and the risks involved, it would be dangerous work. For that reason, the team was given survival and combat training both at the SAS Regiment HQ in Hereford, and in Saudi. Grantham's information was always going to be vital and, being the only man he would talk to, as well as having the right Police, Army and Cyprus background, Murray was given a lead role. At that time Grantham was still in touch with some of the smugglers, though secretly as the contract on him was still, 'live'. The

Operation was code-named 'Priscilla'. Its brief was to work in utmost secrecy. Even the Head of British Armed Forces - Cyprus, wasn't brought into the circle - something that would later have repercussions for Murray and his team.

Unfortunately - or fortunately, depending on the way of looking at it - the unit arrived in Cyprus around the time ISIL was finally being crushed in Syria - thanks largely, to the bombing missions carried out by UK and US forces. Grantham reported to Murray murmurings of a major gear-up in smuggling operations. Those running things had sensed what might be a once-in-a-lifetime opportunity to take maximum advantage of the chaos everyone knew would accompany the build up of British and Allied Forces in Cyprus and the intensification of military intervention in Syria.

Murray's team went undercover immediately. With only the barest preparation, they embarked upon a series of hectic and often dangerous surveillances, infiltrations and incursions in and around army bases, as well as Syrian and Iraqi towns and villages where those known to be involved in the operation lived and worked. The fall of ISIL proved a defining moment. Using information bought or extracted from ISIL fighters, as well as British military sources, the smugglers had arranged to use disaffected Syrian soldiers and mercenaries to intercept a convoy containing art works originally looted from Baghdad during the Iraq war and which high level officials in the Syrian Government were trying to spirit out of the country. Thought to be part of Syrian President, Bashar Assad's contingency planning in the event he ever had to flee the country, the convoy was being guarded by members of Assad's elite Republican Guard.

Having been tipped off what was to happen,

Murray's team were on hand to witness the Guards' unusually swift capitulation to the smuggler's 'ambush' - money was seen to change hands – as well as the subsequent dispatching of those who remained loyal to Assad and who tried to mount a belated resistance.

As those in the pay of the smugglers carted the twice-stolen booty away, Murray's team began the nerve-racking task of tracking it through the various links in the chain. The operation was to last for six months with the likes of Murray, and his team, which included Red and Kishore, living amongst the bands of deserters and roving mercenaries who at that time were swarming all over the region. At one stage they even found themselves being dragooned into helping the smugglers load part of the haul onto trucks to be taken to a secret cache on the Saudi-Iraq border. Twice during this period, Murray came close to being exposed as a British agent. Luckily, Red was on hand both times to pull him out - once under heavy fire.

A few weeks after the war ended, Murray and his team had all the information they needed. In a series of co-ordinated raids in the UK, Cyprus, and several Arab states, members of the ring - army and civilian - were rounded up. Many were charged and/or extradited and later appeared before British civil and military courts and given lengthy sentences. Others were dealt with in ways Murray never learned of and preferred not to know about. At this point, Murray paused in his tale to take a drink. He could see Gina was fascinated. But now his mood darkened.

'It would have been a good result, but for the missing gold.'

Gina started. 'Gold? My father spoke of money.'

Murray shook his head. 'When people start talking 'gold', the wrong sort of people become interested.'

'What happened?'

'Part of the haul consisted of a consignment of gold bars, looted from the Bank of Iraq just before Baghdad fell. We were led to believe it was amongst the consignments we were tracking, but it never surfaced. After the gang was arrested, no-one would say what happened to it. Some tried to muddy the waters by pointing the finger at us. Some of the military high-ups at that time were pissed off they'd been cut out of the chain of command and embarrassed about the army's role in the affair. They insisted there ought to be an 'independent investigation' into what happened to the gold.'

After another drink Murray continued. 'It was politics and bullshit really, but they got their way. Westgate was brought in and put in charge of an SIB enquiry to look into it. He was out to make a name for himself and I guess he decided we could be his meal ticket. He found a couple of 'witnesses' who spun him a story about the trucks containing the gold being stolen in the night by Englishmen disguised as Arabs – which pointed to us. It was a load of balls of course, but it was enough to get everyone thinking. We were all pulled in for questioning, detained for weeks, but they never found anything – not that there was anything to find. We were eventually exonerated, but it left a nasty taste. Some still believe it was us. Westgate is obsessed with it. He swore that one day he would prove we were responsible. I thought he'd moved on until he showed up at your father's office.'

'So what do you think *did* happen to the gold?'

Murray refilled his glass. He was feeling more relaxed now, surprisingly so, given he was talking about things he'd thought he would never reveal to anyone. 'Who knows? Hidden away by some of the gang themselves maybe. Or Assad loyalists. Personally, I'm not convinced it ever existed. There were a lot of crazy rumours circulating around that time. Everything was blamed on deserting ISIL fighters but there were all sorts of factions operating in that area at the time. Even if it did exist, any one of them could have taken it.'

His tale finished - for now - Murray sat back, awaiting her reaction.

Her gaze stayed on him a good while. Eventually she shook her head. 'What an incredible story. But what happened to you after? You obviously left the army, or the police, or whoever you were working for.'

His face darkened.

'After everything that had happened, good and bad, I felt I couldn't go back to Police work. Not in England at least. I heard reports about some not-very-nice things being spread around back home. Mud sticks, you know? We-.' He breathed deeply. 'Kathy and I - Kathy was my wife - we had a son. He was six. They hardly saw me while all this was going on. We'd always loved Cyprus so we decided to settle here and start over. I'm a carpenter by trade and we thought we might be able to get a small furniture business going. We still had all the money and savings from my time in the Army and those of us involved in the Operation were entitled to some fairly generous allowances. We heard there was a plot of land for sale and went to see the developer, Klerides. The rest... I think you know.' As he fell silent, he could almost see the question forming in Gina's mind. She was a woman.

'Can I ask what hap-.'

'After Priscilla, the Army let us stay on Episkopi while the house was being built. I had to return to Saudi to tie up some loose ends. Kathy and Jack, that was his name, Jack-' Gina gave a sad smile - 'They'd been out for the day to Kurium beach. The way home took them along the road that runs through the base. You know it? The cliff road?' She nodded. 'Some local farmer was driving his broken-down truck towards them when his steering went. The truck veered across the road and when Kathy tried to avoid it she lost control. They went through the crash barr-.' He stopped, unable to finish. He reached for his glass and took a long drink. Gina said nothing, letting him recover.

When he eventually looked at her again, he saw the candle's flame reflected in the dampness in her eyes and had to take another drink. After what seemed a long time, during which neither of them spoke, Irena appeared at Gina's shoulder, hovering as if she needed to speak with her. But after a moment's hesitation she left without asking. Eventually Murray pulled himself round.

Too much of this. Not why I came.

'I said that after I told you, I'd ask if you still feel you can trust me.'

'Yes....'

'And that you had to be honest.'

'I will be.'

'So, do you?'

'Yes.'

'In that case....'

But before he could continue her hand came up and her gaze slid away over his shoulder. Her face changed to one of recognition and she forced a smile to cover the bad timing. Before he could turn there was babble of Greek from behind.

'Yasoo, Ileana,' Gina said.

Murray looked round just as the girl arrived next to him. She was younger than Gina but he saw the similarity at once. Her hair was darker and longer and she still retained the slimness of youth, but there was no doubting who she was.

'Mr Murray, this is Ileana, my sister. Ileana this is Mr Murray.'

Conscious of Gina's formality, Murray smiled up at the young woman. 'Call me Peter. I'm very pleased to meet you, Ileana.'

The appraising look that came into the pretty face matched the one Gina had given him at Dironda's. After a couple of seconds' hesitation, the smile that broke suggested he had passed scrutiny.

'You too, Mr Murray, Peter. And I am sorry to interrupt your dinner, but I must speak with my sister.'

He waved the interruption away. 'Be my guest.'

As he eased back in his chair, Ileana and Gina spoke together. It involved much hand waving and what Murray assumed was the Greek equivalent of 'tushing', from both women. A sisterly argument, though he had no way of knowing how serious. It ended with Gina getting up, the raised eyebrows signalling her exasperation. *Sisters!*

Ileana followed her to the bar where Gina took some notes from the till and passed them to her sibling. After a brief acknowledgement from Ileana that Murray assumed was meant to pass as gratitude she was about to leave the way she'd come in, through the rear, when she stopped and turned back to him.

'Nice to have met you Mr M- Peter.'

'And you, Ileana.'

As she left, the younger woman threw her sister a look that was full of meaning as well as mischief. Gina ignored it and Murray knew he would have to pretend not to have seen it. Then she was gone. A whirlwind, like her older sister.

'I am sorry about that,' Gina said as she sat down again. 'Always she comes out without money. Crazy.'

'But you love her all the same.'

Gina smiled. 'Of course. I have to. Apart from being sisters, we share a house.'

He paused to let things settle, then: 'Now where were we? Oh yes, I was about to-.' But like so many times before, she didn't let him finish.

'You don't have to say anything else. How can I help you?'

CHAPTER 16

Major Glyn Westgate of the Royal Military Police SIB rose from his temporary office's wooden desk and went through to the meagre kitchen. Opening the ancient fridge-freezer he grabbed some ice, dropped it into a tumbler, then poured over a generous measure of the doubtful Bombay Sapphire he'd picked up, cheap, at a Cava in Pafos harbour. Satisfied it was as much as he could do to trick his brain into thinking he was back in his more conducive, Berlin surroundings, he returned to where he'd left off, perusing the photographs the Base Adjutant had brought over, twenty minutes earlier.

He bent the stem of the angle-poise-lamp so that its single spot shone down on the images he'd requested, forty-eight hours before. They were even better than he had expected. Much clearer than the Google Earth images he'd browsed on his laptop, and they weren't bad. The pictures showed the house and land around in remarkable detail. He could even tell that the figure relaxing by the kidney-shaped pool was a blond woman. She would be the model-wife. The one whose early pictures he'd seen, but had been disappointed not to find any more recent.

Pulling his notepad towards him, he cast his eyes down the list of dates he'd noted after going through the papers again. They included those from the file he'd recovered from SIB Headquarters in Berlin, as well as the ones the helpful young lady in Nicosia's snowed-under Land Registry had faxed through to him. He'd been more than a little surprised, but most grateful, when she actually rang back to say she'd managed to find the plans he'd enquired about.

The dates were only a rough guide, of course. There were still some variables his earlier investigation had never been able to resolve. And knowing the vagaries of Cyprus bureaucracy, he knew he should not place too much store on the dates shown in the documents submitted by the builders, either. Nevertheless, there were some interesting correlations. It didn't take too much imagination to see the possibilities. And Glyn Westgate was nothing if not imaginative.

The Army Investigator smiled as he sipped at his gin, savouring both the tangy aftertaste and the feeling that had been growing in him these last couple of days. It told him that this time, his efforts stood a much better chance of bearing fruit than before.

He surveyed the photographs again. Nothing jumped out at him especially. He hadn't really expected it would. Nevertheless, they gave a good enough idea of the overall layout so that when the time came, he wouldn't have to mess about getting his bearings. He wondered how long he would have to wait? Although the instructions from his bosses were open-ended, he knew there would be a limit. After last time, those above would be watching closely and he didn't want to let himself be seen to be hanging around, just waiting for things to happen. He wondered if maybe he ought to start being even more proactive. From what he'd seen and heard, things were already pretty stirred up. It would not take much to stir them even more.

But before that, he needed to latch onto Murray

again. He'd driven by Murray's rental in Kato Pafos's Limnaria district several times the last couple of days, and though he'd clocked the two Russians in the supposedly nondescript white van staking out the place, he'd seen no sign of Murray. He'd obviously gone to ground. Westgate wasn't worried. He had a good idea where he might be holed up. Even if he was wrong, Pafos wasn't the sort of place where you could lay low long. Especially if you had things to take care of that meant putting yourself about, as he was certain Murray needed to.

Westgate allowed himself a self-satisfied nod of congratulation. His efforts so far had started some of the balls rolling. It shouldn't be hard to get the rest moving as well, particularly if he helped things along with a little push here and there. He drained his glass, then headed back to the kitchen for a refill.

CHAPTER 17

Klerides sounded apologetic -genuinely. 'I rang straight after he'd gone, Mr Murray but could not get through on your mobile.'

Murray watched as the regular, Friday morning BA flight to Gatwick climbed out over the sea before making the right turn that would take it North-West along the coast, the first leg of its fifteen-hundred mile journey.

'Not your fault Nik, I was otherwise engaged. Tell me again what he was after.'

'He wanted details from your property file. Copies of our agreements, letters, correspondence, that sort of thing. He seemed very interested in dates.'

'What did you give him?'

'Nothing. I told him everything was with our solicitors, to prepare our case, and he would have to go through them.'

'Good answer. Anything else?'

'He said he knew of the trouble I'd had with Mr Podruznig and that he would protect me if I cooperated.'

'And what did you say to that?'

'I said I did not know what he was talking about and did not need anyone's protection.'

Murray nodded. For a property developer, Klerides

was remarkably principled. Some would have leaped at the chance to ingratiate themselves with the British Armed Forces. He hoped things wouldn't soon blow up in a way that would cause him and his brother problems. He bore no grudges.

Before ringing off, Murray thanked him for the update and asked Nik to keep him informed on any other approaches. He said he would.

Murray turned to Red, sat under the faded, Coca-Cola sun umbrella.

'Westgate. He's asking about the house. Checking dates.'

Red's face remained impassive. 'He's becoming a bloody nuisance.'

'But not one we can do anything about, unfortunately.'

'Oh I don't know....'

Murray read the message, but remained non-committal. He still liked to think that the Westgate problem would disappear on its own, eventually. Deep down, he knew he was being wildly optimistic.

Superintendent Pippis Iridotu was angry. And he hated being angry. Especially with either of his two daughters. He didn't mind so much when it was their brother, Chris. Boys are supposed to be shouted at, how else do they learn to be men? And he always felt worse when the source of his anger was his eldest. Gina had a habit of reacting as if nothing had happened. It was infuriating.

'I don't see what there is to get upset about, Papa. He had a meal, paid for it, and left. Just like everyone else.'

Pippis wasn't going to let her get away with such an obvious lie for a single moment. 'So you sat at other customers' tables talking for three hours also, did you? It must have been a very long night.'

Surprised by his knowledge, Gina thought quickly. She would speak to his informant when she got home that evening. At nineteen, Ileana shouldn't need lessons on the importance of sisterly discretion.

'Why shouldn't I talk with him? He was a customer. I talk with all my customers. You know that.'

Pippis's voice rose. 'BECAUSE I TOLD YOU NOT TO. That is why.'

'You told me not to get involved with him. Talking is not getting involved.'

'Then why do you now come to me asking questions? Is that not getting involved?'

'I am just curious that is all. He did not seem to me as you described him. Such a man does not shed tears when he speaks of his family.'

Pippis exploded. '*HOW CAN A POLICEMAN'S DAUGHTER BE SO NAIVE?*' His arms windmilled as he spoke, hands emphasising every word. 'A man puts on a show of being sad, and instantly you want to mother him.'

'Do not be ridiculous, Papa. Do you not think I can tell when a man is putting on a show? Like I said, I was just curious.'

Pippis gave a derisory snort. 'I seem to recall someone else who aroused your curiosity. How many wives and children was it? Three, and seven? Or was it eight?'

'That was only because I wanted to find out the truth about him.'

'And what an excellent job you made of doing so.'

This time, Gina thought carefully before responding. The incident when, to her father's embarrassment, the police were called to deal with the man's second wife who turned up at Gina's apartment late one night, hurling abuse and invective that made even the two

105

young policemen who came to arrest her blush, was not easy to brush aside. Still, she did her best.

'I am not a child Papa. I knew exactly what I was doing then, just as I do now. I am not in a relationship with this Mr Murray. I simply want to know if his story about this Russian stealing his home is true or not. You always say yourself that we must watch out for these Pontians.'

'Meaning that it is my business as a *policeman*, Gina. I do not intend that all the women in my family become Miss Marbles and start investigating gossip. When I want gossip I will ask your mother. Or that Dironda everyone seems to listen to.'

Despite her father's fierce manner, Gina had to suppress a smile. Apart from mispronouncing the famous detective's name - the old, English TV series was running on PIK1, horribly sub-titled of course - she had not realised that Dironda's reputation had spread as far as the local Chief of Police himself. Realising that unless she altered course she would never succeed in her mission, Gina switched tack. A buff folder lay on the side of his desk. She wondered if it was the one.

'Let us not argue, Papa. I am sorry if I caused you any alarm. But I can assure you, I have no plans to see Mr Murray again, unless it is as a paying customer.' Mentally she crossed fingers. If he spotted the distinction between current arrangements - none - and future intentions - lots - she could be in trouble. He didn't.

Still, he was suspicious. His eyes narrowed. 'You could refuse to serve him if he turns up again.'

She made a, *Don't be stupid,* face. 'Business is not so good I can afford to turn away good money. ' She sidled up to him, kissed his cheek. 'But I promise not to raise the subject again.'

'Good.' He glanced at her but didn't return the kiss. He needed to cement victory first. Even so, he signalled his willingness to bridge-build. 'That is more like what a father is entitled to expect from a dutiful daughter.'

She turned to go. 'See you tonight, Papa.'

After the door closed, Pippis Iridotu spent a long time looking at it. He turned back to his desk. The folder he had been going through - again - when she walked in was still there. For some reason he felt the sudden urge to put it somewhere safe. He went to his desk, opened the bottom drawer, and dropped the folder in before looking back up at the door. His eyes narrowed. Reaching into his trouser pocket, he took out his keys, reached down, and locked the drawer.

The nagging urge momentarily satisfied, he sat at his desk and pulled towards him the in-tray he needed to get through before he could finish up. He bent his head and started reading. But after a few minutes he realised he was sitting upright in his chair, looking at the door again, wondering about her abrupt departure. He looked down at the drawer again. It was still closed. Still locked. The folder safe from prying eyes.

He knew he was missing something. He wished he knew what.

The other side of the door, Gina perched cross-legged on the desk, smiling down, warmly, at Woman-Sergeant Andri Pahiti. Andri didn't return it.

Instead, the sergeant was sitting back in her chair, arms folded, regarding Gina with a look that was intended to convey this would be the last, *the very last*, time. She was also trying to come to terms with what she had just agreed to do. But she knew the pull Gina had with her father. She also knew the man she worked for and his opposite number in the adjoining Limassol

Division, where Andri's husband, Laslo, worked shifts, were good friends. It took Laslo a good hour or more to get to work, and back, each day from their home in Peyia village, the wrong side of Pafos from Limassol. Superintendent Pippis was known for the pride he took in not interfering in posting decisions involving friends and family of those close to him. He had spoken, many times about how he abhorred the sort of patronage he'd witnessed coming up through the ranks. Too often, it led to officers landing jobs for which they were ill-equipped. For that reason, he always left such matters to his Chief Inspector second-in-command. But Andri knew enough about her boss's eldest daughter to be in no doubt. If Gina said she could get her father to make an exception in Laslo's case, she believed her.

'*Thank* you Andri,' Gina said. Knowing a reply wouldn't be forthcoming, she didn't wait, but simply turned and wooshed out of the ante-office, as was her fashion.

As she gazed at the doorway through which Gina had vanished, Andri had no way of knowing how closely her wary musings mirrored those of the man the other side of the door. Not for the first time, she wondered whether it was time she gave up her privileged position as the Superintendent's gatekeeper, and returned to the sort of police work that, in truth, she no longer had a great hankering for but at least would allow her to sleep nights. Then she thought about how much easier things would be if Laslo worked from Pafos Divisional Police Headquarters rather than Limassol. Tucking the dilemma over her own future away for consideration another time, she started to think about where she had tucked away the box containing all the spare keys she had managed to gather during the two years she had worked for Pippis Iridotu.

CHAPTER 18

The men's names were Piotr and Olaf. Georgian by birth, like Lantzeff himself, they had been specially chosen for their assignment. A twenty-four-seven house watching job calls for a certain single-mindedness. Especially when the only relief comes in the form of a once-a-day thirty-minute swap-out for a proper toilet break - the plastic bottles in back having to suffice between times. Fortunately, single mindedness is an attribute Georgians are reputed to possess in ample measure, or so Lantzeff always claimed. Which was why, presumably, he had chosen them. And carrying out the second part of the assignment - bringing the Englishman in if he showed himself - called for the sort of other attributes for which the former pair of Spetsnaz were noted. Fearlessness, strength, and well-honed combat skills.

So far, the men's dedication to their task had helped maintain the state of alertness Lantzeff had assured them was necessary if they were not to incur both his wrath, and that of Podruznig himself. The result was that after three days, their tally of 'false alarms' ran to two frightened postmen, an Electricity Authority meter-reader, and a holidaying couple from the UK who, most unfortunately for them, had the wrong house-number for the old friends they were seeking to surprise with an unannounced visit. Following Piotr and Olaf's frightening interrogation, the Brits didn't hang around to try to confirm the right address, but left as quickly as their hire car would take them. And credit to the two Georgians, during their long periods of observation, they had noted other occurrences they thought may be relevant to their task, but weren't quite sure.

Like the grey Honda.

Having been absent attending to another 'persuasion' mission' the past week, the pair had no first-hand knowledge of the events that had led to their present assignment. What they *did* know was that during their absence, every member of the team had been spoken to, personally, by Lantzeff, as were they on their return, and given clear warning as to what would happen if they let their guard slip over this particular problem. They also knew that the man they had been told to watch out for was connected with the incident in the kitchen they heard about the night they got back. And though no one had said as much, they assumed he was the same man who - so rumour had it - escaped a run out to the wilderness. True or not, it still had everyone talking. They had since discovered that Nikolas hadn't returned from that trip either. Which, he being a fellow Georgian, was a shame. Finally, they were aware also that the two Siberians who had been on watch the night of the kitchen incident were no longer around either. The official word was that they had been, 'sent home' - but everyone liked to think they knew what that meant. Several members of the team had seen them getting into the four-by-four that was to take them to the airport. Lantzeff drove, accompanied by two more of his longest-serving team members. The word around was that the three returned in far less time than an airport run would have taken.

Piotr and Olaf didn't find such rumours particularly disquieting. In their line of business these things happen. But it did make them determined not to suffer a similar fate to that of the Siberians - whatever it was.

Which was why they had noted the details of the grey Honda that had cruised past the target premises on the first day, and twice again since, even though the ex-military-looking driver clearly wasn't the man they were waiting for. True, their report back to Lantzeff didn't mention the fact that the driver also appeared to have spotted them. And when word came back that it traced back to British Sovereign Forces registration, they had wondered if, perhaps, there were a few too many things about which they had either not been informed, or did not fully understand. They just hoped the fact of their being seen wouldn't prove significant in a way that would bounce back on them.

It was early afternoon on the third day - they were just finishing the baguettes and coffee that had been brought to them by the elderly Asian vendor who ran the kiosk on the main road - when they saw the jeep. It did not match the details of the one they'd been told to look out for, but given the way it slowed as it drove past the house – it had come from behind, passing them on their right, they both came instantly on alert.

They watched it turn at the bottom of the street, before coming back and slowing to a stop outside the house. Neither man said anything, but adrenalin started pumping the moment the man in a bright red-shirt and wearing a baseball cap and sunglasses stepped from the passenger side, rounded the Jeep's bonnet and crossed the narrow pavement to the front door.

Despite his attempt at disguise, their training meant they had little trouble matching the Englishman to the photograph they'd been given. Dropping their

111

Styrofoam cups on the floor, they shifted in their seats, waking the muscles that had lain dormant for hours, readying themselves to act.

The man in the red shirt lifted a key to the lock but, about to insert it, he paused as if some sixth sense had alerted him to danger. Looking round, he stared at the white van parked thirty metres further up the street. For a moment, time froze, the man in the baseball cap looking straight at them, Piotr and Olaf wishing themselves invisible.

Suddenly, their quarry exploded into action. Spinning round, he dashed back towards the jeep which hadn't moved, its engine still running. They heard him yell, "GO, GO, GO," then he was diving into the back just as, with a squeal of tyres, it leaped forward.

Piotr barely had time to turn the engine before the jeep shot past, the man in the cap and glasses glaring at them from the back, though he just had time to register the driver's ginger hair. By the time they turned the van around, the jeep was already turning left at the other end of the street. Putting his foot down, Piotr raced after while Olaf radioed control, asking if any others were near enough to assist in the chase.

As Piotr made the left turn, he saw the jeep charging down towards the T- junction at the far end, the man in the red shirt and glasses still watching their progress through the jeep's rear window. Flooring the accelerator, he set off in pursuit.

As the Russians' van turned at the T-junction and disappeared, Murray raised himself from behind the low garden wall that fronted the houses on the left. He turned his shoulder to ease the pain suffered when his diving roll from the jeep took him into the palm tree in the middle of the lawn. Red had barely slowed when he dived out, while Kishore, wearing an identical shirt, cap and glasses took Murray's place in back.

As the roar of engines faded in the distance, Murray jogged back towards the house. Although they'd agreed ten minutes would be enough - after which Red would look to shake off his pursuers - he didn't want to hang around any longer than necessary.

The doors and windows at the front were secure. But as Murray skirted around the side and saw the fly-screen covering the back door swinging loose on its hinges, he knew what to expect. Sure enough, he found the wood around the door's lock splintered. He only had to push the door lightly for it to swing open.

Stepping into the small kitchen that opened onto the living area, he saw at once that the place had been trashed. Kitchen cupboards had been emptied, their contents spilled, smashed and strewn around the floor. In the living room, the cushions on the sofa and chairs had been slashed, stuffing hanging out, more strewn around. The display-unit-bookcase had been pulled down. His books and the few of Kathy's knick-knacks he'd chosen to put out lay scattered and broken. But whilst he felt anger towards those responsible, there was little sadness. The house was a furnished let, taken after the funeral while the Sea Caves house was still being finished - and before Podruznig arrived. It had never been anything more than a place to lay his head. Most of his and Kathy's stuff was still in storage, thank God.

As he stepped further into the living area and looked around, surveying the mess, he saw the message scrawled on the left-hand wall. In large, dripping red letters it read, "BIG MISTAKE." For several seconds he stood before it, mulling over the significance of its message. Then he turned and headed upstairs.

The upper rooms - two bedrooms and a bathroom -

were in a similar, ransacked state with drawers and cupboards emptied. The mattresses had been pulled off the beds and given the same treatment as the sofa. A musky-sweet odour hung over everything and he recognised the cologne Kathy had brought him back from her last visit to her mother in the UK. Sure enough, on checking the bathroom he found it, smashed on the tile floor. But though it was what angered him most - Kathy had always liked it - he didn't dwell on it.

Returning to the main bedroom, he poked his head into the built-in cupboard. The small safe that had been bolted to the floor had been prised off its anchorages and the door was wide open, the photographs and other documents it contained strewn around. Not bothering to check it, he turned back to the bed. Stepping over and around the clothes and bedding littering the floor, he grasped the bottom of the wooden bed frame - still heavy even without the mattress - and pulled it away from the wall. There was a loud screeching noise, like fingernails on a chalk-board, as the legs scraped across the tiles.

Moving to the headboard he reached behind, feeling for what he knew would still be there when he saw the bed hadn't been moved. His fingers made contact and he ripped the plastic sleeve away from the duct-tape holding it to the back of the headboard. A quick glance was enough to confirm that its contents - money, passport, other documents - were undisturbed.

Retrieving a hold-all from the back bedroom, he stuffed it with clothes and the few personal effects he didn't feel like leaving, slipped the plastic sleeve into the side pocket then returned downstairs. After taking one last look around - there was nothing of value he couldn't replace - he left the way he'd come in. He didn't bother trying to secure the door. When the letting agents saw the mess, his bond would be forfeit anyway. Before stepping out into the street, he double-checked to make sure there was still no sign of the white van - though if it had returned Red would have rung. Confirming all was clear, he checked his watch. In another minute Red and Kishore would shake off their pursuers. Ten minutes later they would pick him up from the agreed rendezvous outside the Paphos Beach Hotel along the coast. Just time enough. Swinging the bag over his shoulder, he set off, double-time.

CHAPTER 19

Hunkered in the high-backed chair he'd stolen from the office of a retiring Nicosia police chief, Superintendent Pippis Iridotu studied the English Army Major briefing him on the latest developments. He found it interesting that Westgate only made eye-contact when emphasising a point he deemed important.

Like his tale about Murray supposedly breaking into Podruznig's house and daubing some sort of message on the wall.

When Pippis showed scepticism - Murray didn't come across as the sort given to rash actions - Westgate insisted his information was good, but would not reveal its source. When he went on to say it fitted with things he knew about Murray but which, unfortunately, he was not at liberty to share with the Commander, Pippis remained sceptical. He didn't seek to argue, however, conscious that right from the off, Westgate had always painted Murray as a man with no redeeming qualities whatsoever. It made him recall how, when Murray first came to him to discuss his options for dealing with his house problem, he was open enough to admit that he had left the army on 'not the happiest of terms', and that if Pippis chose to dig, he would have little difficulty finding people prepared to 'diss' him. Ileana explained that evening what 'diss' meant. Murray also stated that just as many would swear that he had been unfairly maligned. Whilst his work had taken him to some dark places, he was a man who, generally, respected the rule of law.

Murray's predictions had proven accurate in both respects, which was why Pippis preferred to rely on his instincts. And while he had been forced to revise his early assessment in the light of what he later learned – mainly from Westgate – he still remembered those first impressions. A man with a past that wasn't free from shadows, but who was basically honest, had been wronged, and now wished to resolve his problem in the least disruptive way possible - preferably within the law. He was also conscious, though it irked him to even let it enter the equation, of what Gina had said, and she was rarely wrong about such things - ex lover-boy excepted.

Nevertheless, he was still prepared to keep an open mind. If Westgate's accounts contained even a spark of truth, it was troubling. An incident such as the wall daubing he'd described would be bound to provoke a response. Given the Russian's history, it would unlikely take the form of waving a flag of truce and an invitation to Murray to discuss how they may resolve their dispute, amicably. He also remembered what Ileana had said when she'd let slip about Gina talking to 'an Englishman' at the Taverna. One who looked, 'a bit beaten up.' The last thing Pippis needed was that sort of escalation. Who knew where it could lead?

He turned his attention back to the army officer, now talking about enquiries he had made with some of Klerides' workmen, the ones who'd put down the footings.

'When I asked if they had seen anything strange going on while they were there, I got an interesting reaction. At first, I thought they were about to tell me

117

something, but then they clammed up. Like they had been told to keep their mouths shut.'

Pippis snorted. 'These builders. They were not Cypriot?'

'No. They were-.'

'Let me guess. Albanians. Or Syrian.'

Westgate frowned. 'Albanian. Why?'

Pippis snorted again. Without imported labour, the recently reinvigorated building boom that, alongside tourism, was the mainstay of the country's economy, would falter. 'They are like the Irish once were in your country. Or perhaps the Poles, more recently.'

'And?'

'Did you enquire as to whether they are here legally?'

'Is that relevant?'

'It is if you are going to read things into why they did not like to speak with you. The developers know what is going on and warn them never to talk to the authorities. I am surprised you got any of them to even admit they speak English. Go back tomorrow and try to find them again. I suspect you will not.'

Westgate shrugged it off. 'You may be right, or not. Either way, it just adds to the overall picture. Believe me, Superintendent, I am sure that what happened to Murray's family isn't the only reason he's so keen to get back into that house.'

Pippis nodded, as if prepared to accept Westgate's analysis, at least for the time being. After several more minutes spent going over what Westgate either knew or suspected, the meeting wound to a close.

'If I hear any more, I will let you know at once,' Westgate said.

'Thank you, Major, please do that.'

Pippis' smile was as wide as ever as he showed Westgate to the door. Whatever his uncertainties, it was always as well to keep the wheels on which his relationship with the British Military Authorities ran, well-greased.

In truth, the Divisional Commander was becoming increasingly irritated by Westgate's transparent attempts to keep him involved and 'updated' about the whole affair. He was beginning to think the matter was not one the police should be involved in at all, or even overly concerned about. Unless, of course, Murray or the Russian started trying to kill each other, in which case that would be a different matter. But until then, who cares about the British Army's problems? In any case, fantastic-sounding stories about missing gold were, probably, just bait aimed at arousing his interest. He reached for the door handle.

As the two men came out Gina, dressed in a startling red and white polka-dot dress, hopped off her perch on the edge of Andri's desk. When she turned, Pippis saw that his daughter seemed unusually flustered. About to comment - it was such a rare event - the sound of a drawer suddenly banging shut drew his gaze to Andri. She was blushing. They'd obviously been gossiping over something juicy. He suspected that if he now reached down and opened the drawer Andri had banged shut so clumsily, he would find one of those celebrity photograph magazines women read these days, even Maria, his wife. He decided not to embarrass them.

'Miss Iridotu,' Westgate said, in his best Army-Officer manner. 'A pleasure to see you again. You seem to spend almost as much time here as your father.'

Still recovering, Gina returned him the polite smile Pippis recognised as the one she kept for those visitors to her taverna she knew she wasn't likely to see again. It didn't take her long to get her voice back.

'He needs keeping an eye on, Major. If he didn't have

119

Andri and I to look after him, he would never get any work done.' As the two men acknowledged her humour with the polite chuckle it merited, she turned a scolding look on her father. 'Not another meeting about Mr Murray is it Papa? Really Major, wouldn't you think the Pafos Divisional Police Commander would have better things to do with his time than get involved in property disputes?'

Pippis just caught Westgate's look of surprise. But even he wasn't sure which of them Gina's message was aimed at. He glared at her. But when Westgate turned to him, the innocent smile also seemed at odds with his words.

'Your daughter is obviously well-informed about what is happening around the district, Superintendent. Perhaps I should employ her as my assistant?'

Irritated by Gina's speaking out of turn and embarrassed by her disclosing knowledge of his affairs, Pippis's retort was less considered than it would normally be. 'Your money would be better spent on a meal at her Taverna, Major. You would be surprised what sort of people turn up there.'

Westgate's eyebrows lifted. At the same time Gina's eyes blazed and a fiery redness came into her face. Too late, Pippis realised what he had said. Westgate turned to her.

'Ah yes. I remember your father mentioning you run a restaurant.'

'A taverna actually, Major.'

He smiled at her. 'I'm not sure I would know the difference. Perhaps I might try it some time. Do you have a card?'

Her clutch-bag was in her hand. She didn't move to check it. 'I am sorry. No.'

In the silence that followed, Pippis and Gina glared

venom at each other. Andri kept her head down. Westgate smiled from father to daughter, before realising his presence was no longer needed.

'I'll be off then.'

Westgate's gaze was fixed on the Police Station's main entrance. It was hot as hell in the car and he was sweating his balls off, but he hadn't put the air-con on as that would mean running the engine and he didn't want to draw attention to himself should she appear. He'd settled for rolling the Honda's windows down. It barely made any difference.

It had taken him only as long as the short walk back to his car for him to run through the several possibilities that flowed from the loaded exchange he had witnessed between the Police Commander and his sparky daughter. All of them interested him.

One thing his investigator's instincts told him for sure. Gina had met Murray. The way his name came so readily to her lips, it was obvious she'd had dealings with him. Leaving the station, he'd remembered she was around the day he surprised Murray in the Superintendent's office. Probably invited him to her restaurant – Taverna, snooty bitch – he wouldn't be surprised. And where might that have led? If his reading of the situation was correct, she'd been irritated to find them still discussing Murray, almost protectively so. Which would hardly be the case if all she knew was what he had fed her father. It was all *most* interesting.

He'd been waiting for half-an-hour now and was beginning to wonder if she'd left the station via the door round the other side after all. It was the one she would use if she'd walked in from the Old Town. But he'd taken a gamble on her having driven there, in which case her car would be one of the many parked along

Ypolohagou Avenue, where most visitors parked. Whatever had drawn her there, he doubted it was a mission that would keep her too long, not the way she was dressed. In which case-.

The striking figure in the polka-dot dress that suddenly rounded the pole-barrier at the station entrance ended his speculation. As she started to walk, quickly, in her high heels up the tree lined avenue towards him, he sank into his seat, thinking on an excuse for still being there should she spot him. His fears vanished as she stopped at the red Mercedes sports convertible that had been top of his list of 'possibles', and got in. With only the briefest glance behind – typical Cypriot - she shot out of her space and drove off. Even before she'd covered the hundred or so metres to the junction with Posiedenos Avenue, Westgate's Honda was where single-mobile surveillance best practice said it should be; two cars behind.

As she turned left, Westgate made ready to follow as soon as he could squeeze past the cars in front. Having picked her up, he didn't want to lose her, especially not now, with his suspicions still on course to be proved correct.

While waiting he'd used the time to run through the various criteria that would fit with his several hypotheses about why she may have been there, at the exact same time as him. As she'd left the station compound, he'd only had in her plain sight for a few seconds. But it was long enough for him to spot that at least one of those criteria was met.

The package in her hand had looked like a large envelope. The kind that could contain the sort of papers you might find in a police file - or copies. There'd been no sign of anything when he'd come out of Iridotu's office. The only thing she was carrying was the bag she

couldn't even be bothered to check for a business card -
not that he had any real interest in visiting her *'taverna'*.
Not as a paying customer at any rate.

Of course the envelope could contain anything. It
may be nothing at all to do with Murray, or Podruznig.
In which case he might be about to waste a whole lot of
time - perhaps days - on a wild goose chase. On the
other hand…

As he reached the junction and pulled left, prompting
a loud blast on the horn from the driver of the battered
pick-up behind, Westgate fixed his eyes on the brightly-
coloured sports car he could just make out in the line of
traffic heading out of town. Pressing his foot to the
floor, he headed after her.

CHAPTER 20

It was late afternoon when Westgate eased past the end of the cul-de-sac in the heart of Pafos's Konia district, just in time to see her pull into a driveway halfway up on the left. He continued on, turned, then parked up where he could see the end of the road if she came out again.

Apart from the fact that most of the houses around were big and expensive-looking - probably subsidised by Daddy - Westgate wasn't surprised to discover this was where she lived. Konia is popular among those locals whose work involves regular contact with tourists and the ubiquitous ex-pat Brit population. Given that most of the district's residents are Cypriot, they welcome the break.

Grateful for the opportunity to ease off – however long it may last – Westgate reached into the back for the water bottle and bag of bananas he'd picked up on his travels, then settled down to wait.

Most of the two hours since he'd picked her up leaving the police station had been spent ducking, diving and hanging back while she made stops for groceries, shoes and, presumably - the last being a beautician's - cosmetics. As far as he could tell, the envelope hadn't left the car.

As afternoon turned to evening, Westgate stayed alert, checking out the many cars that turned into the estate, bringing those with day jobs home. It wasn't hard to spot them as locals in their smart Mercs and BMWs - Brits tend to go for SUVs. And there is something about a Cypriot behind the wheel of a car that, even from a distance, distinguishes them from ex-pats.

By seven-thirty, dusk was falling. Knowing darkness would follow quickly, Westgate reasoned that if anything was going to happen, it would most likely be soon. Assuming her, 'Taverna', was open that evening, it wouldn't be long before she left to check things out. Following his gut, he got out and wandered round the corner to stroll, head down, past the house. At the end of the cul-de-sac he found an unlit spot between two gateposts where the view was good, and he was shielded by overhanging trees.

Now able to study the house for the first time, he could see it fitted the pattern for the area. Two floors, upper veranda, flat roof, medium-size garden, small driveway, lots of enclosing greenery. Lights showed in some of the windows and now and again he glimpsed someone, though he couldn't tell if it was her, or someone else.

He'd been there less than ten minutes when a jeep turned into the road to drive, slowly, up towards him. He could just make out the driver leaning across the passenger seat, as if checking house numbers. It stopped across the back of her Merc. Though not Murray's, he recognised it as one he'd clocked outside the Dive Centre a couple of times before they all disappeared. He congratulated himself on his foresight.

The driver stepped out. It was Murray. As he approached the front door, Westgate noted he was empty-handed. She must have been expecting him, as the door opened at once and he went inside. Less than five minutes later he came out again. He was carrying a large envelope.

Westgate made sure he was well-hidden as Murray drove down to the turning circle, made a fast three-pointer, then drove back down, slowing to give a brief wave as he passed the house. At the bottom of the road he turned left, and disappeared. Westgate knew that if he sprinted back to his car, he might still be able to catch up. Murray would lead him to wherever was now base. But it also risked drawing attention to himself. Besides, he'd seen enough. For now.

In the muted light from the bedside lamp, Murray swigged a Keo bottle as he leafed through the papers. The information they contained was more revealing than he'd expected. Some he'd seen before - documents from the same Military Intelligence source he tapped into when he first learned about Podruznig - others were new. He sent mental congratulations to Iridotu. The Police Chief's contacts were better-placed than Murray had given him credit for.

The papers included what looked like extracts from Podruznig's BRCR - Russian Criminal Record Bureau - file, detailing his early run-ins with the police and Communist Party-run Courts. There was also a lengthy profile which, judging by the Americanisms, had come from a US-based source, CIA probably. The US agencies had invested heavily in monitoring the Oligarchs since Putin came to power, as well as those associated with them. But of most interest were the several papers that carried the hall marks of having come from an FSB Intelligence File. The Federal Security Service - its English title - is the domestic successor to the KGB.

Comprising what looked like extracts culled from a variety of sources – some carried margin-references Murray recognised as relating to CIA, MI5, MOSSAD, as well as others – each of the dated entries was recorded in two languages, Russian and English. Murray recognised the technique as one used extensively within what eventually came to be known as, SEMU, the Slavic Economic Monitoring Unit.

Originally set up within the KGB prior to its break-up in the early nineties, the Unit's official aim was to analyse and report upon the implications for Federal Security of the trend, begun under Gorbachev in the eighties and continuing under Yeltsin through the decade following, towards greater economic freedom and the so-called, 'democratisation of Government'. The phenomenon would, eventually of course, come to be seen as more smoke and mirrors than any genuine reforming movement. But within two years of its establishment, SEMU's work became almost wholly focused on something no intelligence agency - especially those of the old Soviet Union - had experienced before.

The rapid growth of what collectively became known as the Russian Mafias, the simultaneous emergence of the Oligarchs, and the relationship between the two, was not something anyone, least of all the world's intelligence community foresaw. To most observers, it was clear that those clinging to the reigns of power within Russia during those turbulent times were in two minds as to whether the changes they were witnessing were a force for good, or bad. Many were in no doubt that extending the country's economic reach to parts of the world where Russia's influence was low, was undoubtedly beneficial. At the same time however, power bases emerged, both within and without Russia, that were not only capable of matching anything the KGB had to offer in terms of resources and expertise, but were perceived as containing within them the seeds of revolution on a scale that could make the end of the

Romanoff Dynasty look like a minor tweak in political direction.

SEMU's brief was to gather intelligence on what these various factions were up to and predict where things were headed. By this means, the hope was that if and when the revolution came, the executive of the day - whoever it might be - may have enough ammunition to act swiftly against those with the potential to lead such a movement. In the end it all came down - as such things always do in Russia - to dirty tricks and blackmail. And the SEMU Intelligence Files were full of it.

Murray was familiar enough with the sort of shadowy, if not downright dead-of-night, activities that underpinned the rise of most of the Oligarchs. In particular, the Arabian side of the organisation Operation Priscilla had set out to smash, was known to have close links with branches of the Russian mafia. Murray had heard only recently how, having seen the success one of their ilk had enjoyed by investing in the English Premier Football League, several of those who had once been of great interest to MI5, CIA and the FSB were now looking to do the same - though through less well known 'intermediaries.' It came as no great surprise to Murray, therefore, to learn that Podruznig was linked - in some cases by strong evidence, in others only rumour and innuendo - to more than his fair share of double dealings, blackmail, disappearances - and murder.

What was a surprise, however - and the more he read the more he sat up, even going so far as to place his bottle down so he could give the documents his fullest attention - was the detail the SEMU clerks had included within what were only supposed to be summary log entries. In some cases, Murray found it hard to imagine the original documents - wherever they now lay -

containing much more than those he was reading.

Names, dates, places, detailed assessments. They were all there. Together, they provided a detailed account of not just how Podruznig had acquired his wealth and risen to the position of power he now enjoyed, but also how he'd used that power to maintain his position, whilst also pursuing the acquisition of the things he needed to satisfy his peculiarly idiosyncratic interests. Of particular interest was an account attributed to someone with strong connections inside the murky underworld that surrounds the Black Sea port of Odessa.

Eventually Murray finished reading. He didn't so much put the last sheet down, as let it slip from his fingers so that it drifted down, like a feather on a breeze, to join the others strewn over the bed.

For a long time he stared, fixedly, at a spot on the wall across the room, registering nothing but the thoughts and possibilities racing through his brain. Eventually, remembering his beer he reached for it. But as he brought it to his lips he paused, mind still mulling over the implications of what he'd read. Two words, more breathed than spoken, passed his lips.

'Bloody hell.'

CHAPTER 21

Finished stripping what little grazing there was between the rocks lining the trail, the herd leader, an old Billy with a broken right horn, lifted its shaggy head, ready to move up to the trees that promised shelter from the baking, midday sun.

The track was one the herd travelled intermittently. Depending upon the time of year, a moon's passing was usually enough for the grasses to grow sufficiently for the route to be worth re-visiting. And being the keeper of the collective herd-memory, the Billy knew it as a safe route up to the trees where shade now beckoned. But as he made ready to move he stopped, suddenly, left foreleg up and cocked - a warning to those following.

Nearing the end of his allotted twenty-year-or-so lifespan, the Billy's sight was no longer as keen as it once was, But his scenting ability was acute as ever, and it had alerted him to danger. It spoke to the presence of an invader, an animal smell that was not a natural part of the rugged landscape they were crossing. He peered about, checking the scrubs either side of the trail, trying to pick out what he knew was there, but which was, somehow, invisible to his gaze. As the scent came again, a picture formed of the creature they encountered now and again during their meanderings but which they always tried to avoid, wary of its unpredictable nature.

But right now he could see nothing that fitted with what his instincts told him was near. The shapes and hues all appeared normal. Chalky rock, grey scrubs, sandy earth, grassy tones. Nevertheless, he trusted his senses enough to know he was not mistaken.

Moving off the trail, he hop-skipped several yards up the slope, at the same time sending out the low whistle-grunt that would signal to the others they should follow his lead. Reaching a higher-lying track, he stopped again to sample the air. The scent was still there but weaker now, not growing in his throat as it would be if the invader were following. A few yards further on, it disappeared altogether. Satisfied he had led his charges away from danger, the old Billy lowered his head and returned to his grazing.

Some distance away, down the hillside towards the coast, Valerik Podruznig descended the steps outside his front door to where the freshly-polished BMW X7 xDrive stood, gleaming in the sun. A faithful charger awaiting its King. Rounding the shining expanse of bonnet, he ran his fingers, lovingly, over the hot metal. As he did so, a ripple of pleasure coursed through him. He pursed his lips in an expression of satisfaction.

It was six months now since Podruznig had taken possession of the purchase that, as much as any other in his mind, signalled what he had achieved in the face of adversities that would have overwhelmed lesser men. Though he first placed the order many months before, the cost-doubling modifications and customising Podruznig had insisted on, meant that the vehicle's gestation in its - of all places South Carolina - womb, had taken longer than normal.

But despite having had half-a-year to get used to it, he still found that physical contact brought a glow of pleasure that bordered on sexual in its intensity. He felt it as a charge that ran through him, speaking of both the pleasures he'd taken clawing his way to his present position, as well as those he looked forward to experiencing in the years ahead - the ones that come with success.

All his life, the man who was born in the small collective south of St Petersburg that was so anonymous it merited only a district reference - DY13 - had dreamed of owning a 'top-of-the-range' mark. Even when, as a young boy, he fought off those much bigger than him for the right to buy the last loaf of bread on the frequently-bare shelves of the collective's only grocers, he was determined that one day he would own something that would mark him as, Special.

Admittedly, there were more expensive and luxurious models on the market, particularly the Lexus and Porsche equivalents. But this, the much sought-after BMW X7 xDrive, fitted the bill, exactly. With its high driving position, reserves of power, and lofty air of Germanic supremacy - not to mention the Get-Out-Of-My-Way statement it made when on the road – the X7 reflected the qualities Podruznig now stood for. Strength. Dominance. Efficiency. In Valerik Podruznig's view, the likes of Rolls Royce, Bentley, Aston Martin, were just toys. Better- suited to retired financiers, failed would-be-James-Bond dreamers, and little boys with too much money and not enough imagination to know how to use it.

The X7, on the other hand, spoke of someone who knew how to make things happen in this world. Someone who meant business . Someone who would not be pushed aside. An Achiever.

As he rounded the car's nearside, he spied a piece of lint, a thread from the polishing buffer by the look of it, caught in the chrome strip lining the front wheel arch. He tutted, loudly. He hated such sloppiness, and would remember to mention it to Lantzeff. But as he bent to remove it, the barest draught of a breeze passed somewhere close to his right ear. At the same time a resounding 'CLANG' rent the air and the car seemed to give out a little shudder.

Podruznig blinked, trying to make sense of what had just happened - and found himself staring at a neat round hole in the lower wing a mere twelve inches to his right. For several moments he was too disoriented to do anything but stare at it, his brain struggling to rationalise what had just happened. Then another 'CLANG' sounded, and the BMW rocked again. At the same time a second hole appeared - in the door this time, a few inches below the handle.

As realisation hit, a scream of rage erupted from Podruznig's throat. At the same time, he spun round to face towards the hills of the Paphos Forest, a good mile distant, and which looked down over the house that was now his home.

'BASTARD,' he yelled. Even as he vented his defiance, his eyes scoured the miles of chalk and scrub that made up the uniform and ruggedly beautiful landscape. The shout was followed by a stream of guttural abuse and cursings - in Russian, as well as English.

From behind and out of the house, alerted by their employer's cries, armed men appeared, the alarm in their faces evidencing their readiness to deal with whatever they found. Experience had taught them it could be anything from a missed garden weed, to a full-blown assault - real or perceived. Most had their automatics already drawn as they spilled through the door, thrusting them out in front, two-handed, eyes swivelling in all directions as they searched for targets.

What none were prepared for was the sight of their leader waving his fists about his head like a demented shadow boxer, screaming into the air at some invisible foe. Unsure of themselves, or what action was required, they stopped, looking round again for an enemy before exchanging puzzled and, in most cases wary, glances. As Lantzeff appeared in the doorway, and primed by years of training, he took the initiative, leaping down the steps to reach his boss's side.

'What is it, Valerik? What has happened?'

Even he was shaken by the face that swung to meet him. So twisted with fury was it, Lantzeff feared for a moment that he might even, for the first time, have to defend himself against his employer's rage. He seemed even angrier than that morning in the kitchen - if that were possible. This time it seemed to be taking him to an extreme even Lantzeff had not seen. Podruznig kept making strange, jerking half-turns towards the car, back to Lantzeff, then the gate, then back again. At the same time he appeared to have lost the power of coherent speech, babbling snarls and oaths that contained what sounded like random scatterings of, 'Bastard,' and 'Dead,' repeated, over and over.

It was during the few seconds this process was taking place that Lantzeff picked up on the wild glances Podruznig kept throwing at the X7. What did the fucking car have to do with anything? But then he realised that some of Podruznig's wild gestures were also directed towards it, as if trying to draw his lieutenant's attention to something. As Lantzeff's eyes finally lit on the hole in the wing, the other in the door, understanding dawned. At the same time, Podruznig managed finally to put his words in some order of semblance. And Lantzeff was in no doubt that the command they formed was intended to be carried out - to the letter.

'DEAD. DO YOU HEAR ME, URI? I WANT THE BASTARD DEAD. DEAD, DEAD, DEAD.'

The sun was lowering over the sea when the trucks turned back in through the gate, Podruznig was waiting, hands on hips, face dark-crimson. And as Lantzeff stepped from the lead vehicle, he knew that, as before, he had to be careful. The Russian was closer to breaking-point than he could ever remember. Nevertheless he met the man's glare evenly as he made his way over to reiterate what he had already reported over the radio.

'Nothing but goats,' he said. 'The area is too big. It would take an army to search it properly.'

He didn't wait for Podruznig's response - that he was still furious went without saying - but turned to cast his gaze over the hills he and his men had spent several hours scouring. All afternoon they had criss-crossed the undulating slopes, searching through scrub, checking out any rock formations that looked like they could provide natural cover for a shooter. But they had found nothing - just as Lantzeff had anticipated when Podruznig began issuing his raging demands that every man at his disposal, 'Get out there, find the bastard, and bring him to me.'

Not that Lantzeff had argued against. The state Podruznig was in, he would have brooked no objections, even from the Siberian. And Lantzeff wasn't that stupid. Easier to disappear for the afternoon along with the others. Let Podruznig calm down a little, then they could talk, sensibly, about how to respond. Nevertheless, he had made sure that two of the team remained behind, though discreetly, to provide cover should it be needed. What had happened didn't have the feel of a feint-and-

135

draw tactic, but he wasn't going to take any chances.

It was now obvious to Lantzeff and, he hoped, Podruznig as well, that the Russian had never been in the shooter's sights. To hit a target twice in succession at this distance - even something X7 size - called for a degree of skill that had to mean the sniper was well capable of hitting a man had he chosen to do so. If more evidence were needed, the shot-out CCTV camera the morning of the graffiti provided it.

No, this was a deliberate attempt - and a clever one Lantzeff had to concede, though privately - to hurt Podruznig in a way no physical attack could ever achieve. To intimidate. To wind him up. To show that someone was far from ready to give up. Which meant that something had to be done, and quickly.

As the rest of the team trooped back to their basement quarters, for the most part heads down, lest they be singled out by their boss's accusing glare - they all knew how he hated failure - Podruznig came forward to stand next to his second-in-command. As he spoke, his gaze stayed on the hills, as if his tormentor might yet choose to expose himself.

'So what am I supposed to do now, Uri?' he growled. Lantzeff sensed the struggle for control taking place within him. 'Am I supposed to hide away inside my own house, while this *PIZDA* decides whether to put a bullet in me? Or my wife? My daughter even?'

Lantzeff chose his words carefully. 'I will find him Valerik, I promise you. I will not rest until this man is dealt with. He will regret he ever thought to challenge you.'

Podruznig turned to him, eyes still manic, face contorted. 'Then do it Uri. But this time make sure it is done in a way that sends out a message. I want anyone who thinks they can stand up to me to know that no one, *but no one,* opposes Valerik Podruznig.'

Lantzeff nodded. 'Do not worry Valerik, they will.'

The two men turned to head back to the house. But as they passed the X7 - still parked at the bottom of the steps - a loud 'CLANG' resonated around the compound and the car shook. They both whirled round to face the hills, now darkening in the evening gloom.

Like a wounded animal defying a would-be predator, Podruznig let out a scream that, seconds later, would bring everyone running out again to see what new outrage had occurred.

'BASTAAAAARRRRD.'

CHAPTER 22

For many women, Saturday morning is a time for dressing up and heading to the shops. And not just to shop. Meeting friends. Taking coffee. Gossiping. They are now all part of, 'The Shopping Experience.'

To this end, Pafos's Kings Avenue Mall, on the big roundabout heading down towards the harbour area, is as glitzy, modern, and designer-label stuffed as any to be found in towns and cities all over Europe. Nevertheless, many Pafos women - at least those who prefer something more 'traditional' - have always preferred the Old Town and the narrow streets surrounding the bustling Market. Here, the fashion stores are complimented by quaint cafes, restaurants, and artisan shops and stalls that cater for all tastes - locals, ex-pats, and tourists alike. In recent years the area has been the focus of major redevelopment and modernisation, making it more popular than ever.

Scorpios, next door to the Market and with a magnificent view out over Paphos Bay, provides a carefully-nurtured mix of them all. By this means, its wily owner, Andreas, an avuncular Cypriot whose slim frame recalls the National-Team sprinter he once was, ensures that whatever the season, day of week or weather, he does brisk business.

This Saturday morning was no exception. By midmorning, shoppers and tourists alike were ready for a break. Andreas, his two daughters and the young Polish waitress he'd recently taken on, were being run off their feet. Very much 'hands-on' when it comes to looking after his customers, Andreas's shirt was already sweat-stained, a fact that some tourists find sufficiently off-putting to wrinkle their noses, but bothers the regulars not at all.

As he weaved his way between the tightly-packed tables, Andreas held aloft the several breakfasts-with-chips he was taking to the bunch of Brits who had taken up residence on the shaded veranda. It was their third round of orders, but while it was good for business, they were starting to become annoyingly loud. Enough, at least, for Andreas to hope they would move on as soon as they'd eaten.

Glancing at the two tables that occupied the prime spot in front of the sliding picture window through which a gentle breeze always blows, Andreas allowed himself an uncharacteristic frown. The group of men who had arrived with the well-dressed Russian woman, her friend and their children, were up to their usual tricks.

Regular Saturday-morning customers, the party always presented Andreas with a quandary. Whilst the women spent freely enough and were no more trouble than any other customers - less so in many respects - their male chaperones, usually four in number as today, were invariably surly. Either that or they were so over-familiar with Andreas's girls as to be offensive - which, in a place like Scorpios, takes some doing. But what annoyed Andreas the most, apart from the fact the men only ever drank one coffee and water apiece however long the women stayed, was the way that, as soon as they arrived, they enforced an invisible 'cordon' around whatever table the women and children settled at, muscling other customers aside or using their considerable statures to 'encourage' them to adjust their seating arrangements - sometimes several times - until the required, "safe-distance" was achieved.

Andreas still wasn't entirely certain who the good-looking, but to his mind overly-made-up, blond was. She and her young daughter were clearly the focus of the men's attention. And though she did her best to pretend they weren't there, it was obvious she was used to having minders around, never failing to consult with them whenever she wished to 'powder her nose' which, by Andreas's reckoning, usually occurred at least three times during their stay.

When they first started coming in, Andreas had wondered if she was some sort of media celebrity - a film or pop star, or the wife of some famous footballer. But when he realised she was Russian - and not one that his daughters recognised from the pages of the gossip magazines they read endlessly - he put things together. Cyprus was known for its sympathetic tax regime, especially where foreign money was concerned. And while quite a few 'celebrities' did indeed have homes around and about - large and luxurious ones - so did many 'businessmen'. In particular, Andreas was aware that the new breed of Russians, especially those from the Black Sea areas, was attracted to the island in increasing numbers. Andreas had eventually concluded she must be married to one of them. Once he did so, he knew he had no choice but to put up with the disruption they brought. The last thing he wanted was to get on the wrong side of those sorts of people.

'They want more coffee,' a voice chirped from the men's table as Andreas passed on his way back to the kitchen. He nodded to show he'd heard but didn't respond further. He hated such rudeness. At least the Brits were usually cheerful, and said, 'please'.

As he slipped behind the bar - the coffee-range was playing up again - he saw the way Melitza, his youngest, was staring daggers at the men and was surprised. Of them all, she was usually the most irrepressibly cheery.

'Something wrong, Chicken?'

She showed a scowling face. 'The one with the beard and that horrible knife tattoo on his cheek. He felt my bum when I walked past. He has done it before, *the pig*.'

At once Andreas felt the familiar anger rising within him. It was made worse by the sure knowledge there was little he could do to stop such abuse, short of risking his restaurant being fire-bombed one night. And while his daughters were wise enough to understand why their father had no choice but to let a certain level of 'mistreatment' go - though there were limits and they knew he was no coward - it didn't make matters any easier.

'I am sorry,' Andreas said to his daughter. 'Stay away from them. I will serve them from now on.'

'It is alright Papa, I am used to it. You look after our other customers. They've already seen off the German family that was at the table next to them.'

Prompted by her insight, Andreas looked out over the bar, checking how his other patrons were reacting. He had seen the wary glances from some as the party of Russians settled themselves. But apart from the ginger-haired man with the weather-beaten face and sunglasses sitting in the corner on his own, most seemed to have now lost interest. The man had arrived some thirty minutes before. In that time he had ordered two Cyprus coffees - 'plenty of sugar' - while reading his paper and making calls on his mobile. Long experience had taught Andreas to always keep a discreet eye on those who do not fit the usual customer profile. He had noticed how the man's gaze kept turning to the Russian women, as well as their minders.

Andreas gave his daughter a reassuring smile, then leaned sideways and kissed her cheek. Seventeen, and already she knew the realities of managing a business such as this. Just as well. With no brothers, the day would come when she and her sister would have to run things for themselves. As he began to shoot steam through to clear valves, he even managed a chuckle. 'Maybe you should put up that sign again.'

Several Saturdays before, Melitza and her sister had waited until they'd seen the party approaching before putting a sign up in the bar they had prepared without Andreas's knowledge. Written in Greek, it read, 'NO RUSSIANS'. Andreas didn't notice until the group was about to walk in, and only just managed to snatch it down before they would have seen it - though he doubted any of them could read Greek. He hadn't been amused, though they'd joked about it since. He continued. 'Only this time you'd better mention men with beards and tatt-.'

Melitza's warning hiss stopped him just in time and he looked up to see the woman approaching, the bearded man following.

As was the routine, she stopped at the door to the stairs leading up to the toilets while the man went up to check. What did they think, Andreas mused, as the man clumped up the stairs? That kidnappers lurk in places such as this? As she waited, she flashed Andreas the smile that always reminded him of the sort he used to get from the hostesses when, during his days on the athletics team, a heavy day's training was invariably followed by a crawl around Nicosia's bars and over-priced nightclubs. Nevertheless he made a point of returning it. He didn't have a problem with her. Just her minders.

Her smile vanished as the man returned from his scouting mission and nodded to her, stepping aside so she could squeeze passed his ample frame.

As he listened to her mounting the stairs, Andreas suddenly realised the man was glowering at him. He wasn't sure whether it was because he had seen them exchange smiles - *such a crime* - or had caught Andreas's reference to beards after all. Either way, Andreas made a point of returning the stare just long enough to convey the fact he wasn't intimidated, before turning away to see to the coffees. It wasn't much, but it was the best he could do under the circumstances.

Marianna Podruznig closed the outer door to the ladies behind her. As she turned, a draught from somewhere blew through the coiffure she'd had done at no little cost, earlier that morning. It caused a lock of hair to stray across her cheek, prompting an irritated, 'Tch.' Her regular eight o'clock slot at Revolution, the popular salon in Messogi run by London-trained Raz, was now an essential pre-requisite to her Saturday morning shopping trips, just as it had been in Moscow, before she met Valerik. As back then, she still liked to look her best when out in public, though she was conscious that such bouts of freedom were increasingly rare these days. She turned to the mirror.

But as she started to tease the wanderer back in place, another breeze blew - from above she now realised. Anxious in case Raz's best efforts were about to be undone, she looked up. A skylight was wide open, the sun shining through. Like every day this time of year, it was stiflingly hot. In the half-hour since her previous visit, Andreas must have opened it to let some air in.

Keen to finish before any more damage was done, she turned and put out a hand to push open the door to the single cubicle.

It happened so fast, she couldn't even follow the blur of action, let alone scream for help.

As her fingers touched the door's surface it flew back and a figure leaped at her from the cubicle's depths. She was barely conscious of strong hands spinning her round, a hardened hand clamping over her mouth, an arm wrapping tightly round her waist, half lifting her so she had no purchase to lever against as she struggled, though she knew at once resisting would be useless.

He was strong. Very strong.

CHAPTER 23

Marianna knew at once what was in store for her. In that instant the fears she had harboured for so long rose to the surface, painting a story that had only one ending. The feeling of regret was overwhelming. She would never see Sasha again. She had always known this day may come, eventually.

In the few short weeks of courtship, such as it was, before she and Valerik married, Marianna had already begun to suspect that being wed to the suave Russian may not be the risk-free enterprise she imagined when he started wooing her with promises of a life of luxury, free from the anxieties that beset most ordinary married couples. By their three-month anniversary, those doubts had hardened to certainty, and Marianna was fully aware of the extent of the mistake she had made.

Not only did Valerik's protective attitude towards her change almost entirely in that surprisingly short time, out went any pretence at romance as well. The flowers, the gifts, the jewels. All he needed, she soon realised, was her presence in bed, or wherever else he decided she should open her legs for him when the other pleasures he craved were, for some reason, denied him. Worse even than that was the realisation that she was set to live the rest of her life - at least until such time as he tired of her and turned her in for someone younger - as a virtual prisoner.

Strangely, given how she hated the brutish Siberian, Uri, and felt uncomfortable whenever he was around, it was he who first opened her eyes to the realities of her position. It was Uri who pointed out that by marrying Valerik, she had placed herself in jeopardy so great it would, in his words, 'be a miracle' if she survived to see her thirtieth birthday. She was then in her eighteenth year. And it was Uri who, that day soon after Sasha was born, when she had objected to his cloying attentions and those of his ape-like companions, who sat her down - pushed would be a better description - and spelt things out to her. Until then, she had been blind as to the the extent to which Valerik's position of power was founded as much on fear, as on the rubles that flowed from the myriad enterprises he seemed to have hands in. Nor had she realised that the risks Valerik, and by extension she, now faced, were not just of the sort associated with the plush boardrooms and corporate headquarters she visited on those occasions Valerik wanted to display her to his 'business' colleagues. As Uri appeared to take delight in telling her as she cowered on the sofa that day, cradling baby-Sasha in her arms, the numbing fear growing, the far greater risk was from those who would come in the dead of night. Or whilst they were driving somewhere, eating out at some restaurant or attending some function where Valerik had decided it was more important he be seen at with his wife on his arm, rather than whichever ingénue was current flavour of the month.

Bomb, bullet, knife. Kidnap, murder rape. Not just her, but Sasha as well. This was the reality Uri awakened her to that day. And it was Uri who made clear that never again would she leave the house without a posse of guards to accompany her wherever she went - even to the toilet. They would ensure that whatever she and Sasha did, she would never lead the life she had imagined would be hers when she agreed to wed the oh-so-charming suitor who set his sights on her all those years ago and wouldn't give up until she forswore her mother's sound advice and said, 'Yes.'

And now it was happening. Just as Uri had said it would. Without warning, from nowhere. In the very place in fact she had come to look forward to as the once-a-week antidote to the unremitting bleakness of her marriage. A place where, taking coffee with her only real friend Ria, watching Sasha playing and giggling with Ria's daughter, Anna, she had felt able - for only an hour or so each week admittedly but better than nothing - to experience something close to 'normality'.

All this flashed through Marianna's brain as she waited for the blade she was sure would soon come. In the cubicle's mirror, through glazed, panicked eyes, she could just make out the two of them, locked together like limpets, him standing behind her, hand over her face, squeezing, not too hard but enough to stifle any sound that might come from her throat, his other arm wrapped tight about her waist, restraining her. She couldn't see any knife yet, nevertheless she was sure it was there, it had to be. She knew it could not be a kidnap. Strong though he clearly was, even he would not be able to lift her through the skylight, not without running the risk of her screaming her lungs out. And escaping with her down the stairs where they all waited, was not an option.

Which left only murder or, if he was quick, rape. Or both.

Even as the awful realisation hit her, she was amazed by the way her mind was still able to work in the face of such horror. Never having been trained to react otherwise and coming from a simple background, Marianna had always assumed that if the worst ever happened and she found herself in such a position, she would panic to the point where she would simply stop functioning. She had imagined herself, crumbling into a whimpering mass of pathetic womanhood, begging to be spared, more especially, for her daughter to be spared. But Sasha was safe downstairs, watched over by men who, whilst they often frightened even her, Marianne knew would never allow anything to happen to their boss's only daughter. Fear alone would see to that.

It was this knowledge Marianna now realised - that her daughter was safe and not about to suffer the same fate as herself - that stalled her panicking. And not just that. As she waited for him to make his move, she realised that not only was she not scared by the thought of what this man would do to her. In some way she could not fully comprehend, she actually *welcomed* it. It would be painful of course, of that she was sure. But after all the years of abuse, humiliation and torture, mental as well as physical, of living life as a virtual prisoner, cut off from her family and friends, not able to bring up her daughter in the way her instincts told her was right - a material want for nothing is no substitute for the gift of two parents who love each other - death, even a painful one, would be a release of sorts. With that thought, Marianna stopped struggling, though she had barely been aware she was, and waited for the knife to do its work.

'I said, do you understand me?'

The voice sounded, soft and low in her ear, already strangely familiar. *But how can that be?* He was speaking English. Good English, without any accent she recognised. She didn't know anyone who spoke like that. As the voice came again - 'Answer me. Do you

148

understand?' - she suddenly realised that all the time she had been struggling, musing on what was about to happen and why, words had been sounding in her ear. Which was why, when the voice finally registered it sounded familiar. Soft, yet no less forceful, he had been urging her to calm down, to stop struggling. Telling her he was not going to hurt her, or her child. Had he said something about just wanting to talk, or was that just the imaginings of a hysterical soon-to-be victim? Yet she didn't think she was hysterical.

She froze, and for the first time gave attention to his words.

'I just want to talk. Do you understand? Nod if you understand.'

She nodded.

She felt the grip round her waist loosen, slightly, though the hand clamped over her mouth kept up its pressure. She wondered about trying to make use of the greater freedom to try to break free, but thought better of it. He could tighten his grip again in an instant. Besides, she was beginning to think that perhaps, just perhaps, things were not as she had first thought. Could it be that she may even live through this? After all, if he had intended to kill her he could have done so by now.

'I am going to take my hand away from your mouth, but I don't want you to scream. Nod if you understand.' She nodded. 'You won't be in any danger, but you mustn't make a noise. Nod if you understand.' She nodded again.

She felt the hand lift away and it was all she could do stifle the reflex that made her want to scream out as soon as she knew she could. She swallowed, hard, and stayed silent, frozen to the spot. As the hand moved further away from her face, the pressure round her waist also fell away. She turned to face him.

She recognised him at once.

CHAPTER 24

Though Marianna Podruznig's previous and only sighting of him had been fleeting - the day he panicked them all with his charge to the gates - she had got a good enough look when he turned his face up to the window. She had thought then he didn't look much like the deluded madman Valerik had spoken of. In fact, she'd thought his ruggedly-handsome features, together with the easy way he carried himself - remarkable given what was happening - spoke more of someone who got things done through a quiet determination, rather than threats of violence. She also remembered how, on that occasion, she thought there was a certain sadness about him. Something in his face as he came up the drive. The way he stopped to stare at the fountain. It had made her wonder if Valerik had told her everything when he described how the house's previous would-be purchaser had defaulted, time after time, on his agreement with the builder, Klerides.

But even if she had been right, there was no trace of sadness in him now. In its place was a grim determination, offset by a look that seemed intended to convey he meant her no harm. She was almost convinced.

'Wh-what you want?' She kept her voice low, almost a whisper. She didn't want to provoke him.

'Like I said, I just want to talk.'

'About what?'

'Your husband. You. Your daughter. The house.'

'The house is nothing to do with me. You must talk to my husband.'

'I'm afraid the time for talking may be over.'

She remembered his latest attack, a few days before and surprised herself again by daring to let the anger she'd felt then show. 'You should have thought about that before you started shooting at us. My daughter plays in our garden. You could have killed her.' As she spoke, his eyes narrowed, almost a puzzled look. 'Please do not treat me like an idiot,' she continued. 'I get enough of that at home.'

He raised an index finger. It was a curious, yet under the circumstances somehow convincing, way of marking conviction. 'Believe me. I would never do anything that might cause harm to you, or your daughter.'

'So you think that shooting holes in my husband's car is not dangerous? What if she had been there? She could have been inside for all you know.'

For what seemed a long time he didn't answer, but stood looking down at her, as if digesting her words. *Or working up a defence?* Eventually the quizzical look faded. She thought she caught the merest hint of something else in his blue eyes – surely not amusement? But then it too was gone.

'As I said, I would not do anything to harm you or your daughter. My argument is with your husband.'

'Then please, argue with him and leave me and my daughter out of it.' She turned, emboldened enough now to make to leave. But his hand stretched over her shoulder to press against the door.

'That is what I intend to do. And why I am here.'

She turned back to him. Though preventing her from

leaving, she had no sense now that he posed any threat to her. For the first time she began to relax, curiosity taking over.

'What do you mean?'

He hesitated, as if weighing his words. 'Your husband is not the sort of man who responds well to argument.'

Her tongue ran around her lips. A nervous reflex. She never, ever, spoke about Valerik to others. She didn't dare. Too many spies. 'Maybe not. But that is nothing I can do anything about.'

'And I cannot give up what is rightfully mine.'

She was about to argue, but knew this was not the time. 'So what does that mean?'

'It means things will get worse.'

She squared up to him as far as she was able. He stood a good six inches over her. 'I am not frightened by threats, Mr...-.' She struggled to recall the name Valerik had mentioned.

'My name is Peter. And I am not trying to threaten, or frighten you. I just want to make sure that innocent people, like you and your daughter, do not end up getting hurt because of your husband's wrongdoing.'

Now it was her eyes that narrowed. 'What do you mean, wrongdoing?'

He took a long deep breath. 'What has your husband told you about me?'

At the bottom of the stairs, Max turned, looking up to see if there was any sign of her. He could not understand how women could spend so long, so often, just taking a leak. *What the fuck do they do in there?*

He looked across to where the others sat waiting, and saw the other woman, the one with the even bigger tits and the snotty kid, glance in his direction. Even she seemed to be becoming impatient. As Max waited, Ivan, their team leader for the day, lifted his head and spread his hands. *What gives?*

Max shrugged back. *Search me.* Ivan shook his head, showing his disdain for the former Chechnian soldier. The only representative of his country in the entire squad, Max sometimes felt the ribbing getting to him - but the money was good. He threw Ivan a look he hoped would say, *If you're so fucking clever why don't you go up there and drag her out?*

A minute later, Ivan raised himself from the chair to wander over.

'What the fuck's taking her so long?'

'What the fuck do you think? Playing with herself for all I know.'

Ivan sneered, looked back at the other woman and the two girls, before turning back.

'Go tell her to move her arse. I'm supposed to take Mr P. to Limassol this afternoon. If I'm late back, I'll blame you.'

'Fuck-all to do with me.'

'Just tell her.'

Muttering oaths, Max turned and started up the stairs.

At the table in the corner, the ginger-haired man reading his paper stretched out a finger and pressed a button on his mobile's screen.

Marianna stared up at the Englishman, still not sure how much she should trust him. His story had the ring of truth about it. Yet if it were true it would mean... it was all *her* fault. Was that possible? Her crestfallen look must have betrayed her thoughts as he suddenly gave a half-smile.

'It wasn't your fault, Mrs Podruznig. Your husband wouldn't have told you the house was already spoken for.'

'But if I had known, I wouldn't have-'

'You didn't. Don't worry about it.'

She looked puzzled. 'So why are you telling me this n-?'

His hand came up to her mouth, but lightly, shutting off her words. As she'd been speaking she'd caught the sound of a low buzzing somewhere. They waited. Seconds later she heard footsteps on the landing.

A knock, hesitant, on the door.

Alarm flooded her face.

'Mrs Podruznig? Are you alright?'

She took a steadying breath. 'Yes Max, I'm fine. I'll be down in a minute.'

Through the door came a grunt of acknowledgement, but no sounds of him moving away. After several seconds there was another knock.

'Mrs Podruznig?'

She feigned annoyance. 'What now?'

A pause. 'Are you-? Is someone else... in there?'

'Don't be stupid Max. Go away. You're becoming annoying.'

'Sorry Mrs Podruznig, just checking. I'll see you downstairs then.' She let him wait.

'Yes.'

Another pause.

'Okay then.'

They heard his heavy tread descending the stairs. She breathed out.

'I still don't understand what you want from me. I have no control over what my husband does.'

He nodded, thoughtfully, as if coming to a decision.

'I wanted to warn you.'

'Warn me? About what?'

'About what will probably happen.'

Fear in her face now. 'What do you mean?'

'I am afraid that people may start getting hurt.'

'Which people? Me? My daughter?'

'That is why I'm here. I wouldn't want that.'

'You think Valerik would?'

'Let's put it this way, if things became more... heated, would he let you move away? To somewhere safe?'

She thought about it. She didn't like her conclusion.

He read her silence. 'That is why it would be better if you and your daughter weren't around.'

Her eyes widened. 'You are telling me I should leave my husband?' He didn't answer. He didn't need to. Suddenly overcome with shock, she could hardly put words together. Her breath started to come in gasps. 'I could never-. He would never-. He would find me. He would-.' He pressed a finger to her lips, quieting her. She had been on the verge of panicking. The thought of what he would do. He had told her many times. 'If you ever try to leave, or take Sasha away....' She couldn't even complete the thought. It was too terrible.

'I know things about your husband, Mr Podruznig.'

'What... sort of... things?'

'What he does... to you.' She felt herself beginning to blush. 'And about... the girls.' Reddening even faster, she shook her head, trying to blank it out.

'I can help you Mrs Podruznig.'

She looked up at him sharply. 'What makes you think I need your help?'

He waited what seemed a long time before answering. 'Are you saying you don't?'

She swallowed. So many things whizzing through her mind all at once. Shock. Fear. *Hope.*

She bowed her head, looking at the floor, biting her lip. She looked up into his face. It was a strong, kind face. A face that for the first time in a long time - and in entirely different circumstances - she may even be

156

tempted to kiss. 'Why would you help me?'

He smiled at her. A nice smile as well.

'Because I think you may be able to help me.'

'Help you? How?'

Ivan had had enough. This was becoming ridiculous. It was bad enough having to hang around listening to their gossip, the stupid kids' babbling, never mind waiting all this time while she takes a dump, changes her towel, whatever. He marched over to Max.

'Well?'

'She said she'd be down in a minute.'

'That was five minutes ago. What's she doing up there?'

'How do I know? She's talking to herself.'

Ivan stiffened. 'What do you mean, talking to herself?'

'I don't know I just heard her, talking to herself.'

'On her phone?' Ivan looked back to where she was sitting. It wouldn't be the first time she had tried to contact her family without permission. But her mobile was where she'd left it, on the table.

Ria saw them looking, got up, came over.

'Is Marianna alright? She seems to be taking a long time?'

Ivan regarded Max as if he were a simpleton.

'Talking to herself?' He shook his head, disdain showing. 'Come on.'

The pair mounted the stairs.

As they reached the top, Max thought he heard a scuffling noise. Ivan stopped at the door marked with a woman's outline, knocked once, hard.

'Mrs Podruznig?'

Silence.

'Mrs Podruznig?' He tried the door. It was locked.

'Mrs Podruznig?' Louder now, growing urgent.

He stepped back, about to throw his weight against the door, when it opened. She was standing in front of the mirror putting the finishing touches to her hair. She turned to give the two men a scolding look.

'Really. Can I not be left in peace while I put right what the wind has done to my hair?'

Ivan looked at her, blinking, unsure what to say. Her hair had seemed alright to him. And far as he could remember there'd been only the lightest of breezes when they arrived. But Hell, what did he know about women's hair?

Jamming her comb back into her handbag she stepped out, giving them both a final, withering look.

'*Men.*'

As she stomped downstairs, Ivan muttered to Max. 'Whore-bitch.'

From the top of the stairs, Max watched his team leader follow her down, before disappearing into the bar. He turned, looking across the landing at the door to the ladies, now closed. Re-tracing his steps he stopped outside again. Taking a breath, he pushed against the door. It swung open. The washroom was empty, the door to the inner cubicle pushed closed. He stepped inside.

Standing back from the cubicle, he reached inside his waistband, ready, just in case. Then he gave the door to the cubicle a hard shove and tensed. The door swung back with a bang to reveal, nothing. Max relaxed.

He took one last look around then, satisfied everything was as it had been when he checked it before she came in, he turned to head back downstairs. He didn't look up. Even if he had, all he would have seen was a closed skylight.

Downstairs, Ria scoffed at Marianna's complaint about the wind ruining her hair. *What wind?*

'Nonsense, Maria. It's fine. In fact, it's *gorgeous*. You are becoming too fussy about such things. That is what happens when you have too much time on your hands. You must get out more.'

Marianna smiled at her friend, showing how grateful she was for her supportive comments.

In reality, Ria's well-meaning words barely registered. Rather, Marianna's attention was all on Sasha as, laughing and smiling she showed her best friend, Anna, her new mobile. And as she watched the beautiful little girl with the pixie nose and long blond hair, all she could think about was her future, *their* future, what *he* had said to her, and what he had asked her to *do*.

CHAPTER 25

The black Samsung was Podruznig's 'business' phone. He was surprised therefore when the voice he didn't recognise said, 'It doesn't matter who I am, just shut up and listen.' This in reply to his demand the caller identify himself. Not taken to following orders - certainly not from some idiot who thinks he's safe on the other end of a phone - Podruznig put even more into sounding threatening than usual.

'No one talks to me like that. How did you get this number? I'll-.'

'You'll do nothing. And if you want to find the man you're looking for, you'll shut the fuck up, RIGHT NOW.'

Podruznig had learned long ago how not to miss an opportunity, however it may be packaged. Biting back words, he clamped his lips together. He would deal with whoever this prick was in due course.

'That's better. Now, have you got a pen?'

As Podruznig listened and scribbled, his eyes narrowed. He didn't ask how the man knew what he was telling him, or how he even knew of his interest. He didn't care. All men have enemies. Had it not been so, he could never have achieved so much in such a relatively short lifetime. And by the time the caller rang off, Podruznig had managed to put aside thoughts about discovering his identity and how he'd managed to get his closely-guarded number - for now at least.

For minutes he stood there, phone in hand, not moving, face turned to the sea, sparkling away, peacefully, beyond the curved windows. His eyes were glazed as the thought-processes the call had set in motion whirred and clashed, as they always did when something excited him. And the information the caller had imparted was, definitely, exciting.

'URI,' he yelled, eventually, still not turning.

Seconds later, the wooden doors opened. Lantzeff stood there, primed, waiting.

'Get Shokov here. Now.'

Though surprised to receive such an order without having been party to any prior discussion, Uri didn't question why Shokov was needed. Given the Muscovite's particular area of expertise, the answer to the question was self-evident. And given recent events, Uri could think of only one target towards whom Shokov's skills may be directed. But he did wonder what had happened to prompt such a command? Nevertheless, he didn't probe. That would appear weak. An acknowledgement that on this occasion, his boss's resources may have proved more effective than his own. Instead he nodded once, and left the room, closing the door firmly behind him.

Wasting no time, Lantzeff made his way, swiftly, to the basement command centre. From there he could not only begin the task of tracking Shokov down – the last he'd heard he was involved in something in Madrid - he could also re-run the CCTV footage to see what had happened in the run up to him being summoned. He was all but certain it had to be a phone call. There had been no visitors that morning, and Podruznig wasn't the sort to sit around contemplating options once he had enough information to come to a decision.

A few minutes later, as Lantzeff watched his employer taking the call on his mobile, the duty operator, one of the Ukrainians, confirmed it was the only one in the previous fifteen minutes.

Lantzeff congratulated himself on his foresight in convincing Podruznig that it was in his own and, especially, his family's interests, to allow the whole house to be monitored, twenty-four-seven. The camera in their bedroom was, of course, fitted with an 'off' switch, though Lantzeff was now convinced that given the regularity with which Podruznig 'forgot' to switch it off, he had to be deriving some perverted pleasure from knowing that the 'games' he got his wife to play every now and then were not only being witnessed, but also recorded. And despite his low regard for her, Lantzeff was equally certain that she was wholly ignorant that her humiliations were being so captured. Slut though she undoubtedly was, even she would be horrified if she ever learned what went on in the Command Centre those times her husband chose to let those working for him see how adept he could be at bending her to his will. Lantzeff was just glad that, so far as he knew, none of the recordings had appeared on-line yet. Given their content, it was only a matter of time. He sometimes wondered what Podruznig's reaction would be if and when he found out. Outrage, followed by retribution, swift and brutal, would fit the usual pattern. But given the way Podruznig seemed to be almost deliberately leaving the way open for such a betrayal, Lantzeff was no longer so sure.

Despite the recording's visual clarity however, it didn't include audio. Perhaps wisely, Podruznig had insisted that his conversations should always remain private.

After noting the times shown on the screen, Lantzeff crossed to the other side of the room, behind the operator. Checking to make sure that the Ukrainian's attention was back where it should be, on the bank of screens, Lantzeff pulled open one of the flaps that covered the wiring and control boxes governing the CCTV system.

Lantzeff had warned his staff many times, under pain of dismissal or worse, that no one but he was allowed to touch the highly sensitive, 'CCTV, Tuning Regulator.' So far, the warnings had worked. He hoped it would continue. If word of the extra level of monitoring he had arranged to be installed *alongside* the CCTV ever reached Valerik, there would, he was sure, be hell to pay. Picking up the earphones he kept there for the purpose, he cupped one to his ear, at the same time setting the digital clock so that the scanner-recorder would playback whatever signal it had locked onto at the time the call came in. As the figures mirrored that shown on the video, Lantzeff settled himself on the side of the desk and listened. And as he did so, a leering smile spread across his face.

CHAPTER 26

After refilling both their glasses, Gina rose from the table to move to the bench-seat overlooking the garden. Murray waited a minute, debating within himself, before moving to join her. She moved her skirt, making way for him.

'It is a beautiful night,' she said.

'And a hot one.'

Her bare shoulders lifted as she gave a light shrug. 'It is July. You expect snow perhaps?'

He drank his wine. All around, the scent of the jasmine she had told him over dinner was her favourite, hung in the air.

'Thank you for that wonderful meal. It's been a while since I've eaten like that.'

'I am glad. A man like you should be able to eat well.'

Not sure if there was some sort of message there, he shot her a sideways glance. The three-quarter moon was behind her. Its silvery light cast a halo around her silhouette. Her head was back as she looked up at the stars, mouth open in almost childlike wonder. It brought home to him, again, how beautiful she was. Not for the first time that evening he thought on how different this Gina was from the self-assured restaurateur-cum-policeman's daughter he had known thus far. It made him wonder what other sides there were, whether he would ever get to see them.

Though the bench was made for two, he was conscious that the way she was sitting his larger-than-average frame was pressing against her. Instinctively, but perhaps also to relieve the tension that had crept into him, he moved his arm so it rested on the back of the bench, behind her. As she surveyed the heavens, her hair brushed over his skin. It tickled. Thus far he had been comfortable in the evening warmth. Suddenly he was conscious there was sweat above his top lip.

'I ought to thank you as well for your help. I should have mentioned it bef-.' The finger she pressed to his lips as she turned, stopped him.

'Not tonight. This is your night off, remember?'

After a moment's pause he nodded, gave a wry smile.

When she'd called with her invitation to dinner she had added a stipulation. 'But we do not talk of houses, or Russians or policemen, yes?' It had sounded good to him and he'd agreed, readily. But come the night, he'd found it harder than he expected. He was way out of practice making polite conversation. All through the first half of the evening, he'd had to keep reminding himself of their agreement. Up to now almost all his contact with her had revolved, one way or another, around his problem with the house, Podruznig, and his dealing with her father. But putting his personal difficulties to one side meant he had no choice but to relate to her as not just an interesting person in her own right, but also - no getting away from it - an attractive - make that *very* attractive - woman. It created a conflict he was still struggling with.

As the evening wore on, the wine helped. And while he remained determined not to make a fool of himself, he couldn't escape the feeling that even if he did, she wouldn't object. But he was also scared of waking in the morning feeling like he'd done something unforgivable. Okay, some would say two years is long enough. Others, not.

As he turned to take in the pretty face next to him, he found her already staring at him. He had slumped low in his seat, and the way she was twisted round, she loomed over him, moonlight filtering through the dark tresses framing her face. He raised the hand on the back of the chair, letting the tips of his fingers play through her soft hair. Suddenly, it was not the jasmine, but her musky fragrance that was all around. She dipped her head, bringing her face closer to his, a wave of hair falling across her cheek. She was lovely. He swallowed, feeling the panic beginning to rise.

A door banged inside.

'HELLO-OO?'

Gina bolted up, eyes wide with first surprise, then disappointment, finally, annoyance. As the clicking of heels on tiles sounded within, a growl, fierce but low, came from her throat.

'Urrrghhh.'

As Gina shot to her feet, Murray turned in time to see a smiling Ileana, slim-waisted in her white cut-offs and wearing a glittering top that showed inches of midriff, pull open the sliding glass door to step out into the garden.

'I am not interrupting anything I hope? Hello, Peter.'

'Hello Ileana,' Murray answered, suddenly conscious of a different conflicted feeling - relief, mixed with disappointment. 'Not at all. We were just enjoying the beautiful evening.'

While Murray and Ileana chatted, idly, Gina's silence was deafening. And though the smile stayed on Ileana's face, Murray was painfully aware of the daggers flashing from her elder sister's eyes. Eventually Gina joined in the conversation.

'I thought you were going into town tonight?'

'I was. I am,' she corrected herself. 'But my car is in the garage. I need to borrow yours.'

'What? Take my car on one of your nights out? You think I am stupid?'

'I will look after it, Gina. Honestly. I am supposed to be meeting Mario later. I need a car.'

'What is wrong with a taxi?'

As Ileana pouted - 'Gi-na!' - Murray made to go into the house, sensing he was playing gooseberry.

'It is alright, Peter,' Gina said. 'Ileana won't be staying.'

To Murray's surprise, her sister turned her appeal on him, as if he had some say in the matter.

'Tell her, Peter. I will look after it, won't I?'

Put on the spot and caught out by her unexpected familiarity, Murray was, for once, lost for words. His gaze wavered between the two women, uncertain what his answer should be. 'I er... Well, I... Erm...'

Gina turned her gaze on him, a pencilled eyebrow arching. *And what has this to do with you?*

Suddenly realising he was now being subjected to the fierce scrutiny of not one but two attractive women, Murray felt himself begin to redden. For long seconds both women stared at him, demanding his support. Then, without warning, they both burst out laughing. It made him feel even worse.

'Oh, Peter.' Gina held her stomach. 'Your face!'

He turned to Ileana. Her hand was over her mouth, trying to suppress loud giggles. Murray's initial reaction was to wish he was somewhere else. But as their unsuccessful attempts to control their mirth continued, the inevitable happened. His embarrassment dissipated, replaced by a deprecating smile that, despite his best efforts, and to his horror, began to turn into a chuckle.

Seconds later the dam broke, and Peter Murray laughed like he had not laughed for a very long time.

Eventually each managing to reassert some semblance of control, they picked up the remnants of the conversation.

'That was very bad of you to embarrass Peter like that,' Gina chided. As she spoke, she dabbed a tissue at her eyes, trying to rescue her makeup.

Ileana hung her head, like a chastened schoolgirl. 'Sorry. *Peter*.' It set off a whole new round of laughter.

'Enough,' Murray said eventually, feeling the urge to show some manly control. Though beneath the surface, the smile lingered.

'Yes,' Gina said. 'Enough. My stomach is hurting.' She rounded on her sister. 'Go Ileana! Take my keys. Just make sure it comes back without any scratches.'

Ileana squealed her delight, and gave her sister a hug.

'Thank you Gina. I promise I will look after it.' She turned to Murray. 'Goodnight, Peter. Gina was right, you do have a nice smile.'

He nodded, but didn't rise to the bait. 'Enjoy your evening Ileana.' As she made to go back inside he added; 'Don't stay out too late.'

As she turned to flash him a mischievous smile, Gina ushered her out with a smack to her rump.

'GO.'

Alone again, they turned to each other. He was about to say something when Ileana returned.

'I am sorry, Peter. I need to get Gina's car out.'

Remembering he had parked across the driveway, blocking her Mercedes, Murray fished in his pocket.

'I'll move it.'

'No need. Give me your keys and I'll do it. I have disrupted your evening enough already. I'll leave them on the table in the hallway.' He handed them over.

With a final, 'Goodnight,' she left once more, pulling the glass door shut behind her.

After she had gone, Murray let out a long sigh.

'I'm not sure which of you is worse. God help the men you two marry.'

Gina smiled. 'Whoever said we will marry? Perhaps we shall stay single. That way we can have more fun.'

Sensing the playfulness he had seen more of that evening than ever before about to return, and remembering where they were before Ileana arrived, Murray thought a diversion was called for.

'How about if I make coffee? I think I'm ready for one.'

This time her smile was more knowing than humorous. 'That would be nice.'

As he went into the kitchen, Gina headed for the bathroom off the hallway. He was filling the coffee pot when he heard her shout. He poked his head round the door.

'Sorry Gina, what was that?'

'I said, 'Ileana seems to be having trouble starting your car.''

He stopped to listen. Sure enough, the noise of an engine turning over, not firing, sounded from the road out front.

Murray froze.

During his time undercover, he'd learned the value of a car that always started first time. The habit had stuck. Now he made sure that whatever he happened to be driving, it was always well-tuned. In that moment, the words of the lanky SAS Instructor who took them through their week-long survival training came to him.

And watch out for anything out of the ordinary. The slightest sign could spell danger....

Murray dropped the coffeepot and exploded from the

kitchen, racing for the hallway.

'ILEANA!'

Gina came out of the bathroom.

'What is it?'

Ignoring her, he rushed past and wrenched open the front door.

'ILEANA GET-.'

The last thing he registered was a blinding flash and a blast of intense heat, then he was flying back down the hallway, taking Gina with him.

Part Two

NEGOTIATION

CHAPTER 27

The well-dressed man in rimless glasses leaned forward in his chair, brought his hands together, and gave the official a withering look. 'So tell me, Vagit, what is your explanation this time?"

Nervous as always in the man's presence, Vagit Gudenov, the Odessa Port Authority Manager, swallowed hard, at the same time resisting the temptation to wring his hands. Instead he concentrated on trying to come up with a compromise that might satisfy his inquisitor's demands yet still leave the way open for the kickback that up to thirty minutes earlier he had been expecting would be his before the day's end. As he searched for an idea, Vagit's mind was, for once, not preoccupied with the humbleness of the surroundings.

The stinking, grubby office overlooking the dock was mainly used by the foremen and loading supervisors who gathered there several times a day to iron out differences, drink tea or something stronger, and while away the odd hour perusing the Chinese porn magazines the salts dropped off. The latter activity was, of course, essential to the process of ensuring that no operation completed in a shorter time than the Gang-bosses had allowed for. Though the dockers were on piece-rates, work these days was plentiful and the chief concern of those in charge was to make sure no one did any more than they had to.

Gudenov hated the foreman's office with a passion. Not only did it smell of stale sweat and the grease that, like such places the world over, was embedded in the worn square of carpet covering the centre of the floor, it always brought back discomfiting memories. His own, sweet-smelling, leather and mahogany retreat on the third floor of the Port Authority Building the other side of the quay was the antithesis of where he now stood. But his infrequent trips dockside always served to remind him of his early days as a dock-labourer, the lowest of the low, at everyone's beck and call. And though he had worked, fought, schemed and scratched his way to the pinnacle of the Port Authority's rigid hierarchy, Gudenov had no nostalgia for 'the old days'. Proud of what he'd achieved, he nonetheless preferred to forget his humble origins. Back then, the docks had been a vile and dangerous place to work. Apart from the horrendous state of the equipment they were required to operate - serious injury, death even, was a regular occurrence - the place always swarmed with party informers. There had never been any shortage of men and women willing to supplement their meagre pay-packets by drawing some bumptious official's attention to the latest tittle-tattle regarding doings around the world, sparked by news brought in on the latest tide. Agents from the local KGB contingent, as it was in those days, were never away from the place.

But worse than the memories, was the fact that whenever Gudenov was called to the office, he invariably found himself on the defensive.

Under normal circumstances, he rarely had cause to

visit the place. As far as he was concerned, his duties now consisted of making telephone calls, attending meetings and signing whatever documents Vatlava, the pretty secretary he was screwing, placed in front of him - after the contents of the accompanying envelope had been removed, counted and added to the ledger only he and Vatlava knew about of course. So why risk getting oil stains on his expensive shoes, or seagull-shit on the English-tailored suits he preferred to wear, by actually visiting the dockside? He knew what went on there well enough, he didn't need reminders.

It was why Gudenov could never understand why the man now sat behind the desk, still waiting, patiently it appeared, for his explanation, seemed to enjoy coming here so much.

For the past year, ever since ownership of Northwest Shipping passed into Anatoly Kaskiv's hands in fact, what began as the occasional drop-in - just to say hello and become acquainted with how things worked, Gudenov at first assumed - had grown to the point where it was now happening once a week, sometimes twice. It was not good. Not good at all. Apart from the disruption that accompanied Kaskiv and his entourage's arrival on the dockside, each visit also brought with it the inevitable phone call.

'Vagit? I wonder if you could spare me a few minutes?'

It meant Vagit having to drop whatever he was doing - on one, memorable, occasion it had been Vatlava - to drag himself across the dockyard, avoiding the slick puddles and crap that lay all over, to climb the rickety wooden steps to the office. There he would find Kaskiv, as usual poring over papers spread across the desk, flanked by his courtiers, all doing their best to look like they shared his sudden passion for all things maritime.

And while he waited for the man who had summoned him to speak, sometimes even to acknowledge his arrival, he would try to work out what this week's interrogation was to be about. It always began more or less the same way.

'Sorry to drag you away Vagit, I am sure you are very busy,' - *patronising bastard* - 'But there is something here I do not understand. Can you please explain…?' Which is when Gudenov would spend the next hour - sometimes longer - trying to make the former steel worker who everyone said had the best business brain in all Ukraine but who Gudenov thought of as rather dim, understand why dock-work was not like any other business. Of course the task was made doubly difficult by the fact that Gudenov's instincts warned him against mentioning that, like most ports in the former-USSR territories, and especially those on the Black Sea, the Odessa Dockyard worked by means of a long-established system of kickbacks and patronage. It meant that cargoes were handled in strict order of priority, depending upon the thickness and speed of arrival on the Authority Manager's desk of the package required to accompany the Bill of Lading.

For that reason, Vagit frequently found himself in the impossible position of having to defend a handling schedule that anyone with a modicum of intelligence could see made no sense at all. And though there were times when Gudenov was certain his inquisitor was fully aware of how things worked and was merely tormenting him, there were others when he was equally certain the man was so naive as to make him wonder how such an idiot could have amassed the fortune he had.

Today it was all about Vagit's decision to give priority clearance to a Japanese cargo vessel, the MV Toyota, over Northwest Shipping's MV Coral Blue, a decision he would never have made had he been made aware, (a) the Coral Blue was now part of Kaskiv's Northwest fleet, and (b), that he would that day be visited by the man himself. Already, he couldn't wait to get back to his office to sack his prick of an administrator, Karloff. He had had enough. If he had told the man once he had told him a thousand times, he was to let him know whenever a Northwest ship was in.

But the thing Gudenov really couldn't get his head round was that Anatoly Kaskiv was wealthy. Immensely wealthy. And though he had never visited the place, Gudenov had no trouble imagining that Kaskiv's own office in the plush concrete and steel edifice that was his new Corporate Headquarters, just outside Odessa, would make even his office look barren. So why spend so much time here? Staying for hours to immerse himself in the minutiae of running a shipping line that by all accounts was not even one tenth of his business empire? It didn't make sense, unless the claims of some of Kaskiv's detractors were right. That he suffered from a type of attention disorder that meant, like a little boy in a toyshop, he couldn't resist the temptation to play with whatever was at hand. Gudenov could only hope that the phase would soon pass and that Kaskiv's attention would soon move elsewhere. In which case the sooner the better, for everyone.

'Well?' Kaskiv demanded, jarring Gudenov out of his wishing and back to the present.

Gudenov, took a deep breath. 'What you have to understand, Patron Kaskiv, is that-.'

'What?'

'Well you see, it is not as easy as simply following the order of berthing....'

'Why not?'

Inside, Gudenov grimaced. 'There are other things

that must be taken into account-.'

'Such as?'

'Such as…' An idea came to him. Fanciful maybe, but it would do. 'The Wharf Ladies.'

Kaskiv started, and looked to his entourage. Smirks were already passing between them. His ever-present contingent of advisors and bodyguards always enjoyed the spectacle of watching Vagit's weekly squirmings. And whilst they thought he was nothing if not imaginative, the only reason most kept coming back each week was to see what sort of hole he would dig himself into this time.

'Please explain, Vagit. Exactly how do prostitutes affect your handling schedules?' Unlike his posse, if Kaskiv saw anything amusing in the direction Gudenov was heading, it didn't show.

'You see Patron, it is like this….'

'Carry on.'

'Well as you know, the ladies belong mainly to the Coptic Church, yes?'

'I am sure I have no idea, but if you say so I will not argue.'

'But most of the sailors who land here are Muslim.'

'So what?' Kaskiv's impatience began to show.

'Well if you knew anything about dock work-' As Kaskiv's eyebrows rose Gudenov hurried to cover his gaffe. 'As of course you do, you know that Muslims would never allow themselves to work-' Outside, the noise of some commotion suddenly carried through the window. The wah-wah of a siren amidst shrill shouting. Gudenov ventured on. '-Never allow themselves to work in an environment where-' A horn blaring. More shouting. Kaskiv's people moved to the windows to see what was happening. 'Where there may be a risk of-' Kaskiv's minder-in-chief, a bulky Russian named

Bogdanof, came forward.

'The Police, Anatoly.'

Gudenov let his words trail off. Police? Now what could they want? Kaskiv wasn't moving though his gaze remained squarely on the now silent Port Official. If he shared any of Gudenov's concern about the police's unexpected arrival, he didn't show it. There seemed even to be a trace of a smile at the extremities of his mouth. Nevertheless Gudenov was relieved. There were no problems involving the police he knew of that couldn't be sorted with a few crates of Khortytsa. And their arrival at that particular moment was, for him, fortuitous.

'Excuse me, Patron. I must see what they want.'

But Kaskiv's eyes held him. 'Do not worry Vagit. I know what they want.'

'You do?'

'Yes.'

Vagit swallowed. There was something unnerving, disquieting even, about Kaskiv's even manner. 'Then... may I ask what it is?'

Kaskiv rose, slowly. 'They want-'

'Yes?'

'You.'

Gudenov froze, his mouth gaping. The colour drained from his face. There was silence in the room. For long seconds the two men regarded each other. The sound of heavy, plodding feet mounting the steps came to Gudenov's ears. Had there been a hole beneath Gudenov's feet, his stomach would already have dropped through it. *My God, surely they have not found out about-*. On the verge of panicking, Vagit caught himself as he saw the broad smile that suddenly broke across Kaskiv's face. On cue, those around burst into laughter.

Gudenov looked at them, then back at Kaskiv. They were all shaking their heads. A couple wiping at their eyes. Kaskiv rose. Coming round the desk he draped an arm around the shaking Port Manager's shoulders.

'I am sorry, Vagit. I was joking. It is not you they are here to see. It is me.'

The words barely registered in Gudenov's ears as he fought to recover himself. *What was that? Did he say a joke? The BASTARD.*

The door opened behind him and he turned. Framed in the doorway, the ample frame of Colonel Boris Kiryenko of the Odessa Militsiya, more than filled out the sky-blue shirt that was his new uniform - the Ministry of Internal Affairs' latest attempt to distance itself from its old Soviet roots. As always, the policeman looked suitably serious. Gudenov heaved a sigh of relief. If it was Kiryenko, then it certainly couldn't mean trouble for him. *Thank God.*

'Come in Colonel,' Kaskiv said, beckoning to the Police Commander. 'We are expecting you.'

The policeman nodded at Gudenov as he passed. 'Hello Vagit.'

Relief turning rapidly to annoyance, Vagit's response was bordering on curt. 'I was not expecting to see you here today, Colonel.' What he meant was, *Why did you not tell me you were coming? What do you think all those deliveries to the villa in the hills are for? Goodwill?*

And the policeman's face was a mask as he stopped to address him. 'My business today is not with you, Vagit.' He turned back to Kaskiv.

Silence now fell in the room. Eventually Gudenov realised everyone was waiting for him to leave. He jerked himself into action.

'Excuse me Patron, I must- Er…. I have to return to my office. People waiting. You understand.'

'Of course,' Kaskiv said, benevolently.

But as Gudenov reached the door Kaskiv hailed him.

'Oh, Vagit.'

He turned.

'I still look forward to hearing the end of your explanation concerning the Coral Blue.'

Gudenov smiled. 'Whenever you are ready, Patron.'

Closing the door firmly behind him, he let out a long breath before starting down the steps. As he neared the bottom, where the Colonel's car waited, single blue light still flashing, the policeman's driver-body guard, called to him.

'Hello Vagit. Do you have that case for me yet?'

Lost in thought, Gudenov didn't answer. Nor did he pay any attention to the figure in the back of the car and who, had he done so, would undoubtedly have aroused his curiosity. Instead, Gudenov was trying desperately to dream up a plausible reason why Muslim prejudices towards prostitutes might necessitate having to rearrange cargo-handling schedules.

CHAPTER 28

From the window of the dock foreman's office, Anatoly Kaskiv watched Vagit's scurrying figure disappear between the gantries before turning to face the policeman.

'You have brought him?'

Kiryenko jerked his bear's head back towards the door. 'Downstairs.'

Kaskiv pursed his lips. 'Is he genuine?'

Kiryenko shrugged. 'All I can say is, I am satisfied he is who he says he is. Our Intelligence boys have been able to check that much. Beyond that, who knows?'

Kaskiv waited, thinking. Eventually he said, 'Bring him up. I will speak with him.' As Kiryenko turned, Kaskiv added. 'Alone.'

Words of protest sprang from his team. Bogdanof came forward. 'I cannot allow that, Anatoly. I-.'

But Kaskiv was ready. 'Not this time Viktor. This, I must do alone.'

Seeing the set of his master's features, Bogdanof relented, but made sure Kaskiv could see it was begrudged.

By way of response, Kaskiv grasped his arm, feeling the hard muscle beneath the sleeve. 'I appreciate your loyalty Viktor, but please, trust me. I know what I am doing.' Bogdanof said nothing.

As they all filed out, Kaskiv settled himself behind the desk. As always, he felt comfortable here, more so than his ridiculous office in the new building which, in a rare moment of weakness, he'd let himself be talked into commissioning. No, this was far more his sort of place. Somewhere he could remember who he was, where he was from, how things had been before Sissi's death. And he was glad he'd arranged the meet here, away from all the prying eyes and ears at his organisation's HQ. Even so, he needed to be careful. There was something about the message that had arrived telling him he should grant the man's request to speak with him alone, that had set his antenna buzzing. A footfall sounded outside the door. In the next few seconds he would know if his instincts were correct.

The door opened and the man, a westerner, entered. He seemed to be limping.

There was nothing in the face or demeanour that told Kaskiv anything, not immediately. He had the obvious bearing of a soldier. Hints of a maybe-dormant athleticism. The eyes were sharp, but cool. No sign of nerves. But these were qualities many were capable of displaying. Of themselves they mean nothing. On the other hand, the cuts to his face - they looked recent. Together with the bandaged wrist and the limp - more a stiffness now he'd had time to weigh it - it pointed towards some recent trouble. And while that didn't mean anything either, it spoke of someone who at least knew how to survive.

For several moments the two men eyed each other, gauging. Neither offered a hand. Eventually Kaskiv nodded to the old office chair under the cracked window. The man shook his head.

'I've been sitting for twelve hours. I'm fine here.'

Kaskiv nodded. English, as he'd been told to expect.

'As you wish.' He came straight to the point. 'Colonel Kiryenko says you have information that will interest me.'

The man nodded.

'Concerning my daughter?'

Another nod.

'And how did you come by it?'

A barely-discernible shrug. 'Contacts.'

Kaskiv suppressed a smile before shaking his head. The standard answer. He sighed.

As well as the results of his own, detailed investigations, Kaskiv had long ago become familiar with the various agency reports. They were all the same. Speculation, nothing definite. Never enough for him to take the decisive action he had always longed for. Already, he doubted the man could tell him anything he hadn't heard a hundred times before. He placed his hands flat on the table. He was a busy man.

'You asked to speak with me alone. I am here. What have you to say?'

Despite all his doubts, Kaskiv was impressed when his visitor didn't prevaricate but came straight out with it.

'The man responsible for the death of your daughter is standing at the bottom of those steps.' He made a half-turn, towards the door.

Kaskiv held a breath, then let it out as he shook his head, the familiar feeling of disappointment taking root. He was foolish to have expected otherwise. 'You think people have not suggested him before?'

The man didn't seem put off by Kaskiv's show of scepticism.

'I am sure they have. But the source of my information would know, whereas others wouldn't.'

Already weary of the conversation - would the pain never end? - Kaskiv gave a short, mocking laugh.

'Then in order to convince me, you must name your source.' Again, the face showed no surprise.

'Fair enough. Her name is Marianna Podruznig.'

Kaskiv froze. And as his scepticism disappeared in a flash, he decided to give the visitor his full attention.

CHAPTER 29

Major Glyn Westgate let rip his exasperation.

'And THANKS. For NOTHING.'

Not that the faceless official in the Nicosia Passport Office heard. Westgate had slammed the receiver down a split second earlier.

For close to a minute he glared at the phone, jaw cradled in one hand, fingers of the other drumming on the desk, impatient. He hated being thwarted. And right now it seemed it was happening at every turn.

For the best part of the past three days, working from one of the two portacabins that, tucked away in a remote corner of Episkopi Sovereign Base Garrison served as the SIB Office, the army investigator had been making phone calls. None had taken him anywhere. Twice during that period he'd given up, grabbed his car keys, and taken off to re-visit all the places he could think of, all the while knowing it would be a waste of time. He was running out of options.

He wasn't so much surprised to find himself in this position as annoyed. It had always been likely that at some point they would all go to ground. He just hadn't expected it to be so soon. Or sudden. But then he hadn't foreseen the bomb either.

Of course, he moved as soon as he heard the news on the BFBS radio, but that was a full eight hours after the event, and by then he was shut out, completely.

His first port of call was the Pafos Police Station, but it was locked down tight as a drum. Even those on the gate weren't saying anything, under orders so strict that even his usually-sufficient credentials were not enough to bypass them. He couldn't even get hold of Iridotu on the telephone, never mind get to see him - though that was perhaps not surprising either, given what had happened. The station itself was buzzing with activity and he could imagine the sort of things that would be going on within the thick stone walls. He could also guess at the numbness and anger those inside would be feeling over what had happened in a town that had a reputation as one of the more tranquil - and safe - among the Mediterranean's holiday resorts.

Much of the overt speculation, understandably, concerned terrorism. Some of the news reports were still speculating an Al-Qaeda or ISIL connection, though others had ruled it out quickly, worried how such a rumour might impact tourism. But as soon as Westgate learned the location, his investigator's instincts told him the real story.

Getting nowhere with the police and sensing from all the activity what might be about to happen, he headed back to the base, grabbed a CROPS kit and went and staked out the house, lying low in the hills with everything he needed for a prolonged Covert Rural Observation - just in case it turned out to be a protracted wait. As it happened, the circus arrived within four hours of him setting up, just as the sun was rising. It was still less than twenty-four hours after the blast, which wasn't at all bad considering the levers Westgate suspected Iridotu would have had to pull to get a warrant.

And judging by the size of the police convoy that

rolled up the main road from Coral Bay and turned left onto the track leading to the house, Westgate would have bet it contained just about every Crime Investigation and Search and Forensic Resource available to the Cyprus Police Force.

From his prime vantage point, equipped with field glasses, night-scope and video, Westgate watched the whole thing unfold before him.

To begin with, the house erupted at the police's arrival. Westgate got the clear impression that if the men on the gates hadn't opened them when they did, whoever was leading the convoy was prepared to bulldoze his way through. It was Podruznig himself who came down the steps to greet them, flanked by the big Siberian and two other minders. He looked suitably astonished of course, mixed with just the right amount of, *why-am-I-being-persecuted-like-this* resentment.

But within minutes, after seeing the way the Russians offered only token resistance, objecting not-too-strongly before giving in and becoming almost welcoming, Westgate realised what was going on. Notwithstanding the magnitude of the miscalculation by which the daughters of the local Police Commander himself were caught in the blast, the police's likely response had been factored into the Russians' plans from the start.

Over the next few hours, Westgate monitored the operation's progress. Separate Search and Forensic Teams were allocated to different parts of the house, garages and outbuildings; others to the grounds, front and rear. And though the police were clearly pulling out all the stops, Westgate guessed what the outcome would be. Whatever illicit materials might once have lain around the house – weapons, components, bomb making equipment, documentation - anything that could possibly justify arrests, detentions or even 'voluntary questioning' - they weren't there now. The disappointed, and in some cases exhausted, looks on the faces of the various Team Leaders as, one by one, they reported to the Mobile Command Vehicle the police had set up in front of the house, confirmed as much. During all the searching, Westgate saw not so much as a single cardboard box or black plastic bag - the staple of police-search operations the world over - come from the house or anywhere else. In fact the only things he saw being carried out were used Crime-Scene kits taken back to the Forensic Teams' Land Rovers. Given that a trained Evidence-Gatherer can usually find something in the most innocent of households that is capable of being made to look sufficiently ambiguous to invite further enquiry, it was remarkable. Confirmation, if any were needed, that Podruznig had left nothing to chance.

Throughout, Pippis Iridotu remained notably absent. Wisely, he appeared to have stayed away, not risking putting himself in a position where he could later be accused of 'contaminating' the investigation. In any case, Westgate assumed, other things, not least family, would still be occupying his attention. Instead, the Operation appeared to be being led by another Commander from Force Headquarters at Nicosia. Westgate remembered meeting him once, briefly, when he was introduced as a former Chief of Detectives who was now Head of the Force's Operational Support Division. Westgate was impressed that despite the heightened emotions that would undoubtedly be running through the whole Force, the Chief Constable - no doubt the Government as well – had made sure his force's response was at least seen to be as professionally impartial as the circumstances allowed for, whatever may be going on elsewhere.

Some seven hours later, as the last of the convoy rolled away, leaving only the Command Vehicle, Westgate saw the man in charge of the operation square up to Podruznig at the bottom of the steps. As he handed over the documentation he was required by law to leave justifying the search - Westgate made a note to remember to get hold of a copy - he and Podruznig exchanged words. It made Westgate wish he'd included a directional microphone in his hurriedly-put-together requisition to the base's Special Ops Quartermaster. Whatever was said, the anger that was still evident in the Police Commander's face, as well as the smugness on Podruznig's, was indication enough that things would not stop here. Which meant that Westgate needed to get back into the loop, and quickly, hence all the telephone calls.

But despite all his efforts since then, Westgate was no nearer finding out what was going on than when he'd turned up at the police station. And having now had sight of the Army's Intelligence Assessment concerning the incident and which he'd contributed to - it was classified 'C' for 'Criminal', as opposed to 'T'-'Terrorist' - he feared that even the official, 'Service Approach' to Cyprus's Interior Ministry wouldn't work either. He'd initiated the contact through the office of Head of Armed Forces-Cyprus, as soon as he couldn't get hold of Iridotu. But he was beginning to think that even that may not be enough to break through the information clamp-down that was presently reigning - at least not quickly enough for his purpose.

And he was yet to discover anything he could use to bargain his way back in. Murray's companions were no longer at the villa overlooking the airport, and following the police raid, Podruznig and his team weren't venturing out. Everyone, it seemed, was holding their breath. Worst of all, Westgate could hardly believe that the information he most needed was still evading him.

Whether or not Murray was still alive. And, if he was, where was he, and what was he doing?

In the immediate aftermath, the rumour was he'd died. The official reports spoke of three fatalities. But no one was giving out names. And though the Pafos General Hospital was under heavy police guard, he couldn't even get confirmation of any casualties. Having organised similar, 'diversion operations', himself, aimed at convincing certain parties that the dead were still alive or vice-versa, Westgate knew the police presence didn't necessarily signify anything. For that reason, he'd also tried following some of the girls' neighbours and approaching them away from their homes - entry and exit to the streets around the scene being still under strict police control. But those he spoke to either couldn't, or wouldn't, add to what was being reported, eyeing him with a suspicion that suggested they would be on the telephone to the police as soon as he left.

It underlined the importance of being careful, especially in the present climate. If he drew too much attention, he would succeed only in making himself a target. He could end up being detained and held incommunicado while suspicious investigators considered what part, if any, he may have played in things. And despite his official position, he wasn't confident that dropping Iridotu's name would necessarily open any doors. All the signs were that the police family had closed ranks around their Commander. He imagined Pafos Police Station's white, ceramic-tiled cells at that moment being stuffed full of potential 'sources' the police had picked up off the streets, all sweating litres while the investigators waited to see what, if anything, they may be persuaded to add to what was already known.

Now, almost a week after the explosion, Westgate was

grudgingly impressed. He hadn't come across such a wholesale dearth of information since the corruption investigation he'd overseen in Rwanda - and that was only because the local populace firmly believed that the Hutu Rebels the Government Forces were seeking, counted amongst their number, 'Ju-Ju Men' who saw and heard everything.

Tired and, for the moment, beaten, Westgate rose and crossed to the water cooler. Refilling the plastic cup - the first went straight down - he turned to peer between the slats of the blinds that covered the reinforced windows through which the afternoon sun still poured. Having ordered the other two SIB NCO's out - no point risking others picking up where his true interests lay - he was, thankfully, alone. The only noise - a dubious rattle - came from the ancient air-con unit high up on the wall above the cluttered notice board. As in many military establishments abroad, no one was sure if the a/c contributed anything by way of keeping the temperature down - the thermometer on the opposite wall read twenty-nine

. But Westgate was as oblivious of the heat as he was of his shirt clinging to his back and arms. Instead his attention was focused on the questions going round and round in his head.

Was Murray alive? And what would happen next?

CHAPTER 30

By the time the group settled down to business, it was late into the afternoon, the still-baking sun about to disappear behind the house served by the enclosed courtyard in which they were gathered.

There were six in all. It had taken the best part of a week to bring them together. The last had arrived only that morning, on a hastily-booked KLM charter bringing tourists from Amsterdam's Schipol airport. Though none were tied to anything that might be regarded as 'regular employment', their backgrounds and particular range of skills meant that most had to nonetheless engineer their release from whatever it was they were doing when news of the bombing arrived.

They should have been seven but as best they'd been able to find out the one they called 'Blink', a Welshman who knew more about munitions than the rest of them put together, was somewhere in West Africa. Niger someone said, working for Trollian, the global Risk Management company that nowadays seems to somehow get involved in just about any conflict around the world people could name – as well as many they could not. Word was he'd got himself mired rather more deeply than was wise in some local tribal difficulty that had been holding up the laying of an American oil company pipeline the past two years. It wasn't that the men worried particularly whether Blink was still alive or not, death was an occupational hazard in their lines of work. But risk assessment was something they always had time for - natural enough given the part it played in keeping them alive. Anything pointing towards conditions worsening in those places they earned their living was therefore of great interest. The fact that in this case, the evidence might be the loss of one of their number - Blink - was of course a matter for regret. But it wouldn't be the cause of any great wailing or gnashing of teeth as it might with some tight-knit groups. Not so far as most were concerned at any rate. A quiet gathering in some corner bar, followed by a boozy reminisce over the occasions that had been memorable, accompanied by solemn head-shaking and intonations of the, 'What a shame, what a waste,' variety, was about as much as any of them could expect from a band they nevertheless counted as their closest friends.

There was one exception however. And he was Peter Murray.

When news of what had happened reached them - wherever they happened to be - none hesitated more than a minute in making the decision to haul themselves to Cyprus at the earliest opportunity. Not only was Murray the one who had brought them together in the first place, they all, one way or another, owed him much. The unexpected news – a couple hadn't even heard about Kathy yet - was therefore a cause for genuine concern, if not quite, perhaps, for the reasons some may imagine.

As the bluff, black Mancunian, Moss Side Billy, the last to arrive, settled at the table under the two lemon trees and pulled a tab off a Keo, the joshing and tom-foolery that had prevailed through most of the afternoon died away. It was replaced by an expectant hush as they all waited to see who would take up the running. Without Murray, they were essentially leaderless. And though Red was the most obvious replacement – he knew the griff about what was going on, and in military terms was the 'ranker' - it was the slim-framed Geordie, 'Wazzer', who rose to take another can from the cool-box, timing things in a way that drew everyone's attention, and thereby laying claim to be first to speak.

'Strikes me,' he started in his pronounced twang, ripping the tab and lifting the can to his mouth. 'Strikes me, that this guy, Podruznig.' He turned to check he'd got the name right. Red nodded. 'This guy Podruznig needs to be sorted, but propa'. Nun of this, 'now let this be a warning,' bullshit. I'm talkin' once and for all. Final. Nah messin' aboot.'

As he returned to his seat, several heads nodded in agreement. Though this was the first time they'd sat together to discuss next moves, most had taken Wazzer's stance pretty much as read as soon as they heard what had been happening with the house - especially when they learned about Murray. The questions were, how to make it happen, and when?

The fact that Wazzer had gone straight to the nub of the problem - Podruznig - rather than regurgitating the tragic chain of events that had blighted Murray's life the past two years and played no little part in reuniting them, came as no surprise. The past three days had seen enough lamenting over the affair as well as several conversations of the, 'Why didn't he just ace him to begin with?' variety. By now they all knew enough about what had been going on to make further discussion on the subject redundant. They were where they were. How they'd arrived was immaterial. All that mattered now was the right exit strategy. Having let Wazzer open, Red took up the running.

'Before we start talking about sorting people, I think we need to bear in mind what Peter's wishes on all this were.' There was a low chorus of reluctantly-concurring murmurs.

'So what were they then?'

Red turned to the fresh-faced young man with close-cropped black hair sitting away from the main group. The soft Irish accent and wire-framed glasses lent the speaker something of an academic air, akin to that of a poet, or teacher. But they all knew him better. Each of them had heard if not seen for themselves the way Ryan O'Donnell acquitted himself in close-quarter combat. On this occasion, the titanium-steel hunting knife with the black ivory handle he always carried was displayed openly in the Samsonite scabbard on his belt. As he waited for Red to answer, he winked across at Billy. Everyone knew they were friends.

'He didn't want blood spilled in the house,' Red answered.

The Irishman smiled, wickedly. 'Then we'll have to catch it and get rid of it somewhere else.'

It prompted chuckles in the others, apart from Kishore. Of them all, the ex-Gurkha tended to keep his thoughts to himself. Not on this occasion.

'Peter was serious. The house was Kathy's dream.' An edge crept into the Gurkha's voice. 'I wouldn't want to see her memory besmirched.' Red's hand landed on his shoulder.

'Easy Kish. I know how you feel, and I agree we shouldn't do anything Peter wouldn't have wanted us to, though you may have to explain to this pig-ignorant lot what 'besmirch' means.' It brought on smiles, easing the tension that had arrived from nowhere.

But Wazzer and Ryan weren't alone in wanting to get on with things. A voice that was more growl than

Queen's English said, 'I didn't come all this fuckin' way to pussyfoot around.'

They all turned to stare at the thick-set man who had spent the past five minutes rocking back on his plastic chair's legs, saying nothing. The oldest of the group, James 'Bear' Jocelyn had the cauliflower-ears and beat-about-the-face features of a nineteenth-century prize-fighter or rugby-scrum hooker. He'd arrived from the Lebanon the day before. Once a professional boxer, he'd quit the ring to enlist in the army the day his doctor told him the reason he could no longer 'hear' every note of the Opera arias he loved even more than boxing, was due to 'shake' damage to the auditory cortex in his left temporal lobe. He liked to think he got out in time but, given his propensity for getting into fist fights whenever the opportunity arose, those who knew him best were doubtful. Unlike the young Irishman, Red let him continue.

'I met Kathy and I always had a lot of respect for Plod.' 'Plod' was Murray's nickname in the group. More concurring murmurs. 'But I'm fucked if I'm going to piss around trying to persuade this Russian bastard to fuck off. Let's just recce the place and do it. We all agreed didn't we? Three years? Well that was three years ago. It's time.'

Red scanned the faces. During Priscilla, they'd rarely disagreed over what needed to be done. But back then things had been clearer. That was a military-run op. And say what you like about Murray, he'd been a master at managing consensus. Now it was different. While they all had a stake in achieving what Peter himself had been working towards - the Russian's departure - they would all, if asked, take a differing slant on the best way of bringing it about. And for all the SAS's reputation for pulling rabbits out of hats, Red knew it wasn't to be achieved by charging into things without the requisite Appreciation Of A Situation that allowed for effective contingency planning. It was what was needed now. He told them so.

'Fair enough,' Bear responded as Red finished. He pulled his chair round, ready to begin. 'Let's get on with it. Then we'll do what we came to do.' The others followed his lead, Kishore included. It signalled agreement.

A few minutes later, Red stood at the head of the table, meeting the steady gazes of the men who had once all delighted in taking the piss out of their 'poofy code-name', Priscilla-Six. He looked for signs of more challenge in the faces but couldn't see any. For the time being, it seemed, they were happy to work under his direction. He wondered how long it would last. How long he could hold them together without Murray. He began.

'Okay. There's some work still to be done yet. Ground-mapping, head counting, that sort of thing. We'll talk about that later. For the time being we'll start with what we know.' He reached for the folder he'd brought to the table, took out a sheaf of photographs, handed them to Kishore to pass round. 'This is our biggest problem. His name is Uri.'

As he gave them a few seconds to familiarise themselves with the giant Siberian's photograph, ex-Sergeant Mike 'Red' McGeary's gaze flitted from one to the other. As he did so, the half of his brain that wasn't thinking about the briefing he was about to give, mulled over the two questions to which he didn't have answers. The first was how their plans could be affected by whatever the police were doing? The other was which of their number would still be around when it was all over to share in the spoils?

CHAPTER 31

Lifting his cap, Kyriakos Mikros used his shirtsleeve to wipe the sweat from his brow. It was the hottest part of the day and the rocky outcrop that was his post offered no shelter from the afternoon sun's incessant glare.

Leaning his rifle against the bleached stump of a fallen cedar, the young man reached down to pull his canteen from between the crack in the rocks where he'd stored it, safe from the sun's heat, soon after his dawn arrival. Pulling out the cork stopper, he lifted it to his mouth, relishing the mountain spring water's refreshing coolness. After a few glugs, he paused long enough to check that nothing was moving in the valley below. Satisfied, he finished his thirst-quenching, re-plugged the canteen and returned it to his make-do cool-box. Taking up his weapon, he cradled it across his chest, the way he'd been shown as a child, but resting his weight on the other leg this time.

A few paces back along the outcrop, would have taken Kyriakos to where the shadows of the tall fir trees fell across the steep, rocky slopes. Yet the thought of sheltering from the sun didn't occur to him. The long speech delivered to them all by his Uncle Pippis, that Sunday morning they gathered in front of the farmhouse to hear his grave pronouncements, had spelt out clear enough what was required - and what to expect should any be found wanting. And not just Pippis.

Afterwards, when the 'business-talk' was over and the women were bringing out the food - despite the sombre atmosphere, the elders insisted that family traditions must carry on - his father, Vasillis, pulled him to one side.

'I know what you and your cousins are saying Kyriakos. But you are the eldest. I am relying on you to put your feelings aside, and ensure that the family's wishes are carried out.'

Kyriakos stood tall. If he resented being reminded of his responsibilities, he did not let it show. 'You do not have to worry about me father. We all know what needs to be done.'

Had Kyriakos been harbouring any doubts about his mission, the look of pride that showed in his father's eyes in that moment would have dispelled them. It was a difficult and dark time for everyone - the darkest most had known - but the twenty year old was determined to ensure that not just he, but the rest of the younger ones as well, abided by their elders' decision - at least until such time as it was all over. Then he and his cousins would be free to act in the way they had discussed, assuming of course that the focus of their anger was still alive by then.

At the foot of the valley, away to his left, movement on the gravel road that ran up to the farmhouse caught Kyriakos's eye. Straightening, he brought the binoculars round his neck to bear on the silver speck at the front of the dust cloud. He recognised the Mazda pick-up at once. Even from way up here, he could make out the driver, his cousin, Anton. Tracking ahead of it, he sought out the farmhouse on top of the hill far below, training the lenses on the front door. As he did so, the noise of the approaching vehicle finally reached him, its gearbox straining as it reached the steepest part of the approach.

As in all mountains, sound carries easily in the low Troodos. Sure enough, as Kyriakos watched, a man, older, grey-haired and with the sort of tanned-leather complexion that is common in mountain-folk emerged onto the wide, covered porch, coming forward to where he could observe the vehicle's approach. The binoculars were powerful and Kyriakos had no difficulty making out the old service revolver in the man's right hand. Out of the house behind him, came a younger woman. She was wearing dark glasses and drying her hands on a cloth. The man waggled the gun at her, as if telling her to go back inside. She ignored him.

Unslinging his Uncle George's favourite hunting rifle - a Czechoslovakian-bought Ceska Zbvrojovka 550 - Kyriakos laid himself across the flat rock he had picked out earlier. Bending his right knee in classic sniper fashion, he fitted the smooth walnut stock to his shoulder and settled himself. When he was happy he was set, he let his breath out slowly, at the same time sighting through the scope his uncle had warned him he was to treat with the utmost respect, having cost more than the rifle.

As the car crested the rise to come level with the house, Kyriakos followed it the last few yards until it stopped alongside the porch, driver's side to him. Neither the grey-haired man nor the woman came forward, but remained under the shade. As both front doors opened, Kyriakos ignored Anton, focusing instead on the man levering himself out of the passenger seat to stand, stiffly, upright.

Working as he did in the accounts department of one of Paphos's bigger property developers, Kyriakos's marksmanship skills were not as developed as his mountain-born cousins. Nevertheless, even for him, it presented an easy shot. As the scope's cross-hairs settled on the side of the man's temple and Kyriakos's finger curled so it fitted, snug around the trigger, he couldn't stop the smile that came into his face.

CHAPTER 32

Thirty-two years of age, Anton was tall and slim. He wore the flat cap that was common in those parts and a light jacket that bulged under one arm. As he came round the bonnet, the old man's face broke into a smile. Stepping down the porch, he came forward to embrace the younger man.

'Kalimera, Anton. Welcome!'

'Kalimera, Grandfather,' Anton said, returning the old man's hug.

Releasing his grandson - one of many - the older man let the smile drop as he turned to face Anton's passenger, now also coming forward on stiff legs. He nodded a curt, 'Kalimera.' The minimum courtesy demanded.

'Kalimera,' the man replied.

Mounting the porch, Anton paused to accept the woman's hug, words of welcome and kisses, before letting his grandfather lead him inside.

At the foot of the steps, Anton's passenger looked up at the woman who, every time he now saw her, sent shivers up and down his spine. It was a week since they'd parted, but even though he couldn't see her eyes behind the dark glasses, he could tell she had not changed. The light was still absent. She smiled at him, weakly.

'Hello, Peter.'

He tried returning it. It wasn't easy. 'Hello Gina.'

At first she hesitated. Then, as if to head off the uncomfortable silence that threatened, she descended to stand before him. She was still wearing the surgical collar, her hair piled high to stop it catching. Up close, he could see that the livid blue bruising round her eyes was yet to fade, and he felt again the anguish of knowing he was its cause - when the back of his head crashed into her face. He hoped it wasn't just wishful thinking that the injuries seemed less pronounced than a week ago.

She tried another smile. More warmth this time. 'Welcome back.'

'Thank you.' He nearly added, '*Glad to be back*,' but thought better of it.

For a moment they stood looking at each other, both fishing for the words. In the end they gave up and settled for a hug and the light kiss Gina planted on his cheek. Chaste though it was, Murray was glad none of the family were on hand to witness it. Then he remembered. He turned to look up at the mountain above them. As if reading his thoughts, she stepped round him, eyes searching the slopes. Suddenly, she raised an arm above her head and waved. High above, a figure rose to show himself amid the rocks, acknowledging her greeting by raising his rifle above his head, Apache style.

Though the sun was behind him, Murray thought he recognised young Kyriakos, one of her many cousins. As Gina turned to go inside - 'Let's get you out of the sun,' – he let his gaze linger on the family member rostered for 'guardianship' duties that day. He could still remember the look on Kyriakos's face - others as well - when he first met them all at the family gathering following the blast. Now, the way Kyriakos held the rifle aloft, framed against the sky, Murray could just make out it was fitted with a telescopic sight. And though he was aware of the younger man's brief, he wondered just what

Kyriakos had been doing up to the moment Gina waved at him. Suppressing the thought - if any of them were minded to vent their feelings there was little he could do about it anyway - he turned to follow after her.

CHAPTER 33

Situated on the first floor of Pafos Police Headquarters, the Divisional Training Room enjoys a pleasant aspect over Kennedy Square and the Town Gardens. Bordered by cafes and restaurants, the square is a popular gathering place for locals and tourists alike. The former meet there to conduct business-in-the-sun over coffee and rolls, the latter to soak up the atmosphere of the Old Town's buzz and bustle. Across the road from the square, flower beds stocked with local flora line the station's western wall.

When not in use, the Training Room has long been a favoured hang out - literally - for staff to enjoy a smoke with their morning break. There, they lean from the tall windows to carry on shouted conversations with those they recognise across the square - or passing motorists. In days past, male officers would also enjoy rating, on a scale of one-to-ten, those female passers-by they chose to favour with their attentions - which meant most of them. Nowadays the tradition is less observed.

Some weeks before, the Force's latest attempts to enforce its No-Smoking Policy in all its buildings - thereby bringing it in line with the rest of the European Union - had led to what some said was a 'ridiculous' debate, when the 'window hangers' sought to argue that they were not actually smoking on the premises. Seeing the matter well down his order of priorities, Pippis had, perhaps wisely, skirted round the issue. He'd sensed his staff's strength of feeling over a policy some claimed impacted upon their much-needed work-breaks, while also threatening to undermine the station's well-established 'links with its community.' Eventually, under pressure from his HQ's Health-and-Safety-obsessed Personnel Department, Pippis had arranged a meeting with all concerned to resolve the matter.

It never took place.

The day the meeting was scheduled, Pippis authorised the Training Room to be converted into a Major Incident Room for the biggest criminal investigation in the Pafos Police's history. Those staff still with enough time on their hands to worry about the No Smoking Policy - in reality very few - were forced to seek solace elsewhere. The problem disappeared overnight.

Not that Pippis had given the matter a thought since the night of the explosion. Which explained why, despite his presence *and* that of the force's Assistant Chief Constable, Operations, several of the detectives, index clerks and typists were at that moment puffing away, oblivious of the crime they were committing.

When he first arrived - ostensibly to show his support and catch up on progress, but also under strict orders from the Island's Chief of Police to assess, personally, how Pippis was holding up - Assistant Chief Constable Akis Mavromatis nearly made the mistake of commenting on the fact the policy was being ignored. Worse in his eyes, the Divisional Commander himself appeared to be leading the revolt. Thankfully, both for common sense and Akis's credibility around the force - he still hoped to one day make Chief Constable - his ambitious policeman's instincts sensed danger before he opened his mouth. For the longer his briefing session wore on, the more he realised the level of commitment among the Investigation Team. He also became aware of how high was their determination to see justice done, for the sake of their Commander if nothing else - at which point the Assistant Chief congratulated himself on his wise decision to say nothing. Had he chosen otherwise he now realised, he might have found himself flat on his back, gazing up at the tall windows from one of the pretty beds of African Violets beneath, wondering if another bomb had gone off.

Nevertheless, Policy matters apart, the ACC had largely succeeded in his mission. After listening to Pippis's patient retelling of the history between the Englishman and the Russian whose presence on the island was now such Big News at Headquarters, and seeing for himself what the investigation had so far produced, he was in little doubt that Pippis's early assertions were correct. The bomb was, quite clearly, intended for the Englishman, Murray, rather than Pippis's family. Furthermore, despite the absence of direct evidence, Akis was also satisfied that the man behind the bombing was almost certainly Podruznig, as Pippis had been stating from the start. But whilst he could understand, completely, why Pippis had authorised the search of the Sea-Caves property that had attracted such strong complaint from the Russian Embassy at Nicosia, he could also see that all Pippis had was circumstantial evidence. If the Russians pressed their complaint, the Chief would be hard pushed to justify their actions. And whilst everyone wanted to give Pippis their backing - under the circumstances how could they do otherwise - it didn't mean he wouldn't be hung out to dry if such a course was needed. They had discussed the matter at length at Headquarters, and were all agreed. Regrettable though it may be, long-gone were the days when countries like Cyprus could get away with a shrug and a philosophical, 'It is the way we do things here.' Not in these days of Human Rights, Civil Litigation and the so-called 'European Courts of Justice.' Unfortunately, in terms of bringing the guilty party to book, things weren't looking so good.

A former detective himself, Akis knew that not all crimes are capable of being investigated to a conviction. And whilst levels of crime in Cyprus were rising and changing - less 'tourist' crime; more organised fraud, money laundering, forced prostitution and burglary, mainly perpetrated by immigrant groups - the island's Police Force was not well-equipped when it came to dealing with the likes of Podruznig. Nevertheless, as Akis listened to Pippis's account, he began to realise that, despite his expectation that he would quickly spot something vital that had been overlooked in the emotional heat of the moment, the opposite was the case.

As far as he could tell, the investigation had been everything it should have been - even allowing for the personal dimension that had led some at Headquarters to suggest that Pippis ought to be taken out of the equation. Furthermore, Pippis's Chief of Detectives was one of the most experienced investigators around. The way he had set up the enquiry and how, under Pippis's direction, he was managing things were, as far as the ACC could see, by the book.

The only trouble was, the evidence they were seeking was yet to come to light. And if he was reading what Pippis was telling him correctly, there was diminishing likelihood it would do so. Which made him wonder why, given that his own family were amongst the victims, Pippis didn't seem too concerned when he acknowledged the possibility that Podruznig and his henchmen might, ultimately, escape legal sanction. Eventually, made conscious of the passage of time by Pippis's constant checking of his wristwatch, Akis asked the question that was uppermost in his mind.

'So, what message would you like me to take back to the Chief?'

For long seconds Pippis continued to play with the elastic band he had taken to twiddling with during the latter part of the Assistant Chief's visit. When he eventually looked up to meet his senior's quizzical look head-on, Pippis's eyes were as cold and lifeless as those of the sea bass that grace the metal slabs on Pafos's ancient Fish Market. And Akis Mavromatis wasn't at all sure what to make of it when Pippis answered in a voice that was almost too calm, 'Tell him, Pippis has things in hand.'

After the man from Headquarters had gone, Pippis turned to Andri. The woman who was privy to most of his secrets was sitting to attention, already awaiting whatever order was to come her way. It was as if by being ready, she thought she might ease some of the burden weighing so heavily on the man she had enjoyed working for these past four years. Seeing the willing look on her face, Pippis was struck by an overwhelming feeling of guilt. For in that moment, he realised just how much he had always taken the woman who looked after his daily affairs for granted. Suddenly, he remembered the issue Gina had raised with him, an age ago now it seemed, concerning Andri's husband, Laslo. And right then Pippis decided he would, after all, speak to his opposite number at Limassol about the matter. Gina had been right. It *was* the least he could do. But other things needed his attention first.

'I'll be out the rest of the day Andri. Let me know if

anyone is looking for me.'

Andri nodded and smiled, proud to know he trusted her to cover for him on those occasions when matters outside of his Divisional Commander duties called on his time. She liked to think that she had just about perfected the fine arts of delay, avoidance and diversion. In fact it was one of the more challenging aspects of her job to rapidly come up with some new-yet-plausible reason why Pippis was not in a position to be reached/return the call/come to the phone, when one of the force's Chief Officers or another senior colleague was looking for him. She never sought to delve, which was why it took her so long to rule out another woman - and for which she gave thanks. She would never have been able to look Gina in the eye again. Instead, Andri was happy to accept that in a close-knit town like Pafos, a man in Pippis's position has many other calls on his time, apart from his official duties.

But that day, as Pippis left, having allowed the ACC enough time to be well clear of the station, Andri didn't need to wonder where he was going. She knew for a fact it would be the same place he had visited every afternoon for the past two weeks. And if anyone did suspect and tried to make anything of it by suggesting he was abusing his position by taking off for a few hours each day, she would be more than happy to put them right.

CHAPTER 34

Rising from the padded comfort of her wooden steamer, Marianna Podruznig left the other mothers to their chatter and went over to the drinks table the caterers had set up under the big yellow awning. As she waited for the young Asian girl who had come with the food to finish preparing her iced lime-juice, Sasha's voice, shrill with excitement, broke into her musings.

'Watch mama. I'm going to jump the furthest.'

Turning, Marianne just managed the requisite smile of encouragement in time before her daughter launched herself from the side of the pool. She landed with a splash and a scream amidst the shrieking gang of girls. At once, a fierce debate broke out over whether or not the birthday girl had broken the record set by Lizzy, the tallest, moments before.

In no hurry to rejoin the other women - she had noticed how their voices dropped the moment she was out of hearing - Marianna made a show of enjoying the children's pool-play. For the next few minutes she made sure her laughter at their antics was interspersed with appropriate words of warning about not straying into the deep end, or holding each other under the water too long, as would be expected from an attentive parent.

But less than half of Marianna's attention was on making sure the girls were having a good time. The greater part still dwelt on the matters she had been struggling to get her head round ever since that awful day when the fears she had been doing her best to suppress for so long, became reality.

What concerned her wasn't just the way the police arrived out of the blue to invade her home and rifle through even her most private and, she had thought, hidden possessions - including Sasha's toy-boxes and collection of stuffed animals. Rather, it was the effect the visit - coupled with whatever words the policeman-in-charge whispered in Valerik's ear before he left - had on her husband, that was causing her to lose sleep.

Marianna had long ago accepted that she was never going to be anything other than the trophy-wife she knew Valerik was looking for the day he asked her to marry him. She wasn't *that* stupid. But though she had been realistic enough to know she would always take second place to Valerik's business and other interests, she was prepared to settle for the crumbs Valerik tossed her way every now and then and which he knew were essential to maintaining the façade of a happy family. The crumbs included expensive gifts for her and Sasha, dining parties at the island's swankiest restaurants, private-arranged access to Lara Bay so Sasha could witness the turtles hatching. All designed to give an impression of a normal happy family, living the dream that comes with a place in the sun.

But since that day, even those meagre hand-outs had ceased. And the more she thought about it, the more the words of the Englishman who had surprised her that day in Scorpios returned to haunt her. *When his ship starts to sink and his back is to the wall, you and your daughter will simply be so much baggage, to be jettisoned along with the rest of the ballast.*

Okay, she wasn't sure if Valerik's back was to the wall

yet. He didn't give that impression and besides, he would never tell her if it was. But she had wondered long and hard about the 'Pafos Bomb Outrage' that had dominated both the news, *and* everyone's conversation the last couple of weeks. More and more, she found herself wondering if her husband may have been connected to it after all - despite all his denials.

During the house search, Valerik had made a point of keeping her away from the officers, telling her to stay in her room and making sure Uri was present to make sure she kept her mouth shut. Afterwards, he told her next to nothing other than it was simply part of the local authorities' ongoing campaign to harass Pontians such as himself. And she regarded it as acutely patronising when he simply told her, 'not to worry about it.' But she *had* worried. Especially as the bomb happened only days after the Englishman's dire warning that, 'things may soon start to get worse'.

And things definitely were worse. Valerik had barely spoken to her or Sasha these past two weeks. And though she had managed to get him to agree to her hosting a party for their daughter's seventh birthday - '*Whatever you like* ': then, when she pressed, *'I said I'll be there, if I'm around'* - he was yet to go beyond the brief wave he had managed across the pool when all their guests arrived. And he was *still* talking into his mobile.

Behind her dark glasses, and without turning from the children, Marianna shifted her attention to where he still paced, beneath the old Carob tree that grew at the top of the cliff. A short distance away, Uri was waiting for him to finish, so he could deliver whatever important news had brought him marching, swiftly, from the house, just as Valerik took yet another call. He was still waving his arms about, all the while keeping up the flow of dialogue that the wind kept snatching away before she could make any of it out.

Seeing him like this, so distracted he couldn't even find time to welcome guests to his own daughter's birthday party, made her wonder what the other women made of it all. Laughing at her stupidity for putting up with it she suspected. Then again, they were not so different. Married to men of uncertain financial heritage. Children attending the same, expensive Russian School in Mandria as Sasha. Little or no say in how they run their lives - or their children's.

Valerik had been like this the best part of the day. Several days, in fact. Making phone calls. Meeting with Uri and his men, or with others Uri's lot brought to the house - sometimes late into the night. Marianna had no idea what was going on and little hope of finding out, certainly not now that her minders seemed to be paying closer attention than ever to her movements - both in the house and during her trips out. Even when seeing to her toilet, she had found herself scanning the walls, fixtures and fittings, wondering how she would know if some surveillance device was, even at that moment, keeping tabs on her. More than ever before, she felt trapped and alone. Worse than that, even though right now it seemed illogical, she feared for her and her daughter's futures.

As she felt the dampness at the corners of her eyes, Marianna suddenly realised she was in danger of letting the true depths of her despair show through. She took a deep breath to rally herself. If she wasn't careful she would find herself on the end of yet another 'reminder' from Valerik of what to expect should she fail to live up to his increasingly bizarre expectations.

Calling to the girls one last time to, 'Be careful,' – to anyone watching it would be in keeping with her coming out of motherly birthday reflections - Marianna

Podruznig went to rejoin the other mothers. As she neared the group she listened for the sudden change of rhythm that would mark them moving to a different topic of conversation.

Across the other side of the pool, out of the women's hearing, the last thing on Valerik Podruznig's mind was his daughter's birthday party, though Uri's sour comments about how the Hell he was supposed to manage security when the place was full of screaming kids, were an occasional reminder.

Instead, he was juggling two important phone calls. One was from the scheming German who ran the airline he had bought into last year, and who was droning on about the impact on their operation of the latest EU pronouncements on CO_2 emissions. As if he cared about CO_2 emissions. Why couldn't he just run the fucking business for God's sake? That was what he paid him for wasn't it?

The other, more interesting call, was from the man he had spoken to twice before. The one with whom he seemed to share a common interest, though he was yet to work out exactly why. Whoever he was, it seemed to suit his purpose as much as Podruznig's to keep him informed about the matters they discussed. Even if on this occasion his information was as disappointingly sparse as that coming from Podruznig's other sources. Not that it mattered.

The week before, Podruznig had wasted days trying to find out what was going on, ensconced with Uri and his other advisors in the basement command bunker, running useless 'what-if' scenarios. Eventually, he had concluded that whatever further actions the police may or may not be planning, whether Murray was dead or alive - his instincts told him the latter - the only certainty lay in taking the initiative. It did no good hanging around, waiting to see what may happen next. He needed to seize control, to start directing things. Which was why he'd decided to bring in a specialist.

Putting the German on hold again, Podruznig gave the other caller his full attention. The conversation that followed was guarded, full of allusions and coded references to, 'unfortunate incidents'. You never know who may be listening in, even on an encrypted line.

As it drew to a close, Podruznig remembered the pitch he had thought of following their last contact. 'Thank you again my friend. But tell me, when will we meet? I feel I should reward you for your assistance, even if the outcome of our last collaboration was not quite what we expected.' After a moment he added, 'No, of course I do not hold you responsible. It was an unforeseeable development.' *Like Hell. If that bastard Shokov had any common sense he would never have set a device outside the Chief of Police's daughter's house. It was bound to trigger a reaction. He should have shown patience. Wait until Murray left. Follow him, then set the damn thing.* Too late now. But at least he won't be making those sort of mistakes again. He continued his phone call. 'And I do understand your position. I look forward to hearing from you.' As the man rang off, he went back to the German. 'Klaus? Something has come up. Call me back later.' Snapping his phone shut he turned to Uri, who was listening hard into his own mobile. 'Well?'

After a few moments Uri came off the phone. He pulled a face and shook his head. 'We cannot trace it. He is using some sort of relay through Amsterdam.'

Podruznig tutted. 'Such clever bastards these days.'

'We should have that copy of the FSB's new tracking software by the next time he calls. It should give us a better result.'

'I hope so Uri. I am becoming tired of these failures.'

Uri noted the implied criticism but said nothing. He could barely wait to get his hands on the man whose unlooked-for interventions were, like Murray's before him, undermining the stock he had spent years building up in Podruznig's service. It would be an occasion for celebration, Uri's own, special brand of celebration. He returned to the subject that had brought him out to speak to his boss just as the unidentified man had telephoned.

'Our visitor has arrived. He is downstairs.'

Podruznig's eyes lit up. 'Excellent. I shall speak with him at once. From what our friend says there may not be much time.' He turned to head inside.

'Er, Boss?'

He turned to Uri. 'What?'

The Siberian nodded to where the party was continuing across the other side of the pool. His wife was waving. The cake had just been brought out, the children gathering round.

'Shit.' He turned to Uri. 'Two minutes. Then call me with an urgent call from Moscow on the house phone.'

Then he set of across the garden, smiling broadly.

CHAPTER 35

As Murray and Gina entered the room, he was shocked by what he saw. And though he witnessed it for only seconds, it was enough to remind Murray that despite the coolness that had been to the fore during their most recent exchanges, he and Pippis Iridotu now shared a common purpose.

For as they walked in, the Divisional Commander for the Pafos Police division rose quickly from his kneeling position at the foot of the bed. Turned away to face the windows, a hand lifted, wiping across his eyes and face.

'Oh Papa,' Gina cried.

She rushed to him, wrapping her arms round him. As she did so, Murray could see her eyes brimming again. For several seconds, the big man did his best to hold out, but had no chance. For close to a minute, father and daughter hugged each other tight, as each tried to stop the tears they both knew they ought to control, for now at least.

Eventually they released each other, Gina to dig into her bag for tissues, Pippis to turn a stoney-but-blotchy-red face on Murray. As Murray took the hand offered, he made a point of holding the policeman's gaze seconds longer than would be normal. For all that the commander's public persona may be based upon a reputation for stoic dependability and coolness under pressure, there was no shame in showing emotion under such circumstances. Something else they now had in common.

And Murray was not surprised when Pippis dispensed with the niceties to simply observe, 'So. You are back.' Whatever the two now shared, and despite the undercurrents they may acknowledge were there, friendship was not part of it, not yet at any rate. For now, they were business partners, nothing more.

By way of response, Murray turned to the bandage-swathed figure on the bed. Gina was already there, taking her sister's remaining hand. Like last time, it was hard not to let his eyes be drawn to the most obvious evidence of the catastrophe that had befallen Pippis's second daughter - the flatness of the bed where her right leg should be. He couldn't help remembering the last time he'd seen her, skipping out to go dancing. Not for the first time, he had to steel himself against the guilt that swooped in.

'How is she?' he said, quietly.

Pippis sniffed. 'No change. She is still being ventilated. They say we must still wait.'

Gina bent to deliver a kiss to her sister's cheek - the only part of her face not covered by the breathing mask and bandages - before whispering something in her ear. Then, straightening, she crossed herself, and lifted the rosary in her hand to her lips.

For a few moments they all stood in silence, each with their thoughts. Having given up on religion before his teenage years, Murray was surprised to find himself as close to appealing to some higher authority as he could remember. There had been no such opportunity with Kathy and Jack.

As Gina said the silent prayers she had come to deliver, Murray took small satisfaction from knowing that at least the state-of-the-art care Ileana was receiving, gave her the best chance of recovery she and her family could hope for. He was also conscious of the irony that Ileana probably owed her life to the tensions that still exist between the Republic of Cyprus and the Turkish-occupied sector in the North. Though decades have passed since the Turks invaded, the potential for military conflict remains, at least as far as the politicians are concerned. Which is why conscription to military service is still compulsory for all Cypriot males when they turn eighteen. It also explains why maintaining an effective and efficient military capability is always a non-negotiable element during the international community's ongoing attempts to broker a settlement between the two sides. This in turn means that, unlike most other European countries where pressure on Government budgets is such that the once unthinkable is no longer so, Cyprus's two Military Hospitals – one just outside Nicosia, the other in the hills above Pafos – are maintained at an ever-present state of readiness. Constantly updated with the latest equipment and kept ticking over with a core of medical staff, they train and exercise regularly to always be ready to deal with victims of war – which of course includes bomb and shell injuries.

In reality, and apart from the ministrations of the hospital's staff for which Pippis thanked them every day, Ileana was alive due to two strokes of fortune. Murray suspected it would be months, maybe years, before it became clear whether that fortune was 'good' or 'bad'. That depended first on her continuing to live, then if she did, how she adjusted, mentally and physically, to the reduced body that was now hers.

The first piece of good fortune - if that is what it was - was the fact that evidence from the scene pointed to the bomber having learned their skills in the theatre of terrorism, rather than assassination. He, or she, had used a motion-gravity ignition-device rather than an electrical one. Had it been the latter, the bomb would have exploded as soon as Ileana turned the key in the ignition. She would have died immediately. But a motion-gravity device relies on a flow of liquid-mercury to complete the electrical circuit, which in turn sets off the detonator. Such devices require forward-thrust to set the mercury moving, which is why the carrying vehicle usually manages to travel a short distance before exploding – the time taken for the mercury to complete the circuit. From a terrorist's viewpoint - which often calls for maximum death and injury, preferably encompassing the general public - such devices are ideal as they give the target time to move from say a private garage, into a more public environment, before the device explodes. In Ileana's case, her second stroke of 'fortune' lay in the fact that after the engine eventually caught, she only moved Murray's jeep a distance of a few metres - enough to clear Gina's drive - before stopping and getting out. She was already walking away when the mercury completed its journey and the jeep exploded. Though less than ten metres from the source of the blast, the impact upon her young body was considerably reduced from what it would have been had she still been inside. And though the blast was enough to strip much of the flesh from her back and, particularly, her legs - flesh from the discarded right one now being used to help repair her left - the two hedges and three fences she was blown through actually absorbed much of the impact. As the paramedics who worked to extract her from the bushes she was found lying in at the scene were heard to observe, 'She may owe her life to the bougainvillea.'

A touch on his arm snapped Murray out of his reverie. He looked around. Next to him, Pippis turned his tired eyes from his daughters, to Murray. He nodded towards the door.

'Gina needs to be with her sister. Let us talk.'

Squashed into the plastic bucket-seats in the small waiting area opposite Ileana's room, Murray filled Pippis in on his Balkan expedition. Pippis listened with silent interest as Murray spoke of what he had learned, and of the discussions he had had in the shabby office overlooking the Odessa dockyard.

When Murray finished, Pippis stayed silent for several minutes. Murray didn't press. Having received Murray's account, and listened carefully to the ideas Murray had formed between fitful dozes on the fishing boat bringing him back to Cyprus - another branch of Pippis's large family - the policeman would want to be certain as to his next move. Once things started, there would be no turning back.

Eventually, Pippis placed his hands on his knees and levered himself out of his seat. Murray rose with him, so that both men stood in the middle of the room, looking at each other. Pippis took a deep breath, which had the effect of bringing him back to his full height. Since the explosion, he seemed to have shrunk in stature. Turning his head right, towards the east-facing window, he let his gaze roam over the distant Troodos foothills. Eventually he turned back to Murray, still awaiting his response. He put out a hand. Murray took it.

'Then let us do this thing,' Pippis said, 'And bring an end to it.'

CHAPTER 36

Though the basement 'briefing room' was air-conditioned, Podruznig was finding that just looking at the man who went by the name, 'Lamaar', made him feel several degrees warmer. The new arrival was wearing a heavy brown suit, jacket fastened in the middle, long-sleeved white shirt with button-down collar, and plain green tie. Despite the unseasonal attire, he bore no outward sign of being bothered by the heat he must have experienced on the way there. Cold-blooded, Podruznig thought.

Older than the Russian had expected – or was it just the way he was dressed? – the man was six feet tall, athletically built and, judging by the slow pirouette he made when Podruznig entered from behind, given to saving his energy for when he needed it most. The longish face was angular, pock-marked with what could have been the childhood ravages of chicken-pox, or something similar. The cheekbones were high and his short, blond hair stood straight in a flat buzz-cut. Standing stiff, and straight, Podruznig thought he looked like he was made of steel. On first making eye contact, the striking green eyes seemed to take in everything about Podruznig in a single, flashing glance, before reverting to a calmer, almost stupefied look. But he made no effort to speak and remained board-stiff until

Podruznig proffered a hand. He put out his own to let Podruznig grasp it briefly before withdrawing it, as if he feared some form of contamination. Given his occupation, the man's overall appearance and manner suggested someone who didn't care for the company of others, lacked social skills and was interested only in getting the job done. Podruznig felt reassured.

'Welcome,' Podruznig said in English, showing him to a sofa that stood against the wall. As with the handshake, Lamaar hesitated, looking at it as if it might be booby-trapped before sitting down. Every action seemed to require careful forethought.

'Thank you for coming at such short notice.' The man's head jerked upwards in acknowledgement. 'Uri has given you details of the targets?'

The dragon-eyes flicked left to Uri before returning, as if on springs. Another head-jerk.

Podruznig turned to Uri. Their eyes met in unspoken agreement. This was, The Man. He continued. 'Let me emphasise one thing. Circumstances dictate that the problems you have been made aware of, be resolved as soon as possible.'

The response was a slow, lizard-like blink followed by, 'I do what has to be done, when it can be done. I do not cut corners.' He spoke with an indeterminate European accent. Traces of French and Slavic. Some Italian maybe.

Podruznig weighed him through narrowed eyes. The man was a professional. He respected that. 'Also, you should know I do not countenance failure.'

The man's eye's flared, briefly, then died. 'If I did, I would not be here.'

Podruznig returned the man's stare, as if to stress that at the end of the day, he would be the one to judge. In reality he was impressed. Uri was good and had proved himself many times over. But this Lamaar.... He was of different stock altogether. If only he had more like him on his team. What he could achieve….

'Uri will show you where to stow your gear and provide you with what you need.' The man rose, the meeting over. 'Questions?'

He shook his head, stood there, waiting.

'This way,' Uri said. He led him down the corridor to the bunk-rooms.

As he watched Lamaar disappear - from the back he somehow seemed wider about the shoulders than he looked from the front - Podruznig allowed himself a smirk before turning to go back up stairs, already looking forward to returning to the interests he had been neglecting of late. His daughter's birthday party was not among them.

Ahead of Pippis's HRV, dust still hung over the unfinished road's gravel surface, marking another vehicle's recent passing. In the passenger seat, Murray leaned forward to peer up at the slopes ahead of them, looking for signs of the spotters he knew were there somewhere. Behind them, Gina lolled. She had found her visit to her sister's bedside exhausting, emotionally draining. She badly needed quality sleep.

'It will be my brother, I think,' Pippis said in answer to Murray's unspoken question. 'Vasillis said he was shutting shop early to get here.'

Murray remembered Pippis mentioning the butchery his brother's family ran on the Polis Road. He leaned forward, checking the wing-mirror on his side. Some way behind was another cloud.

'And that will probably be Chris,' Pippis said, looking in the mirror.

'Your son?'

'My uncle.'

'The one with the garage?'

'The one who runs The Neptune, at Coral Bay.'

Murray nodded. He knew of four Chris's so far - though he expected there were more. The other, a nephew, worked in the Municipal Offices next door to the Police Station.

'How many are coming?'

Pippis waved a hand in the air, conjuring numbers. 'Twenty maybe. Twenty-five? Perhaps thirty.'

Murray stared ahead. He had no idea how far Pippis's family extended or how many he had called to what would be the second gathering since the explosion. During the earlier meeting, when Murray first met most of them, the names had just kept coming; several Chrises and Georges; Kyriakos, Pambos, Nickolas, some Peters, Stavroses, Davids, and more. He gave up trying to remember them all once the numbers crept past twenty. And when Pippis spoke of 'thirty,' Murray guessed he was referring just to men-folk. If the women came along as well, and with the children - which was likely - God knows how many that would make.

As he calculated numbers, Murray resigned himself to experiencing the same mix of hostility and hospitality as last time, perhaps more of the former if it included some who were yet to meet him. He knew without having to be told that his presence amongst them, the part he was playing in the events now unfolding, presented many in the family with a dilemma. By nature, Cypriots are among the most welcoming and friendly of people. It was why he and Kathy had chosen to settle here. Before him, his own ex-service parents. But it could not be ignored that, however the facts were presented, what had befallen Ileana and Gina traced back to their involvement with him. He couldn't blame those who found it hard to comply with their elders' counsel not to hold Murray to account, but to welcome his commitment to helping them achieve the justice they were looking for - whatever form that may take. And while he appreciated the efforts of the likes of Pippis, who was doing his best to keep up the pretence that Murray was, for now at least, an honorary member of the family, he couldn't help but be aware of the simmering anger some were holding in check. He didn't like to dwell on how things might pan out when it was all over. Assuming he was still around to find out.

But thoughts of Pippis's family brought to mind another matter, one he was still mulling over. His Black Sea trip had been managed with the connivance of a family member who worked in the Immigration Department. It meant he'd been able to avoid channels that may have been being monitored. Looking out at the spectacular Troodos scenery flashing past, he said, 'You've got a big family, Superintendent. Do they all live in the Pafos district?'

He felt rather than saw the policeman's searching glance. Once you got to know him, the laid-back official the policeman most often presented was far from the true Pippis.

'Most, but not all. Cyprus is a small island. As you know, we have big families. Limassol, Larnaca, Nicosia. We are all over. This is good for holidays, yes?'

Murray ignored the joke. 'Nicosia eh?' He said it like he was impressed. It prompted another glance.

'What is it you need, Mr Murray?'

As the HRV bumped and rocked over a particularly uneven stretch of 'road', Murray hung on, then turned to give him a look that was deliberately nonchalant.

'Don't suppose any of them happen to have connections with anyone in your Intelligence set-up do they?'

Pippis eyes narrowed. After several moments, a wry, slight smile – the first in some time – showed.

CHAPTER 37

By six o'clock, most had arrived. As the women stoked the oil-drum barbeques and prepped the food that would follow, the children helped lay tables under the olive trees. The men retired inside.

The discussions were lengthy, and heated. Conducted mostly in English, for Murray's sake, he was conscious that whenever it turned Greek it probably meant they were talking about him. And it seemed he wasn't the only one surprised when at such times it was usually Pippis who stepped up to defend him. He saw the whispers that passed between some. As far as Murray could tell, Pippis seemed to be in the chair, though it was his white-haired father, Galios, who did the summing-up. The old man still owned Gina's taverna, as well as the farm and its adjoining winery. At ninety-three, Galios was still the proud possessor of a head of hair so thick Murray would have been glad to sport it in his twenties. When Galios spoke, everyone else fell silent. And on the rare occasions someone dissented from his view, they did so with utmost respect. And Galios always had the final word.

How much of it had been worked out before and they were simply going through the motions, Murray had no idea. But the debate when it raged and the different points of view offered up for consideration seemed genuine enough. But bit by bit, stage by stage, the different elements were agreed. And despite the obvious dangers involved, Murray sensed a mood of excited anticipation taking hold amongst those present. It reminded him of the briefings he had presided over during Priscilla. Several times he caught some of the older men nudging each other, exchanging knowing winks and sly smiles. 'Like the old EOKA days,' he heard one say, a reference to the island's struggle for independence from the British during the 1950s. Murray didn't like to point out that ruthless though the British Army was perceived to be during its period of occupation, it was nothing compared to what Podruznig and his henchmen were capable of. He just hoped he hadn't overlooked anything. Provided people played their part, it should all fall into place. But then he remembered what he hadn't dared share with Pippis, or anyone else for that matter. It was the one thing with the potential to threaten their chances of success, and the one he couldn't predict. He had no choice but to hope that when the time came, he would be able to deal with it without it affecting everything else. Nevertheless he harboured deep feelings of guilt about keeping Pippis in the dark.

As the discussion progressed and as if to underline Murray's dilemma, the biggest point of disagreement seemed to centre round not what needed to be done, but how far Pippis ought to be involved in it. If anything went wrong and he ended up implicated in a scandal, he stood to lose more than all of them. His brother, Vasillis, was particularly concerned.

'But there is no need for Pippis to get involved,' he argued. 'We all know what needs to be done.' For once, Vasillis saw a positive in Murray's involvement, even referring to him by name. 'As he said last time, the benefit of Mr Murray being here is that if anything goes wrong, it will be seen as his doing. Why put yourself at risk?'

Grim faced, Pippis made ready to answer, but old Galios held up a hand. The room fell silent. For the first time, the old man rose to his feet, using his stick for support.

'I have discussed this matter with my son at great length. It is true that some would love to drag the name of Iridotu through the dirt if Pippis is found to have acted outside the law. His career, his reputation, his personal life, would be destroyed, saying nothing of any other ill that, God forbid, may befall him.' Murmurs of agreement sounded round the room. 'For myself, I fear that risk greatly.' At this point he turned to face Murray. 'Yet we are talking about putting ourselves in the hands of this man, who I know some blame, for this whole situation.' There was another low murmur. 'He is not one of us. How do we know we can trust him?' He turned full circle in the centre of the room. Wherever he was going, Murray couldn't help but be impressed. The man was a born orator. 'But I also know that it is Pippis and Maria who have suffered the most in all of this.' Here his voice almost faltered. Gritting his teeth he kept going. 'Indeed, it is for that very reason we are here, to help them put right the wrong done against our little Ileana and, of course,' he held out a hand, 'Gina.' Heads turned in the direction he'd indicated. For the first time Murray realised she was standing just inside the door, her eyes riveted on her grandfather. 'But it is also true that the Englishman himself has been wronged.' Gina's gaze switched from her Grandfather to Murray. 'And he also seeks justice.' Galios paused to ponder, looking at the floor. 'These are complicated matters. Ileana is my granddaughter, and I know what I feel in my heart. But more important than that, Pippis is her father. I think therefore that none of us have the right to tell him what to do, or to question his judgement over this affair. He will do what he feels he must.' The nodding of heads seemed to signify general agreement.

'As for you Mr Murray,' Murray's head snapped up as he felt the harsh stares that turned in his direction. 'Pippis tells me he trusts you.' Murray glanced across to where the policeman sat, watching. 'Therefore I also trust you, and I say we welcome your help in this matter.' A commotion at the back of the room made everyone turn. A door banged shut. Murray wasn't sure who had left but he couldn't see young Kyriakos anywhere. Galios continued, unaffected. 'But let me say this. If, when it is over, I discover that you have failed to consider what is best for my family in all of this, then you will find the House of Iridotu as fierce an enemy as this Russian.' This time as the old man fell silent, there was no murmur of agreement, only an intense quiet.

Murray rose and came forward. He turned to address them all.

'I have said this to Pippis and now I say it to all of you. This situation has come about because the Russian wronged me, and my family. Now he has wronged you also. We are all therefore victims of his disregard for the law and his contempt for human life. But I make an oath to everyone here. Whatever happens, whether I find the justice Galios refers to or not, I swear I will not rest until Pippis and you all, have gained the satisfaction you also seek.'

There were several nods, one or two even began to clap but stopped as Pippis rose to come forward, stopping in front of Murray. To Murray's surprise he wrapped his arms round him in a brotherly embrace that was clearly meant as a signal to all. As more spontaneous applause broke around them, Murray, embarrassed, looked for Gina. But she had gone.

Afterwards, when it was all over, the necessary decisions taken, responsibilities clarified, Murray went looking for her. He found her along the goat track that led behind the farmhouse, sitting on a rock, smoking fiercely as she gazed up at the mountains at the head of the valley. Behind them, the dying rays of the sun that had already set over the rest of the island picked out the British Army's golf ball-style listening station on top of Mount Olympus, Cyprus's highest point, painting it orange-yellow.

As he approached, she stubbed out her cigarette, grinding it into the rock several times, making sure it was dead before flicking it away. In high summer, in the mountains, fire is an ever-present risk. She didn't turn to acknowledge his presence but went back to her mountain-gazing.

'Mind if I join you?'

She shuffled right a bit, but said nothing. He sat beside her. She had dispensed with her collar the day before and her hair was down, blowing softly in the late breeze coming off the mountains. It reminded him of how she'd looked that night in her garden, before Ileana arrived. He remembered the feelings she'd revived in him. But that was then.

'Tell me what you're thinking,' he said, though he had a fair idea.

As if she'd been waiting for the invitation, she turned on him. There was just enough light to make out the tracks on her cheeks.

'Why don't you go home Peter?' she said.

It wasn't the answer he'd been expecting. 'That's what I am trying to do.'

'I don't mean here. I mean England.'

He paused. 'I know what you meant. But my home is here now.'

She was breathing hard, trying to stay in control.

'People are going to get hurt.'

'What is going to happen will happen, whether I am part of it or not.'

'But if you were not here it would have to be done differently. Then my father would have to-.' She stopped, as if anticipating his reply.

'What? Use his authority? Bring Podruznig before the courts? You know that will not happen, Gina. That is why-.'

'That is why you are all acting like little boys? Running around playing war games? Why do men always think violence is the answer to everything?'

Murray was surprised by the bitterness in her voice. He had assumed she wanted to avenge her sister as much as anyone. He said so.

'I do,' she replied to his question. 'But not if it means my father putting himself at risk this way.'

Murray looked into her face but the light was fading rapidly now and he couldn't see what was there. He wanted to ask if it was just her father she was worried about, but was scared that whatever her real feelings, the heat of the moment might lead her to say it was.

'Your father knows what he is doing Gina.'

'But do you?'

He took his time answering, stung by the implication. Before the explosion she'd trusted in his abilities. 'I suppose you will just have to wait and see.'

She gave a mocking grunt. 'Wait and see? Is that the best reassurance you can come up with?'

Murray didn't answer, he couldn't. For a long time there was silence between them. The vehemence in her tone had surprised him, but he knew he had no right to expect anything else.

Suddenly and to his surprise, she collapsed in on herself, dropping her face into her hands, shoulders hunching. Caught unawares, he thought about putting his arms round her. But he left it too late. Taking a deep lungful of air she rallied, coming upright again. But her mind was clearly still in turmoil.

'So much has happened…. I do not know what it is all about any more…. Ileana is still alive. A house is just a house. Tell me Peter, why are you doing all this?' She turned to him, her hands feeling their way down his arm, searching for the reassurance she so obviously needed. He waited a while before speaking.

'I cannot speak for Ileana. That is for you and your family. But-.'

'Yes?'

He reached into his back pocket. 'Give me your lighter.' She passed it across.

It took a couple of attempts, but as the flame steadied, Gina leant in to see what he was cupping in his other hand. It was a leather billfold, a photograph showing in the plastic window.

The woman had long blond hair, and was stunningly attractive. It was the first time Gina had seen her, or the beautifully-handsome little boy pressing up against her to get into the shot. Despite the fact he was smiling broadly, Gina had no trouble seeing his father in him. They stayed that way, looking at the picture in the flickering flame, until the breeze caught it again and it died.

It was almost pitch dark now and Murray could barely make her out. He felt her hand settle, lightly, on his shoulder. It stayed there a while. Eventually, she rose to her feet. She didn't say anything, but as she walked away her hand brushed, gently, against his cheek.

As he listened to her pick her way carefully back along the now dark path to the house, Peter Murray sat on the rock, staring out into the pitch dark of the mountain night. As he did so, his thumb rubbed, back and forth across the billfold's plastic window.

CHAPTER 38

The two men came round the side of the house, heading towards the black SUV parked at the bottom of the steps. Nearly a mile away, former Marine Lance-Corporal William Desmond Hines, more commonly known as 'Moss-Side Billy', checked his watch - 07.15 - before rolling left so he could check them out through the binoculars propped on the stand. He was familiar with all of them now, bar one, and a quick glance was all he needed. Sure enough, they were the same pair Wazzer had reported the previous day at this time, and Ryan the day before that. The pattern seemed established.

Rolling back right to where he'd set the Cougar against a rock so he could get at it quickly if needed, he pressed and held the 'talk' button.

'Dress Circle to Bookings, over,' he said, softly.

Kishore's response was instantaneous, as always. 'Go Dress Circle.' .

'Zero seven-one five. Werewolf and Dracula out. Looks like the Sugar run, over.'

'Roger that. Confirming Werewolf and Dracula. Standing by for Goldilocks, over.'

Shaking his head at the ridiculousness of the exchange, Billy checked through the binoculars again but there was still no sign of the little girl's green blazer or her golden hair. *Having an extra bowl of Cheerios* he thought.

He still wasn't sure who had devised the horror/fairy-tale code; Wazzer probably. It was him who'd come up with Priscilla. Something to do with some film Billy had never heard of. About the desert and fucking transvestites of all things. But Billy had to admit, though they'd all taken the piss, it worked fine. By now they all knew the scary-looking one with the slicked-black widow's-peak as Dracula; the guy with the hairy arms, Werewolf, and the tall one with the lurching gait, Frankenstein. The giant Siberian with the scar, Podruznig's right-hand man? Igor of course. And so on. For a mapping and counting op. like this it did the job. Another day or so and they should have all they need. Now if he could just get some more on The Mummy - the one who kept himself well wrapped up whatever the temperature but who'd rarely been seen since he arrived a couple of days before - they could knock all this logging stuff on the head and concentrate on getting ready for-.

The sudden sound of stones, skittering somewhere away to his right made Billy tense. About to check behind, he jumped as a dark shape suddenly burst into view, cutting across his vision to lope and skip away down the hillside.

'Fuck me,' Billy breathed out, as the goat settled again several yards away. 'I'll have you for chops, you bastard.'

He laughed at himself, easing the tension that was suddenly in him, glad that none of the others had been on hand to witness his jumpy reaction. Nevertheless he was annoyed he hadn't heard the goat's approach sooner. It went to show how quiet some animals can be. It must have been grazing behind him when he moved. What with the lizards treating him like part of the landscape every time he went doggo, he would be happy to be the hell out of it. He was just glad there were fewer snakes than he'd expected, and those he'd seen were only the harmless, black ones. Lizards he could stand, but snakes gave him the shivers.

Movement far below brought him back to the present, and he bent to the binoculars again. But they'd shifted out of line. He must have banged them when the goat made him jump. Taking them from the stand, he brought them up and to bear on the front of the house. But in this new position, he had to lift his head, stretching so he could sight over the low wall of rocks camouflaging the hide.

As he took in the flash of green skipping down the steps, he felt something run across his neck. But after the goat thing he forced himself not to overreact to what he was sure was just some other member of the local fauna. Nevertheless he reached down to brush whatever it was away, keeping the binoculars trained.

Something wasn't right.

His fingers made contact with something slick and warm and he felt the first stirrings of panic as the image of a snake came to him; one of the green ones this time. He looked down.

At first he couldn't work out what he was seeing. Something dark, and liquid, pooling beneath him. Had he managed to split open his water bottle as well when he moved? But as he raised himself to let more light in he realised that whatever it was, it was a deep shade of red. Suddenly he gagged and for the first time felt the spurting against his hand. He brought it up. It was covered in blood.

What the fuck?

Instinctively his hand went to his throat, and his fumbling fingers disappeared into the gaping wound that was now there.

'JESUS.'

He jack-knifed round but even before he could bring the figure into focus, he recognised the onset of the sickening, light-headed feeling that follows quickly in cases of catastrophic arterial hemorrhaging. The sudden change of position opened the slit further and, as another spurt of his rapidly diminishing blood supply cascaded before his eyes, he finally got a good look at the man sitting calmly on the rocks behind, wiping his still-bloody blade on the gaiters of his combat trousers.

The cold green eyes of The Mummy stared back at former Marine Lance-Corporal William Desmond Hines, watching, dispassionately, as the dying Mancunian's body began to convulse in the pre-death spasms that are characteristic of a ruptured carotid. And for all the interest in the dying man's struggles that was reflected in the killer's face, he could have been watching paint dry.

In that instant Billy knew who, and more importantly what, The Mummy was. He hadn't heard a fucking *thing* for Chrissake. Hadn't even *realised* it was his throat being slit. So quick. So deadly.

Even as consciousness began to drain away, Billy's training kicked in. He had to warn the others. But, trying to reach for the Cougar, he could barely get his arm off the ground, and he knew. It was already too late.

The last things Moss Side Billy saw were the killer's striking green eyes staring at him, waiting for him to stop moving, so he could move on to whoever was next. And as Billy's own eyes flickered shut for the final time, the last thing he heard was Kishore's tinny voice saying, 'Bookings to Dress Circle. Any sign of Goldilocks yet, over?'

CHAPTER 39

It was getting on for two years since Murray had last visited the picturesque village of Lofou in the hills above Limassol. In that time it had changed little - apart from the fact that Valuka's builders were now working on a whole new set of properties.

Valuka Erigos was the enterprising owner of the Lofou Tavern. Ten years earlier he had returned to his home with a first-class honours degree in Business Studies from Sheffield University. Since then he had transformed the village.

Following what many Southern-Cyprus dwelling, 'Greek' Cypriots, still refer to as the, 'Turkish Invasion' in nineteen-seventy-four - and which led to the island's present North/South-Turkish/Greek divide - most of Lofou's mainly Turkish villagers were forced out. Over the years the homes they abandoned fell into ruin. Lofou's fortunes fell yet further when many of the families left behind decided there was easier money to be made down on the coast, where the tourists were, than up here, picking almonds and growing olives. But the cycle of decline was interrupted by Valuka's return. He spotted the potential at once.

Quietly, so as keep his strategy hidden as long as possible, Valuka started buying up the old properties and converting them into smart weekend and holiday apartments. These he rented out to those tourists who were looking for a more, 'Authentic Cyprus Holiday Experience', as well as the houses' original owners. By then they had realised - too late - that rather than the bustle of the coastal resorts, somewhere quiet in the hills was just what they needed to recharge their batteries.

By the time of Murray's first visit, during Priscilla, Valuka owned more than half the village and was adding to his investment by providing his guests with food and drink at any of the three eating-houses he also ran - not forgetting the coffee and gift shop. As a place where the Priscilla team could regroup off-base and away from prying eyes, Lofou was ideal, having all the key pre-requisites; privacy, easy access and, most of all, a plentiful supply of good food and Keo.

After checking with Valuka - 'Number 205,' he told him after Murray prised himself from his welcoming embrace - Murray wound his way through the narrow cobbled streets until he found the stout wooden gates which, together with high stone walls, ensured each block of apartments benefited from its own private courtyard.

He rang the bell. After a short wait the gate opened a few inches. A face peered out. He recognised it at once.

'*Jesus-fucking-Christ*,' the Irishman said.

Murray knew something was badly wrong as soon as the gates closed behind him. The way they were all sat around, heads down, told him. The last time he'd seen them like this was after the fire-fight where they lost 'Sailor', their local Saudi guide. A snap head-count came up with two less than he'd expected. But he let them get the backslapping and declarations of the, 'we-all-thought-you-were-dead' variety out of the way before asking. The sombre mood returned at once, and it fell to

Red to break the news.

'Someone's aced Billy.'

Murray felt the same awful gut-wrench he'd experienced twice in his life, the last being when he heard Ileana trying to start his Jeep. He waited while the first wave passed.

'How?'

Red told him what they either knew or had pieced together. Wazzer and Ryan had found Billy's body when they went to see why he wasn't answering his radio. 'It must be someone pretty special to take Billy like that,' Red said.

Murray nodded. Not the big Siberian with the scar then. He was a gun-or-bare-hands type. But he decided to leave the question of why they were out there when they thought he was dead to another time. Besides, he could guess.

'This was pinned to him.'

Red passed across the bloodied piece of paper. Written in a neat, precise hand, the message read, "ONE AND COUNTING."

Murray read it several times, letting the implications behind the words settle. 'Any ideas?' he said.

Red's hesitation told Murray he wasn't sure. 'A handy-looking guy arrived a couple of days ago. We've only clocked him twice since. But from what we saw he had all the right credentials.'

'A specialist?'

'Could be.'

Murray took a deep breath. Someone like that could ruin all his plans.

'Fuck.'

'That's what we thought,' someone said.

Murray looked round to where Bear was sitting on a planter made out of an upturned barrel, cut in half and painted white. The question in the former pugilist's face was, *What you going to do about it?*

For a while, over Keo and whiskey, they lamented their loss. Apart from anything else, Billy was the one they'd all relied on for new jokes. Eventually, as in the old days, Murray moved to bring them round.

'We all know the drill. When something like this happens, we do a check.'

He looked into each of the faces. They all returned his gaze steadily. No comments, no dissenters. He wasn't surprised. They weren't the sort who would be put off by a little thing called death. Whatever they'd originally come for, it was now deeply personal.

Murray looked for the sheaf of papers he'd come with, having picked them up off Klerides after running the builder all round Pafos to make sure he wasn't being tailed. They were on the chair where he'd dropped them on hearing about Billy. Clearing the empty cans and bottles off the table, he spread them out. As the others recognised them for what they were, they crowded round. Murray didn't have to wait for their attention.

'Let me bring you up to date.'

CHAPTER 40

Coming away from the hospital - still no change - Pippis headed for the Traffic Division Headquarters out at Yiroskipou. Earlier that day, he'd checked the duty-roster to confirm the officers he was to meet with were working, though he hadn't rung to warn of his coming. If anything went wrong and Internal Investigations got involved, he would rather there were no footprints. As he drove, Pippis juggled in his mind the several problems that were increasingly eating up his time. Chief among them by a long way of course, was Ileana.

Pippis was more than grateful for everything the military medics were doing for his daughter. They had also worked hard at reassuring Maria and himself there was every chance that when she woke, and in time, she would be the same bright, young girl they had raised - once she adjusted to the fact of her missing limbs.

But Pippis knew enough about doctors not to set too much store by words that, on the face of it, sounded heartening, but actually reflected a worrying uncertainty. He had picked up the way the consultant just managed to stop himself saying, 'if' rather than, 'when', when he talked of Ileana waking up. And Pippis knew that in medical speak, 'No reason we know of why...' – in this case why Ileana should not recover without brain damage – amounted to little more than, 'We are in God's hands.' Which was why Maria was spending so much time at Agios Georgiou - the Church of St George – on the hill above where they lived. And though it had been many years since Pippis had invested any real meaning in his Sunday prayers, he was doing so now.

And when he wasn't thinking of his beautiful young daughter - swathed in bandages and plaster, breathing through a mask, fed nourishment and being medicated via an array of needles and tubes - there was the other matter. The one that right now, was keeping him going through the day. At least it held out the prospect of some form of closure – which was more than could be said of the investigation he was running. He meant no slur on the hard-working officers under his command, but his suspicion was that the enquiry had as much chance of success, as him becoming the Island's next Chief of Police - despite what his Deputy Chief Constable kept saying during his regular 'Performance Reviews.'

But while the twin shadows of Ileana and the 'family affair' as it was now being referred to, dominated his waking hours, his day-to-day responsibilities still demanded attention, despite Andri's best efforts to field them. In particular he needed to review the draft Operational Order for the forthcoming Aphrodite Festival the following weekend.

The annual Opera Gala performed in front of Pafos's famous Medieval Fort on the Harbour – this year it was to be Verdi's 'La Traviata' – is the premier social event of the Island's summer season. Attracting as it does locals and tourists in large numbers, the festival is renowned as the event no member of Cyprus's social or political elite can afford to miss. It is also the biggest in the Pafos Police calendar, as well as the one the Chief Constable himself likes most to be seen at. For that reason if no other, Pippis never failed to give the forty-odd-page order produced by his Events Planning Team his closest attention before signing it off. This year, he had special reasons for checking that the fine detail met with his approval.

Professional duties apart, Pippis also had to keep reminding himself that he was still a father and husband. And that in between everything, he needed to make time for Gina, Chris and Maria - especially Maria. The night before, she had fallen as deep as he had seen her since the explosion - the twin effects of exhaustion and worry. Day by day, the hours she was spending at her daughter's bedside, speaking words of hope and encouragement that were yet to elicit any reply, were taking their toll.

All this whirled through Pippis's head as he pulled up at the traffic lights at the junction of Makarios and Hemfer Avenues, focusing on the right turn he would be making fifty metres through the junction. Such was his preoccupation, he didn't think twice when a movement in his mirror drew his eye. Behind, a battered pick-up truck seemed to have a problem, the driver having got out to raise the bonnet to make some adjustment to the engine. Had Pippis been paying more attention, he may have read something into the way the man yelped and jumped as his hand made contact with something hot, causing him to drop whatever tool he was holding. Bending to retrieve it from under the spare-wheel mounting on the back of Pippis's car, he was momentarily lost to Pippis's sight - which was why Pippis remained oblivious when the man reached under the back bumper and pressed a small, black box to the underside of the vehicle's chassis. Pausing only to make sure the magnetised case was holding secure, he stood up, finished attending to his engine, slammed shut the bonnet and returned to his vehicle.

By the time the pick-up moved off again, Pippis was already through the junction, getting ready for his right turn, thoughts already on what he would be saying to the men he was about to 'bump' into.

CHAPTER 41

On the hills overlooking Episkopi Bay, to the west of Limassol and close to the Episkopi garrison, the ruins of the ancient city-kingdom of Kourion provide a fascinating glimpse of Cyprus's complex history. Founded by the Greeks and added to over the ages by Venetians, Arabs and Romans, the World Heritage site comprises archaeological treasures that bear comparison, on a smaller scale, with sites in Rome or Pompeii.

The most spectacular of Kourion's attractions is the carefully-restored Greco-Roman Theatre, with its stunning, sea-view backdrop. Also used in ancient times for occasional gladiatorial contests, it is now a popular summer venue for open air musical and theatrical productions. So beautiful is the panorama from the theatre's steeply-raked steps, visitors often linger far longer than intended to wallow in the richness of their surroundings.

On the face of it, Murray was doing exactly that. In reality he was waiting. And though he had been sitting there over thirty minutes, not once had he checked the time, nor turned to scrutinise the tourists and snappers milling around him. His gaze was fixed on the sea's far horizon. His thoughts however, dwelt a little nearer.

At the base of the cliff upon which the theatre stands, lies Episkopi Beach. Popular with base personnel as well as tourists, it boasts a line of three, fine sea-food restaurants. They all serve excellent fish and chips, though regulars always argue that 'theirs' is the best. The middle of the three, the 'Blue-Chris' was Murray's and Kathy's particular favourite. And it was while Kathy was driving back to the base one day having lunched there, Jack dozing in the seat next to her, that she met the battered, old, fruit farm truck with the steering mechanism that was about to fail, disastrously, coming towards her.

Murray had never been back there since the accident. But having arrived early for his rendezvous and taken his spot on the steps, he had wondered, several times, if he would pluck up the courage to just wander over and gaze down on the place that had been in their, 'top three' of the island's many attractions. He was doing so again when a voice said, 'Mr Murray?'

He turned. A couple of metres to his left, on the tier above his, a man stood looking out over the sea, just as Murray had been doing. Sporting a tangle of curly black hair, he looked to be in his thirties, though the dark glasses made it difficult to tell. His clothes - white-linen shirt open to the navel and khaki cut-offs - contrasted with his dark complexion. And the rubber flip-flops were the sort Murray couldn't stand. The ones with the annoying strap that sits between the big toe and its neighbour. Murray recognised the look. He saw it often around the smarter hotels in high summer. It was, he thought, carefully calculated to achieve the right balance between laid-back beach-bum, and smart-but-casual Adonis. The Shirley Valentines loved it. That said, given their choice of meeting place, it was less obtrusive than the ubiquitous cream suit favoured by most Arab

Government Officials these days.

'Thanks for coming,' Murray said.

Already satisfied, it seemed, that he was talking to the right man, the newcomer stepped down to Murray's level. To a casual onlooker they would simply be strangers sharing the view of the sun dancing on the sea, perhaps exchanging suitably impressed comments on the surroundings. And as the man spoke he turned, slowly, as if noting the Theatre's architectural features.

'Your friends, the Iridotus, know the right people, it seems.'

'So it appears, though right now I'm not sure they count me as, 'friend.'

Turning back, the man stood with his hands splayed on hips, looking towards the sea again. After waiting long enough to dispel any impression they might be together he said, 'Why am I here Mr Murray?'

Murray's face hardened. The fact he'd come at all meant he knew damn well why. 'You've looked me up. You tell me.'

The man smiled, wryly. 'Hmmm… you do have an interesting history.'

His English was excellent, even down to the accent. Oxford, or Cambridge, Murray guessed. But he had neither time nor patience to play run-around. 'So how much do you know?'

'As much as we need to,' the man said

'I suppose that includes Operation Priscilla?'

Behind the glasses, the thick eyebrows arched upwards. 'Ahh, Yes. *Priscilla*. Such a silly code-name. Whoever dreamed that up?' He didn't wait for an answer but continued. 'A bit of a cock-up by the standards of your country I would say. But it seemed to get there in the end.'

'Apart from one or two… unresolved issues.'

'Such as?'

Murray shot him a glance. 'Are we going to fuck around all afternoon? 'Cos if we are, I'll need a drink.' It had the desired effect. The man's posture changed. He turned to face Murray, directly.

'I take it you are referring to certain property in which my Government may have an interest?'

Murray met the man's enquiring stare. 'I need to know if that interest is ongoing?'

Even behind the glasses, Murray saw the eyes narrow. 'It could be.'

From behind, Murray heard the sound of children's laughter, approaching. 'In that case, let's find somewhere quieter where you can buy me a beer while I tell you a tale of woe.'

Turning, he began to mount the steps but had to dodge aside to avoid the young boy who came skipping down, his older sister in pursuit. Following them, but well-behind, their mother shouted down to them, 'BE CAREFUL. You nearly knocked that poor man over.'

As Murray made his way back towards the small kiosk near the entrance that sold beers as well as ice cream, the Arab official loitered behind, exchanging friendly smiles and jokes with the children and, when she arrived, their young and attractive blond mother. Then, spotting a man who looked like the children's father approaching down the tiers, he made his goodbyes before flashing the young mother a practised smile, and following in Murray's steps. As he reached the theatre's top-most tier, he spied the man he'd been dragged off a delicate operation in France two days before to come and meet, already at the kiosk and reaching for his billfold. Lifting a hand to his ear as if to scratch it, the man spoke to those listening.

'It sounds like they may have been right for once. Make the call, then put everyone on standby.'

As he started his engine, Pippis looked up. The four officers - three men, one woman - were at the upper-floor window, watching his departure. He wondered what they might now be saying to each other, what they would be thinking, but then he stopped. Whatever it was, he was certain they would not be regretting their decision, quite the opposite in fact. They were all good, experienced officers. They had grasped what he was putting to them more quickly than even he had expected. And he'd sensed no doubt or hesitation when, after checking with each other, they turned back to him and, in unison, nodded their affirmation. Driving out the gate, he let out a long breath. One more cog in place.

He had never really doubted their cooperation, not after the way they'd performed during the previous summer's operation against the gang of Bulgarian Sex-Traffickers who thought Pafos was just the place to expand their operation. 'Nip it in the bud. Do whatever it takes,' was the command that had come from on high. The Chief himself relayed it to Pippis in a way that left no doubt over the depth of the Government's concerns. If such things were allowed to take hold, the effect on the Island's tourist industry could be calamitous.

And together, Pippis and his small-but-hand-picked 'Task force' had nipped it, albeit not all their methods were reflected in the reports that went back to Police HQ, along with the requisite deportation dossiers. On that occasion, the four he had just spent an hour talking to weren't particularly bothered about not sticking entirely to laid down 'procedures', so long as the outcome was in their homeland's best interests, which Pippis assured them it was.

The late afternoon traffic was building as Pippis turned his HRV out through the station's gates, this time heading for the motorway and the hour-long journey that would take him back to the place that was beginning to resemble an Operations Control Centre – which in effect is what it was. Putting his foot down, he turned his thoughts to what he would tell those waiting, and wondering how Murray had got on.

But even had he not been so distracted, there was nothing about the pick-up, several cars back and falling even further behind as Pippis gathered speed, that would have drawn his attention. The same applied to its steely-eyed driver, who kept glancing at the GPS monitor affixed to his dashboard. And Pippis could not have foreseen the further anguish it was set to bring to him and his family.

CHAPTER 42

From his position behind the bar where he was pretending to clean the already immaculate counter-tops, Andreas monitored the Russian woman's progress as she downed her first cappuccino of the morning. Her initial visit upstairs always followed soon after, and he needed to judge his timing. Sure enough, as her minder returned from his scouting mission, she rose to come forward. Andreas left it until she was about to pass the bar before stepping out with the basket of toiletries, holding them in front in a way he'd calculated would draw her gaze. The look on his face was suitably apologetic, embarrassed even.

'I am sorry Madam. Melitza was supposed to take these up earlier. I will do it now.'

Her polite smile said she wasn't above looking after herself. 'Give them to me. I will take them.'

'Are you sure? That is very kind.' He handed her the basket. About to turn away, he stopped. 'By the way, I managed to get some more of that Indian Coconut Soap you seem to like.' He pointed at the colourfully-wrapped package in the middle of the basket.

Behind her, Ivan loitered but paid no heed. The last thing he was interested in was toiletries. Even had he been, he would not have seen the puzzled look on his charge's face and which greeted Andreas's words.

Marianna Podruznig glanced at the basket's contents then back up at Andreas, just in time to catch the strange look he gave her before he turned back to his polishing. Clutching the basket, she climbed the stairs.

In the small cloakroom she made sure the door was locked, firmly, before taking out the item Andreas had indicated. The sticker-seal looked like it had been disturbed. She unwrapped it. It contained nothing but what it was supposed to - soap. For a moment she thought she must have misunderstood. But about to confine the wrapper to the litter bin, she glimpsed the markings on its inside. Unfurling the waxy paper, she read the message.

'Take what Andreas offers. On the night, be ready. P.'

The wave of panic that washed over her was so dizzying she had to lean on the sink until it passed. Then she re-read the note, breathing deep as she digested both the words themselves and their unstated, but portentous meaning. It was going to happen. Just like he had said it would. She didn't know whether to be fearful, excited, hopeful, or all three. Fear was dominant.

She flushed the wrapper down the toilet then saw to her ablutions. Her actions quickened as the moments passed, as though she feared someone might suddenly burst in and discover her duplicity. Settling herself as best she could, she checked herself one last time in the mirror before returning downstairs.

As she re-entered the bar and made her way back to her table, no one could have guessed the bombshell that had just landed in her lap, or the feverish activity now taking place beneath the calm exterior. Accepting Ria's offer of another cappuccino with a nod and a smile, she lit a cigarette and drew on it deeply.

It was five minute's later, when Andreas brought their refills that the promised offer arrived. It was in the form of an envelope. He held it out to her.

'I hope you do not mind, Mrs Podruznig.' She glanced up at him, surprised. She hadn't even realised he knew her name. 'But I remember you once mentioned how you enjoy the Opera.'

As Andreas held the envelope open to display its contents - two gaily-decorated tickets for the Aphrodite Festival Performance that coming Saturday night - she ignored the look of astonishment on Ria's face. Seated at the next table, Ivan rose and came forward to see what was going on. Andreas continued.

'A couple of German customers were planning on going, but one of them took ill and they have flown home. They asked me to pass on their tickets to some of my regulars. I wondered if perhaps you and your daughter would like to accept these two?' He nodded towards Sasha, seated at the adjacent table with Anna, both engrossed in their mobiles.

'What is this?' Ivan's spade of a hand reached out to take the envelope. Delving inside, he pulled out the tickets, turning them, suspiciously, in his fingers.

Andreas made to explain again. 'I was just saying to Madam. Some of my German customers-'

'I heard what you said.' He made to hand the envelope back to Andreas. 'She cannot accept gifts. She would not be able to go anyway.'

Sensing her opportunity about to be snuffed out, Marianna Podruznig took a deep breath but still managed to make it sound casual. 'Do not be so rude, Ivan.' She reached up and plucked the envelope from his grasp. 'We should not refuse such a generous offer.' Glancing at Ria, she saw the look on her friend's face.

Opera? You?

Ivan began to dig his heels in. 'My orders are that-'

'I know what your orders are, Ivan, but leave it to me.

I will explain to Mr Podruznig. He will understand.'

Not convinced, but not particularly interested either in arguing the toss over such a trivial matter – *let the boss decide* – Ivan shrugged his hefty shoulders before wandering back to his table, As he went, she heard him mutter something about, 'Opera-shit.'

Marianna looked up at Andreas. There was something in the benevolent-but-sad way he was regarding her that almost made her want to burst into tears right there. She swallowed hard. 'This is very kind of you. I will ask my husband. If we are able to go I am sure we will enjoy it greatly.' With a final smile, Andreas turned away and headed back to the bar.

When he was gone, Ria checked over her shoulder – the men were laughing over some comment of Ivan's - before leaning into her friend, conspiratorially. 'Since when have you been interested in Opera?'

Marianna looked up from stuffing the already-precious documents into her bag; God forbid she should lose them. 'What do you mean? I have always liked Opera. You know that.' The quick glance at her minders and the inflection in her voice was enough to tell Ria she was supposed to play along. They often used code when speaking of matters she did not wish her minders – and husband - to know of.

Ria's eyes narrowed as she drew on her cigarette and she gave a sly smile. 'Oh yes, I forgot. And of course, it is 'La Traviata.' Marianna let her face show her gratitude. But after another quick check behind, Ria lowered her voice. 'But I expect to hear what you are up to soon.'

Marianna nodded as she picked up her coffee-cup. 'Don't worry Ria, you will.'

For the rest of their morning's stay at Scorpios, as Ria spoke of her mother's illness, shopping and the dinner party she was to host that weekend, it was all Marianna could do to appear interested. Almost all her attention was on trying to work out how she would set about talking Valerik into letting her and Sasha go to the Opera.

CHAPTER 43

Starting with his shoulders, then moving down the rest of his body, the man called Lamaar flexed his muscle-groups the way he always did when normal movement wasn't possible. And though the process would have been barely visible to even someone close, the sequence of tensing, flexing and relaxing was enough to ensure that, should the need arise, his body would respond the way it was supposed to - and at once, despite having lain still for over an hour.

From his hide amidst a clump of low-growing junipers, Lamaar followed the comings and goings at the farmhouse below through the Atom Red-Star Russian-Military binoculars that were an especially-prized part of his kit. They were a trophy from a necessarily-brief contact with a Russian General in the Steppes some years before. And though there was no question anyone had witnessed his arriving at his chosen hiding place – once again, his Afghan-Mountain training had come in useful – he was glad he had approached over the top from the adjoining valley, rather than the route indicated on the GPS. Had he done, he was sure he would have been spotted, though he was yet to pick out the watcher he was certain had to be lurking somewhere in the surrounding hills.

That the Farmhouse was central to whatever the

policeman was planning, Lamaar was also now certain. The several vehicles and the number of people milling around – so far he had counted more than a dozen – were too many for a location as isolated as this. And given everything that had happened, Lamaar doubted they were organising some family social event. But the clincher was the fact that since he'd arrived to take up station overlooking the back of the house and the road leading up from his right, he hadn't stopped seeing weapons. As well as the twin-barrelled shotguns, carried by the two young men who came out of the house to enjoy a smoke in the sun soon after he settled, there were several rifles stacked, teepee-style at the side. Half an hour earlier, an old man had come out to attend to the generator at the back. Even he had a pistol tucked in his waistband. Lamaar was yet to see the policeman, though his HRV was parked up out front, still sending out the signal that had led Lamaar to the valley. Presumably he was inside.

Turning his binoculars to the hillside opposite, he made another scan, searching for the evidence that would indicate where the spotter was. When he'd surveyed the valley earlier, he had concluded that the slope opposite, overlooking the front of the farm, was the most obvious place. The way the road weaved up from the south, it gave the best vantage point over any approach from that direction. Another reason to congratulate himself on his decision to choose another route in.

As his sweep reached the rocky outcrop he had picked out earlier, he stopped, inspecting it in more detail this time. Apart from being a natural look-out spot, the low branches of the pine trees behind showed signs of disturbance. And while he couldn't rule out mouflon – he'd spotted several of the mountain sheep ranging the higher slopes around – instinct told him it more likely marked the passing of something taller.

For several minutes he focused on the area around the outcrop. But much of it was screened from view by the boulders that made it such a natural shelter. Seeing no further signs he was about to move on when suddenly, from behind a rock right in the middle of his field of vision, a man rose to his feet. He must have been lying there all this time not moving, like Lamaar himself. But unlike Lamaar, he hadn't been trained or disciplined to know that if your job is to watch, that is all you do. Youngish, wearing a green cap and a bright blue bandana that protected his neck from the afternoon sun, the man stood looking down at the farmhouse. He was holding a mobile phone to his ear. He waved.

Lamaar swung the binoculars down and left, focusing in on the house. At first he couldn't see anyone. But then a woman came into view, returning the young man's waves as she spoke into her mobile. She was heading away from the house, towards the path that led across the valley and over the stream, from where it rose sharply until it disappeared into the trees.

Lamaar knew it was her as soon as she came into view. The age was right and the way she walked, stiffly, told him as much. She held a basket over her right arm that was covered in a colourful check-cloth. Judging by the spotter's enthusiasm and her cheery response, Lamaar guessed it contained items the spotter opposite would find most welcome after a long, hot day on the hillside.

As she followed the path away from the house and down the far slope, she was lost from his view. But a few minutes later she reappeared, climbing the slopes beyond the stream. As he watched her making her way along the path, leaning forward now to counter the steepening gradient, Lamaar took in everything about her. The rounded contours of her body under the white top and loose skirt. The occasional flashes of firm, toned leg whenever she lifted the skirt to step up or over some hazard. The thick, shiny-dark hair that was caught in a ponytail and held in place by a wooden clasp. And on those occasions she turned his way, he noted the shape of her breasts under her top, imagining what they would feel like in his rough hands, mentally weighing them, judging their size. As he watched, the tip of his tongue emerged to run around the thin lips, like a gastronome savouring a meal placed in front of him by his favourite headwaiter. He adjusted his position to re-distribute his weight, relieving the sudden pressure that had come, unbidden, below his stomach.

The binoculars Lamaar was so proud of stayed on her until she became lost from view amongst the trees. Somewhere there, the path would turn to the right, following the contour of the hillside to where it emerged behind the outcrop opposite. Switching his gaze back, Lamaar saw that the man was no longer to be seen. Settled back down again behind the rocks he assumed, his attention re-focused on the approach up through the valley while he awaited her arrival. Lamaar snorted his disdain. The thought had probably never occurred to them that their mountain hideaway might be susceptible to being breached from above. *Amateurs!*

Packing away the binoculars, he made ready to vacate the place he had chosen as his OP the past hour, checking the sun, gauging distances. He would have to move fast if he was to secure his objective. But her progress would be slow - hampered by her injuries and her cargo - and she had some distance to cover before she reached her goal.

As he set off, making sure to stay low and behind

what cover was available, the thought of what the next couple of hours would bring brought a smile to Lamaar's face. He was after all, a professional. And he enjoyed his work.

Westgate ended the call, put his mobile away, and returned to his coffee. It had cooled during his lengthy discussion and he downed it quickly. Hailing the waiter, he ordered another, before settling himself in the comfortable wicker armchair. Around the corner from the sea front, the harbour area Costa Coffee shop's elevated position is ideal for people-watching. Along the pavement outside, throngs of holidaymakers from the hotels lining Poseidonos Avenue were heading for the harbour area's bustling centre, with its multitude of shops, bars, and restaurants. But Westgate wasn't interested in people watching. He was reflecting on his conversation.

The man had sounded even angrier than normal. Understandable, given the delay. But Westgate was pretty sure it was only for effect. He would calm once he thought things through. After all, it wasn't Westgate's fault that information was so sparse. None of them had factored in the complications over the Russian's involvement. And given they had waited so long for things to start moving again – Murray's gang had stuck it out far longer than they had ever imagined - it made no sense to risk drawing attention to their interest by running around asking questions. Besides, the contact he had managed to make recently meant his chances of picking up on anything significant were much improved - as he'd discovered when he learned of what had happened in the hills overlooking the house. He hadn't pushed for details, it wouldn't have been professional. But when he referred to the house being watched and the comment came back about there now being one less to worry about, the inference was clear.

That Murray's gang were still interested in the house raised two possibilities. The first was that Murray was still alive and following through with his plan. The second, that he *was* dead and the others were doing so on his behalf. Either way, it didn't matter. Given the way things were shaping up, the eventual outcome would, he was sure, be the same. What he needed to focus on, was making sure that when the pieces stopped falling and the smoke cleared, he was in a position to step in - right place, right time - and do what he was being paid for. When that happened, his patient persistence would, he hoped, be rewarded in the way it so deserved. It had been long enough coming.

As the pretty Japanese waitress poured his second coffee, Westgate thought about whether it was too soon to call again. Their last contact had been two days before, but his instincts told him the pace was picking up and he shouldn't leave things too long. He could easily come up with some bullshit story to justify it. Some sighting, or interesting-sounding piece of background. The tone in the man's voice was usually enough to tell how things were going, or if there were any new developments.

Grabbing his phone, he punched in the divert-code the Comms. Officer at the base had given him, followed by the number he'd memorised. After a short delay, the familiar voice answered. He sounded calmer than last time. Perhaps something positive had happened for a change. Either that or he was ready to barter information.

'It's me,' Westgate said.

CHAPTER 44

The sun was dropping behind the mountain backing the farmhouse as Murray pulled up. He knew at once something was wrong. Pippis, one of the older Chrises, and another of his nephews were just setting off, fully armed, along the path that wound across the valley. Seeing Murray arriving, they stopped while Pippis jogged back. He looked as concerned as the first time Murray saw him after the explosion.

'Gina took a basket up to Kyriakos three hours ago.'

Instinctively, Murray's gaze switched to the outcrop. There was no one in sight.

'She hasn't returned and they aren't answering their phones.'

As if to prove it, Pippis turned to fire his rifle into the air. He waited only as long as it took for Murray to see there was no response from up on the outcrop, before he turned to rejoin his companions. 'We must hurry.'

'I'm coming with you,' Murray said.

By the time they emerged from the trees onto the outcrop, dusk was falling. Far below, the lights showed bright in the windows of the farmhouse. There was no sign of Kyriakos or Gina. The four fanned out to search.

It was George, Pippis's nephew, who found Kyriakos's body amidst the rocks that formed a natural shelter on the southern edge of the outcrop. He all but collapsed as he hailed them. 'HERE.' They scrambled over to join him.

Kyriakos was still sitting upright, his back against the large boulder. He was facing out down the valley, his rifle beside him. His white shirt was stained red from the blood that had gushed from the wide slit in his throat. There was no sign he had even had time to move, let alone put up any resistance. Just like Billy, Murray thought. About to say so, a heart-rending cry from Pippis stayed him.

'GINA.'

Turning from Kyriakos, Pippis set off, searching frantically around the outcrop. They all joined him. Murray could sense the Policeman's terror that he would find her, having suffered the same fate as her cousin. For himself, he was all-but sure they would not. For several minutes they scoured the immediate area around the outcrop and surrounding trees. Eventually it was Murray, going over the ground already covered by the younger Chris, who found the food basket, on top of the rock where it had been left for them. Chris had missed it in the semi-darkness. No one criticised.

The basket's contents were undisturbed, but on top of the cloth, weighted by a stone, was a note. Written in a neat, precise hand, the message turned Murray's blood cold. He read it to the others.

'THE BOY MAKES 2. IF YOU COME AFTER HER SHE WILL BE 3.'

Murray handed it to Pippis. 'He's got her,' he said, grimly.

Pippis held the paper between shaking fingers, reading its devastating message for himself. Then the

Divisional Commander for the Pafos Police Division lifted his eyes to the emerging stars and gave out a howl of torment that reverberated and echoed off the mountains for what seemed an age.

'GINNAAAA.'

By the time they reached the farmhouse everyone knew what had happened. After hearing Pippis's fearful cry echoing down off the mountain, some of the younger men had rushed out and up the hill to lend aid in whatever way was needed – only to meet the party returning, carrying Kyriakos's body between them. One of them raced back with the terrible news.

The older women wailed as fresh hands, working under Galios's direction, took Kyriakos from his exhausted bearers and carried him inside. Few words passed between them, though Murray could tell the dam would not hold long. Vasillis hadn't arrived yet. He was on his way, but already the smell of vengeance hung heavy in the air. When someone raised the question of what they were going to do about Gina, Pippis silenced them with a curt, 'See to Kyriakos, then we will talk.'

During their silent descent down the mountain, Murray had sensed, rather than seen, the change in Pippis. The anguish, grief and fury that had been fuelled by Kyriakos's murder and the killer's note, lasted only as long as it took Murray to cajole them all into holding off declaring their intended response until after they got Kyriakos off the hillside. As they began the grim task of carrying him down - not easy in the dark - they'd all lapsed into silence. But Murray kept his attention on the man whose daughter was now in peril, and could only admire the man's fortitude in controlling whatever emotions were coursing through. His stoicism seemed to convey itself to the others, stemming Chris and George's

268

questions about what they would do once they got down.

By the time they neared the farmhouse and the family came out to meet them, Murray sensed Pippis's quiet determination more keenly than he had after the explosion. He didn't need to ask how much notice Pippis intended to take of the killer's note. But for all that Murray was aware he might soon face a fresh wave of resentment from certain quarters, his concern remained on ensuring that whatever decisions were taken, nothing happened that might endanger Gina. It wouldn't be easy. The desire to avenge Kyriakos and stage an immediate rescue – if such a thing were even possible – would be strong in all of them. He just hoped that the likes of Galios and Pippis were not too enraged to recognise that decisions taken in the heat of battle didn't always stand up to scrutiny. With Gina a hostage, now, above all, was the time for cool thinking.

As the rest of the family disappeared inside with Kyriakos, Pippis motioned Murray to hang back.

'My family are angry. Already they talk of revenge.' Murray nodded. 'The note spoke of two. What does it mean?'

Murray told him about Billy, regretting he hadn't contacted Pippis at once to warn him that Podruznig had brought in a professional. Pippis wasn't interested in recrimination.

'We all thought we were safe here. We were wrong.'

'Which raises a question.'

Pippis stared at him a moment, then the penny dropped. Turning, he walked swiftly to where the cars were lined up in front of the house. Murray followed.

They found it easily. Murray had used trackers during live ops many times and reasoned that having the highest public profile, Pippis was the most likely target. As he pulled the small box off the back of Pippis's HRV and showed it to him, the policeman displayed no regret, only the same steely determination as he observed, 'So it was me who led him here.'

Taking the device from Murray, he flung it down and ground it into the gravel with his heel. The failure to preserve what could have been vital evidence signalled to Murray well enough that whatever action Pippis was now considering, it wasn't the sort that would end in a court case – not unless it was to be him in the dock.

On the way down, Murray had wondered whether, in light of Kyriakos's death, Pippis would now ditch what they had recently discussed in favour of a full-scale police response. They were after all, now dealing with a murder and kidnapping as well as the bombing. But Podruznig held an ace card - Gina. Murray figured that at all costs, Pippis would wish to avoid anything that might alert whoever was holding her to the fact something was being planned. Besides, Murray was pretty sure that even if a police operation did result in some official sanction, Kyriakos's murder, coming on top of what had happened to Ileana, meant it would not be enough to satisfy the family. The juggernaut was rolling. Murray could imagine only one thing stopping it.

He knew he was right when Pippis turned to him and said, 'We do not have much time. Where will they take her?'

Murray thought a moment. The Sea Caves house was almost too obvious. But it was secure, and anywhere else would mean Podruznig having to split his forces. If his intention was to intimidate his enemies into leaving him alone – the Intelligence File Murray had seen showed he had used the tactic many times over the years – it had to be there. In saying so to Pippis, Murray took care not to voice his other, worse fear, that Podruznig may decide to

270

kill her anyway. He remembered what he'd read about Podruznig's past misdeeds - and what he'd learned during his Odessa trip.

Pippis took his time digesting it. It was obvious to Murray what he was thinking. If they went ahead and something went wrong, she could still end up dead.

'Pippis.'

They turned. Galios was framed in the doorway.

'Your family needs you.'

'A moment Papa.' He turned back to Murray. 'I have no time Mr Murray. My family needs me to be strong. You have experience of situations like this. Tell me. What should we do?'

Murray's gaze swung between Pippis and old Galios, still waiting for his son to instruct them as to their response. Clearly, the priority was Gina's safety. But could that be guaranteed? And though right now it was way down his order of priorities, there was still the other matter to consider. On the face of it, it was all too difficult. Not enough time.

'Pippis?'

'I am coming Papa. Mr Murray?'

Murray's mind raced, re-playing everything that had happened so far. Everything he had learned about Podruznig. Seeking out options. He recalled that first day he had visited the house with Klerides. The panic he'd triggered. Their reception. The walk up the drive to meet with Podruznig. His being snatched, and taken out to the Akamas for 'disposal'. His meeting with Marianna Podruznig at Scorpios. The-. Wait. She had said something about-.

'They need you Pippis.' Galios was becoming impatient.

'Peter?' -- the first time he had used Murray's given name

He remembered. He dug in his pocket, took out his phone.

'Go to your family Pippis. But don't let them rush into any decisions. I'll join you shortly.'

About to say something, Pippis bit his lip, turned, and went to join his father. Arms about each other, they went inside. The door closed behind them. Murray called Red.

'Wassup Plod?'

Murray brought him up to date. When he finished, Red repeated the words he'd already uttered several times as he'd listened. '*Jesus Christ.*' Then, 'So what do you think the chances are of-?'

'Who doubled with Billy on the obs on the house?'

'The obs? Mainly Wazzer I think. Ryan did a bit but-'

'Is Wazzer there?'

'Hang on.'

As he waited, Murray mentally crossed his fingers. If he was right, they would have to work out the details, and he might need another stroke of luck on the part of Pippis's family. But there was nothing wrong with the basic idea. It had worked well enough for the Greeks at Troy.

A few minutes later, as Murray walked in, Pippis was addressing his family, arrayed about him. Silence fell as Murray came through the door. Even Galios seemed to be looking at him differently now. *Too much pain, even for him.* Murray spoke directly to Pippis.

'Do you know anyone who works for Charalambos Pilakoutas?'

Part Three

SETTLEMENT

CHAPTER 45

The Charalambos Pilakoutas Group is the biggest, franchised car dealership in Cyprus. It trades in most of the up-market marques - BMW, Rolls Royce, Jaguar, others. Kodras Shikkis had been Service Manager at the Pafos branch of the group's BMW Division since gaining promotion from Lead-Salesman on the basis of his organising skills and, especially, his observed ability to cope with pressure. The latter quality was particularly important as one of the post's key responsibilities involved handling dissatisfied customers - usually those unacquainted with the fact that the word often used to describe the Cypriot work-ethic mirrors the Spanish - mañana.

But in the six years he'd been doing the job, nothing came close to what hit him when he arrived at his office at his usual seven-am to find his phone already ringing. Thinking to ignore it – his secretary didn't start until eight – he changed his mind when he saw it was the line from Nicosia Group Headquarters. *At this time of the morning? Unheard of.*

When he picked up and heard the booming voice of the group's senior Operations Director, Marinos Tsaliki himself and not his secretary, Nova - 'Is that you Kodras?' - he snapped to attention.

'Mr Tsaliki? What can I-?'

Not allowed to finish, Kodras could only listen as the man who was second in the group's hierarchy only to its chairman, spelt out, in precise terms, the reason for his call. It began with, 'Listen carefully Kodras. I am calling directly on behalf of the chairman himself.' It ended with the sort of question Kodras usually answered straight off the top of his head. Thankfully, his instincts told him that on this occasion, it would not be good for his career if he had to ring back and admit he'd made a mistake. For that reason, Kodras uttered the words he took pride in having always avoided since his first day in the job.

'I am sorry sir, I do not know.'

Tsaliki maintained a steady calm. 'In that case, Kodras, this is what you will do.'

As Kodras wrote down the step-by-step instructions, responding to each with a crisp, 'Yes sir,' his collar grew damp. He had no idea whether what was being demanded of him was deliverable – *has he forgotten it is Friday?* - but his chairman's tone left him in no doubt. If he did not succeed in what was being asked of him, he may as well start reading the Situations Vacant pages of the Cyprus Mail.

When he was finished, Tsaliki said, 'Any questions, Kodras?'

'No sir.'

'Then get on with it. And let me know when it is done.'

As he hung up, Kodras knew that despite himself, he had told one lie. He did have questions. Lots. But none were relevant to the success of his mission, only to understanding why he was being asked to carry it out - and what could be so important as to make his Director late for his regular, Friday-morning seven-o'clock round of golf at the exclusive Aphrodite Hills Resort?

Shelving his curiosity – he needed to get things moving – Kodras made his way through to the garage and out back to the low prefabricated building that was the bodyshop. On his way he passed the service mechanics eating their first breakfast. In high summer they start at six so they can finish before the sun is at its fiercest. He didn't respond to their cheery chorus of, 'Good morning Kodras.'

As he slipped between the plastic strip-curtains hanging over the bodyshop entrance, the sweet smell of acrylic hit him. Leonidis Evripidou, the bodyshop foreman, was standing in front of a Jaguar saloon that was up on the ramps. It was minus both front wings and its bonnet. He was sipping Cyprus coffee from a small cup while giving instructions to the shop's two young panel-beaters who were standing, hands in the pockets of their blue overalls, looking suitably bored. They all turned as Kodras came in. Their faces evidenced their surprise. Leonidis and Kodras knew each from their salesman days, which was why Leonidis didn't try to hide his amusement at seeing his boss out and about from his luxurious office so early.

'My God, Kodras. Has Peta finally traded you in for someone who can give her what she needs?'

Having married a woman ten years younger than himself, Kodras was used to the occasional ribbing his good fortune sometimes generated. But on this occasion he ditched his usual retort about Leonidis's six children and his own wife's proclivities.

'The X7 Leo, the one belonging to the Russian. Is it finished yet?'

The smile on Leonidis's face vanished. Simple courtesy demanded at least some attempt at banter before business. But whatever the cause of his boss's bad mood – Peta no doubt – he wasn't about to let

Kodras take it out on him. He raised his cup towards the back of the bodyshop where the object of his boss's enquiry was still gathering dust. 'We are waiting for the door panel.'

'And?'

'And what?'

'Has it come in yet?'

'Limassol were supposed to be getting one yesterday. They said they'd let us know if it came in.'

'And?'

Amused again at seeing Kodras so exercised, Leonidis decided it was time to bring him down. 'What do you mean, 'And'? It is Friday Kodras. Tomorrow is Saturday. What is the problem?' But instead of calming, Kodras's face grew red.

'The problem, Leonidis, is that I have just taken a telephone call from Mr Marinos Tsaliki, ringing on behalf of the chairman himself. Leonidis stiffened. The younger men took their hands out of their pockets, smiles disappearing. 'He has ordered that it-' He pointed at the X7. 'Be made ready by tonight.'

Leonidis's jaw dropped. 'Tonight? Do not be ridiculous Kodras. How can it be ready by tonight? We don't even know if we have the panel.'

Kodras stepped forward a few paces and in a way no one at the dealership had ever heard him speak before - low and menacing - said, 'In that case Leonidis, I suggest you find out.'

'But what if it hasn't arrived?'

Kodras remained firm. There was no question he was going to allow Leonidis to let him down in this. 'In that case, you will send one of these two-' He jerked a thumb at the panel-beaters - 'to pick it up from wherever it is, and I mean, *wherever*. Then you will work on it until it is ready, and then I will ring Mr Tsaliki and tell him what a fine job you have done.'

Leonidis tried one last time. 'But we close at four. I am taking Iroula to see her sister in Nicosia for the weekend.' But even as he spoke the words, the look on Kodras's face – like the voice, one he had never seen before – told him that on this occasion, Kodras was not going to give way.

'Let me tell you something Leonidis,' Kodras said. 'And then you can ring Iroula and you can tell her. I, you and these two will not be going anywhere until that-.' He pointed at the car again. 'Is finished and ready for delivery.'

A few minutes later, back in his office, Kodras let out a long breath. He couldn't remember a time when he'd had to take such a hard line. Usually it was a case of getting back to the customer and explaining how some third party had failed in their promise. *'I am sorry, but you must understand, such things are beyond our control.'* Not this time. But at least the car's wing was in stock. As he'd left the bodyshop the two fitters were scurrying about, putting the Jag away, making ready to fetch the X7 from its dusty nest. Kodras checked the clock on the wall. If Leonidis didn't ring in the next five minutes to confirm the door-panel was also in-stock, he would go over there again and check what was happening.

Sitting back, Kodras reviewed his actions since the phone call and did some calculations. So long as they had the part before late morning, there should still be time. Fitting was straight-forward, and the paint they used these days was quick-drying. Not ideal by any means – it would normally be left twenty-four hours to go off before polishing and finishing - but on this occasion it would do. At least then he could ring Tsaliki and inform him of his success.

Satisfied he had things as much under control as was

possible in the circumstances, Kodras decided it was time to find out what had precipitated the crisis. But as he reached for the telephone, he had no way of knowing that, after a morning spent ringing his contacts, both at Group Headquarters and elsewhere, he would be no nearer knowing what lay behind his chairman's extraordinary intervention than he was right then. Nor could he have predicted that in the days and weeks following, the information would continue to elude him. In fact, like Leonidis, the two panel-beaters, and everyone else who heard about it during the course of that morning, Kodras Shikkis was destined to never find out what lay behind what he would always remember as the most frenetic day of his working life.

CHAPTER 46

As Marianna Podruznig put her case to her barely-listening husband, her heart beat so fast she had to call on all her reserves of guile to disguise the fact.

'And it would be good for Sasha,' she reasoned. 'She has never been to anything like this, and there are so few opportunities these days.' As before, Valerik waved away her plea as if it were a fly around food. Whatever was on his mind and had been since the rumpus the previous evening, was clearly still his top priority.

Marianna had no idea what had happened. She knew only that halfway through the sumptuous dinner she had prepared - the first part of her plan to soften him up - Uri had suddenly burst in to whisper something in Valerik's ear. It brought him bolt upright, eyes widening like saucers. Pausing only to throw down the remains of the Chateau Boyd Cantenac she had ordered in specially from her favourite Cava up near the market, he tossed her an already-distracted, 'Something has happened I must attend to.' Then he followed Uri out, closing the doors behind him.

Rushing across the room to put her ear to the door, her mind's eye followed their muffled voices into the kitchen and down to the basement. *Now what?*

She didn't see him again that night.

When she rose in the morning, the signs something

serious had happened were everywhere. Valerik was nowhere to be seen - probably already ensconced with Uri below somewhere. Looking out of the window, she saw Uri's staff bustling about the place as if expecting some sort of attack, carrying things from the garage-storeroom to the gate-house, rushing to and fro, in and out of the basement. There seemed more guards on the gate than normal, others stationed around the compound. Later she would discover that Uri had even stationed someone up in the roof-turret. Before she could finish dressing, Ivan knocked with a message from Valerik. Sasha was not to go to school, and they were to confine themselves to the house. Also, they were to stay away from the basement – not easy given that the main access was via the kitchen.

'Do not be ridiculous,' she responded, already sensing something with the potential to ruin her plans further. Time, especially, was against her. 'Tell Mr Podruznig I need to see him as soon as he is free.' Ivan's derisory snort as he sloped away left her fearing he would ignore her instruction.

But the message must have got through, as around lunchtime Valerik appeared to ask what she wanted. The way he didn't even try to disguise the fact his mind was on other things simply confirmed the conclusion she had already come to. Right now - maybe always - she and Sasha were nothing but an inconvenient distraction, to either be ignored altogether or, at most, given only the consideration needed to let him get on with what was important. Like ensuring that he got his own way in life, no matter how others suffered.

She knew now it was this increasing egotism that lay behind the ongoing vendetta with the Englishman - not that she could ever dare voice such an opinion. Apart from supposedly having no knowledge of the matter -

he had remained tight-lipped about it from the start - if she as much as tried to broach the subject, to point out to him that they had other houses elsewhere, bigger and more luxuriously appointed even than this one, he would be instantly suspicious. He would want to know who she had been talking with to even have a view on the subject. And as there was no one she could point at who knew enough to discuss it – he would discount her bodyguards at once – she risked putting herself in a dangerous situation. If he pushed and got so much as a whiff she was keeping something from him, he would not hesitate to use more persuasive methods. Maybe even hand her over to Uri. He'd probably even enjoy doing so. Determined though she was, Marianna had not been brought up to be the sort who can withstand pain, at least, not for long. Certainly, any hint of a threat towards her daughter and she would tell anyone anything they wanted to know. For these reasons, she had no option but to keep her mouth shut, play dumb, and continue to hope she may yet manipulate him into letting her and Sasha go to the Festival. But as he dismissed her latest appeal, Marianna knew she was struggling.

'Anyway,' he said, 'Since when are you interested in Opera?'

It was a good point, though she didn't dare concede it. 'It is not just the Opera,' she countered. 'There are other things going on as well. A fair. Street entertainers. The Parade. She has never seen anything like that.'

'What about the Gorky festival? You took her there didn't you?'

'For God's sake Valerik, that was six years ago. She was three.' She took his surprised look as a small victory, of sorts. 'You cannot keep her cosseted all her life. Or me, for that matter. It is not fair on us.'

Seeing the way his eyes flared at the implied criticism,

she knew she had to be careful. If she went too far, he would simply walk away, as he was wont to when he tired of listening to her pleadings - whether for more freedom, flexibility, *love*. 'You have your business to keep you busy. But since we moved here, Sasha and I hardly get out at all.'

'That is a lie,' he snapped, impatience now showing. 'You see Ria every week.'

'For coffee and shopping. It's hardly what you would call a special treat.'

As if sensing the balance of logic was with her, he made to brush the matter aside. 'This is not the right time. Something has happened.' *So I can see.* 'It requires my attention. I cannot be distracted to make arrangements for you and Sasha. Wait a few days, then you can go wherever you want.'

Though it confirmed what she had been seeing all morning – *Whatever can it be?* – she had no choice but to press on. 'But the Festival will be over by then. It will be too late.' She put on her most kittenish look. 'Come Valerik, a trip to the harbour hardly involves much trouble. It is only the same as our Saturday morning run into town. And we will not stay for the second act. Sasha will have seen enough by then anyway. It would only be for a couple of hours.' The way he hesitated, searching for another point in his favour rather than outright dismissal, she sensed an opening. 'And whatever it is that requires your attention so badly, I am sure you will be better off if Sasha and I are not around.' His eyebrows lifted. *Another hit.* 'And if you need us to come home, I will come at once, no arguing.'

As he turned to her, anger still yet to show, she felt a surge of hope she might actually be winning. But before he could say anything there was a sharp knock on the door and Uri walked in. Her heart fell.

No. Not now.

'I am sorry Valerik.' Though he addressed his master, Marianna saw the way his suspicious eyes slid to her as if to say, *Now what are you up to?* She met his gaze without turning away, certain he'd timed his intrusion deliberately.

'What is it Uri?'

'The garage has just called to say your car will be ready later today.'

His face changed. It actually lit up. 'It will?'

Marianna quashed a frustrated groan. As she thought, the news was hardly earth shattering, though the enthusiasm in her husband's voice said he thought otherwise. She saw the moment that might have been beginning to slip away. *And I was so close.*

'When can they bring it back?'

'They mentioned tomorrow, but I told them they would have to wait. Right now I don't want unnecessary callers coming and going.'

'Nonsense, Uri. I have waited long enough as it is. Ring them back and tell them tomorrow will be fine. It is not motor dealers we need to be careful about.' Then, as if realising he might have said too much, he turned to her, glancing warily at Uri.

'Go to this Festival thing. Take Sasha with you. But you will return at once if I need you here.'

Marianna's heart leaped. The good news about his beloved car must have turned him. 'Of course, my husband.'

Podruznig turned to Uri who was looking aghast. 'That is all Uri. Thank you.'

As Uri left, she felt, rather than saw the look of hate in his face. She did not get the better of the Siberian very often. But on those rare occasions she did, she loved the feeling. This one was special, for all sorts of reasons.

Alone again, she moved to stand close to her husband, smouldering in a way she had not practised in a long time, sensing the need to reassure him. 'Thank you Valerik. You are a good husband and father.' As she reached down, she pretended not to notice the flash of surprise that came into his face. 'And when you have more time, then perhaps….' She turned her face up to his, lips apart, ready. His head began to dip towards hers. But suddenly, as if remembering his priorities, he pulled back.

'Enough of this. I have no time right now.' He headed for the door. 'When you see Ivan, send him to me. I will give him his instructions.'

'Of course Valerik.'

As he left the room Marianna let out a long sigh of relief, but she resisted the temptation to jump for joy. The CCTV sees everything.

CHAPTER 47

Approaching the iron gates, Kodras Shikkis had never been so nervous in his life. He had no idea what was going on at the house overlooking the Sea Caves, and he did not want to know. All he had been told was, he should follow the instructions he had been given, to the letter. He had been here only once before. The day he delivered the X7. That experience was enough to discourage him from making the, usually obligatory, two-week follow up visit, just to make sure the customer was satisfied with the product and service. Unfortunately, events of the past twenty-four hours meant he now had no choice in the matter.

The first evidence this was the case had come in the form of yet another telephone call from Tsaliki – less than an hour after Kodras had rung him late the previous afternoon with the good news that he had succeeded in his mission and the car would indeed be ready on time. Of course, in telling his boss this he made no reference to Leonidis - by then in dire straits with his wife - or the two exhausted panel-beaters.

As with Tsaliki's first call, the second was instructive in nature, informing Kodras what he was to do next and giving notice of the visitors who would soon be arriving to brief him further. At that time, all Kodras knew was that he was to act as if his visitors' instructions were coming from the chairman himself - which puzzled Kodras no end, but made sense when the visitors arrived and he recognised one as the local Chief of Police, Superintendent Pippis Iridotu, himself.

As the Superintendent marched towards Kodras's office with two men Kodras had never seen before in tow, Kodras just knew that the mysterious sequence of events that had started with the phone call that morning was far from over. Within minutes of the Police Chief's arrival, it became clear that harrowing though the day had been thus far – the door panel the beaters had to fetch all the way from Limassol had proved more troublesome than expected – things were about to get a whole lot worse.

His suspicion proved correct when Superintendent Pippis began to lay out what would happen the following day, starting with Kodras's return to the dealership first thing Saturday morning. Kodras still hadn't worked out how he would ever placate Peta for having to cancel their attendance at the Pre-Festival Reception at the Municipal Hall that afternoon. For the first time in his life, he had managed to secure tickets for the event - and early enough to give Peta plenty of time during which she could drop the fact into as many conversations as she could without making her gloating appear too obvious. Worse, he still didn't know if he would be free by the time the Opera began. For all he knew, once this present task was finished a whole new set of instructions awaited him. He was beginning to feel like he had been selected as the dupe in some convoluted game, the end purpose of which would remain, forever, a mystery to him – which in fact, wasn't far from the truth.

But for all his doubts, fears and questions, Kodras was not about to defy the wishes of his company chairman. Certainly not Superintendent Pippis. Things had changed greatly since his country joined the EU. And they were still changing. But not so fast that people like Kodras could afford to not cooperate with the police when asked to do so.

All of which explained how Kodras found himself delivering the Russian's supposedly pristine BMW X7 eDrive that Saturday afternoon, instead of donning his best suit and stepping out to the Festival Reception with his sexy young wife on his arm. The fact he had been told to wait two hours *beyond* the time he originally gave Podruznig's number two, the Siberian Uri, when he rang to arrange delivery, made the whole thing even more mysterious.

As he pulled up in front of the gates, checking his mirror to make sure that the demonstrator X7 following behind to take him back was not so close as to run into him, one of the gates opened just wide enough for someone to step out. Kodras swallowed hard as he recognised the big Siberian and steeled himself. The man with the scar made him jittery at the best of times. As he approached the driver's window, Kodras prayed to God he wasn't about to wet himself.

'You are late,' Uri barked the moment Kodras let the window down.

'I-I'm sorry,sir.' Kodras said. 'We had to make sure the paint was dry before-'

'Never mind. Just take it in. And be quick.'

'Yes sir,' Kodras said.

As Uri motioned to someone and the gate swung open, Kodras tried not to let his embarrassment show. His nervousness had actually led him to address the muscle-bound idiot the way he would his chairman. *Get a grip of yourself Kodras.*

Kodras drove through and up the drive, at the same time checking behind to make sure that his companion hadn't been stopped. The two cars pulled up in line, at the bottom of the steps. As Kodras stepped from the car, Podruznig himself came down the steps to meet him. He sighed with relief. So far, everything had happened as he had been led to expect it would.

'Hello Mr Podruznig,' Kodras used the cheery voice he reserved for home deliveries as he put out his hand. Podruznig ignored it.

'You were supposed to be here two hours ago.'

'I am very sorry, sir. It was just that-'

'It is as new I hope?'

'Of course sir, see for yourself.'

As he had been instructed – he would have done it anyway – Kodras led the owner around the vehicle, showing him the panels that had been replaced, explaining to the less-than-interested Russian the reasons for the delay. As Podruznig examined the bodywork, running his hands, lovingly, over the buffed metal, Kodras sensed the Russian's enthusiasm was less marked than he remembered it. In fact, apart from checking that the vehicle was in its original, unblemished condition, Podruznig seemed almost distracted. But not too much.

'What is this?'

Kodras leaned forward. Podruznig was pointing at a dulled area of paintwork low on the front wing.

'It is just polish that has not been dusted off. Do not worry Mr Podruznig, it will soon come up.'

The look on Podruznig's face conveyed his obvious feelings on the subject. 'And I am supposed to do that myself am I?'

Though again what he expected, Kodras still gulped. If getting on the wrong side of the Superintendent was something to avoid, the same went for this man, only more so. 'One minute Sir, I will attend to it.'

Leaving Podruznig glaring at the blemish in disgust,

Kodras went over to the other X7 and returned with a bottle of cleaner and a bright yellow duster. 'I am sure this will get rid of it.'

As he bent to the task, Kodras was conscious of Podruznig's close scrutiny, as if waiting for a chance to prove that the service manager's optimism was misplaced. As Kodras rubbed at the spot, a voice came from behind.

'Have you asked him, Kodras?'

Kodras lifted his head to glance at the other driver. He was wearing a brightly-coloured cap and dark driving glasses. 'Be quiet Ulysses. You will have to wait.' He returned to his buffing.

'What is wrong with him?' Podruznig said.

Kodras didn't break from his task. 'Ignore him Mr Podruznig. He wants to know if he can go to the bathroom. It is his own fault. He should have gone before we came out. There, you see? It is coming off.'

'Kodras. I am desperate.'

'I said, you'll have to wait, Ulysses.' He gave Podruznig an apologetic look. 'I am sorry about this, Mr Podruznig. He has not been with us long.' He poured more cleaner onto the cloth and went over the blemish again. 'That is better. It is nearly all off now.'

Again the voice sounded. 'Ask him Kodras.'

About to show annoyance, Kodras was beaten to it.

'Oh, for God's sake,' Podruznig said. He waved up the steps. 'Go take a piss. There is a bathroom just inside the hall.' He indicated the open door at the top of the steps.'

'Thank you sir,' Ulysses called, already moving as he tipped his cap..

With the spot disappearing, Podruznig's attention returned to making sure there were no other blemishes. As he circled the car, Ulysses mounted the steps and headed inside.

'HERE,' Podruznig shouted in disgust. 'There is another one here.' He whirled on Kodras who all but turned white as the Russian pointed at another discolouration on the sill. 'Does no one bother to check these things Kodras? What sort of outfit are you running here?'

Kodras tried not to quiver in the face of the man's anger. 'I am sorry, Mr Podruznig. I can assure you someone is supposed to make pre-delivery checks. Rest assured I will deal with him personally as soon as I get back.'

'I should think so. I expect better service than this from a dealership like yours.'

'Of course, sir.' Feeling sufficiently chastened for it to be no act, Kodras focused on getting rid of the offending mark as the fuming Podruznig looked on. But the second spot proved more troublesome than the first. It took several applications of cleaner before the stain was finally gone.

'There,' Kodras said, straightening up. 'All done.'

By this time, Podruznig had circled the vehicle several times more, but without finding anything else to add to his displeasure. Kodras was glad. He couldn't wait to get away from the place. As he'd been cleaning he'd sensed the edginess around the compound, picking up signals from the faces of the men he saw dotted about. They all looked like they were waiting for something, a definite sense of unease in the air.

He turned an apologetic face on his customer. 'By way of amends Mr Podruznig, I will send a couple of men out tomorrow to give it another good clean and polish.'

'Do not bother, Kodras.'

'No-no, it is the least I can do.'

Podruznig's response was almost a snarl. 'I said, don't bother. I will have it cleaned when I am ready. Now please leave. I am very busy.'

'Of course Mr Podruznig.'

Pausing only to give the Russian a salute that bordered on tugging at a forelock, Kodras started towards the other car.

Suddenly Podruznig remembered. 'Where has that driver of yours got to? He has not come out yet.'

Kodras turned to see Podruznig looking up at the front door, clicking fingers at one of his men, urging him to go root Ulysses out. Kodras waited until the man was halfway up the steps. 'It is alright sir, he is here. Hey, Ulysses.'

Podruznig turned in the direction Kodras had called. Over by the gates the man in the cap and glasses was sharing a smoke with a couple of Podruznig's men. At Kodras's call he waved and started over. Podruznig grunted away his mistake 'In that case take him and go.' Business over, he mounted the steps and entered the house. There was no goodbye wave of gratitude.

As Ulysses turned the other X7 round and headed for the gates, Kodras snapped his seatbelt and pulled the lap-strap tight. As the same time, he let out a long sigh of relief.

'Now get us the Hell out of here, Ulysses. As fast as you can.'

CHAPTER 48

According to the announcer who was repeating everything twice - in Greek then English - attendance that evening was a record for an Aphrodite Festival performance. Over two and a half thousand, which is a lot for a small harbour like Pafos's. The semicircle of tiered seating erected in front of the old, Lusignan-built Fort was jam-packed. Behind, lining the quay and the approaches to the harbour, hordes of rubbernecking tourists and local families mingled, lured by the prospect of hearing for free, what the cream of Cyprus society had paid good money for.

As the Orchestra of the National Opera Company of Poland - this year's guest performers - tuned up for the first act, Marianna craned right and left, looking for anyone who may appear to be trying to attract her attention. But apart from Ivan and his partner, Sergei, stationed at the exits either side of the section where she and Sasha were seated, all she could see were joyful festival goers, romantically-inclined couples, garrulous groups, or parties of over-dressed dignitaries settling themselves into their seats in readiness for what the announcer kept promising would be, 'An event unlike any you have experienced before.'

Marianna didn't know what to expect. The brief message hidden in the soap-basket gave no hint as to what might happen – if anything. Though she tried to maintain the pretence of being caught up in the jovial atmosphere – for appearance, as well as Sasha's sake – she was finding it hard to keep up the deceit. And given the way Ivan and his team were watching her every move, her conviction was growing that the whole thing was impossible, especially in so public a place as this. Not only were her minders on alert, but so were the scores of police and stewards swarming everywhere. She was beginning to wonder if she had been foolish to imagine that the Englishman would risk further danger, just for her and Sasha. What were they to him after all, apart from his enemy's family, not that Valerik attached much importance to the fact? She had even wondered if it might all be some sort of trick, aimed at using her and Sasha as a bargaining tool.

'It's starting Mummy.'

As Marianna turned a smile on her wide-eyed daughter, the feelings of guilt swooped in again. Not for the first time, she wondered if she was doing the right thing. The little girl waiting, excitedly, to experience her first ever Opera could have no idea her life may be about to change.

As the lights dimmed, a hush fell over the audience, though a far off murmur indicated that those watching from the fringes would be less respectful. A few moments later, as Verdi's haunting Prelude began, Marianna settled back in her seat. She had no choice now but to wait and see what the evening would bring.

'You're hurting Mummy.'

Marianna turned. Sasha was holding up the hand Marianna was clutching, a pained expression on her face.

'I am sorry, *lapushka*.' She relaxed her grip and gave her daughter another reassuring smile, though it didn't match how she felt inside. She turned back to the stage, where the events that would end in tragedy were about to unfold. She hoped with all her heart they would not prove prophetic.

Lamaar closed the bedroom door, locked it, then put the key in his pocket. Turning, slowly, he faced the woman perched on the edge of the bed. Her face was full of fear, and the way she was just sitting there, wrists and ankles bound in rope, presented an image he found… interesting. So much so, he lingered at the door a few moments, enjoying the spectacle, letting his imagination work. He was after all, in no rush.

It was rare that Lamaar got the opportunity to spend time with his victims. Most of his commissions required only the most fleeting contact, if any at all. It reflected the way things had changed since his first ventures into the profession that had proved more lucrative than his time in *La Legion*. Nowadays, even people requiring his services like to still think of themselves as 'civilised', and therefore beyond requiring that the commissions they send his way be made to suffer additional tortures. Not like it used to be. There was a time when the 'client's' suffering was often more important than their removal. On the odd occasion Lamaar met someone in the same line of business as himself and they talked about it - not that he was one for talking – he would sometimes quip that it all changed with the Human Rights thing. It was the nearest Lamaar ever came to a joke. In reality, the difference was due to the increasing sophistication of police investigation methods. The longer the time spent with the victim, the greater the chance of leaving some incriminating trace - hair, DNA, prints - that may prove his undoing.

Not that Lamaar worried unduly about such things. If he ever suspected a contact may prove compromising, he had a simple solution. Dispose of the body. He had done so many times, and in ways he liked to think were nothing if not imaginative. Farming equipment was particularly versatile. In truth, a good percentage of his commissions required that the body be never found. And while in such cases the brief sometimes called for the victim to not suffer unduly - *such hypocrisy* - he didn't always comply. After all, who is to know?

As he went about getting things ready, drawing curtains, making sure the necessary accoutrements were to hand, the thought came that the woman on the bed may fall into that category. He had no instructions other than to bring her up from the basement and ensure against her escape - moving her had proved impossible while the woman and kid were around. But from what he understood about what was going on, Lamaar could not envisage any way the Russian could afford to let her live. Especially not now that he had let her see him.

Lamaar had known right away that was stupid. But he was beginning to realise the extent of the Russian's arrogance. Over the years, he had met many who relied on muscle and fear to get their way. As a philosophy, it was dangerous and misguided. A throwback to the days when strength and power were all. And whilst some now realised that today's climate calls for a different, more subtle approach, others – the likes of Podruznig - were yet to learn the lesson.

It was why Lamaar had already decided he would not be hanging around to see his contract through. Day by day, it was becoming evident the Russian was bent on colliding with his enemies, head on. It probably explained why he had told Lamaar to take the woman if he came across her.

At the time, Lamaar had not fully appreciated how unstable the Russian was. Had he done, he would have left her. But the way he raved at her in the basement the night before, threatening her with graphic descriptions of what would befall her if she did not disclose what she knew of her father's plans, or if he attempted any rescue, Lamaar realised that, contrary to the Russian's assertions, things were not as 'under control' as they should be.

In fact, Lamaar was not sure just who, if anyone, was controlling events. Which meant anything could happen. He had survived this long by ensuring that things happened in ways that, if not entirely predictable, could at least be catered for through careful planning. But that wasn't possible in the present circumstances, which was why sense told him that he ought not to delay too long in distancing himself from what he saw as a delicately-balanced situation.

But not yet. There being no immediate danger, he could afford to dally. Which brought him back to *Her*.

As he paused to remove his jacket, hanging it over the back of a fancily-upholstered chair, thoughts of what may be possible in the time available, triggered a sly smile. Seeing it, the woman's eyes widened further. It pleased him to see how quick she was. The bright ones were always more fun.

Podruznig had said he was to 'look after her.' He had not expanded, nor had Lamaar pressed for clarification. Clearly, the Russian believed that the simple act of holding her was enough to forestall any attempt at rescue.

Lamaar was not so sure. What he did know was, before he left the Russian's employ, he would have to deal with her. It wasn't just Podruznig's face she had seen.

When, without any warning, Podruznig whipped off her blindfold down in the basement, Lamaar had been standing right in front of her. As with bodies, he was always careful about making sure no one could connect him to a crime. It applied to the mercenary in the hills, as well as the soldier on the mountain. And on the few occasions some inadvertent witness may have been able to link him to a client, they tended to meet with 'accidents'. And he wasn't about to break his rule just because her father was a policeman. It meant that whatever he did with her, it didn't matter. No one would ever know. Even if Podruznig discovered what he was up to, he was hardly in a position to complain, not if what he had heard of the Russian's own proclivities was true.

As he approached the bed, ready to begin, she reared away as far as she was able. And as he closed on her, the acute sense of smell he had realised years ago was his own special gift, picked up the particular traces of pheromones in her sweat that told him she was terrified. *The Smell Of Fear.* It excited him even more.

'W-what are you going to do?' she said. As she spoke, she began to scrabble away across the bed, trying to escape his reach. But tied the way she was, she succeeded only in putting herself in the middle of the bed - which suited his purpose.

The change in her, from the defiant woman of the night before, to this scared, helpless little girl, brought another smile to his face. Then, she had shouted defiance at the Russian, telling how he would pay for kidnapping her, killing the boy. But that changed when the Russian left her in Lamaar's sole care. She seemed to sense, almost at once, that unlike Podruznig, Lamaar was not bound by other considerations. And he knew she could tell, just by looking into his eyes, what he was capable of. He had come across women like that. They were rare, but always memorable. And in answer to her query about his intentions, he made no attempt at deceit.

'I do not yet know what I am going to do my dear. But I assure you, it will give me the greatest pleasure to find out.'

CHAPTER 49

About to climb into the back of the four-by-four that would take them home, Marianna paused to take one last look around, scanning faces as she had been doing all evening, searching for any sign of the Englishman, or anyone else who looked like they may be acting for him. But apart from the two young policemen she had caught ogling her on a couple of occasions, no one looked like they had anything on their minds apart from enjoying the spectacle, the music and the festive atmosphere.

In fact, apart from the usual sprinkling of men in the seats around hers and who, out of sight of their partners, turned their admiring gazes on her every now and then, no one had appeared to take much interest in her at all, apart from the policemen.

She remembered Ria had once spoken of how some elements within the local force were prone to use their positions to find an excuse to engage lone, attractive women in conversation. It usually resulted in a request for their telephone number - for 'official purposes only' of course. What dismayed Marianna most about the ruse, was the number of times it seemed to actually work. Even Ria admitted, eventually, to accepting the young officer's invitation for 'drinks' the time he stopped her to warn her about her speed while driving along the coast road.

As she took her last look round before settling into the back seat, Marianna suspected that the pair standing under one of the palms lining the harbour was of that ilk. When she'd stepped up into the Mitsubishi, her skirt rode up. She just caught the way they leaned into each other, no doubt swapping some remark that would prompt the inane, macho chuckling she hated. If it did, she never got to see however, as Ivan closed the door to the outside world. In her mind, she likened it to a prison gate, slamming shut.

Drawing Sasha to her - she had nodded off halfway through the first act - Marianna let out a sigh. Whatever the Englishman might have planned, if indeed he ever planned anything, it was too late now. Ensconced with her guards, she was going nowhere, apart from home. At that moment, the uncertainties over her and Sasha's futures that had plagued her these last few days, returned. Taking a tissue from her purse, she dabbed at the tear that was forming. Emotions swirled within her. Chief amongst them was disappointment - *he seemed so genuine in his promises* - but relief was there also.

She had always feared what may transpire if the Englishman followed through on his promise. He had said there may be a period when she would have to stay hidden. Stupidly she now realised, she had fallen for his assurances. God alone knew what he planned to do with the information she had given him. Her duplicity could bring disaster on them all. Not just Valerik, but herself and, worst of all, Sasha. She cursed herself for her naivety.

At the time, she believed the Englishman when he said that if she trusted him, he could arrange the freedom she craved. When it was all over, he said, she and Sasha would be able to start a new life, free from the humiliations Valerik subjected her to, the obsessive control he exercised over every aspect of their lives. Most of all, and it was what finally swung her, he said she would not have to worry about any threat of reprisal. That even if Valerik ever discovered where they were, or that she had conspired in her own liberation, factors existed that meant he would never be able to harm them. He didn't say what those factors were, and she didn't ask. At the time, it came like an answer to all her prayers, and she did not think on it long before giving her agreement. What a fool she had been.

At the end of the harbour service road they turned left, following the direction indicated by the traffic policeman on point duty who was so busy talking into his radio he barely looked at them as they passed. The route would take them along the Tombs of the Kings Road back to Coral Bay, the Sea Caves, Valerik, and the life she had, for a fleeting, foolish moment let herself dream she may escape. Taking the sleeping child next to her in her arms, she stifled the sob that threatened as she hugged her as tight as she dared without waking her.

CHAPTER 50

For Pafos International Airport Air Traffic Control, Aphrodite Festival Saturday is the busiest day of the year. Apart from it being the middle of the high season, with holiday flights arriving non-stop from dawn to late into the night, they also have to contend with more private aircraft – props, jets and helicopters – than the rest of the year put together. For that reason, Senior Controller Kleanthis Savva always scheduled himself for duty throughout the day, starting at six and finishing only when the last of the Festival traffic had left.

This year was as hectic as any he could remember, having got off to the worst possible start when an early-morning charter to Manchester reported an engine failure whilst taxiing out to the runway. By the time the problem was traced to a faulty indicator on the flight-deck, two hours had been lost and the day's schedule was already shot to pieces.

Nevertheless, under Kleanthis's steady direction and thanks also to the willing support he lent his stressed-out staff so they could still manage their much-needed smoking-breaks, the team gradually managed to stitch the battered schedule back together. By late afternoon, flights were arriving and departing more or less in their proper order, if not quite on schedule. In Kleanthis's view, and given the circumstances, half-an-hour was neither here nor there.

By seven-thirty in the evening, with all the filed arrivals on the tarmac, Kleanthis felt sufficiently confident everything was under control he could take a break himself. He had not eaten since breakfast. Handing control to his number two, Santos, a young man with much still to learn, but who was showing promise, and after logging the fact on the command and control system, he headed down to the staff restaurant in the main terminal building. There he grabbed a black coffee and a warmed ham and cheese ciabatta, opened his paper, and chilled.

It was twenty minutes later, as he was climbing the steps back up to the Control Tower, that he happened to glance back over his shoulder, alerted by the reflection of a flashing light in the windows above. He was horrified to see a line of police cars approaching across the airfield, blue lights strobing the tarmac, bouncing off the glass-sided Departure Hall behind. Kleanthis's heart leaped into his mouth. Some emergency must have kicked off during his absence. Why had Santos not notified him? The radio he carried on his belt had been on all the time. Racing up the remaining steps, he burst into the control room.

Sitting quietly in their seats, everyone stopped their idle chat to turn and look at him, surprised by his explosive entrance. Flummoxed, Kleanthis looked across to where Santos was leaning against a desk, drinking water from a bottle as he watched the Cyprus-Italy Euro-Championship qualifier on his mobile - an offence that would land him and, probably, Kleanthis, in prison if a Civil Aviation official happened to walk in. Not that there was much chance of that on Festival Saturday.

'What's happened, Santos?' Kleanthis called.

Alarmed, Santos jumped up. 'What do you mean?

Happened where?'

Kleanthis could scarcely believe it. '*THERE.*' He gestured through the darkened windows. '*Out there,*' he repeated.

As one, the whole of the control room evening shift turned. As they saw the convoy approaching, jaws dropped. For a moment nobody moved. Then everyone scrambled to their stations.

'Check and report flight status,' Kleanthis shouted to the controllers peering at their screens as if expecting to see some impending disaster they had somehow missed. 'Santos, get onto Larnaca.' The bigger of the island's two international airports, Larnaca invariably heard about things before they did. 'See if they know something we don't.'

'At once Kleanthis.'

As everyone jumped to, Kleanthis picked up the hotline to the Airport Duty Manager's office. He would know what the police were doing here. Why hadn't he rung him? About to press the call button, Kleanthis stopped as his eyes lit again on the approaching line of vehicles. For an emergency, the convoy was proceeding at an unusually steady pace, particularly given how the local police are known for putting their foot down in response to the most routine calls. 'What the…?'

As the convoy pulled up below the control tower – no screeching of brakes or squealing of tyres – Kleanthis's instincts took over. He returned the phone to its cradle. The doors of the lead police car opened and uniformed figures eased themselves out. They didn't run, or seem in too much of a hurry as they headed for the steps. Kleanthis turned to his team. The rows of shaking heads, blank faces and choruses of, 'Nothing here,' confirmed it. Whatever had brought the police to his tower this night, it was no air-emergency.

He just managed to get everyone focused back on their screens – all routine, the post-festival exodus wouldn't start for a good three hours yet – when footfalls sounded on the steps outside. The door opened and a bulky figure came in, followed closely by the airport duty manager Kleanthis had been about to ring.

Kleanthis stared, open-mouthed. He knew Superintendent Pippis Iridotu from the Church of Saint George they both attended on the hill, and the occasional fetes their wives collaborated in organising. But he had only ever seen him in the control tower once. That was during that debacle of a Major Incident Exercise eighteen months ago. What could possibly have brought him here, and on this night of all nights? Surely he should be down at the harbour? He had lost count of the times he had heard Pippis tell how he liked to be on hand to ensure the Festival Policing Operation went smoothly – even if it was from the front row seats he always managed to obtain for himself and his family.

Shocked, Kleanthis hesitated, half expecting the door to open again and a shock-wave of Civil Aviation officials to burst in. In the absence of an emergency, a snap inspection - which would in any case have been entirely unprecedented - was about the only thing he could think of that might justify such a high-powered visit. But the door remained closed.

Suddenly Kleanthis realised the policeman was staring at him, hands open, as if saying, *Well, Kleanthis? Are you awake?*

Pulling himself together, Kleanthis swallowed and managed a nervous, 'Superintendent?' He glanced at the duty manager. His face was a mask of non-information. 'What brings you here? I am-. We are-'

Pippis held up a calming hand. 'I am sorry to arrive unannounced, Kleanthis. And I have already apologised

306

to Mr Stavrou.' He half-turned to the duty manager, still giving nothing away. 'I am here to meet a private flight.'

Kleanthis blinked in surprise. 'A private flight?' He reached for the clip board that had been his bible through the afternoon and early evening. 'But you are too late, Superintendent.' He ran his finger down the lists, confirming he wasn't mistaken. 'The last notified flight arrived two hours ago. And I checked all the VIP attendees in myself. No one said they were expecting to see you.'

'That is right, Kleanthis,' Pippis said. His voice was calm, authoritative, reassuring. The tone he was famous for. He half turned again, as if to acknowledge the point a second time to the Duty Manager. Kleanthis noticed that the man seemed to be looking at the floor, as if what was happening was something he wanted no part of. 'But you see,' Pippis continued. 'The flight I am meeting is not on your list.'

Kleanthis took a second while he confirmed to himself he had not misheard. 'Not on the list? But that is impossible. A flight cannot land unless it has filed a plan through Larnaca. And all flights filed are-'

'Yes, yes, Kleanthis I know all that. But you see, this particular flight has not filed a plan.'

Kleanthis shook his head. Not only was such a thing illegal, it was unheard of. It didn't make any sense. But as his brain searched for an explanation, he remembered an article he had read some weeks before in the Pafos Times. The police were promising to clamp down on the Balkan smugglers who were increasingly using Southern Cyprus as their gateway to the rest of Europe.

Drug-dealers. That had to be it. But to attempt a land-drop-run here? And on this night of all nights? Such a thing would be doomed to failure from the start. It would be madness. Even if-

Kleanthis stopped. Pippis was shaking his head, as if reading his thoughts.

'It is not what you are thinking Kleanthis. Come let us speak.' Draping a heavy arm round the smaller man's shoulders, the policeman steered him into the small, glass-fronted Senior Controller's office. The sheepish Duty Manager followed. Pippis shut the door behind them and ushered Kleanthis to sit, which he did.

Over the next few minutes, the rest of the Control Room staff were treated to a spectacle the like of which none of them had witnessed before. To begin with, the policeman spoke, quietly, so that no one in the Control Room could hear, while Kleanthis listened. They all saw the puzzled look that came into Kleanthis's face. It soon turned to amazement, then horror.

As Kleanthis jumped to his feet, his voice rose to a pitch where people could hear snatches through the glass. '...*must be joking*.' '*It cannot*...' '*Who has authorised*...?' He turned to the Duty Manager, as if appealing to him. But the man only shook his head, speaking softly so no one could hear, before returning to studying the carpet. Clearly, whatever was happening he had no say in the matter. Either that or the policeman was giving him none. Eventually, in the face of what, to those watching, looked like the policeman's calm insistence, Kleanthis's objections, if that was what they were, drained away. He fell silent.

A moment later he turned and, as if in a daze, came to the door. Opening it, he called out. 'Santos.'

'Yes Kleanthis?'

Kleanthis beckoned him inside, shutting the door behind him.

Santos's heart thumped as he waited to hear what it was all about. The policeman cleared his throat. 'Tell him Kleanthis.' Santos turned to his boss, who was looking pale.

'Get ready to take charge of an arrival, Santos. Use my terminal.' He indicated the one on his desk.

'An arrival Kleanthis? But where is the notification?'

Not wanting to go through it again, Kleanthis shook his head. 'There is no notification Santos. Nor will there be.' He turned to the policeman, who was looking grave. 'In fact, after tonight, you are to forget all about it.'

Santos was mortified. 'But what if someone asks-'

The policeman cut him off. 'They won't Santos. And even if by some chance they do, you will deny all knowledge. As far as everyone here tonight is concerned, this flight never arrived.'

CHAPTER 51

Even before the Zodiac beached, the four were out, the pair in front grabbing at the painter so they could drag the assault craft under the shelter of the cliffs as soon as the two in the stern were ashore. The beach was shale and steeply raked. In the dark, they needed to avoid any of the op-ruining ankle-breaks a Special Boat Services Captain had once warned was the greatest danger at the beginning of any beach-based assault. Tonight, there was no such disaster. Less than a minute later, they were at the base of the cliffs, Zodiac stowed, gear unloaded, ready to go.

Red peered upwards, mapping the route Ryan and Wazzer had picked out. Two nights before, the pair had spent a queasy couple of hours in the Zodiac, a hundred metres out, videoing the beach and cliffs through the night scope so they wouldn't have to waste time looking for the best way up when they landed. They'd been lucky. Either side of the inlet were deep caves of the sort that stretch of coast is famous for. No way up from there. But in the dark above where they now stood, the cliff was pock-marked with features that provided ample hand and foot holds. Nevertheless, around the thirty foot mark, the sea had cut into the limestone, forming a shallow overhang which would need some rope work. Kishore, the Gurkha, was the climber.

'Up you go, Kish,' Red said, making a stirrup with his hands. 'And try not to peel off this time.' The others chuckled.

'Piss off,' Kishore said. *Three years and they still won't let it go.*

As the Gurkha shimmied, lizard-like, up the rock-face - the first several feet were sheer - the others made ready for the belay that would follow once the first anchor was in. They worked silently, but together, each following the sequence they had rehearsed in the days previous, and again that very afternoon - after the call came confirming it was a 'Go'.

After a few short minutes, a single tug on the rope from the darkness above told them Kishore was ready. Red tapped Wazzer on the shoulder. Wazzer looked up and shook his head. Red and Ryan smiled at each other, knowingly. Sure enough, Wazzer blew his cheeks out.

'Next time can we find a nice, flat beachhead?'

He tugged once on the rope, took a hoist from Red and Ryan's shoulders, then he too disappeared into the blackness.

CHAPTER 52

Twelve kilometres away, the Tombs of the Kings Road heading away from the harbour area was buzzing. Holidaymakers and weekend-revellers mingled as they headed for the bars and restaurants that form the colourful - and noisy - strip lining the main road. Horns blared and drivers whistled as young women in startlingly high heels and meagre dresses dodged in and out the stop-start traffic.

In the back of the car, Marianna paid little heed. Her thoughts were still on what would happen over the coming days, what she was going to do, and what life now had in store for the young girl asleep and, thank goodness, oblivious to everything, in her arms. Though only minutes had passed since leaving the harbour, her stomach was already in knots.

As they jerked to a stop, a burst of invective spewed from Ivan and he gave a loud blast on the horn. Marianna looked up in time to see one of the two skimpily-dressed young women who'd skipped round the front of the bonnet and made him stamp on the brakes, give him the finger. Ahead of them was a line of brake-lights signalling some hold-up. She sighed.

The Tombs of the Kings Road is notorious for accidents, especially at weekends. For months, letters had been appearing in the local edition of the Cyprus Mail, urging the police to do something about the danger, and not just from car-hiring tourists. By tradition, the weekend is when Cyprus's young bloods get to show where most of their wages go, heading down from the villages in the hills to cruise the strips around the Harbour in their BMWs, flash sports cars, or souped-up Japanese imports with go-fast stripes, low sills and roaring exhausts. If it was an accident, Marianna thought, it could take forever to get home, not that she was in any rush. She turned to look behind. The escort car carrying Max and his partner was right behind, as always.

As they crept along, Ivan muttering to Sergei beside him, Marianna strained to look between them, searching for the cause of the hold-up. Somewhere ahead, flashes of blue reflected off buildings to light up the night sky.

'Is it an accident?' she said.

'We'll know in a minute.'

She sat back. Communication was not one of Ivan's strong points. A few minutes later, she checked again. Ahead of them, several police cars, blue lights flashing, lined the road. Whatever it was looked serious, though as far as she could see, there didn't appear to be any ambulances or fire engines.

'What is it?' she said.

'Looks like some sort of road-check,' Ivan offered, before disintegrating into a babble of oaths she preferred to not hear. Ivan's opinion of the police was as low as theirs sometimes appeared of Pontians. She hoped that if they were stopped, the surly Russian wouldn't do or say anything stupid.

As they neared the front of the line, Marianna saw it *was* a roadblock, and a big one. Several police cars and 4x4s were parked around, their lights adding to the strip's garish displays. Officers in reflective-yellow jackets

313

and waving hand-lamps were picking out cars, apparently at random, and pulling them into a slip-road formed out of traffic cones. As she saw the car in front being waved on by the woman sergeant who seemed to be controlling things, Marianna hoped she was about to do the same to them. No such luck.

'Shit,' Ivan declared as the sergeant waved them in. But instead of complying he stopped in the middle of the road and wound his window down. Marianna groaned, anticipating the worst. As the sergeant approached, Marianna saw she was older than most of the officers she usually saw on Pafos's streets.

'Please pull over sir,' she said, politely.

'What is all this about?' Ivan said. 'We are just trying to get home.'

'We won't delay you sir. Just a routine check.'

'Have I done something wrong?'

'Please pull in sir. The officers over there will explain.' She nodded towards the slip road where officers with clip boards and what Marianna assumed were breathalyser-devices were already dealing with other cars.

Still muttering, Ivan made ready to comply. Before doing so he looked in the mirror and raised his hands in an expression of helplessness. Behind, Max flashed his headlights in acknowledgement. Ivan moved forward, at the same time pulling in to the left.

Looking behind, Marianna saw the sergeant wave Max's car through. Presumably they had enough to deal with for the time being. But, like Ivan, Max also stopped. Marianna guessed he was going to tell her they were together. Even further behind, Marianna could see more blue lights. It seemed the whole of the Pafos police force was out this night.

As Ivan pulled into the slip, stopping behind the car in front, Marianna saw the woman sergeant wagging a finger at Max, motioning him to follow her original direction. She did it in a way that made clear she would stand no arguing. Max must have got the message as he began to move forward. As he drove slowly past them he shouted across.

'We'll pick you up the other side.'

Ivan nodded. 'Police wankers.'

An officer with a clip board appeared at Ivan's window.

'Good evening sir. Is this your car?' He spoke in perfect English.

'No. It belongs to my employer.'

'I see.' He peered into the back, spotted Marianna, Sasha on her lap, beginning to stir. 'Is that you madam?'.

'No, my husband.'

'Please wait one moment.' He turned away to speak into his radio. Marianna heard a babble of static but could not make out what was being said.

Turning back to the car, the officer spoke to Ivan. 'Have you been drinking at all tonight sir?'

'No. Can't you just let us on our way? It's late, and the kid needs her bed.'

Marianna shook her head. Having never practised, Ivan's attempt at paternal concern bordered on the pathetic.

'We won't keep you sir.' The policeman sounded like he was reading from a script. Marianna noticed that the car in front hadn't moved, though the officers who'd been standing next to it were no longer there.

'Do you have your driving licence with you sir?'

'Driving Licence? No I don't have my driving licence. No one told me I need to carry it.'

'In that case I am going to have to ask you to take a breath test. Would you mind stepping out of the car?'

Marianna started. Though she was aware the local

police often carried out stop-checks she had never come across anything on this scale before. All those letters to the press must have struck a nerve. Nevertheless, she was surprised the police had the manpower to mount an operation this size on Festival night. As she could have predicted, Ivan began to rile.

'Why do I have to give a breath test? I haven't had a drink all night.'

'It is just routine sir. If you haven't been drinking there will not be a problem.'

Ivan glanced across at Sergei who raised his hands and shook his head in silent warning to his volatile partner. *Don't argue.*

'Ach,' Ivan cursed. 'Fucking politsiya.' He got out and followed the policeman around the front of the car to the pavement.

To her right, Marianna noticed that the traffic seemed be flowing past her window more freely now. As the policeman spoke with Ivan – showing him the device Marianna assumed was the breathalyser, explaining its operation – she twisted round. Another police 4x4 had pulled up behind them. The driver got out, coming over to the driver's side of the car. He stopped at the window and looked in. She recognised him at once. One of the oglers from the harbour.

'Good evening Madam. Is everything alright?'

Marianna was surprised. She had expected a smarmy look, instead he was entirely professional. Sergei wasn't.

'We will be when your colleague lets us go.' He gestured to where his partner looked like he and the police officer were getting into an argument. At that moment Ivan glanced over at them. Marianna could see he was fuming. The policeman seemed to be trying to direct him towards another police car parked in the side street to their left. Given Ivan's attitude, she thought the young officer was keeping remarkably cool.

To her surprise, the policeman at the window flashed Marianna a smile, before moving to join his colleague. The woman sergeant arrived to join them. Then a fourth officer appeared.

Sergei sat up, becoming agitated. 'What the fuck's going on?'

'Language, Sergei,' Marianna reminded him. Sasha was awake now. He paid her no attention. As the officers started shepherding a protesting Ivan towards the police car, he looked across at them in helpless appeal.

'Where are they taking him?' Sergei said. 'What is happening?' He got out of the car to shout across. 'What is wrong?'

Ivan shook his head as he was led, two in front two behind, clearly struggling to contain his annoyance. 'They want to check my fucking details.' Still protesting, he let himself be man-handled into the back of the police car. Marianna was surprised to see the officer from the harbour get in beside him.

'Ach. Fucking bastards,' Sergei muttered. 'We'll be here all night if we're not careful.' Pausing to light a cigarette, he started pacing up and down the pavement next to the car.

Sasha looked up at her mother. 'What is it Mummy? What is happening?'

Marianna brushed hair off her face. 'Nothing, little one. It is just some policemen. Nothing to worry about.' Nevertheless, she was conscious of a nagging feeling that something didn't feel right. Peering ahead, she could see no sign of Max's car. The lines of traffic seemed to have cleared. Looking about her, she realised the road block seemed to be gearing down.

A shout made Sergei turn. 'What?'

Another shout, which Marianna couldn't make out.

317

She turned to look behind. The second harbour-policeman was leaning out of the window of the police car behind, beckoning Sergei over.

'Now what?' He flicked his butt away, leaned through the window. 'I'll see what he wants.'

As Sergei reached the car, the policeman got out. They exchanged a few words and she saw Sergei reach into his pocket, pulling out his cigarettes. The policeman took one and lit up. As they spoke, two more officers emerged from the back of the car and sauntered round to join them. Suddenly Sergei was surrounded by uniforms.

What happened next so surprised Marianna, she actually let out a squeal of alarm. There was a blur of movement, a brief scuffle, and then the policemen all seemed to pile into the police car. When the doors shut, Sergei was gone.

Marianna froze, hand to her mouth, unable to digest what she had just seen. Suddenly the police car leaped forward and, with a squeal of tyres, roared off past her window. As it flashed by she glimpsed a melee of bodies in the back. Confused, and suddenly very frightened, she swung round - just in time to see the car containing Ivan also taking off. At the bottom of the street it veered right and disappeared.

Panic rising, Marianna spun round, trying to make sense of what was happening. All the police cars seemed to have disappeared, the road block completely gone, traffic flowing freely again. For the first time since arriving in Cyprus she was alone on the streets with Sasha, without any minders. She waited, terrified what might happen next. Sasha must have felt her anxiety.

'What is it Mummy?'

A figure appeared at her side of the car. The driver's door opened. A thick-set man she had never seen before got in. He had the battered look of a boxer.

As he slipped into the seat he looked at her in the mirror, and winked. 'Alright love?' *English*. His hand appeared over his shoulder. 'This is for you.'

He was holding something out to her. A package. She took it. It was a bar of Indian Coconut-Soap. She opened it. The writing was familiar. The words read, 'Go with them. Do as they say. P.'

About to say something, she stopped as the passenger door opened and the woman police sergeant got in.

Sasha was taking it all in. 'Where are Ivan and Sergei Mummy?'

The sergeant twisted round in her seat. There was something motherly in the way she gazed at the little girl. 'It is all right little one. Ivan and Sergei are gone.' She looked into Marianna's frightened face. 'My name is Andri. Do not worry Mrs Podruznig. You are safe now.'

CHAPTER 53

Valerik Podruznig paced the living room floor, punching numbers into his mobile, listening for a connection, cancelling when there wasn't any, trying others. *Where the fuck were they?*

As the doors swung open and Uri came back in, Podruznig spun round.

'Well?'

Uri shook his head. 'We cannot raise any of them.'

'Radio?'

Again the Siberian shook his head. Podruznig stared.

'They should have been home an hour ago, at the latest.' For once he was unsure of himself. 'What do you think, Uri?'

Uri took a moment to frame his reply. 'We've checked the road all the way back to the harbour. There are no signs of anything. I rang the main hospital, but there are no reports of anything there either. It could still be an accident and they might have been taken somewhere else.'

'I don't want to know about *could* or *might*. I asked what you *think*.'

Uri didn't hesitate. 'I think something is going on.'

'You mean they've been taken?'

'Possibly. Probably.'

Podruznig swung away to face the window. 'Fuck.'

Uri waited. If he was tempted to play 'Told you so,' he decided against, wisely. When Podruznig turned back, he could barely contain himself.

'Who?' he barked.

The question Uri had anticipated. 'How many enemies have you got?' It was as close as he dared to letting his frustration show. If he'd learned to listen to him....

'Gaponenko?'

Uri shook his head again. 'You have too much on him. And the way things are with his lot right now, that Government Investigation.... It wouldn't be the right time.'

Podruznig pondered. He swept his arm round, indicating their surroundings. 'What about all this business? The house? The Englishman?'

Uri looked doubtful. 'He wouldn't have the resources to pull something like this, and besides, we still are not sure if he is alive.'

Podruznig glowered. 'There seems to be a lot you do not know these days, Uri.' The Siberian let it go. 'What about the woman? Has he got anything out of her yet?'

'Not the last time I checked.'

'Where is he?'

'Sleeping, I imagine.'

Podruznig flared crimson. 'SLEEPING? My family is missing and he's SLEEPING?' Uri didn't point out that the man had been going to bed at nine o'clock every night since he arrived. Keeping regular hours, he called it. *Good for the system.* All the men thought he was a prick, albeit a dangerous one. And despite Podruznig's words, Uri doubted his concern really had anything to do with his wife and daughter.

'Wake him up Uri. Now. I want to know if she knows anything. Anything at all, you understand?' Uri nodded. 'I need to know what the fuck is going on.' Uri left, keeping any frustrations he might have been feeling to himself.

When he'd gone, Podruznig returned to his pacing. Whatever was happening, he needed to know what action to take next. He lived by being prepared, ready for anything, not by letting himself be caught out. Not that he was particularly bothered about Marianna, but Sasha... Even so, if someone thought they could get at him through them, they would soon realise their mistake. But he was beginning to think that maybe Uri's recent pleas for caution were right.

His Head of Security had been moaning for some time about the risks they'd been taking of late. Pointing out that things were becoming too complicated. Perhaps he was right. There was enough to take care of with normal business. Maybe all these distractions with the Englishman, the Police and everything had stretched them too thinly. Led him into taking his eye off things. Perhaps it was time to take Uri's advice and rein in. Get back to basics. Start afresh. He'd done it before. Whenever life got too complicated, he'd always found a way to simplify things. Usually by means of a plan aimed at getting rid of the distraction.

He stopped pacing to look up at the ceiling, as if he was looking through it. Well he could think of one complication he could get rid of right now.

He headed for the door.

Deep within the banana plantation that lay on the house's northern side, Red pressed a finger to his ear-piece, double checking to make sure he had heard right. He had. His heart pumped and the adrenalin began to flow. They had been waiting over two hours. Finally, the time had come. He gave the others a double thumbs-up.

As one, they moved forward.

Two minutes later they were at the edge of the field, surveying the perimeter on that side of the house. There were still lights on inside, but they knew that was normal. Red nodded to Ryan. Unslinging the carrier round his shoulder, the young Irishman laid it on the ground, unzipped the nylon cover and took out Cyclops.

About the length of a carbine, but with what looked like some sort of complicated sighting attachment, the device was the latest thing in CCTV-disabling technology. Unlike the previous generation of such devices, it worked not by blinding the camera with a laser beam, but by sending a pulse of magnetic energy that piggy-backed on whatever transmission system was being used - radio or cable - to knock out the monitor at the surveillance end. Developed by the US specifically for covert intrusion and insertion ops, Cyclops's main benefit - which would last only as long as it took for most operators to become familiar with it - was that it made it look as though the problem was monitor malfunction as opposed to camera interference - nearly always a sure sign of attack.

Having worked out that Podruznig's men would not miss a shot-out camera twice, Red had reckoned that for this op, a more sophisticated technique was called for. And he'd had to call in a lot of favours at Episkopi garrison to get his hands on this piece of kit – as he hadn't stopped telling Ryan.

Snaking forward on his belly, Ryan made his way through the grass and low vegetation to the spot, thirty yards from the perimeter wall, they'd decided gave the best shot at the target. Set under the house's eaves, the camera was the middle of three covering this side of the house and grounds, the other two being on the corners. After several days' surveillance, they'd worked out that the middle one covered a seventy-degree sweep that overlapped with the two corner cameras. Lifting the device to his shoulder, Ryan sighted on the lens and pressed the fire button. There was a low, high-pitched whine followed by a click. A red light glowed in the sight. *Bullseye.*

Slithering backwards, Ryan rejoined the others and gave the thumbs-up. They waited.

CHAPTER 54

In the basement control room, monitor No.3 blinked
once, then clicked off. Bohdan Pugach, one of the pair
of Ukranians on duty that night glanced up from the
classic-car magazine he was reading and waited. When
the screen didn't come back on the way they usually did
when the malfunction was caused by overheating, he
swung his feet off the desk and leaned over to the
monitor's on/off button. He pressed it several times.
Nothing happened.

'*Shizer*,' he said.

He checked the other screens. Everything seemed
normal. Bohdan scratched his head and thought about it.
He was certain it was monitor failure - it was completely
dead - but after what he'd been told had happened to the
pair he and Vasyl replaced, he wasn't about to take any
chances. He reached for the radio.

'Vasyl?'

'Yes Bohdan?' Vasyl's voice came back, tinny but clear.
For some reason they hadn't worked out, the Motorolas
worked better at night than during the day.

'Monitor three is down. Go and make sure camera
twelve is okay will you?'

'Have you tried switching it back on?'

'Oh, thank you. I would never have thought of that.'
He followed it up with a curt, 'Just do it. You want Uri to

drag you out of bed in the morning?'

'Okay, okay. Give me a minute.'

Lounging on one of the poolside steamers, having a
smoke while he looked up at the stars, Vasyl Shapko
cursed under his breath. 'Always something.'

He took a last drag then stubbed it out in one of the
planters, remembering to pocket the butt. The last man
to leave one lying around had been docked three days'
wages. He checked over his shoulder before rising. The
lights were still on in the glass-fronted living area, but
there was now no sign of the Big Boss. Earlier, he had
been pacing up and down, making phone calls, and Uri
had been in and out like a dog on a bitch in heat. But he
hadn't seen either for a while now. He wondered if the
wife and daughter had turned up and no one had
bothered to tell them. It wouldn't surprise him. Soon
after their arrival, he and Vasyl realised that as far as Uri
was concerned, Ukrainians merited no better treatment
than mushrooms - to be kept in the dark and fed on shit.

Putting his cap back on, he headed round to the
north side of the house. As he passed camera eleven,
high on the north-west corner, he made an open fist and
tossed Bohdan the usual, obscene gesture. He walked
down the side until he was directly below camera twelve.
The garden-spots lit up the side of the house and he
could see the camera clearly. It looked okay. He checked
the ground beneath his feet. No glass or anything to
suggest something was amiss. He spoke into the radio.
'It all looks okay here, Bohdan.'

'Can you see the lens?'

Vasyl looked up. 'Wait a moment.' Stepping back onto
the lawn he moved back almost as far as the outer wall,
broadening the angle. He shone his torch up. Light
reflected in the glass.

'The lens is fine Bohdan. It must be the monitor.'

'Great,' Bohdan said, sarcastically. 'In that case you are going to have to cover that side of the house. And don't forget to fill the damn log in.'

'Okay, okay. Stop being an old woman.'

'In fact you'd better come in and start it now. That's what we're supposed to do.'

As he came off the radio, Vasyl cursed his partner's pernickety ways. Bohdan always liked to do things by the book. Still, it was probably as well. The monitor failure meant he now had to check the north side every fifteen minutes. And while he could just wait until the end of the shift and make all the log entries then, it was risky. For all they knew, Uri might have sabotaged the monitor just to test them. If he caught them with the logs incomplete - worse, if he was monitoring the whole thing live somewhere - he and Bohdan would be in big trouble.

'Bastard.'

About to make his way to the back of the house, Vasyl thought he heard a noise behind. Starting to turn, he just caught a blur of movement before something hit him, hard and low on the base of his skull, and everything turned black.

As the wiry guard folded, Ryan and Red broke his fall. They couldn't risk an inadvertent radio transmission when it hit the ground, or worse, for the Uzi to fire off a few rounds if the safety was off. Leaving Ryan to get the unconscious guard out of sight, Red wasted no time putting on the man's jacket and cap, stuffing his hair underneath. Slinging the Uzi over his shoulder, he headed back to the pool, timing it so he came into range of the corner camera about when he should have done. He didn't look up but gestured as he'd seen the guard do, before heading for the steps the other side of the garden. They led under the pool to the shuttered doors to the utility and pump rooms. Ignoring them, he carried on down the concrete corridor leading back towards the house. At the end was another, stouter-looking door with a camera above it. Keeping his head down, he pressed the buzzer, at the same time reaching, casually, for the door handle as if expecting it to be opened at once. As a loud click echoed in the narrow space, Red pulled the door open, readying himself for what would follow.

After pouring over the builder's plans for hours, memorising every detail, he knew exactly what to expect. Six feet beyond the door, on the right, a four-foot high wall divided the corridor from the control room. The other side of it was a counter-table on which were two banks of monitors and the CCTV controls. The doorway - actually just a gap in the wall - was five yards further on, but Red knew the time he would take to reach it would be enough for someone to see it wasn't who it was supposed to be and raise the alarm. As he came level with the wall he put his right hand on top and vaulted straight over, eyes already searching for targets. There was only one.

As Red came over the wall between the monitors, Bohdan reared back in his chair and snatched his feet off the desk. Then he was up and reaching for the red button on the wall to his right. He never made it.

The first blow - to his left shoulder - took him down. The second, before he could even cry out, smashed into his left side, above his kidney, making him crease sideways in agony. The third, delivered with practised skill, connected with the back of his neck and he went out, just like Vasyl.

As he pulled out the nylon ties and tape he would use

to bind the unconscious guard, Red's eyes swept the room, taking everything in. At the same time, he listened for signs of any approach. But apart from the man's rasping breath, all was silent. As he pulled the ratchet on the ties tight round his wrists, Red's gaze kept darting to the monitors, weighing what was showing on the screens, getting his bearings, reconnoitring. When the shit hit the fan, they wouldn't have much time. He needed to pick up whatever he could. Tearing off a couple of strips of tape, Red pressed them over the man's mouth. About to tear off another for good measure, he stopped and his head snapped back to the last screen he'd seen. It had taken a moment for the image to register. Leaving the man where he was - he wasn't going anywhere - he sprang across the room, hoping he was mistaken. He was horrified to see he wasn't.

'Oh, Jesus.'

CHAPTER 55

In the pitch dark, Murray rolled his shoulders and rotated his arms to make sure nothing was locking up, before checking the time - again. The signal should have come over an hour ago. Since then his anxiety had built, despite telling himself that any one of a number of factors could account for the delay. As time stretched, he'd had to work hard at not thinking of all the things that could go wrong, and where it would leave him if anything did.

Over the previous twenty-four hours they'd gone over the plan in detail, searching out weaknesses, challenging themselves with all the 'what-ifs' they could come up with. Most times it all held up. On the odd occasion it didn't, they worked out a contingency. By one o'clock in the morning, they'd covered everything they could think of and trooped off to bed, exhausted. But they all knew there were still enough unknowns to give the plan only a fifty-fifty chance of success at best. And with Gina's life at stake, they weren't good odds.

'Come on guys,' Murray said to himself. 'Where the fuck are you?'

As if in answer – miraculously – he felt a vibration in his pocket. He snatched out his mobile. The screen glowed with Red's message. "Secure." *At last.*

Switching on the radio he'd kept off in case it showed

up on some scanner, he spoke into it, softly. 'Trojan, over.'

The urgency in the voice that came back caused his stomach to drop. 'FIRST FLOOR, TROJAN. GREEN. URGENT. GO. NOW.' He'd never heard Red so close to panic.

Like a bullet from a gun, Murray burst from his hiding place but only into more blackness. The downstairs hallway bathroom's light was off. Wrenching at the door lever, he flung it open, not caring if anyone was there. He would just have to deal with them. Red's tone could mean only one thing, and the image it conjured drove him like a missile towards the room they'd designated 'Green' on the plan.

In the hallway, moonlight streamed through the windows either side of the front door, and the light from the lamp on the table at the bottom of the staircase meant he didn't need his head torch. As he took the stairs three at a time, he readied himself to deal with whatever he might meet. Though the longer he could remain undiscovered the better, only one thing mattered now. As he raced he pulled the automatic from his waistband. He would still prefer not to use it, but wouldn't hesitate if he had to.

Certain as he'd been all along that Gina was somewhere in the house, close, it had been even harder than Murray had imagined to resist the impulse to leave the small storeroom off the downstairs bathroom and search for her on his own. If it hadn't been for his training – and the sure knowledge that without a directing steer he would almost certainly be discovered before he found her - he would have succumbed hours ago. But from the moment he settled himself into the cramped space after pulling off the switch with Ulysses - the short walk up the steps, while Podruznig checked the car with Kodras had been the longest in his life - he'd known he was in for a long and difficult wait. Okay, by waiting until the housekeeper would have finished - it was Pippis who suggested giving it a couple of hours longer - the danger of discovery was reduced. Even so, during his hours of waiting, several people had used the bathroom, including the little girl and, on one occasion he was certain, Marianna herself. Each time Murray's heart beat faster and he prayed that the cleaner would have learned long ago to make certain the toilet was always well-stocked with paper.

Gaining the first-floor landing, he swung left into the short corridor that led to the extra bedroom the other side of the house from the others. He hoped to God they hadn't left it too late - or that Podruznig had already concluded the odds were beginning to stack against him, and decided to cut and run.

But though the floor was tile and the soles of his combat boots rubber, his charge up the stairs had been far from silent. He was a few metres from the door that was his target, when it opened and a man stepped out. Murray knew at once who he was. Tall, wiry and dressed from head to toe in black, it had to be the Mummy. The look on the man's face as he came out reflected only interest in discovering who was dashing about the house at this time and why. The way it changed the instant he saw Murray charging at him suggested an intruder hadn't been high on his list. For Murray, the timing was perfect.

He slammed into the dark figure before he had time to even brace himself, driving him back into the door jamb with a forearm-smash into his chest he hoped would be enough to knock all the wind out of him. The 'woosh' of air that exploded from him and his pained expression told Murray it was. As the man bounced back off the frame, already gasping, Murray swung the flat of the gun so it connected, heavily, with the side of his head, sending him sprawling. He rolled once, then lay still.

Opening the door, Murray grabbed his ankles, dragged him inside and closed it. Spinning round, he saw her. For only the second time in his life he felt the gut-wrenching anguish that hits when you fear you are about to discover something awful has befallen someone you care about.

Spread-eagled on top of the bed, Gina was naked, the tatters of her blouse and skirt littering the floor. Her eyes were closed and she wasn't moving or making any sound. A cloth gag was stuffed into her mouth. He pulled it out, gently. Murray didn't need to take in the bowl of ice-cubes and the still smoking cigarette in the ashtray to know what had so alarmed Red. Nor as he bent his cheek to her lips did he bother assessing the seeping burns to her body, or try to count them.

But the feathery breath and the fluttering eyelids told him what he needed to know. Taking out his knife, he slashed at the ropes binding her to the bed's corners. The fact that, though now free, she didn't move, spoke of how bad she was. About to tend to her, he heard the sound of movement. Turning he saw that her torturer was already coming round. *Tough stuff.* Bending to him, he secured the man's wrists behind his back with zip-ties, before pulling up his ankles and attaching them to his wrists in a secure hog-tie. Stuffing the cloth he'd taken from Gina's mouth into the Mummy's - more roughly than he needed to - he turned back to her just as she began to stir. Grabbing the coverlet her tormentor had removed from the bed lest it be soiled – so thoughtful – he wrapped it gently round her, at the same time speaking soft words of comfort.

'It's me Gina. It's Peter. I've got you. You're okay

now.' In between he managed to speak briefly into his radio. 'I've got her, Red. Stand by for my signal.'

'We're waiting.'

He stopped to listen for signs of alarm elsewhere in the house. So far there weren't any. Thankfully, they were far enough away from the other bedrooms that the commotion of his clash with the Mummy hadn't carried. But he knew better than to count on his presence remaining secret much longer. Assuming the plan was now unfolding as intended, only minutes would have elapsed since Red gained entry. The fact no one had yet raised the alarm meant that luck was still on their side. At least two contingencies had anticipated discovery before now. As Gina stirred and her eyes blinked open, he dared to hope that another minute would be enough.

'It's me Gina, Peter.'

Her eyes widened. Fear giving way to hope. 'Peter? Oh, *PETER*.'

The number of "Theo"s in the exhausted babble that followed marked it as a prayer of thanks. But there would be time for that later. He needed to get her downstairs. The man on the floor was fully awake now, pulling at the ties.

'Listen to me Gina.' The babbling continued. He shook her, not too hard. 'We have to go. Can you stand?'

The urgency in his voice seemed to register. She nodded, weakly. He helped her to her feet, drawing the cover further round her. But as she straightened, her legs gave way and she collapsed back onto the bed. He gave her a few seconds then tried again. This time she managed to stay upright. Arm around her waist, half-carrying half guiding, he got her to the door. As they passed the man on the floor giving out muffled shouts, Murray aimed a kick into his midriff, regretting he didn't have the time to give it all he would have liked. The stifled cries changed to deep gasps for air. They stepped out into the corridor. Murray closed the door and listened. Still nothing.

'This way.'

Behind the door, Lamaar drew in as much air as his spasming lungs could manage and prepared himself. He pulled his ankles up as close as he could to his wrists. His scrambling fingers pulled at his trouser leg, exposing the leather sheath attached to his shin. Concentrating, he began to edge the knife out, taking care not to let it slip from his grasp.

Murray led her down the stairs. As they made their way, he hoped to God her laboured breathing and the gasps of pain that came each time her wounds chafed weren't carrying. Reaching the bathroom, he ushered her inside and then into the cupboard. There wasn't enough space for both of them.

'Stay quiet,' he said. 'It'll be dark, but I'm right here.' About to close the door, he saw the look in her face. It reminded him what she had been through, was still going through. Gathering her face in his hands he kissed her full on the lips. It had the desired effect. Hope dawned in her face. He shut the door.

'Trojan,' he said into the radio. 'Helen is secure.'

There was a moment's silence. Then all hell broke loose.

CHAPTER 56

Somewhere, an attack-alarm wailed. Lights flashed, inside and out. Like the climax to some science fiction film, a red strobe on the wall above the basement alarm button flashed its hysterical warning.

From the living quarters down the corridor, the remaining eight members of the security team Uri had ordered to, 'Rest, but don't sleep,' burst out, Uri leading. Priming Uzis and cocking automatics, they dashed into the control room. Uri hit the button that shut off the alarm before thundering, 'WHAT IS IT?'

He stopped dead. The room was empty. 'BOHDAN?' No reply. He whirled round, eyes searching. 'VASYL?' The same.

'What's happening Uri?' the call came from behind. The room was filling up fast, everyone as confused as each other. 'Where's Bohdan? Why-?'

'QUIET,' Uri shouted, brain racing.

'Who set the alarm off?'

'Where're Bohdan and Vasyl?'

'LOOK.' A finger pointed at the monitors.

As they all craned forward to take in the blurry images, cries of 'FUCK,' and 'SHIZER,' echoed.

Though pitch dark outside, the high camera at the end of the approach track near the road had an infra red mode - and the picture it was sending back was clear enough. Several cars and pick-ups were lined up on the track and the road above it, the heat from their engines glowing bright. The camera covering the fields in front of the house showed several green blobs - people - edging their way forward. There had to be twenty, or more.

'IT'S AN ATTACK,' a voice cried.

Uri responded at once. 'OLAF. Stay with the radio. Everyone else upstairs. Get to the gate. Man the perimeter. NOW.'

Bodies jostled as everyone tried to get up the stairs to the kitchen - the quickest route to the front of the house. As Uri bundled the last one up, he pieced together what must have happened. Seeing the vehicles gathering, Bohdan must have set off the alarm before rushing outside to help Vasyl mount an early defence. It was against instructions but, given the Ukrainians' limitations, probably understandable. Shaking his head – he would deal with them when the crisis was over – he followed after the others.

As he came out into the hallway heading for the front door, Podruznig was bounding down the stairs. 'What is it Uri?'

Uri filled him in. Always ahead of those working for him, Podruznig glimpsed possibilities. 'The girl. Where is she? Where's Lamaar?'

Uri twigged. Intent on defending the house, he hadn't given her a thought. It must have shown in his face. 'Never mind,' Podruznig barked. 'Take charge outside. I'll check upstairs.'

But even as Uri rushed out the front door and Podruznig turned to retrace his steps, Lamaar's voice sounded from above.

'HE'S HERE. The Englishman. He's taken her.'

Looking up, Podruznig saw Lamaar coming towards

him. For once, he thought, he looked flushed, dishevelled. But before Podruznig could demand the explanation his rising anger merited, Lamaar shot past without stopping. Bright steel glinted in his hand.

'He must still be in the house. Leave him to me. I will find them.' Already at the foot of the stairs, Lamaar turned towards the kitchen and utility rooms – the most obvious hiding places. 'And then I will kill them,' he added.

'NOT THE GIRL,' Podruznig shouted after him. But Lamaar was already out of sight, leaving Podruznig unsure if he'd heard. 'FUCK,' Podruznig spat. It was all happening too fast. Not enough time to put it together. He thought of Marianna and Sasha. It was obvious now their disappearance was all part of it. In which case he had underestimated the Englishman, again. It would be the last time. Leaving Lamaar to ferret them out – it didn't matter who killed him so long as he was dead – he dashed out to join Uri.

As Olaf settled himself in front of the bank of screens, his concentration was on listening to the radio as Uri barked out commands - 'Aleksei, bring up the lights. Stanislav, get some grenades,' - and checking the other monitors, making sure they weren't missing something in the heat of the moment.

As he glanced at the screen showing the approach along the corridor that ran under the swimming pool, he saw the camera was out-of-line - pointing way-too high. He twiddled the joy stick to bring it down, and saw the group of men crowded close up against the door.

'FUCK,' he yelled, and was reaching for the radio switch when something hit him, hard from behind and he saw and heard no more.

Red made sure the burly Russian was out cold before pressing the switch that released the lock on the door. Kishore, Wazzer and Ryan spilled through. As they took in Olaf's unconscious bulk, Kishore threw Red a questioning look. Red jerked a thumb at a door behind him.

'There's another in there. Just as well none of them felt like taking a leak when they found out what was happening.' He pointed at the screens and they gathered round. Inside the grounds, Uri's men were stationing themselves at the gates and the front wall. Out in the field, the green blobs had stopped moving forward, waiting.

'Where's Peter?' Kishore said.

'Back in his cubby hole, but not for long. We need to get up there before they start shooting.'

Outside, Uri and his team were getting ready, weapons loaded and cocked. Red knew that despite their superior numbers, those out in the field had neither the firepower nor the experience for a shootout with Podruznig's gunmen. He spoke into his radio.

'Trojan.'

'Receiving,' Murray's whisper came back. He had no way of knowing who might be near.

'Flush the bog and evacuate.'

'Roger.'

The snap of static as Murray switched off his radio – a precaution against it giving him away as he broke cover - came a split-second before Ryan's warning cry of, 'NO, WAIT.'

CHAPTER 57

'Come on, Gina,' Murray said. 'Time to get you out of here.'

She blinked as he switched on the light. Her grey pallor spoke to her condition. *Dehydrated,* Murray thought. *Blood-sugar way-down.* He cursed himself for not thinking to bring a couple of Mars Bars. They were always handy on an op.

He helped her out, making sure she was well-wrapped before easing the door to the hallway a few inches. No one was in sight. From somewhere - outside he thought - he could hear Uri and Podruznig barking orders, sounds of people running over gravel.

'Come on.' He pulled her into the hall. As he helped her out, the way her eyes widened at something behind him screamed a warning.

The usual response in such circumstances would be, turn, assess, react. But Murray knew that by the time he got to the third stage, it would most likely already be too late. And though he didn't yet know what the danger was, he practised what he'd learned during the weeks of preparation for Priscilla but had never had to put into practice. Dipping right - her eyes dictated his choice, if he was wrong he was dead anyway – he bent his right arm and pulled it tight in to his side, using it as a shield. At the same time he raised his left arm, defending his neck and face as he spun round. It saved his life – for the moment.

Something punched into his upper right arm, but though it went instantly dead, he was still alive - and quick enough to swerve back and out of the way of Lamaar's second, slashing strike. The steel blade whistled past his nose to score through the palm of his left hand. Gina screamed as Lamaar leaped at him. Then he was on the floor with Lamaar on top, pressing his full body weight down on the knife that only Murray's grip on his wrist was preventing from plunging straight down into his throat.

Throughout his life, Murray had always kept himself fit, as had Lamaar. In his youth, Murray played football for the county and later, in the army, rugby. Lamaar never bothered with sport - until he realised that the fitter and stronger he was, the easier he could hurt people. In service assessments of his physical prowess, Murray always scored highly. So did Lamaar. Since leaving the army, Murray worked out regularly. Lamaar worked out every day, sometimes twice. Murray focused on aerobics - running and swimming - his favourite. Lamaar concentrated on strength and speed, pumping iron and using a device of his own invention that involved weights on chains attached to spinning poles that would smash his skull or shatter bone if he didn't duck and dodge quickly enough.

With two good arms Murray might, possibly, have been able to hold Lamaar up. Without leverage, the downward pressure could not exceed Lamaar's total body weight. But when Murray brought his other arm up to support his left, it wouldn't work properly. A quick glance told why. Blood flowed from the wound to the *inside* of his arm. Lamaar's first thrust must have penetrated right through, and though the bone wasn't broken, Murray imagined shredded muscle, sliced tendons. As Lamaar kept up the pressure, Murray felt himself weakening, the knife-point drawing near.

'NO,' Gina screamed.

The knife flashed down, cutting through flesh, cartilage and, most of all, the jugular. Blood spurted in an arc, just like Billy's had done, splattering down on the expensive ceramic, splashing across the coverlet Gina still held around her. She opened her mouth to scream again, but this time there was nothing there.

Murray looked up at Lamaar, his eyes wide in shock and horror. As the blood spurted again, Lamaar gripped at his throat with both hands - the knife gone now - gargling and gurgling as he drowned in his own blood. Then he slipped away to his right, out of his line of vision.

Murray's eyes closed as he lay there, gasping for breath, blood still pooling on the front of his shirt.

'Don't just lie there you lazy bastard, MOVE!'

Murray looked up into the cherubic face that ought to have belonged to a poet. Ryan O'Donnell's left hand was stretched out towards him, waiting for his bloodied former Op Commander to take it. In his right was the titanium-steel hunting knife with the black ivory handle. Blood dripped from its tip.

Murray turned to his right. Next to him, Lamaar's body twitched in the throes of death, the accompanying rattle mingling with the gurgles still emerging from the ear-to-ear gash that for some reason brought to mind a shark's bloody smile. He grasped the hand offered and hauled himself to his feet. He had to take several deep reviving breaths before he could talk.

'Thanks-' *Breathe-* 'Boyo.'

'No need,' Ryan said. He turned to look down at his his victim, '*That* was for Billy, you *twat*.' Then he kicked

342

at the body once, viciously. 'And *that's* from *me*.' Lamaar didn't react.

Murray turned to Gina. She was trembling now. Crying. He went to put his arms round her, but she pulled away, eyes flaring in horror at his blood-soaked shirt. He tore it off and threw it away.

'Let's go,' Ryan said.

Murray had to all-but lift her to get her moving again. They had covered only a few yards towards the kitchen when Red, Kishore and Wazzer came running out. Lamaar's body and the state of Murray told Red the story. He shook his head.

'Just as well Irish here spotted yon bugger coming back, otherwise you'd be dead and we'd all be fucked.'

'Tell me about it.' Murray's head flicked towards Gina, hanging onto his arm. 'I need to get her out of this.'

Red jerked a thumb over his shoulder. 'We're secure downstairs. Give us a couple of minutes.' Murray nodded and led her away.

'Right,' Red said. 'Let's do it.'

The four ran to the front door. As they opened it, Podruznig was sprinting back up the steps towards them. He stopped dead as the stainless-steel barrel of a Heckler-Koch G36 assault rifle appeared in front of his nose.

'Don't move a fucking inch,' Kishore said, smiling his goofy smile.

CHAPTER 58

Over by the gates, still trying to work out what the men in the field intended, Uri spun round as he heard the shout.

'ON THE GROUND, NOW, DO IT.'

At the top of the steps, his master stood with his hands raised in the posture of capture, a rifle barrel pressed to his neck by a ginger-haired man Uri had never seen before. As he took in the others, fanned out around Podruznig, already sighting on their targets, Uri knew at once what not to do.

Not so Stanislav.

A shout of defiance came from Uri's left as Stanislav brought his weapon up. There was a short burst from the weapon of one of the men on the steps. and Uri heard the sounds of first Stanislav's weapon, then Stanislav, hitting the ground. *Stupid*, Uri thought.

Following Uri's example, they laid their weapons down, then did as commanded, lying face down, hands clasped on heads in the posture that maximised their chances of not falling victim to a jumpy trigger finger. Two of the men on the steps came amongst them, securing wrists behind backs with zip-ties. A minute later, the ginger haired man spoke into a radio.

'Red to Zeus. Compound secure. It's over.'

When, a minute later, the Englishman appeared

through the front door, the girl at his side, Uri cursed the day he hadn't killed him when he had the chance - and made another promise to himself.

As Murray came out, Kishore was already opening the gates. Headlamps beamed and the noise of engines starting up came to him. He looked across to where Red was securing Podruznig, still snarling defiance. As Podruznig saw Murray emerge, he stopped to pin him with a stare.

'Do not think this is over Englishman. My reach is as long as my memory.'

Letting go Gina's arm, Murray crossed to stand square in front of the Russian, the way he had that first day. Their gazes locked.

'It's about time you learned to listen,' Murray said. 'And to read the writing on the wall.' The Russian's eyes narrowed, as if working out if it might be an oblique reference to the kitchen graffiti that started everything.

Through the gates came a convoy of vehicles, led by two police SUV's, blue lights flashing. They stopped in front of the steps. Pippis stepped out and rushed over to Gina. As they hugged each other, Galios Iridotu helped his elder brother, Papos from one of the cars behind. They shuffled forward to gaze on the face of the man responsible for their family's pain.

As his lip curled into a sneer of contempt, Podruznig turned to hail Pippis in a voice still full of defiance.

'Know this, Polizei. If your family thinks they can avenge themselves by killing me they are mistaken. My murder will hang over your family like a curse. Even here, the police cannot get away with such things.'

Pippis broke away from Gina to come and stand before him, like the others. For a long time he gazed into the Russian's face. Murray thought he could imagine some of what was going through the policeman's mind, but not all. One-armed or no, he steeled himself, just in case he needed to step in. There was no need. When he spoke, Pippis's voice was matter-of-fact, as if he'd been preparing for the moment for a long time, but now it was here, felt it an anti-climax.

'The only thing I and my family will ever be guilty of, *Pontian*, is breaching Civil Aviation Authority Regulations.'

Podruznig's eyebrows knitted together in puzzlement.

Pippis turned to retrace his steps back to the second police car in the convoy. He opened the back door. A man wearing an expensive grey suit, collar and tie got out. As he straightened up and Podruznig got his first good look at him, his jaw dropped.

'Hello Valerik,' Anatoly Kaskiv said, smiling. 'Good to see you again.'

As sight of the man he hadn't seen since leaving Odessa registered in his brain, Podruznig's mouth gaped. Other men - Kaskiv's bodyguards - materialised in the background. Their eyes were everywhere, particularly on Red's still-armed assault team.

Knowing what to expect, Murray shoved Podruznig forward. As they neared the car, Kaskiv stepped to one side. 'Perhaps you might like to say hello to an old friend Valerik?'

Presented with the inside of the car for his inspection, Podruznig bent to look. What colour still remained in his face drained away as he saw the bound and gagged figure of Viktor Bogdanof, Kaskiv's long-serving, chief body-guard. As Podruznig turned from one to the other - Bogdanof, Kaskiv, Murray, Pippis - Murray noted how his Adam's-apple was suddenly pronounced, his eyes those of a hunted deer, now cornered.

As if recognising the moment he too had waited a long time for, Kaskiv came forward. The way he started, by gesturing theatrically at Murray, Murray suspected he intended to make the most of it.

'Of course, Valerik, I had no idea whether to trust Mr Murray here when he first came to me with this story about you, and Viktor, and my little Sissi.' At mention of Kaskiv's dead daughter's name Podruznig swallowed. 'At the time, some hinted that you could, in some way, be responsible. "He likes them young," they said. I never realised just how young. Or your taste for those substances that help your imagination roam where it likes to go.' Kaskiv's voice lowered an octave. 'From what I hear, Valerik, that must be a very dark place. One no woman, young or otherwise, should ever be made to visit.' His face was like stone as he added, 'Like my Sissi was.'

Podruznig took a step forward. 'Anatoly, I-'

'SHUT THE FUCK UP!' Kaskiv's hand whipped across Podruznig's face, the crack of the contact echoing back from the house. Podruznig stood there, stunned. In all his life he had never had to take it as he was having to now. Kaskiv resumed.

'I was foolish Valerik. I demanded proof. I said that for all your weaknesses, you were loyal to me, and my family. Besides, I knew that with Viktor here being the efficient truth-finder he is, you would never risk something so stupid. You would know that I would tell him to leave no stone unturned. Which of course I did. So when he told me you were not involved, I believed him.' At this point Kaskiv turned to look into the car. Bogdanof's sweating face stared back at him, terrified. 'The thought never even entered my head he would lie to me. That, knowing your guilt he would keep it from me.' He turned back to Podruznig, and the words he spoke next were as chilling as any those close enough to hear would ever remember. 'But then I was not to know that Viktor was with you that night. The night you persuaded him to try out your obscene substances. The night you both decided to see if my Sissi possessed the qualities your fucked-up brains imagined.'

Kaskiv paused in his delivery, as if to calm himself, not wanting to give vent to what every bone in his body was crying out for. At least, not yet. In the silence that followed no one moved or said anything, not even Podruznig. Kaskiv took a deep breath.

'No Valerik, I knew none of this. Not until Mr Murray here came to see me....' Podruznig spun round on Murray. The look on his face said, *But how-?* Kaskiv continued. 'And told me that he knew it to be true because....' Podruznig's eyes grew wide. *Surely it could not be.* '..Your wife told him so.'

For a couple of seconds, Podruznig just stood there, then, like the collapse that follows the final blow, his face caved. *Marianna.* In that moment, a man's image floated before him. Oscar Nazarov. Uri's predecessor. A ruthlessly efficient soldier, enforcer and bodyguard, but one who was, nonetheless, always kind to women and children. Shot dead during an encounter with a rival faction years before, he alone knew the truth of what happened that night. It was Nazarov who protected his employer by spiriting him away from the scene, despite his disgust and horror. And Nazarov was the only member of his team Marianna ever had time for, the only one with whom she ever talked. Before Sasha's arrival, it was invariably Nazarov who accompanied Marianna on her long walks. They'd have talked...

Up to that moment, Podruznig had clung to the idea that once away from here, he would convince Kaskiv it was all a plot to oust him. That all Murray and the policeman had done was feed off the rumours that had always been around. He knew now that would not happen. The bitch had betrayed him, just as Uri had always said she would. He should have-

'And in case there was any doubt, Valerik,' Kaskiv was determined to finish. 'I had our good friend, Viktor, here confirm it. He seemed to think that if he could lay the blame on you and that shit you gave him, I would be more understanding. More merciful.' As he took hold of the car door he looked back at the man lying trussed on the back seat. 'I cannot imagine what gave him that idea.' The muffled pleadings that leaped from the back of Bogdanof's throat cut off as Kaskiv slammed the door shut.

As if at a prearranged signal, two of Kaskiv's men came forward to stand either side of Podruznig, gripping his arms.

Realising what was about to happen, Podruznig turned a desperate face on Pippis. 'You cannot let them do this. You are the Police.'

Pippis was as impassive as Murray had ever seen him. 'Do what? They were never here.'

'Come my old friend,' Kaskiv said, signalling to his men. 'We have a plane to catch. To Odessa.' The men dragged Podruznig, screaming, towards one of the cars.

'BASTARDS,' Podruznig yelled. 'I WILL-.'

In the dark, Murray didn't see what happened that stopped Podruznig's protests. A door opened. There was a brief struggle. It slammed shut. Then there was only silence.

Kaskiv turned to Murray. 'Thank you Mr Murray.'

Murray gave an acknowledging nod, but made no answer. None of it had given him pleasure. An agreement had been concluded, that was all. Besides, he knew enough about Kaskiv's own past to hope they would never have to do business again.

Kaskiv seemed to understand. He turned to Pippis, nodded his goodnight. 'Superintendent.'

By now Galios, Papos and Gina had gathered to him. Pippis stood there, arms about them, rock-like, as he too nodded a silent farewell.

This part of the night's business over, Kaskiv climbed back into the police car he had stepped from. Pippis signalled to the officer leading the convoy. As it pulled away, lights still flashing, the others followed. No one spoke as the visitors from the Black Sea that were never there turned left through the gates onto the kilometre-long track that would take them and their prisoner back to the main road, the airport and, by dawn, Odessa. When the last vehicle had passed out of sight, Pippis turned to Murray.

'I hope you have a key, Mr Murray. The house is yours again.'

CHAPTER 59

Dawn's first light was showing behind the hills of the Pafos Forest by the time Murray and Gina returned to the house. In the close to three hours since they'd left, their wounds had been treated and dressed. The level of service on offer at Pafos's General Hospital shot through the roof when Pippis arrived and collared the night-duty doctor. But while Gina's injuries were more superficial than they looked - Murray feared that the real damage may not show until later, and then not to her body - they'd wanted to keep him in, 'for observation.' The hole in his ribcage where the knife had penetrated through his arm, might lead to complications they said. His lung could be pierced. Murray took several deep breaths to show them they were talking bollocks, and told them he wasn't staying anywhere, though he kept to himself how it nearly killed him to make it sound convincing.

As Gina drove them away in the replacement Merc provided by her insurance - she had ordered her father to have it brought to the hospital and insisted she was fit to drive - Murray slipped the sling off his neck and tossed it into the back seat. He pretended not to notice the admonishing look she threw his way.

As they drove in through the gates, he was surprised to discover that the only way he could cope with the emotions that hit him was to close his eyes. They stayed shut until Gina pulled up at the bottom of the steps. Apart from it being the first time he'd been able to drive straight in without being challenged, he was conscious that whatever his confused feelings for Gina Iridotu, it should, rightly, have been another woman next to him. And while he was glad Gina had returned with him, he worried about how she may react when she learned the truth. He hoped he hadn't miscalculated.

As they got out, he heard noises, poolside. They told him all he needed to know. But he resisted going to look while he checked out the hallway. He was glad to see someone had kept their promise.

Bad enough that he'd failed in his initial aim of keeping it out altogether - it had probably never been on the cards anyway - but if death had to come within, as it had, he wanted its stay to be as short as possible. He didn't intend to ask what they'd done with Lamaar's body, but trusted it wouldn't wash up on the beach below any time soon. Giving Gina a wan smile, he headed round back.

Even before he turned the corner, he pictured the image that would greet him. It was close enough. The four men were standing over a pile of earth next to the pool, each little more than a silhouette in what was left of the night's shadow. As he and Gina drew near, he saw they were waiting for him. They'd have heard them driving in.

Murray approached the hole and peered in. It was about five feet deep, enough at the time that the builders wouldn't unearth it. By then, all the footings had been long finished, the shell of the house already up, the pool already dug. In the hole's dark depths, Murray could just make out that they had already begun to excavate beneath the wooden crate that lay there, exposing the lifting chains threaded under. But there was no sign yet of any block and tackle. Given the crate's size - and weight - Murray wondered if it would be enough.

'Didn't expect you back so soon,' Red said.

'We went first-class,' Murray said, not looking up. 'That's the nice thing about Cyprus. Authority and patronage still work here.'

The four waited while Murray completed his inspection. Eventually, he turned to them. The way they were lined up, ready, he could imagine what each was thinking. Where *does* friendship begin and end?

A noise to his left made him turn. Next to him, Gina was staring into the hole. She looked distraught. As bad as the times he'd caught her dwelling on Ileana, he thought. Her hand was over her mouth, doing her best to stifle the sobs of disappointment that were trying to escape. As he looked at her, she lifted her head so their eyes met and he saw what she was thinking. It lanced straight into his heart.

'Time's pressing Plod,' Red said. 'And it'll take us another hour yet to lift the bugger out. Why don't you and Gina go and-'

'It was my home, Red,' Murray said. He turned square-on to the ex-sergeant. 'Mine and Kathy's.' Red didn't move though the others shuffled straight. As always when Kathy's name was mentioned, Kishore looked uncomfortable. *And well he might.*

'I know that, Pete,' Red said. 'Don't worry. We'll put everything back. It'll be good as new.'

Murray was having none of it. 'You should have asked.'

Now it was Red who straightened, but only to show a regretful smile. 'Sure. And what would you have said? Certainly? Feel free? We know you too well for that Peter. And what the eye doesn't see, the heart doesn't worry about.'

Murray shook his head. He looked over at the others. None met his stare. 'You still should have asked.'

Red's expression grew serious. 'We didn't. I'm sorry. Now let us-'

'It was you.'

Red hesitated, becoming wary. 'What was me?'

'The paint job in the kitchen. Shooting up his BMW. You did it.'

The former SAS man stood his ground. There was too much to lose not to face things. 'It was just meant to give him the jitters. Help him come to a decision, that's all.'

Anger crept into Murray's voice. 'Come to a decision? Well that certainly worked well didn't it?'

'Peter, I-.'

'His decision was to see me off.' Red said nothing. 'And when that didn't work, then what happened?' He turned, holding out a hand as if introducing her. 'Go on, explain to her why her sister was blown up, why her cousin was murdered, why she was tied up while a bloody psycho used her as practice.' He cast about him, letting his anger go. 'Why all this, tonight?'

Red said nothing, glaring back at Murray while the others stayed out of it. Murray caught Gina's confused look.

'You mean-?' She stopped, pointing into the hole. 'So this- This was not you?'

For a moment Murray returned her questioning look, before turning it on Red. He waited. At last Red spoke. He had no choice.

'You're right love. This was- is, nothing to do with him. This was us.' He gestured to his comrades. 'And believe me, we are all sorry for what your family has suffered.'

'But not sorry enough to walk away,' Murray said.

Now Red was defiant. 'You know better than that, Peter. It took a lot to get this over here.'

'I can imagine.'

'And you know we aren't just going to give it up.'

Murray nodded. 'That's what I thought you'd say.' The hand in his pocket felt for his mobile. He thumbed a button.

'If you knew it, why did you bother asking?'

'I just thought I would give you the chance.'

'Chance? To do what?'

'To give it up peacefully.'

As the implication registered, the men's stances altered, though subtly. A hollow laugh sounded from Red's throat.

'I don't think you're in a position to make threats Peter. Not with her here.' He nodded to Gina. 'And especially with only one arm.'

Murray shook his head. 'I'm done with threats.'

Red relaxed a little. 'Good in that case-'

'But I'm not.'

They all turned.

The other side of the pool, Major Glyn Westgate and three men in battle-fatigues were pointing weapons at them, exactly as Red's team had covered Podruznig's men hours before.

For several moments there was only silence, then Red turned on Murray.

'Westgate? You sold us out to Westgate?' The disbelief in his voice was clear.

Murray blanked him, saying nothing, gauging.

Westgate's assault rifle swung right as Kishore edged towards the table where their G36s lay. 'Don't be stupid, Corp.'

Kishore froze.

Satisfied his squad had them covered, Westgate came

round the pool to peer down into the hole, just as Murray had done. 'I have to say, that was awfully good of you. Saves us a job.'

Red's fists balled and his lip curled. 'If you think you're just going to waltz in here and, *UUMMPHH*.' He doubled up as the stock of Westgate's rifle jerked back into his midriff. As Kishore and the others reacted, Westgate brought his weapon up, as did his support.

'Ah-ah. Let's not have any unpleasantness. I'm sure Peter would rather not have his swimming pool contaminated with his friends' blood. Am I right Peter?' Murray still said nothing, waiting.

Recovering, Red turned a disappointed face to Murray. 'I thought that after the way they fucked us over, you'd had it with the Army?'

Murray kept his gaze steady as he weighed things. 'I have.'

'So why-?'

'Oh don't worry Sergeant McGeary,' Westgate chipped in. 'Your erstwhile leader hasn't struck any deals with anyone. In fact I suspect he's as surprised to see us as you are. Right Peter?'

Murray shrugged. 'Maybe, maybe not.'

Westgate smiled. 'You don't change do you? You always did like to give the impression you were one step ahead. Well not this time I'm afraid.' Seeing Red's puzzled expression, he continued. 'You see, this,' - he indicated his companions - 'Isn't quite what you probably think it is.'

Murray's head lifted. *I knew it.*

Red exchanged wary glances with his team.

'You see, it would be nice if I could stand here and tell you how good it feels to have succeeded for Queen and Country. That after three years of patient watching and waiting, Her Maj's Armed Forces will now see justice done by returning the goods you've so kindly delivered back to their rightful owner. Good for International Relations and all that, wouldn't you say sergeant?'

Now it was Red who stayed quiet, eyes narrowing, realisation beginning to dawn. 'Unfortunately that's not quite how it is.'

'Priscilla.'

It was Murray who had spoken and they all turned to him. Westgate smiled.

'What about Priscilla?' Red said.

Murray nodded at Westgate. 'He's not here on the Army's behalf, Red. He was part of it all along.'

Red looked from Murray to Westgate and back again, as did Kishore. Gina simply looked confused, everything way over her head. Then Red put it together. 'He was part of the Priscilla organisation?' He turned to Westgate. 'You two-faced bastard.'

Westgate's smile stayed. 'Well someone had to watch the backs of those at the top. And being SIB, I was in an ideal position. And let's face it, the gold might just as well be in my employers' hands as some quasi Middle East President... or yours.'

'And of course,' Murray added. 'The rewards just happen to be a tad higher than the army's.'

Westgate smirked. 'In the words of someone I forget, "You may think that, I couldn't possibly comment".'

'You toffee-nosed twat,' Kishore said. 'So you've been fucking the army over all this time?'

Westgate sneered his reply. 'Just as you did when you decided to take the gold.'

'We didn't steal it from the army. We took it from Isil. They were the enemy, remember?'

'I think that's a rather dubious distinction, don't you?'

'Maybe so, but I never betrayed my country.'

But Westgate was tiring of the argument. 'Given that

we're standing here arguing about something that doesn't rightly belong to any of us, I could contest that, but I won't.' He motioned to his squad. 'Now, if you'll kindly lie yourselves down like your Russian friends did a couple of hours ago, we'll-.'

'LOOK OUT PLOD.'

Kishore hurled himself over the earth-pile towards Murray as a gunshot rent the still morning air. As Murray spun around to see Kishore flying towards him, he caught a fleeting glimpse of the giant Siberian, Uri, stood atop the cliffs, the discharge from the gun in his hand still snaking.

Away to his right, and before Uri could move to get another clear shot - he probably hadn't even seen them in the half-light - the nearest of Westgate's gunmen responded as per his training, dropping to one knee and sending an arc of fire through the bushes towards where the shot had come from. Uri clutched at his side, staggered backwards, then disappeared over the cliff he must have climbed after evading Pippis's mop-up team. About to use the diversion to make a grab at their weapons, Wazzer and Ryan stopped as Westgate's rifle rounded on them.

'Don't.'

On top of the earth mound, Murray cradled Kishore, his hands already red from the blood seeping through the back of Kishore's shirt. 'You stupid little bastard, what did you do that for?'

Grimacing with the effort, Kishore gasped out his reply. 'Bad enough Kathy's not here,' he wheezed. 'You've got to live her dream, Plod.' His eyes closed, and he died in Murray's arms.

For a long time no one spoke, or moved. Murray held Kishore like the friend he was, despite the gold. Eventually Westgate broke in.

'I'm sorry that had to happen, Peter. I'd rather everyone had walked out of here intact.' Murray rocked back onto his heels, still cradling Kishore's body. Westgate motioned to his team as he'd started to before.

'Let's get this over with.' He turned to Red, Wazzer and Ryan. 'Now you lot can-.'

'It's too late,' Murray interrupted.

Westgate misunderstood. 'Don't be difficult Peter. There's plenty of time yet. And whatever you say, we're not leaving here until-.'

'That's not what I mean.' Letting go of Kishore, he stood up.

'Then what-?' Westgate stopped, following the direction Murray was pointing, out to sea where the sunrise over the Pafos hills behind was beginning to chase the dark away over the horizon. Even as Westgate looked out over the water, the white light that could have marked an aircraft dropping towards Pafos Airport changed course, brightening as it turned towards them.

'What the…?'

Everyone watched in silence as the ball of light grew, rapidly. It must have been a trick of the air-currents over the sea, as it wasn't until it was within a hundred metres that they heard the thrup-thrup-thrup of the rotors.

CHAPTER 60

As realisation hit, Westgate opened his mouth to instruct his team. He didn't get a word out. The cold metal that suddenly jammed into his neck stopped them in his throat. Glancing sideways, he saw the automatic in Murray's hand.

'As you said earlier, Glyn, let's not do anything stupid.'

Westgate's men turned to him, looking for direction in the face of a situation Murray knew would not have figured in their pre-op briefing. But when they saw what was happening, they froze. They weren't paid to make the sort of decisions this new development demanded. At the same time, Murray saw the way Ryan looked at Red, motioning towards their weapons. Red shot Murray a glance. It took him only a second to read Murray's face. Which was when he knew. He turned back to Ryan, and shook his head, his face betraying his thoughts. *We're fucked.*

The 725 Cougar helicopter- the upgraded version of the old-but-reliable Puma - slowed to a hover as it cleared the cliff edge. The down-draft hit first as a breeze then, as it made landfall, a full-blown windstorm. They had to lean into it to stay on their feet.

Even before the Cougar touched down on the stretch of bare ground between the pool area and the cliff-edge, its occupants were already bailing out. In their black jump-suits, balaclavas and body armour, and carrying the sort of kit all except Gina had seen before, those watching had no difficulty marking them as Special Forces. The only question on everyone's mind was, whose?

Around twenty in number, it took them less than thirty seconds to secure their drop-objectives. Half deployed around the house, guarding against any further interruption. The rest split into two groups, one covering those already present, the other forming a cordon round the hole. None of them spoke. They didn't need to. It was obvious what they'd come for, and that they were ready to deal with any resistance. As everyone waited to find out what would happen next, a figure swung himself out of the helicopter to cross towards where Murray and Gina stood, Red next to them.

Unarmed, and wearing fatigues rather than battle dress, the man's relaxed manner hinted at non-military status. But it wasn't until he neared that his middle-eastern features became visible in the half-light. Picking out the face he recognised, the man Murray had not seen in the flesh since their meeting at the Kurium ruins, but had communicated with several times since, approached. About to smile, he stopped when he saw Kishore's body. A look of regret came into his face.

'We came as soon as we got your signal, Mr Murray. I am sorry if it was not soon enough.' The others turned, faces registering varying degrees of shock.

Murray sighed and put up the gun he'd kept on Westgate during the Iraqi Golden Division's landing. He just wanted it all to be over.

'You said five minutes. It was close enough. I'm not complaining.'

'Nevertheless, I am sorry.'

By now Red was coming round, working things out. This time he was nearer the mark. 'You had this set up all the time?'

Murray's response was a twitch of an eyebrow.

Red realised what it meant. 'So you must have known about the gold?'

Murray pursed his lips, considering his answer. 'The more I thought about it, the more I realised the timing fitted. If it was anywhere, it had to be here.'

By now everyone was looking at him, as if seeing him for the first time. The one man they'd always intended would never know, had known all along.

'You sly bastard.'

Murray saw the irony in his former colleague's accusation, but let it go. He looked down at Kish's body. He liked to think that, eventually, they may all come to feel like him. *It wasn't worth it. It never would have been.* But he knew they wouldn't.

'Shall we get on now Mr Murray?' the Iraqi Agent said.

Murray looked up at him, then the others, then down at Kishore. He nodded. 'Take it and go.'

They used the helicopter to lift the crate out. It saved messing with hoists and blocks. As it hovered above the house, they all watched as the crate some of those present had schemed and waited on for three years, was winched inside. When the helicopter landed again and the remaining Golden Division troops broke stations to re-board, the man leading the recovery mission came back to Murray. He held out a hand. Murray took it.

'Our Government thanks you, Mr Murray.' Murray nodded, but said nothing.

The sky was a deep shade of early-morning blue as the

Cougar headed out over the sea. It flew West then, when far enough out, turned North-east in the wide arc that would take it and its cargo home. They watched until it was out of sight.

When it was gone, Murray turned to the others. His arm was round Gina's waist. His eyes locked first on Red, then the rest of his team, and finally, Westgate. There were questions he still needed to put to the SIB man, but they would wait for another time. He may have to look for him by then, but he doubted it would be too big a problem. Besides, he may even enjoy tracking him down. So might Pippis for that matter. As for the rest of it, he wondered if his feelings would change in time. He wasn't sure he wanted them to. Treachery is treachery, no matter how you dress it up.

Gathering himself so he looked less like some walking wounded, and more like the soldier he was, he addressed them.

'Now, I'd appreciate it if you'd all get the hell off my property.'

Later, when they had all gone, taking Kish with them, Murray and Gina stood at the edge of the cliff that looked down on the caves that Murray had once looked forward to exploring with his son. Weary to the point of exhaustion, Gina hung on his one, good arm, head resting on his shoulder.

The sun was up now, turning the sea many colours of blue. The water was dotted with fishing boats from Coral Bay and the little fishing port of Agios Georgios, a little way along the coast. They would be bringing in the catches that in a few hours would find their way to table in the more honest of Pafos's many eating houses - the others would serve the remains of yesterday's haul. After a while Murray stirred, conscious that the woman whose

363

face had been playing through his mind, was not the one by his side.

He turned to look at her. The low sun played through her hair. She was still beautiful. More important, she was alive. He took a deep, cleansing breath.

'Things to do,' he said.

She read through it. 'Will you be alright?'

He flexed his injured arm before nodding. 'I think so.'

'That is not what I meant.'

'I know.'

She looked into his face, reading the thoughts that dwelt there, as women do. There were no surprises. She smiled up at him. He returned it. Raising herself, she kissed him, lightly, on the cheek.

'Call me. When you are ready.'

About to give an excuse, he caught the look in her dark eyes. Suddenly, it was like he was seeing them for the first time. Then he realised. Now it was over, they were no longer business partners. Perhaps they never had been. He opened his mouth to speak, but closed it again as an image popped, unbidden, into his head. It was the night he'd sat in her Taverna, sampling the Meze. He'd never got round to reading the rest of the menu. He wondered what it would be like. Extensive, he was sure.

He forgot about excuses.

'Count on it.'

He never knew how long he stayed there after she had gone. It was a budget-airline holiday flight, coming in low over the sea that brought him out of it. Who knows? he thought, as he watched it drop. There may be some on board looking to invest their hard-earned savings in property somewhere. Perhaps even nearby. Developments were springing up all over again now that the financial crisis was over. Stirring, he made his way across to where the old carob tree stood on the edge of the cliff, twisted, gnarled, but most importantly, still there. He wondered how he would respond if he met some would-be investor and they asked, 'Recommend buying round here would you?' He almost smiled as he thought on some choice answers.

Stopping beneath the tree's branches, he reached around the trunk, running his hand over the rough bark, feeling for what he knew was there. As his fingers made contact with the close-cut grooves he closed his eyes. He didn't need to see them to read the words.

"PETER AND KATHY FOREVER XXX"

And beneath them, ten years later, in a younger, less assured hand.

"AND JACK XXX"

Finished reading his son's epilogue, Murray slumped down onto the shiny roots that showed through the bare soil. But he kept his arm round the trunk, as if fearing to let go in case it toppled over into the sea. Reaching into his back pocket, he removed his bill fold and took from it the photograph that was always there. He gazed down at the smiling faces, brought it to his lips, then slipped it into a crack in the bark, next to the story that had begun so many years before.

And as the tears came, he lifted his head to look out over the glistening sea.

It was going to be another, blisteringly-hot day in Pafos.

The end

Enjoyed reading? If you would like to consider posting a

review, please bear in mind that reviews are the lifeblood of authors as they help to keep our books visible to new readers, *and* they give us a better understanding of what you like in a story. You can post a review by visiting the book page, HERE, and clicking on the number of ratings next to the yellow stars.

Coming next…..

Coming in 2020 - The next in the DCI Jamie Carver Series…

THE WOMAN ACROSS THE STREET

Is she, or isn't she?

Newly arrived in Brackers Lake, sixteen-year old Brandon Sawyer is missing Brooklyn. He hates everything about the sleepy Upstate New York town his family has moved to. But when his father volunteers his services to help clear the yard for the woman who lives on her own across the street, life suddenly becomes more interesting.

Across an ocean, three thousand miles away in the offices of the Special Murder Investigation Unit, a detective sits, alone, in the semi-dark. He is staring at a photograph purporting to show that someone he thought was dead, is alive, and living somewhere in the United States. The detective is wondering if it is genuine, or someone's idea of a sick joke, and coming to a stark conclusion. There is only one way to find out.

Taken in hand by 'Peter', daughter of the town's sheriff, Brandon learns that 'sleepy' Brackers Lake may not be quite as sleepy as he thought. Peter's father is still investigating the mysterious death, two months before, of a local councilman, the circumstances of which suggest that behind the town's pretty lace curtains and picket fences, lurks a dark, secret.

When Brandon's teenage curiosity over his part-time 'employer' lead him and Peter to make a bizarre discovery that is beyond their youthful understanding, he fears that he may, unwittingly, have put himself and his friend in deadly danger. But when they seek help and discover that those to whom they would turn may themselves be involved, they realise they must face that danger on their own. And when it does, finally, strike, they can only wonder how, and from where, help may come.

Have you discovered Robert F Barker's Detective Jamie Carver Series yet?

If you enjoy suspense-filled crime fiction, you'll love these stories of a detective who struggles to shake off the shadow that hangs over him, and the sometimes dark, even disturbing, investigations in which he gets involved. Start with Book #1, <u>LAST GASP - HERE</u> - or to find more about all of Robert F Barker's books, visit his <u>AUTHOR PAGE - HERE.</u>

FREE DOWNLOAD

Get the inside
story on what
started it all...

Get a free copy of, *THE CARVER PAPERS*, - The
inside story of the hunt for a Serial Killer, - as
featured in LAST GASP. Click on the link below
to find out more and get started

http://robertfbarker.co.uk/

Robert F Barker was born in Liverpool, England. During a thirty-year police career, he worked in and around some of the North West's grittiest towns and cities. As a senior detective, he led investigations into all kinds of major crime including, murder, armed robbery, serious sex crime and people/drug trafficking. Whilst commanding firearms and disorder incidents, he learned what it means to have to make life-and-death decisions in the heat of live operations. His stories are grounded in the reality of police work, but remain exciting, suspenseful, and with the sort of twists and turns crime-fiction readers love.

For updates about new releases, as well as information about promotions and special offers, visit the author's website and sign up for the VIP Mailing List at:-

http://robertfbarker.co.uk/

Printed in Great Britain
by Amazon

53519907R00227